Forgotten Heir

BLUEBLOOD VAMPIRES BOOK THREE

MICHELLE HERCULES

INFINITE SKY PUBLISHING

Cover illustration: Jemlin

Paperback ISBN: 978-1-959167-09-9

One

MIRANDA

I've been racking my brain, trying to find a way to help Aurora out of her forced engagement. I know my sister; she doesn't covet the High Witch position badly enough to marry someone she loathes. There must be another reason she's willing to go through with the charade.

I've read all the spells in my grimoire and haven't found anything useful. Since I'm not the next in line to become the High Witch, my training is not as intensive as Aurora's. My knowledge is limited. I have no choice but to raid Mom's office and look through her books.

As the High Witch, she maintains a nocturnal schedule to better serve her boss, King Raphael. So, I must wait until she's out of the house. But tonight, she decides to lock herself in her office instead of walking out after sunset. Crap on toast.

It's almost midnight. Niko has long since gone to sleep, and I pretend to have done the same. My eyes are getting droopy though. If Mom doesn't leave soon, I'll have to postpone my snooping around until tomorrow.

I'm minutes away from falling asleep when I hear the front door open and shut. Finally!

I jump out of bed, suddenly energized by my mission. On my

tiptoes, I creep to her office. The door is ajar. Mom keeps her most dangerous books protected in the safe, so locking the door is unnecessary. But I don't need them—at least I hope I don't. I just want a spell to make Calvin repulsed by the idea of marrying Aurora. There won't be any repercussions for her if he's the one who calls off the wedding.

After spending half an hour speed-reading through Mom's books, I find one hex that could work. The only problem, I quickly realize, is that it requires an ingredient I won't find in our pantry. The only place where I might find it is the Nightshade Market, which only opens from midnight to six in the morning. I have to pay a visit to it now and take advantage that Mom just left and most likely will be away for hours.

I jot down the recipe and then return to my room to change. By the time I leave the house, it's already one in the morning. At this hour, it doesn't take long to reach Salem Common where the Nightshade Market's hidden entrance is. The park is deserted, but even so, I pull my hoodie over my head, keeping my face hidden in the shadows. I'm not allowed to be here, especially alone. It's not the safest place in Salem.

Once I reach the bandstand, I recite the spell that will reveal the Nightshade Market to me. Technically, I'm not supposed to know the words, but it's common knowledge among the young witches and mages in the coven. Sometimes I think the elders withhold information solely for the sake of being pains in the ass.

This is not my first visit to the hidden place. I've been here before with my friends. The first time, I wasn't prepared for the feeling of falling out of the sky and ended up flat on my butt. This time, I brace against one of the columns and lock my knees tight. The spell takes a few seconds, enough to leave me light-headed for a moment. I take a few deep breaths before I step out of the bandstand and enter the infamous Nightshade Market.

At first glance, it looks exactly like a regular street market. There are rows of booths and tents in different sizes and colors.

But soon I can feel the magic surrounding the place. It's strong and seductive.

Not knowing where I might find what I need, I choose a random artery and begin my search. The missing ingredient is an herb, so I stop by every tent that sells those. After maybe twenty minutes wandering the market, I begin to realize what I'm looking for is not as common as I thought. No one I've asked has it or has a clue where I could find it. If I can't locate it in the next half hour, I'll have to look for another spell that doesn't require something so rare.

A commotion ahead draws my attention. I hear a vendor curse at a vampire for using compulsion, which puts me on high alert. Bloodsuckers usually don't come here unless they're accompanied by a witch or mage. Curious, I push through the crowd to see who has enraged the man. When I reach the front of the circle of onlookers, I catch Aurora and Saxon disappearing around a corner.

Hell and damn. What are they doing here?

A tall blond vampire follows them, and I do the same, urgency propelling me. I didn't expect to find him blocking my path after I rounded the corner. I stop in my tracks, almost colliding with his back.

"Fuck! Guys, cut it out," he says, exasperated.

I walk around him to see what my sister and Saxon are doing and freeze. *Shit.* They're all over each other, yanking at each other's clothes like animals in heat. Aurora would never act like that unless she was possessed or bewitched.

Her body glows from within, and then she blasts Saxon with a powerful electrical charge, but even so, he doesn't let go of her.

"What happened to them?" I ask the vampire next to me.

I need to know so I can maybe try a counter spell.

"They're mates."

"Son of a bitch. I don't know any magic that can stop them. Brute strength is the only solution. We need to separate them now."

He looks at me with wide eyes, and holy moly, talk about male perfection. I shouldn't have noticed his looks given our current situation, but he's too striking and I'm not blind. Perfectly sculpted face, bright sky-blue eyes, and lips that are like a beacon to me. My throat becomes suddenly dry and all my thoughts get scrambled. Lucky for us, he only hesitates for a second before jumping into action. With a hard yank, he pulls Saxon off Aurora, and then jumps back when Saxon bares his fangs at him and roars.

Fuck. He's gone berserk. He's going to attack Mr. Perfect for interrupting the mating. I should have known. Quicker than lightning, I shove my hand in my bag and grab a crystal. Saxon pounces, but I'm able to create a protective barrier in front of us at the last second. Saxon hits the invisible wall and the impact sends him flying back. He hits the ground hard and doesn't move.

There's a buzz in my ears and my hand holding the crystal tingles with residual magic. *Holy shit, I can't believe I was able to pull that off.*

"Did you do that?" Mr. Perfect asks me, piercing through my post-spell haze.

"Yeah."

"Thank you. You saved me from getting shredded to pieces."

I glance at him, and once again, I can't help being stunned by his beautiful face. He's a vampire, but he feels otherworldly.

"Sure," I reply.

I realize I'm staring like a fool. I should look away, but I can't. He has reeled me in with his bright eyes. To be fair, he's staring at me as well, almost as if he's intrigued by me. I snort in my head. Yeah, very unlikely. Maybe I have dirt on my face.

"What happened?" Saxon asks, breaking my connection with Mr. Perfect.

"You and Aurora went crazy," he replies.

"Can someone explain to me what the hell is going on?" I ask, even though Mr. Perfect already told me Aurora and Saxon are mates. But how in the world they got to the point where the urge to mate overwhelmed everything is still a mystery.

Aurora steps in front of Saxon, pulling the torn pieces of her jacket closer. "Not until you tell me what you're doing here, Miranda."

Ah, shit. Maybe I should have kept my mouth shut. We're no longer alone and I can't confess in front of all these witnesses the real reason I'm here. I'm saved from coming up with an excuse when Lucca and Vivienne come running.

"What now?" Saxon asks as he jumps back onto his feet.

"You need to get Vivienne and Rikkon to the institute at once. Jacques is here and he's not alone," Lucca replies.

Rikkon? I stare at the blond male again. He feels like a vampire, but looking closely, I see his resemblance to Vivienne. Why is he pretending to be a vampire like his sister?

Aurora, Saxon, Lucca, and Vivienne begin to argue about what to do. With Tatiana momentarily out of the picture, Jacques is their number one enemy. Lucca and Saxon want to stay and fight, Aurora and Vivienne want to leave immediately.

To me, the solution is simple.

"What if we hex the crap out of Jacques?" I suggest.

Aurora gives me a droll look. "We can't attack him unprovoked, especially you and me. We would be breaking the Accords."

Her remark makes me feel small and stupid. Maybe I should have kept my mouth shut. I don't know much about all the politics among vampires and the magical community.

"He doesn't need to know the hex came from you," Rikkon butts in. "Can't you cast a spell from afar?"

His support causes my heart to do a backflip. I feel giddy, like the schoolgirl that I am. And when he glances at me with a small smile on his lips, I pretty much melt on the spot. My cheeks feel hot like I'm running a fever. This is all so new to me. I'm not prone to going gaga over pretty boys.

"What's the fun in that?" Saxon retorts. "That's sneaky and cowardly."

"This is not a show, Sax," Vivienne replies. "It's life and death.

I'm not risking Lucca's or Rikkon's lives so you guys can dick around in a testosterone contest."

A chuckle bubbles up my throat, but I clamp my mouth shut. I don't need any of Aurora's friends to think I'm an immature little girl.

Suddenly, the weather turns colder, and a shiver runs down my spine. The gust of wind that comes from behind feels unnatural somehow. Aurora looks over her shoulder. Did she sense the wrongness that came with the chilly breeze like I did?

"Where was Jacques the last time you saw him?" she asks Lucca.

"Right at the front of the market. By now, who knows?"

Loud voices can be heard fast approaching us. A section of the crowd surrounding us gets pushed aside, and a scrawny-looking man steps through, followed by two towering men who ooze power. My muscles become rigid in an instant when I recognize what they are: members of the Warlock of Ivern Guild, the most badass and scary mages in our community.

Shit. They don't look friendly.

The scrawny man points an accusing finger at Saxon and Rikkon. "Those are the bloodsuckers who broke the sacred rules of Nightshade Market."

"Sacred rules? It was just a little bit of compulsion," Saxon replies defensively. "No one got hurt."

My jaw drops to the ground. Is Aurora's mate dense? Can't he sense the dark power emanating from the warlocks?

She steps closer to him and hisses. "Sax, don't say another word."

"You're all coming with us," one of the warlocks says.

Automatically, I step closer to Rikkon, not knowing if I want to protect him or if I'm seeking protection myself. A moment later, he takes my hand in his, squeezing a little. I don't want to think too much about this, but hell if the damn butterflies in my stomach don't have a will of their own.

RIKKON

I don't know what prompted me to take Miranda's hand, but it felt good. I can't recall the last time I had the desire for human connection. My memories have been scrambled by the druid spell. I can't trust them, but should I trust this new development?

Lost in my own mind, I miss part of the conversation around us, but I catch when Aurora agrees to leave with those menacing strangers. Saxon is not happy about her declaration, so I butt in.

"At least now we don't have to worry about Jacques anymore."

Both Saxon and Lucca turn to glower at me. Miranda pulls her hand from mine at once, and I try to not let disappointment win. Maybe I shouldn't have reached for her hand anyway. She must know about my recent past. In this lifetime, I'm a thief and a junkie. I've done terrible things to Vivienne and myself, seeking relief from I don't know what. It's a phantom pain, an agony that won't give me peace.

One of the warlocks points a finger in our direction and whispers words that sound familiar, even if I don't understand the meaning. There's an itch in my brain now, the discomfort of a hidden memory trying to break the lock of its prison cell.

A bright green light swallows our group, and for a split second I'm the wind. I'm whole again. The feeling comes and goes too quickly, and when I'm back in this hollow shell, a wave of melancholy hits me hard, dragging me to a pit of despair.

My companions moan as if the quick trip was the worst part for them. For me, it's the arrival and the loss of something fundamental, vital. The need to seek anything to make me numb to this sense of misery returns. I stomp on it. I can't succumb to weakness now. A lot is at stake and I've failed Vivienne too many times.

I survey our new surroundings. We're in a great chamber and judging by the intricate design on the walls and the classic oil paintings hanging from them, I'd guess we're in a place of importance. A woman with dark hair pulled back and a severe expression glares in Aurora's direction. I see the resemblance between them. She must be the High Witch.

Instinctively, I glance at Miranda. She's watching her older sister with apprehension in her gaze. I might not know much about the inner workings of vampires' and witches' politics, but what Aurora and Saxon did at the Nightshade Market is bad news for both of them.

"Aurora Yuki, you have a lot of explaining to do," the woman says in a cold tone.

"About what exactly?" She crosses her arms in front of her chest, visibly incensing her mother.

"What about?" the High Witch shrieks. "You were spotted behaving in a most disgraceful manner with that blond vampire in the middle of the Nightshade Market."

She continues on her tirade, but a sharp pain on my forehead distracts me. I press the heel of my hand against it, trying to massage away the ache. The throbbing recedes to a faint discomfort, allowing me to pay attention to the situation once more.

Miranda takes a step forward. "Rora did nothing wrong. This whole fiasco was all my fault."

"Oh? Is that so?" Her mother raises an eyebrow, clearly not buying Miranda's excuse.

"It's kind of embarrassing, really. I needed an ingredient for a love potion and went to the Nightshade Market to buy it. I met Aurora and her friends there by chance, and thanks to my clumsiness, Aurora and Saxon ended up covered in Venus Dust."

A faint blush spreads through her cheeks. This lie must be humiliating for Miranda, but she still went with it to help her sister. My appreciation for the young witch grows, and once again, I feel the urge to get closer to her, but not exactly in a romantic way. What is it about her that beguiles me so much?

"And you expect me to believe that's what happened?" her mother snaps.

"She's not lying, ma'am," one of the powerful mages who brought us here says.

Wait? Why is he lying? Suspicion immediately takes hold, making me leery of the duo. First the familiar spell they used on us, and now this. *Fuck*. I wonder if I met them before I lost all my memories.

"Are you saying you were there? You witnessed with your own eyes those events?"

"Yes, ma'am."

The High Witch schools her expression into one of impassive boredom. "Very well. You're all dismissed. Except you, Miranda."

My spine becomes rigid at once and I feel like I should say something, intervene. But I'm a nobody, a broken prince from a forgotten land.

Miranda drops her gaze to the floor, seemingly resigned to staying behind. She lied to protect her sister even at the risk of punishment. I did a similar thing once, even though I don't remember. Vivienne told me I defied our mother and chose to cross over to the mortal lands instead of remaining by Queen Maewe's side. I don't regret my sacrifice, not even for a minute. Maybe that's why I'm drawn to the witch girl. We're kindred spirits.

I spare one last glance at her before I'm enveloped once again by the mage's magic. The spell seeps through my brain, scratching at a memory on the cusp of rediscovery. This time, I'm prepared for it and hold on to the tendrils of enchantment for as long as I can. When we land back in our apartment at Bloodstone, the latch trapping my memories definitely has a fissure. All I have to do now is keep applying pressure until it finally cracks open.

Two

MIRANDA

I'm a witch, but I'm also human, even if the non-magical folk disagree. That means, unlike Harry Potter, I don't go to a fancy wizard school. I must suffer the public high school system like everyone else.

Waking up early in the morning after an all-nighter was a bitch. Staying awake in class? Almost impossible. But the worst part of my day comes after regular school is over and I head over to witchcraft training. All young witches and mages must attend the after-school special program in order to learn to master spells and stay out of trouble.

There are currently two covens in Salem: the New Salem coven which I belong to, and the Dark Moon coven, led by the Belmont family. Both have pledged allegiance to King Raphael, however, the Dark Moon's loyalty to the king is weak, and there are rumors they've assisted Tatiana in the past. No wonder my mother is determined to marry Aurora off to Calvin Belmont.

Unfortunately, Aurora is mated to Saxon, so more than ever I must help her get out of the engagement without putting in jeopardy the frail accord between the magical community and the king.

It's my luck that the first person I cross paths with when I enter the Institute for Witches and Mages is Devon Belmont, Calvin's younger brother. He's the spitting image of Calvin, down to the arrogant smirk permanently plastered to his face.

His eyes shine with mischief when he sees me striding down the hallway. He steps into my path, blocking me.

"Where are you going in such a hurry, Mir?"

"Move aside, Devon. I'm not in the mood for your antics."

"Is that how you treat a future member of your family?" He moves into my personal space, and quickly, my blood begins to boil. I'd hex him if I wasn't already walking on thin ice with my mother.

"No matter what happens, you will never be part of my family," I reply through clenched teeth.

His dark eyebrows furrow together. "I know what you were up to last night."

I freeze as a ball of dread sinks into my stomach. That everyone here would know about my foray at the Nightshade Market was a given, but this toad couldn't possibly know the real reason for my visit.

"Giving your sister and that bloodsucker Venus Dust was a low move, Mir, and so fucking dumb. All you did was tarnish her reputation."

Wait? He thinks I did that on purpose? *Shit*. The possibility people would think that never occurred to me. It'd be too stupid as a plan to cancel Aurora's engagement.

"I didn't throw Venus Dust on them on purpose, dumbass. It was an accident."

"No matter what your sister does, she *will* marry Calvin, which means..." He trails his fingers down my arm, leaning closer to my ear. "*We* will be family. Maybe we can even be more intimate than th—"

I grab his hand in a vise-like grip, and make it burn with invisible fire.

"Aargh. Let go of me."

"Ms. Leal. Stop that immediately." The stern voice of Serena LaVerne, one of our instructors, cuts through my rage.

I drop Devon's hand and step away from the jerkface. He cradles his hand against his chest, contorting his face into a grimace.

"She attacked me out of nowhere."

"You touched me without consent."

"Enough!" Serena snaps. "I want to see you both in my office. Now!"

Great. So much for trying to stay out of trouble. I want my mother's attention, but not in a negative way. I sulk after Serena, already knowing Devon is going to spin a tale where I'm the bad guy. At least he gives me a wide berth. I don't regret burning his hand even if that will land me in a heap of trouble.

Serena enters her office, sitting behind the huge mahogany desk that takes up most of the small space. Devon pulls up a chair, but I choose to remain standing.

"Now, I want to know why you attacked Devon, Miranda. You know that's against our protocols."

"Like I said, he touched me without my consent."

"I touched her arm. How does that warrant getting my hand burned?" he complains.

"You did more than that! You made insinuations," I retort angrily.

"Just shut up, both of you." Serena pinches the bridge of her nose. "I don't have time for this nonsense."

"Are you kidding me?" Devon replies, body coiled tight with tension. "Miranda ought to be punished."

"And you ought to keep your hands to yourself. I have eyes and ears, and you have a reputation."

Holy shit. I didn't expect Serena to put Devon in his place. He's a Belmont after all. Then again, I'm not just a nobody either. I'm the daughter of the High Witch, the highest position in the magical community. The corners of my lips turn upward. Devon is getting more purple by the second and that amuses me to no end.

"Wipe that smugness off your face, Miranda. You're no saint either. The only person who manages to be worse than you in your family is Niko."

I bite the inside of my cheek to keep me from offering a reply. Niko is a hell-raiser for sure, and she wears that moniker with pride. But she's the youngest child, and it's what people—even my mother—expect from her. As the middle child, I'm supposed to be the levelheaded one in the family. I'm surprised by Serena's comment. Besides my unauthorized trip to the Nightshade Market, I don't break the rules that often, and I was only caught yesterday doing so.

"Since you're not going to punish this brat, can I go now? I don't want to be late for my potions class." Devon stands up, not waiting for a reply.

"Yeah, you can go now. Not you, Miranda. I'd like a word."

Devon smirks at me on his way out. I have to fight the urge to flip him off.

"So Devon can't be late but I can?" I ask once the door closes behind him.

"This won't take long. I heard you were in the Nightshade Market looking for ingredients to make a love potion. You know that's illegal, and it can have serious, even deadly consequences."

"My mother already gave me that sermon."

"Even so, it's my duty as your instructor to reinforce the message. No boy is worth going through all that trouble, Miranda. The effect of a love potion is just an illusion. Trust me when I say this: wait for the real deal."

My face becomes warmer. I'm sure I'm blushing all ways to kingdom come.

"Yeah, I know. Don't worry. I've learned my lesson. No more love potions for me."

Serena nods. "Good. Now get going. Since I've decided not to punish you, you can't use this meeting as an excuse for being tardy."

I glance at the clock mounted behind her desk. *Shit*. Class starts in a minute. I have to grow wings to make it in time. I wish I had done more than burn Devon's hand. He would look fabulous with boils on his face.

Besides my altercation with Devon, my day at the institute was okay. I had expected my friends to mock me for procuring Venus Dust, or ask who it was for, but they were all more interested to know about Aurora and Saxon. Relationships between vampires and witches are taboo, so I get their curiosity.

But as they asked me about my sister and her mate, my thoughts kept wandering to Rikkon. He took my hand last night, surprising the hell out of me. It felt good, but if it meant more than a simple offer of comfort in a stressful situation, I screwed up by pulling my hand away brusquely when Saxon's and Lucca's attention turn to us. I don't want or need anyone taking the situation out of context.

Aurora was pretty clear later, Rikkon is off-limits. Plus, he'd also never pay attention to me anyway. I'm just a teenage witch, and he's a Nightingale prince. Talk about way out of my league.

Mom told me I was grounded thanks to my stunt last night, but she doesn't know my schedule. Instead of going home after witchcraft training is over, I head to the other side of town for my secret class in martial arts. I can't get the advanced training Aurora gets because I'm not the next in line to be the High Witch, but no one ever said I couldn't learn more about my heritage. Our grandfather was a mage from Japan, not only skilled in the magical arts, but also a badass in sword and hand-to-hand combat. He was a samurai, a fact that has fascinated me since I was a little girl.

I once asked Mom if I could train to become one, but she shot down that idea faster than a bullet. Witches weren't meant to be warriors, according to her. Easy for her to say when she has access to powerful magic that most don't. She doesn't need to turn her body into a lethal weapon when she has all that power at her fingertips.

As soon as I got my driver's license, I secretly enrolled in samurai training given by one of my grandpa's oldest friends. I considered telling Niko about it, but one, she doesn't have the discipline required for it, and two, she has a big mouth. I couldn't risk her blabbing about my secret to Mom by accident.

Despite being bone-tired, the prospect of another martial arts lesson fills me with energy. I enjoy my classes with Mr. Shirogane more than any witchcraft lecture at the institute. I even got a tattoo near my hip bone of the Japanese *kanji* for loyalty, honor, and bravery, the three paramount virtues that infuse *bushido*, the samurai code of conduct.

Mr. Shirogane's dojo is above a laundromat in a busy commercial street near dragon territory. Finding a parking spot close to the building is impossible. I always park a few blocks away and run to his dojo. That's my warm-up.

He only has one other student, Marcello, a non-blueblood vampire who stopped aging at around twenty. He's tall and bulky, packing some serious muscles under his *gi*. He's also an antisocial grump. I'm usually the first to arrive, but when I cross the dojo's threshold, I see Marcello and Mr. Shirogane already doing the warm-up exercises.

"Good evening, Miss Leal," Mr. Shirogane greets me.

"Good evening, Sensei." I turn to Marcello. "Bloodsucker."

He snorts but doesn't offer a comeback. I shake my head as I head to the restroom to change. I started calling him bloodsucker as a test to see if I could get a rise out of him. It's the only word that seems to affect him, even if only slightly, so the nickname stuck.

He joined Mr. Shirogane last year when he moved to Salem from Boston. Quiet and mysterious, it took forever to get him to tell me more about his life. And even after all these months, all I know now is that he wishes to join the Red Guard and he wants nothing to do with the Bloodstone Institute.

A minute later dressed in my *gi*, I join Mr. Shirogane and Marcello on the tatami. They have just finished warming up, but since I ran here and they didn't wait for me to start the lesson, I'll skip that.

"What's on the schedule today, Sensei?" I ask.

He raises an eyebrow. "I see you're choosing to channel your rebellious side tonight, Miss Leal."

"What? I ran two blocks."

Marcello shakes his head and says nothing.

"Oh, spare me the judgmental silence, bloodsucker."

"Quit calling me bloodsucker. *That* is judgmental."

Whoa. That's more reaction than I'm used to. Something must be bothering him.

"It's not judgmental. It's stereotypical. Two different things." I smirk.

"Children, quit bickering. To answer your earlier question, Miss Leal. Tonight we'll begin our *Hyoho Niten Ichi-ryu* training."

"Two heavens, one school," Marcello and I mumble under our breaths at the same time. Then we glance at each other. His hazel eyes are sparkling with interest now, a mirror of my own.

Samurai usually only carried two swords: the katana and the wakizashi. The katana was only used for outdoor fighting and the wakizashi indoors. Until Miyamoto Musashi, the famous samurai who wrote *The Book of Five Rings*, created the *Hyoho Niten Ichi-ryu* technique, which became the characteristic stance of both swords held above the head to attack. The swords work in a consecutive pace: one sword defends, the other attacks in the next step. It's a badass technique that I've been dying to learn since I started my training with Mr. Shirogane.

Marcello and I walk over to the wall where our training swords are mounted. I take mine down with reverence. Before I was even allowed to touch any blade, Mr. Shirogane drilled in my brain the most fundamental principal of the samurai. The sword represents the ethics underlining bushido. The code of conduct of the samurai denounces the irresponsible use of the sword, emphasizing self-possession and prudence.

"This ought to be fun," Marcello tells me with the hint of a smile, holding both swords in hand.

"I'm glad to know you do find joy in something."

He scrunches his face into a grimace. "There's no room in my life for mindless entertainment."

"Yeah, yeah. Woe is me is your motto."

"Mock me all you want. I wouldn't expect anything less from the daughter of the High Witch."

I whip my face to his. "What's that supposed to mean?"

"Nothing, Miranda. Let's focus on the lesson."

He returns to the center of the tatami while I stare a hole in his back. I know I can't make everyone like me, but his offhanded comment hurt me more than it should. I'm not a pampered brat, and I'll prove it to him and anyone who thinks the same.

Three

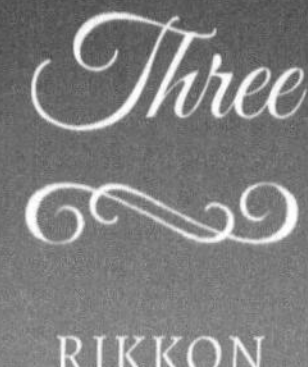

RIKKON

I didn't have a chance to investigate the booth with the dream catchers two nights ago, but now that my visions have returned with a vengeance, I need to find a way to lift the block from my memories sooner rather than later. The pain is crippling, and my body is once again craving relief in the only way it knows how: by taking drugs.

It was hell getting them out of my system when I was in Larsson's captivity. I don't want to go through that again.

The only issue about returning to the Nightshade Market is that I need a witch to take me there, and it only opens at night. Aurora is too busy with Saxon to be any help. Besides, if I ask for her assistance, she'll tell Vivi, and I don't want to involve her. This is something I must do without my sister.

I only know one other witch who might be inclined to help me. Miranda. I could probably find someone else, maybe a rogue mage, but my reason for asking Aurora's younger sister is simple. I recognized a kindred spirit. My memories are all messed up, but one thing I know for sure. I need a friend.

I wait until everyone in the apartment is asleep to sneak out. Through bits of conversation, I learned that there's a way out of Bloodstone through the catacombs. The issue is the five vampire ghosts trapped there that need Nightingale blood in order to break from their cell. I heard them whispering my name yesterday when I was near the stairs leading to the bowels of the institute.

Knowing I might not be strong enough to ignore their call, I borrow Vaughn's noise-cancelling headphones. If I can't hear their voices, then I won't succumb to their thrall.

The hallway in the main section of the institute is pitch black despite the fact that it's midafternoon. I wait until my eyesight adjusts to the gloom instead of using the flashlight app on my phone. I don't want to get caught. But my precaution proves pointless. Once I start walking, the motion-activated lights come to life.

My heart is thumping loudly in my chest, and in the dead silence of the afternoon at the institute, my pulse is all I can hear. I'm risking a lot by venturing out in broad daylight. If someone sees me, there goes my disguise. And that's in the best-case scenario. There's also the danger of getting captured by Tatiana's followers.

When I see the sign pointing to the basement stairs, I put the headphones on and play music as loud as it goes. I'm not one to get spooked by dark places, and yet my adrenaline levels spike with each step I take down to the basement. The corridor has faint illumination, but I'm not staying in the main hallway of this maze. Using the compass app on my phone, I let it guide me in the direction of the old cemetery. That's where the mausoleum is, and the stairs up to the surface.

As I plunge into complete darkness, the air becomes cooler. My skin breaks out in goose bumps, and my heart squeezes tightly in my chest almost as if it senses evil is lurking nearby. A lethargy seems to take hold of me. It feels like I'm treading water. *Fuck.* This can't be normal. Sure, I can't hear anything besides the loud music, but maybe the vampire ghosts have other ways to lure me into their trap.

I glance at my phone to make sure I'm still heading in the right direction. Suddenly, tendrils of cold air seem to wrap around my body. With a grunt I force my legs to move, breaking free from the invisible embrace, and running as fast as I can. My breathing is already coming out in bursts when I finally see the silhouette of an opening ahead. No sooner do I place my foot on the first step of the stairs, than the music in my ears stops abruptly and a chilling shriek pierces through. I fall on my knees, knocking the headphones off my head.

"You can't escape us. We'll be your doom," the disembodied voice tells me.

I jump back to my feet, forgetting the headphones that fell out of sight in the darkness. I need to get to the surface before the ghosts lure me back into the catacombs. A burst of energy propels me upward, and for a moment, I have the sensation that I'm flying until I collide with the wooden door at the top of the stairs.

It opens with the impact, and I fall once again, but this time on my side. My right shoulder hits the solid ground first, and white-hot agony makes me see stars. I roll onto my back, stunned for a moment as I ride the pain and catch my breath. But at least I'm out of the darkness and I can't sense the malevolent presence anymore.

I sit up and rotate my shoulder to make sure I didn't dislocate it or tear a muscle. It's sore, but the throbbing is already fading into a mild discomfort. The phone is still in my hand. It's a miracle I managed to hold on to it during my dash through the door.

It's ten past two o'clock. Miranda will probably get out of school soon. There is obviously more than one high school in Salem, but I did my homework before I left the apartment. It wasn't hard to find her social media profile and the name of her school. It's not stalking if the information is widely available online.

Yeah, keep saying that, Rikkon. Whatever makes you feel better.

For a second I consider calling an Uber, but then I remember I look like a vampire. Even humans will be affected by the spell. I can't let anyone take a good look at me. In hindsight, I should have thought things through. There's nothing for it now.

I get back up, and pull my hoodie over my head, covering my hair. I had the foresight to bring sunglasses too. It's not cold enough to justify covering my face with a scarf. I'll just have to stay away from people and keep my chin down as I head to town.

Before I leave the mausoleum, I look left and right to make sure the coast is clear. The old cemetery looks abandoned, but maybe familiars tend it. I haven't lived at Bloodstone long enough to learn the routine of the place.

To be on the safe side, I sprint toward the road, and on the way to town, I keep close to the edge of the forest. I must be able to hide quickly if the need arises.

It takes me around twenty minutes to arrive at Miranda's high school, but now that I'm here, I feel like an idiot. I don't know what car she drives and spotting her in the sea of students leaving the building might be difficult. There's also the issue that I have to remain hidden. Lurking in the shadows, wearing a hoodie and sunglasses probably makes me look hella suspicious.

I find a tree not too far from the school's entrance and wait, hoping I didn't already miss her leaving. I lose track of time, but my guess is that no more than five minutes have gone by. I'm so focused on scanning the crowd that when someone touches my arm I jerk to the side, hitting my sore shoulder against the tree trunk.

"Fuck," I curse under my breath.

"Sorry. What are you doing here, Rikkon?"

Miranda is standing in front of me, staring with those capti-vating almond-shaped eyes that shine with innocence. At once, a sense of calm washes over me, bringing my heart rate back to a normal pace. But when I open my mouth to answer her, nothing comes out. I'm tongue-tied and I don't know why.

Four

MIRANDA

My head is pounding with the worst headache possible. Our algebra teacher decided to surprise us with a quiz that I was so not prepared for. Add that to the aches from last night's samurai training, and it made for another hellish day in school. God, I can't wait to graduate and leave this hellhole.

It's no surprise I'm in a foul mood when I step outside the building. I still have to go through hours of witchcraft training, whereas my friends are heading to the mall. Blowing off the rest of the day is super tempting, but my conscience won't let me be bad. It reminds me that I'm already in the shitter with my mother. Getting my punishment extended just to fart around at the mall is not worth it.

Halfway toward my car, I spot a dark figure hiding behind a tree. My spine goes rigid as I squint, scanning the guy's aura. Shady characters lurking near the school is never a good sign. But is he a supe or just a human with bad intentions?

It doesn't take me long to register the male is a vampire. Impossible. He would have turned to ashes the moment sunlight touched his skin. That can only mean one thing.

"No way," I mutter under my breath as my heart does a somersault in my chest.

"What's the matter, brat?" a nauseating voice asks too close to my ear.

I spin around to glare at Devon. The idiot goes to the same high school as I do because suffering him at the institute is not enough. Fate had to make me suffer him here too. It seems he hasn't learned his lesson to stay away from me, though. He couldn't have shown up at a worse moment. If he sees Rikkon, he'll create a fuss.

"Nothing," I reply through clenched teeth. "What do you want, pest? Why are you acting like a stalker around me?"

He twists his expression into a scowl. "You wish I were your stalker. You're not my type."

"Is that supposed to make me feel bad? Run along now before I do more than burn your hand."

He snorts. "Do you think I'm afraid of your cheap magic tricks?"

I lift my hand and snap my fingers, creating sparks between them. This fire is not invisible. It's the real deal and it will do more than inflict pain. It will actually burn. Creating fire is the only cool spell I was able to master so far from Aurora's grimoire that Niko and I have been secretly studying from.

Devon places a hand over his chest. "Ooh, you know how to make fire. Big fucking deal. I'm a Belmont. You have no idea what kind of powerful spells I have at my fingertips."

Crap. I shouldn't have goaded the idiot. I'm not afraid of him. He might be a Belmont, but there's no chance in hell his elders allow him access to the family's secrets yet. Witches and mages only pass on knowledge to the younger generations when they have no choice in the matter—meaning, when they have a foot in the grave. Also, if we start a hex war in the middle of the school's parking lot, my mother might ship me to a boarding school far away from here.

"Yo, Devon," one of his friends shouts from the distance. "Are you coming or not?"

He looks over his shoulder. "Yeah. I'll be right there." Then he turns to me. "You're lucky this time, brat. But rest assured, payback is coming for your little stunt yesterday."

"I'm trembling in fear," I retort when I should have simply let him have the last word. I'm trying to get rid of the guy as fast as I can, after all. There's a more pressing matter demanding my attention.

Luckily, Devon doesn't engage and simply saunters away. I don't move from my spot, not even to check if Rikkon is still behind that tree, until Devon disappears inside his car and drives off. Then I pivot around and stride to Rikkon. He's still there with his eyes glued to the front of the school. I expect him to turn around when I approach, but he doesn't move a muscle until I touch his arm to get his attention.

He jumps, startled, hitting his shoulder against the tree.

"Fuck," he mutters, massaging the spot right away.

Way to go, Miranda. You could have called out to him instead of scaring the crap out of the guy.

My heart is beating faster now, and my stomach is tied in knots. Why does he make me so unsteady?

"Sorry. What are you doing here, Rikkon?" I ask through the nervousness, hoping he doesn't notice.

He doesn't answer for a couple of beats, turning the happy butterflies in my stomach into angry hornets.

"I, er..." He rubs the back of his neck. "I came looking for you."

"Really?" My voice comes out high-pitched and I berate myself for being so transparent. "I mean, why? Is everything okay at Bloodstone?"

"As okay as it can be, considering recent events. I was worried about you."

The butterflies in my stomach turn radioactive, fluttering

their wings at the same rapid pace as my heart. *Settle down, damn bugs. Why am I having such an intense crush on Rikkon?*

"You were?" I squeak.

"Of course. Your mother didn't look happy about your confession."

I look away as embarrassment washes over me. I should have thought of a better excuse than a love potion. That lie will haunt me for months.

"No, but she only grounded me. It could have been worse."

"What you did for your sister, taking the blame for what happened, was amazing."

His compliment makes my heart sing. I don't get them often.

He looks left and right in a cagey manner, reminding me that he's not supposed to be out during the day when he's pretending to be a vampire.

"Can we go someplace safe to talk?" he asks.

"Yeah, of course. Stay right here. I'll bring my car over."

I sprint through the parking lot, trying my hardest not to let my imagination run wild. Just because Rikkon snuck out of the institute and risked exposure to see me doesn't mean he's into me. This is not a romance novel.

Shame hits me when I notice the state of my car. I'm not the tidiest person in the world and I tend to use the inside of my vehicle as a dumping ground for, well, everything. At least it doesn't smell. There's nothing I can do about the mess now.

I drive as close to the tree as possible, glad that the majority of students have already left campus. Devon's interruption was good for something.

Rikkon quickly pulls the door open and slides inside. The faint scent of mint and cardamom reaches my nose, adding another layer of things to enjoy about him. It's hard to concentrate when he looks *and* smells that good. *Yikes.* I need to find a major upsetting flaw to balance things out here, since the fact he's a former junkie has done nothing to turn me off.

Distractions aside, I'm dying to know the reason behind his

clandestine visit, but it's better if I drive someplace no one can see me with a passenger.

After a minute, my curiosity gets the better of me.

"So, why did you come to see me?"

"I know it's going to sound weird, but I need a favor."

"Why do you think it's going to sound weird?"

"We've just met."

"True, but you're hardly a stranger I picked up off the street. You're Vivi's brother."

He laughs softly. "I'm afraid that's not much better."

The sound is deprecatory. He must be thinking about his past as an addict. That doesn't sit well with me. Everyone has a past. At least he's trying to get better.

"What's the favor?" I ask to keep the conversation on track.

"I need to return to the Nightshade Market."

My fingers grip the steering wheel tighter. Of all the things he could have asked me, that's the one favor I might not be able to grant.

"Why?"

He takes a deep breath, making me guess he's going to make an important confession.

"I'm looking for something."

Disappointment washes over me. He doesn't trust me enough, but he wants my help. Isn't that the story of my life? *Maybe if you weren't such a people pleaser, folks wouldn't take advantage of you, Miranda.*

"You have to give me more than that," I say.

With a sigh, he looks out the window. He still has the hoodie over his head and the sunglasses so all I can see is the hard clench of his jaw.

"How much do you know about my situation?" he finally asks.

"I know you were Larsson's captive for a while, and you're a Nightingale prince without memories or powers."

"But you also know I'm a recovering addict, right?" He glances at me.

"Yeah. Aurora told me," I reply bitterly. She made sure to emphasize that part.

"I'm not only a junkie, Miranda. I am—*was*—also a drug dealer. It's not safe to be around me."

"Then why did you come looking for me?"

Please say because you couldn't stop thinking about me.

Oh my god. I have to stop watching soap operas.

"Because I'm selfish, and I'm in desperate need of help, and asking Vivi is... not an option right now."

God, Rikkon has to stop making these vague comments. My mind is spinning like a top, wondering why Vivi can't help him. I feel bad for him. I can't imagine being forced into exile and being stripped of your powers to boot. My mother might be cold and mean sometimes, but she'd never be that cruel to us.

But going to the Nightshade Market is not something I can do. It's not only the fact I'm grounded that's the problem. I'd be putting Rikkon's life in danger. Jacques wants Vivi, and if he has a chance to grab Rikkon to get to her, he will. I can't risk it. I don't have an arsenal of powerful spells at my disposal. I won't be any protection to him.

"I'm sorry. I can't take you to the Nightshade Market. It's not safe for us."

He rubs his face. "You're right. I don't know what I was thinking involving you like this. The last thing I want is to put you in harm's way. Maybe you can teach me the spell that makes the market visible."

"But you don't have any magic. Spells are not only about reciting random words."

I glance at him briefly just in time to catch the wince. *Shit.* I shouldn't have reminded him of his lack of powers.

"Why do you want to go back there anyway?" I quickly add.

"The last time I was there, I saw a booth selling dream catchers. There was something about them that caught my eye. I think

I've been there before. Maybe that vendor was the one who sold me the memory spell."

I concentrate, trying to remember that booth. I know I walked by it. The dream catchers drew my attention because they were similar to the ones I'd seen in the window of a shop near Mr. Shirogane's dojo.

"Was there anything about those dream catchers that stood out to you?"

"Yeah. They had little crystals on them that reflected the light in a peculiar manner, like they were creating a pattern around them. I felt drawn to them like I'm drawn to... er, like a moth is drawn to a flame."

His comment makes me look at him again. A blush creeps up his cheeks and now I'm dying to know who Rikkon is drawn to. I'm so jealous that I can't breathe right. *Ugh.* I have to get over this stupid infatuation. I'm nearly eighteen, not a tween.

"Well, we can't go back to the market, but I think I can help you."

"Really?" He turns in his seat, facing me completely. "How?"

I want to peel my eyes off the road once more to bask in his attention, but causing a fender bender is not what we need right now.

"I've seen similar dream catchers before."

"Where?"

"Near dragon territory. Are you allowed back in there?"

He grumbles, facing forward again as he sinks dejectedly against the seat. "Not really. But you said the shop is *near* Larsson's domain, not exactly in it."

"True, but there are plenty of dragons roaming where the shop is. If they see you, are they instructed to punish you?"

Rikkon laughs, and this time, I detect actual amusement.

"No, I won't be punished. But I can't get noticed by anyone anyway. Thanks to this stupid spell, everyone thinks I'm a vampire. I even have fake fangs." He leans closer, showing me his teeth. "See?"

Tingles run down my spine thanks to his proximity. It's an effort not to look. "Yeah, I know."

He chuckles, returning to his side. "Sorry. I forgot you're a witch. You probably know how to brew the potion that made me look like this."

"Probably." *If I ever get the recipe for it.* "I have an idea. What if I glamoured you to appear human?"

"Wait, you want to remove the spell? Can you do that?"

"No, it's a potion spell, so you either have to wait until the effects wear off or you must drink an antidote."

"So you want to place a glamour on top of a glamour?"

"Yeah. Mind you, I don't know if it will work, but it's worth a try."

He shrugs. "I'm game for anything that will make our trip easier."

Oh, Rikkon. Nothing that involves you will be easy, not when I can't stop going hormonal just by looking at you.

Five

There are a million things I want to ask Miranda, but I keep my mouth shut during the rest of the ride. I can't be trusted to not say something inappropriate. I almost confessed that I'm drawn to her. Who does that to someone they've just met? Psychos and stalkers, that's who.

Don't get me started on getting closer to her to show my fake vampire teeth. Could I be any lamer? It's hard to believe I'm an immortal who has lived for thousands of years when I act like an idiot. Do I miss human connection that much?

We're in a busy commercial street that I know all too well. I've sold drugs in dark alleyways nearby. It's why I accidentally crossed into dragon territory. I was too high to realize what I had done and then I got caught. I shiver, remembering my days in captivity. The dragon kingpin didn't hurt me, but the withdrawals were killer. I thought I was going to die.

Miranda parks her car on one of the less busy side streets. It's sketchy as hell.

"Are you sure you want to leave your car here?" I ask, looking out the window.

"Oh, it's fine. I park here every night."

Now she has my full attention. "Why?"

Her beautiful eyes widen as guilt shines in them. "Never mind. Forget I said anything."

"Mir, are you in trouble?"

"Mir?" Her eyebrows arch.

My ears and face burn. Why am I calling her by cute nicknames? Just because I feel comfortable around her like I've known her for years doesn't make it true.

"I'm sorry. I shouldn't have called you that."

"Oh, that's fine. I don't mind. All my friends call me Mir. I was just surprised you did."

"Okay, cool. Anyway, how does the glamour spell work?" I ask to change the subject.

The sooner we visit the dream catcher store, the sooner I can stop making a fool of myself. I haven't felt the need for a friend in so long that I'm messing everything up.

"Hold on. I need to grab something from my bag."

She unbuckles her seat belt then twists around, getting her body halfway through the gap separating our seats. She's awfully close to me now, and the scent of vanilla and strawberry hits me at full blast, reminding me of picnics in sunny meadows, pie, and laughter. A heady feeling spreads through my chest, triggered by the shadow of a forgotten memory.

I scooch closer to the door and farther away from her. I can't let her see how her proximity is affecting me. She already has enough reason to stay the hell away. I don't need to add more to the list.

"Ugh, where's my damn grimoire?" she mutters under her breath.

A smirk blossoms on my lips. She's cute when she curses. I shake my head and force my eyes forward. Thoughts like that shouldn't cross my mind. Friendship is the only thing I can allow myself to have. More than that is dangerous. Not because of my fucked-up past or current situation. It's just a feeling I have in the pit of my stomach that if I ever allow myself to get involved with someone romantically, I'll bring doom and destruction to the world.

Miranda returns to her seat, clutching an oversized bag that, by the looks of it, is completely full.

"What do you have in there?" I ask.

"Everything. Ingredients for potions, extra clothes, food, my *gi*—"

"A *gi*? Are you into martial arts?"

She lifts her face to mine and stares at me with eyes as round as saucers. Then she sighs as if resigned.

"Since I keep saying stuff I shouldn't, might as well tell you why I come here every night. I'm training to become a samurai, and my sensei's dojo is a couple of blocks away."

My jaw slackens. "Wow, I didn't know there was samurai training here in Salem. That's awesome."

She smiles, getting a twinkle in her eyes. "Yeah, it's pretty neat. I love it. But my mother doesn't approve, hence why I have to keep it a secret."

"I won't betray your trust, Mir."

"You'd better not, or I'll kick your ass. Ha-ya!" She karate chops the air.

I can't help the laughter that escapes my lips.

"Yeah, you laugh now. Wait until you see me in action."

She returns her attention to the contents of her bag, moving stuff around inside as she continues her search.

"Do you have class today? I'd love to come."

"I do, but it's at night. Don't you have to be back at Blood-stone by then?"

I curse in my head. "Yep. I forgot about that detail."

She yanks a leatherbound notebook from the bag. "Aha! Found it."

"Is that your grimoire?"

"Yes. It doesn't have a lot of spells yet. The witches have a thing about earning knowledge. So it takes years to fill one of these. But Niko and I have been peeking at Aurora's grimoire in secret." She grins in a naughty way, drawing my attention to the fact that she's really pretty.

"Who is Niko?"

"Oh, that's my baby sister." Miranda drops her gaze to her grimoire and begins to turn pages. "I know I jotted down the spell for glamour not too long ago."

"I'm curious, why would you need glamour to pass for a human?"

"Oh, the glamour spell is not specifically for that. It's pretty generic. Like, I could glamour you to look hideous. Not that I'd ever do that. I mean, it would be a sin to hide that face from the world."

Her compliment makes me smile. I should leave it alone, but I can't help it.

"Oh, so you think I'm good-looking?"

She freezes for a second, then lifts her eyes to mine. "You have a mirror."

Her expression remains nonchalant, but her cheeks have a pink tinge to them now. She's embarrassed and for some reason, I'm loving that.

She returns her attention to the grimoire and a few seconds later, she declares, "Got it." Her eyes scan the page, and then she murmurs the spell a few times before setting the book aside. "Come closer."

I tense on the spot, fearing how I'm going to react to the nearness. She notices and frowns. "I'm not going to bite you."

"I know. It's just... I'm leery of magic." I scooch forward and try not to breathe through my nose. I can't let her perfume get to my head again.

"Don't take this the wrong way, but you're weird."

"Trust me, I've heard worse."

She takes a small glass vial from her bag, and then dabs her index finger with the liquid inside. When she reaches over, I force myself to become as still as a statue. But when she glides her finger over my forehead and cheekbones, goose bumps break out on my arms and I find myself leaning forward.

"Okay, now look into my eyes and try to not freak out, okay?"

"Sure," I reply in a tight voice as I remove my sunglasses.

She captures my face between her hands and whispers words in a foreign language I don't understand but know is ancient. My face tingles where she spread the ointment, and involuntarily, I wince.

"Shhh, it's going to be over soon," she says a breath away from my face.

She misunderstood my reaction. It's not the magic that's freaking me out. It's her touch. It's stirring feelings in me that split me in conflicting directions. I'm torn between wanting more of it and repelling it.

The tingle stops abruptly, and Miranda drops her hands from my face in an equally fast manner. I miss the contact immediately.

"Did it work?" I ask.

She wrinkles her nose and squints her eyes. "I think so."

"You think so? Do I still look like a vampire or not?"

"The issue is, I knew that you weren't a vampire, so the original spell was already screwy for me. I could catch glimpses of your true self. But anyway, there's only one way to know for sure." She opens the door of the car. "Let's go."

To be safe, I put my sunglasses on again, and pull the hoodie over my head before following her out. She's waiting for me on the curb, carrying her large bag over her shoulder. It looks too big for her, too heavy.

"I can carry that for you," I offer.

"Better not. What if I need something from it?"

"Okay." I shove my hands in my pockets. "I guess lead the way?"

Miranda stares at me for a couple of beats without moving,

and I don't know what to make of it. Is the glamour spell failing already?

She blinks her eyes a couple of times rapidly, and shakes her head a fraction, almost as if she's trying to clear a daze from her head.

"Sure, let's go."

I'm curious about what put her in a trance like that, but I know better than to ask. I've done a lot of strange things today.

We walk side by side, but I make a point to leave plenty of distance between our bodies. I don't want to accidentally brush her hand with mine and make her uncomfortable.

Miranda stops suddenly when we reach the end of the street, pressing her hand against my chest. So much for trying to avoid touching her.

"What?" I ask.

"I'm just checking to see if the coast is clear of dragons."

"I already told you I won't get punished as long as I don't try to sell drugs in their territory."

"Okay, but you know tensions are high between the dragons and vamps. It doesn't hurt to be safe."

Her comment reminds me of Saxon's close encounter with a dragon shifter. He almost died. Maybe I'm being too relaxed when it comes to them.

She looks left and right before stepping into the busy sidewalk of the main avenue. I follow her, noticing how much closer I am to her now. I should increase the gap, but I don't.

"No one has batted an eyelash in your direction," she mutters. "I think the glamour spell worked."

"You sound surprised. I'm sure you're more talented than you realize."

She doesn't offer a reply, so I peek at her face. Her expression is closed off, and I wonder if I said something wrong. I should ask, but I lose my chance when she points at a sign ahead.

"That's the shop."

Anticipation and a pinch of worry compete for space in my

head. The closer I get to unlocking my memories, the surer I become that I'm about to open Pandora's box. The doorbell chimes when we enter, but there's no one behind the counter. Maybe the clerk is in the back.

There aren't any dream catchers on display, and inside the small store there are so many trinkets on the shelves and hanging from the ceiling that it's hard to pinpoint any particular item.

"We should split up to cover more ground quickly," Miranda suggests.

"Okay."

She veers to the left, disappearing from view. I take the aisle on the right. I'm almost at the end when I hear the doorbell chime again, and then the loud voices of two men.

"I already told you. I haven't seen that guy in years."

"Bullshit. Don't fucking lie to me, vermin. He was seen at the Nightshade Market two nights ago."

Shit. Are they talking about me?

"So what? The market is hu—"

A crash cuts his reply short, followed by a grunt of pain.

"He was seen in front of your stand. Now, I ask again, where the hell is he?"

Whoever the person at the front is, it's not someone we want to bump into. Slowly, I continue toward the end of the aisle. I need to find Miranda so we can get the hell out of here. When I turn a corner, I almost collide with her. She looks up, eyes wide with fear. I want to reassure her, tell her everything is going to be okay, but I don't speak, not even a whisper. I don't want to risk exposure.

"I don't know," the man at the front mumbles. "I swear. Please don't kill me. I've been a faithful servant of the Queen through all these years."

Miranda's eyebrows shoot up. I don't know who she thinks the man is referring to, but the way the blood drains from her face, I can make an educated guess—Tatiana, King Raphael's nemesis. Her followers consider her to be the rightful ruler of the vampires.

I look around, trying to find an alternative exit since it's clear we can't use the main one. What I find first are the dream catchers that caught my attention at the market. Unfortunately, I won't be able to investigate why they appeal to me. We have to get out of here before we're discovered.

Miranda pulls on my sleeve and points at the opposite direction. I see it then, a door semi-hidden by boxes with a faded Exit sign above it. Without wasting any time, I grab her hand and stride toward it. But in my eagerness to escape, I don't consider all the objects on display on the shelves and Miranda's huge bag. She bumps into an item that shatters on the floor.

"It seems you have customers, Dougal," the assailant says.

Miranda and I break into a run and just as I yank the door open, a gust of wind comes rushing down the aisle and suddenly, there's a tall man with hair past his shoulders and an ugly sneer on his face standing a few feet away from us.

"You've been a hard male to find, Rikkon Gael," he says.

"Go!" I try to push Miranda through the door, but she plants her feet on the floor and doesn't budge.

"I'm not leaving without you."

"Oh, you found yourself a little friend." He reaches behind his back and as he lifts his arm, he reveals a glowing sword that had been concealed until then.

Blinding pain in my forehead hits me then, making me grunt. *No. No. No.* I can't be having a vision now, when I need to protect Miranda from whoever this person is.

He sheaths his sword again and grabs me by the lapels of my jacket. "What do you see?"

"Let him go!" Miranda yells, but the strange man only has eyes for me.

The white-hot pain is still splitting my skull in two, leaving little room for fear. He shakes me and yells in my face, "What do you see?"

I spot movement in my peripheral, and a second later, the man howls in pain, letting me go. I stagger back, catching the sight of a small dagger protruding from his side.

"Come on. Let's go!" Miranda yanks my arm and drags me down the narrow corridor that we hope will lead out of the building.

I expect the man to give chase, but he doesn't. My head is still throbbing as we emerge in the narrow alley in the back of the building, and soon I begin to see double. Miranda appears in my line of sight and captures my face in her hands.

"Are you okay?"

"So much... pain."

"Did he do something to you?"

"No. You need... to get out of here... before he comes after us."

"I'm not going to leave you behind. Come on, lean on me. I'll help you."

I throw my arm over her shoulders and let her drag me out of the fetid alleyway. At least I can still use my legs. Our progress is much slower than I would have liked, but eventually we reach the main street. It doesn't give me comfort though. I don't think the man who attacked us cares about witnesses.

Another bolt of blinding pain makes me double over and I almost cause us to collapse in a heap.

"Rikkon. Oh my god. What's happening to you?"

My jaw is locked tight as disjointed images flash before my eyes. I see darkness and then a grotesque creature with a mouth too big for its face and bug eyes that glow red.

There's no escape.

The thought pops in my head and I don't know if it's mine or the creature's.

I black out for a second, and when I come back to, my face is smashed against Miranda's shoulder as she holds me upright. With effort, I stand straighter, mortified by my display of weakness.

"Are you okay?" she asks, staring at me with concern.

"I will be, in a moment." I look away, unable to sustain her gaze. My face is burning up from shame. "We need to get out of here."

"My car is just around the corner."

Now that the pain has decreased to a faint throb, I can move without assistance. We sprint to the side street where Miranda parked her car, and no sooner are we inside and the doors are closed, than she peels away from the curb, burning rubber.

She doesn't say a word as she navigates the heavy traffic, keeping her eyes glued ahead with the occasional glimpses at the rearview mirror.

"He's not pursuing us," I tell her.

"How do you know?"

"A hunch."

I can't explain how I know that the stranger isn't after us. It's just one of the peculiar certainties I have about things.

"He used your Nightingale last name, Gael. And that sword, it glowed."

I press my closed fist against my forehead. "I think that male was a Nightingale too."

"Oh shit. Are you saying I stabbed a psychotic immortal?" She pries her eyes from the road to stare at me wide-eyed.

"I think so. And thank you for doing that. I didn't know you had a dagger in that monstrous bag of yours."

"Yeah, every witch carries a dagger on them. I thought he was going to cut your head off with that sword."

"I don't know what he intended, but killing me wasn't it."

"How can you know? Did you recognize that male?"

"I just know."

"Another hunch?" she laughs without humor.

"Mir, I'm a weirdo, okay? You were right about that. There are things that happen to me that I can't explain, and knowledge of things I couldn't possibly know is one of them. You just have to take my word for it."

"This is bad. This is really bad. We have to tell Aurora and Vivi about him."

"No!" I yell, making her wince. "We can't tell them, not yet."

"But he's after you, Rikkon. He's dangerous. The others need to know there's a crazy Nightingale hunting you."

"I'm begging you. Keep that secret for a while longer."

"Why?"

"Because telling anyone will trigger a series of events that no one is ready for."

"What do you mean? You're not making any sense."

"I told you. I know things that don't make any sense at first, but then they do."

"This is nuts, Rikkon, but okay, I won't tell them yet."

I rest my head against the back of the seat, feeling drained. "Thank you, Mir."

"Can you see in that bank of mysterious knowledge of yours if that male is going to come after me?"

My heart squeezes tightly in my chest as fear overtakes it. More than ever, I curse this fucking spell that makes me look like a vampire. I don't want to hide at Bloodstone, not when there's a Nightingale hunter on the loose. I put Miranda in this mess, and I can't leave her unprotected.

"No, I don't know that. You have to promise to be extra careful when I'm not with you."

"Wait, I need your bodyguard services now?" she squeaks.

"I'll feel better if you let me protect you."

My motives are not self-serving at all. Being near her makes the darkness in my chest feel less of a burden. But I do also believe that if I'm by Miranda's side, the hunter won't harm her. He wants something from me, but he doesn't need her for anything. I can't imagine he's happy she stabbed him.

"I don't get it. He kept asking what you saw. It made no sense."

"He wants to know what I saw in my vision. He seemed desperate about it. Maybe if I tell him, he'll leave us alone."

"Hold up. You get visions? I thought you didn't have any powers."

"I don't consider what I have as powers. More like a curse. Whenever I have visions, it cripples me."

"Boy, you are a hot mess."

"You have no idea."

Six

MIRANDA

Thanks to the encounter with that crazy Nightingale hunter, I don't return to town for my samurai lesson. Once I dropped Rikkon off at Bloodstone and found myself alone, it was easy for paranoia to set in. I stabbed an immortal, and I know he will come back to exact his revenge. Rikkon offered his protection, but what can he do really? Besides some weird-ass visions that turn him into a hindrance, he doesn't have any other powers to help.

Keeping a straight face during dinner was brutal. I managed to fool Mom, but Niko kept giving me scrutinizing glances. She's a freaking bloodhound when it comes to secrets. As much as it would be nice to share the burden with someone, I can't involve her. God knows what she would do to try to help me.

However, as soon as Mom disappears inside her room to change for work, Niko corners me in the kitchen.

"What's up with you tonight?"

"I don't know what you mean." I keep a straight face while I wash the dishes.

"Bullshit. You've been acting weirder than usual, like you're afraid of your own shadow."

I snort, trying to hide the truth. Niko is spot-on. I *am*

"

spooked. Who wouldn't be? I pissed off a psychotic Nightingale hunter.

"Is it because of what happened to Saxon and that dragon shifter?" she continues.

"I'm not scared, okay?" I snap. "But I can't say what happened to him didn't freak me out."

"Do you know how Rora got to him in time?"

"No, I haven't spoken to her since it happened."

Mainly because I have a secret of my own, and if she asks me about Rikkon, I don't want to lie to her.

"It was thanks to Vivienne's brother."

My hands freeze as I whip my face to her. "What do you mean?"

"Oh, that got your attention fast." She smirks, leaning her hip against the counter and crossing her arms.

"Come on, Niko. Quit the suspense and spill it already."

"He had some kind of vision that Saxon was in trouble."

I feel the blood drain from my face. He had another vision, which means he must have endured excruciating pain again.

"What happened to him?" I ask.

"I dunno." She shrugs. "I didn't ask. I was more interested in learning the details of the dragons and vampire's standoff, but as usual, Rora told me nothing."

As if on cue, my phone rings from the kitchen table. It's Aurora's ringtone. I dry off my hands and grab the device before Niko answers the phone for me.

"Rora, is everything okay?"

"Not really. Is Mom home?"

"Yeah. She's getting ready for work."

"Okay. Tell her I'm coming over. I need to talk to her."

"All right. How is everyone?" I ask, not wanting to single out Rikkon.

"Stressed as hell. But I won't bug you with the details. I'll see you soon."

She ends the call before I can get another question in. I'm

mad that she assumes I'm not interested in the affairs of the supe community. *I'm part of it too, damn it!*

"Why are you glaring at your phone?" Niko asks.

I glance up. "Because I'm sick and tired of everyone treating us like little kids."

Niko's eyes widen. "Wow. I can't believe you just said that. I thought *I* was the rebel in the family."

"No, you're the *brat* of the family."

She sticks her tongue out. "Whatever. What did Rora want?"

"She's coming over to talk to Mom."

"Oh, I bet it's about that sexy vampire of hers."

I step closer to Niko and whisper. "Do you know about Rora and Saxon?"

"Who doesn't know at this point? She almost died to save his life after he got attacked by that dragon shifter. Mom is pissed."

"Calvin Belmont must not be happy about it either. He's a weasel. He's going to try something."

"Eh." Niko shrugs. "If Rora decides to step down from being the next in line for the High Witch job and not marry him, there's nothing he can do about it."

"I wouldn't be so sure."

"Well, we won't know the topic of Rora's conversation with Mom until she gets here." She pulls up a chair and sits down, propping her feet on the chair next to hers. "All we can do is wait."

I knock her feet off, pulling the chair away from her. "You can dry the dishes while you wait."

"God, and just when I thought there was hope for you. You're still no fun."

Fifteen minutes later, we hear the doorbell ring. We were waiting for Rora in the living room, but Niko was faster than me and sprinted toward the front door to answer.

"Oh, you're in trouble," she tells Aurora.

God, she's such a pest. It's all our fault. We spoil her rotten because she's the baby in the family.

"When am I not in trouble these days?" Aurora replies.

"Is that Aurora?" Mom asks from the end of the hallway.

"Yep. The prodigal daughter returns." Niko laughs.

I hit her upside the head. "Stop being so gleeful, brat."

"Ouch!" She turns to glower at me, rubbing the sore spot.

Mom appears in the hallway, sporting her angry face. She stares at Aurora for a couple of beats, then turns around and heads to her office. Aurora follows her, but not meekly. Her shoulders are squared, and her chin held high.

No sooner do they disappear through the door and it closes, than Niko takes a step toward Mom's office. I reach over, grabbing the back of her shirt.

"Where do you think you're going?"

"Let me go, Miranda."

"You're not going to eavesdrop on their conversation."

"Why not? You said yourself that you're sick and tired of being treated like kids."

"And do you think acting like one and spying on them is the way to go?" I drop her shirt when she stops resisting me.

She spins around, leveling me with a death stare. "You're such a hypocrite. When it's convenient for you, you don't mind the gossip I tell you. And you're more than happy to sneak peeks at Rora's grimoire."

"That's different." I cross my arms in front of my chest.

"Yeah, whatever." She stomps toward her bedroom and slams the door shut.

Great. Now I have to deal with a pissed-off teenager on top of everything else that's going on in my life. I return to the couch in the living room and wait until Aurora finishes her talk with Mom. To distract myself, I send Rikkon a text message.

Me: How are you?

It's innocent enough, I think. I didn't expect him to reply right away, so when he does, my heart reacts accordingly by taking off at warp speed.

> **_Rikkon: I'm okay. And you?_**
> **_Me: Fine. No signs of angry immortals at my door yet._**
> **_Rikkon: Please call me if you see anything suspicious._**
> **_Me: I will. I heard you had another vision. Was it as bad as before?_**
> **_Rikkon: Yeah._**
> **_Me: I'm sorry._**
> **_Rikkon: Don't be. I'm okay now._**
> **_Me: I wish I could help you._**
> **_Rikkon: Please don't even think about going back to that shop. It's too risky. I'll find a way to deal with my issue._**

It sounds like he's dismissing me, and that makes me sad. I know it's stupid to feel this way. He's probably super guilty that he put me in danger. I'm busy writing a reply when Aurora storms out of Mom's office and marches toward the front door. I jump to my feet, tossing my phone to the side.

"Rora?" I call after her.

She doesn't slow down, bursting out of the house as if she didn't hear me. I follow her, but when I step outside, she's already in her car. Not a second later, she takes off.

"Shit," I mumble.

"What are you doing outside, Miranda?" my mother asks in a stern voice.

I look over my shoulder. "What did you tell Rora?"

"What happened between Aurora and me is not your concern. Now go back inside and make sure Niko doesn't spend the evening watching YouTube videos."

She unlocks her car door, and unlike Aurora, slides calmly behind the steering wheel. I watch her put the car in reverse and then drive off as if nothing was amiss. Hell, the woman is as cold as ice.

I finally return back inside and check on Niko. Her door is locked, but I hear the sound of the TV. She's angry at me too and it's unlikely she'll come out again tonight. And as for doing what my mother asked, forget it. Niko can watch whatever she wants.

My text conversation with Rikkon comes back to the forefront of my mind. All the members of my family are having issues right now, and I'm not the exception. There's an immortal with a thirst for revenge after me, and I can't depend on anyone for protection.

"I'm alone on this," I say to myself, heading to Mom's office.

I'm not looking for a spell tonight. Instead, I need more intel about the Nightingales and their weapons. Maybe if I can find something about glowing swords, I can also find information about the bearer of it.

The biggest library on supernatural lore is at the Council of Witches and Mages headquarters. But Dad was a history buff, and when he passed away, instead of donating his collection of old tomes to the institute, Mom kept them. Isadora Leal may be cold and aloof, but no one can deny she loved Dad dearly.

A pang flares in my chest thinking about him. He's been gone for a while, but the pain his absence left will never go away. While Mom was busy fussing over Aurora or Niko, Dad always had time for me. I shove the morose feeling to the side and concentrate on the task at hand. Dad's collection sits on the top shelf and to reach them, I need a ladder. Since Mom is also not a giant, she keeps one in the office, tucked in a corner.

I get on with the task by leaning the wooden ladder at the beginning of the shelf. I have no idea what I'm looking for, so I have to read the table of contents of every single volume until I find it. It might be a long night.

Perched on the top rung, I reach for the first book. Its leather cover is weathered, and the golden letters on the spine are faded. I can't read the words. It's thick and it weighs a ton. I have to cradle it in my arms in order to look inside. A quick scan at the table of contents tells me this is not a book about Nightingales. It talks about the history of the samurai and it catches my attention immediately. I'd love to bring it down and immerse myself in it, but this is not my mission tonight. With regret, I put it back on the shelf and continue my search.

It's not until I'm almost at the end of the shelf that I stumble across a small notebook, tucked far back and hidden between two larger volumes. I almost missed it. I take a peek, and immediately, I know this is what I'm looking for. It's not the fact this notebook is so old, it was bound by hand, or the fact its pages are yellowed and frail. A tingle goes up my arm as I hold it. Some kind of spell was put on it. There isn't a table of contents on the first page, just a name scribbled down in ink. Tom Mularkey, if I'm reading it right. *Gee, what a name.*

On the second page there's a poem describing a creature so beautiful, no mortal could look away. Sounds like they're describing Rikkon, but not really. The creature in the poem is obviously female, and her hair is silver like it was spun from rays of moonlight. I can relate to the author of the poem though. Whenever I'm in Rikkon's presence, I can't look away.

I get down from the ladder so I can read the whole thing without fear of falling down. I set everything as it was before, turn off the lights, and head back to my room. There were a few other books left to check, but I know deep in my gut this is the one I was looking for. Maybe it's the spell on the book giving me that certainty, but I can't help thinking about Rikkon's odd gift. I suppose having visions of the future could be handy if it helped avoid a disaster, but not at the cost he has to pay.

Once in my room, I don't turn on the ceiling lights. I'm supposed to be sleeping and I don't want Mom to come home and see the glare seeping from my window. The night lamp is much more discreet. Sitting cross-legged on my bed, I begin to read the notebook in earnest. There's a ball of anticipation in my stomach, almost like glee. It feels like I came across a juicy secret and I can't wait to find out everything.

The first few chapters are nothing but poems describing the Nightingales, their ethereal beauty, yadda yadda. It's not until the middle of the notebook that a passage catches my eye. It describes a group of individuals, highly skilled in combat and hunting. My heartbeat accelerates as I keep reading. Those warriors held important positions in the Aquila court, and all of them carried starfire swords. There's a drawing of the sword, which at first glance doesn't look like anything special. It's not until I read the description claiming those swords were as blinding and as hot as the sun that I realize I've found what I'm looking for.

Not bothering with a text, I call Rikkon right away, but the call goes straight to voicemail. *Shit.* I simply can't wait until tomorrow to tell him what I found. What if this badass warrior decides to pay me a visit tonight?

I jump out of bed and shove my shoes on. Then I head to Niko's room. The door is still locked, but it's dead silent inside. She must have gone to sleep already. I can leave her alone for a few hours. She's fifteen, not a kid. Besides, there are wards around the house, she will be safe. That Nightingale is not after her.

Then why the hell do I feel so guilty for stepping out of the house?

Seven

MIRANDA

On my way to the institute of vampires, I hear firetruck sirens in the distance. The noise wouldn't generally alarm me, but tonight it's an ominous sound. As I approach the imposing building of Bloodstone, I curse my impulsiveness. How am I supposed to get in without Aurora knowing I'm on the premises? In hindsight, even if I could communicate with Rikkon, my meeting with him wouldn't remain a secret. He lives with a bunch of vampires.

I park just outside of the main entrance and try his phone again. I get nothing but his voicemail.

"Great."

Well, there's nothing for it. I shove the little notebook I borrowed from Mom in the inside pocket of my jacket. It would fit in my bag, but this is too precious and accessories can get lost.

No sooner do I step out of my car, than dread licks the back of my neck. I pivot around and scan the forest on the other side of the road. It's almost impossible to see anything in the darkness, but I can still sense a dark presence that shouldn't be there. *Fuck.* Did the Nightingale follow me here? I shove my hand inside my bag and grab a crystal I stole from Mom's collection. I figured I'd need the best power boost I could get.

Besides the sensation I'm being observed, I hear nothing. It's like all the living creatures in the forest went into hiding. Why did this damn school for vampires have to be in the middle of nowhere? Not wanting to give my back to the darkness, I move backward, holding the crystal at the ready. Sadly, I haven't replaced the dagger I lost yet.

A gust of cold wind comes out of nowhere and suddenly, I bump against something solid. With a yelp I jump forward and turn, holding the crystal in a menacing way. In front of me is none other than one of the warlocks of the Ivern Guild, the one who lied to my mother to cover for me.

"What are you doing here, little witch?"

I can't answer him right away. My throat is dry and my tongue is stuck in my mouth.

"Don't you know it's not safe for your kind tonight?" he continues.

"What do you mean?" I squeak.

"Shhh." He cocks his head to the side as if listening to something.

"What's going on?" I ask after a couple of beats.

Even in the gloom, I catch his glower. "I should send you home immediately, but unfortunately, there's no time. You're coming with me."

I jump back. "The hell I am."

"For fuck's sake. Why are the witches in your family so difficult?"

He doesn't give me the chance to reply before green light whooshes out of his index finger and I become boneless. My thoughts scramble, and for a moment, it's like I cease to exist. Then I'm falling down a dark tunnel. I think I pass out for a second, because once I hit solid ground again, my body is in one piece, and the darkness is gone. A strong hand grabs my elbow, keeping me upright.

"Easy there," the warlock says.

I step out of his hold, annoyed that he keeps getting into my personal space.

"Watch the hands, buddy. This is 2020, not 1989."

He gives me a droll stare, like what I said was unreasonable. "Fine. I'll let you fall on your ass the next time."

"There won't be a next time." I glance at my surroundings. We're in a dingy corridor that smells of mildew. "Where are we?"

"Inside Bloodstone. That's where you were trying to sneak in, isn't it? You don't need to thank me or anything."

I cross my arms. "I won't. Why does it look so depressing here?"

He shrugs, a gesture that's at complete odds with his menacing posture. "No clue. I didn't sense any activity in this area. It was the best place to land."

"Why are you here, anyway?"

"That's not your concern. Go on. You didn't come to Bloodstone to chitchat in the dark with the likes of me. Your boyfriend is that way." He sticks out his thumb, pointing behind him.

My face bursts into flames, and I'm glad it's dark in here. "Rikkon is not my boyfriend."

"Don't care. I have more pressing matters to attend to."

With that last parting comment, he goes up in green smoke and vanishes from sight. I can breathe more easily now. Jesus, the guy is intense. I stride in the direction he indicated, hoping not to bump into any bloodsuckers. But as soon as I step out of the creepy area, I can hear the voices of students not too far away. Remaining incognito won't happen. I wish I had a cloak of invisibility like Harry Potter. Unfortunately, I haven't come across a spell that makes me invisible yet—if such thing even exists.

I bet the first grimoire that the Belmont family possesses has that spell. It's not fair that such despicable people have access to that kind of knowledge and we don't.

There's no point in getting bitter about that now, Mir. You have to find Rikkon in this maze.

I realize I have no idea where his apartment is, but I can always try a location spell. I don't have anything of his with me, but I used the ointment to mark his face yesterday. There must be a residue of his signature left on the bottle. Still hiding in a shadowy corner, I pull my vial from my bag, uncap it, and smear my index finger with the oil. Then it's just a matter of picturing him in my mind and reciting the magical words.

The air around me seems to tremble, making my skin tingle. Then a golden thread appears in front of me. It disappears around the corner. If I did everything correctly, following that gold thread will lead me straight to Rikkon. The problem now is evading all the witnesses. I pull my grimoire from my bag and begin to search for some kind of diversion spell. Right in the middle, I come across one of the first spells Niko and I lifted from Aurora's grimoire. We picked this one to master because it would be a great practical joke enchantment. It creates a thick fog, turning visibility to zilch for at least a minute. That ought to do it. I need Mom's crystal to cast two spells at once though.

I'll get in so much trouble if I'm caught, but what's the worst that can happen? I'll get grounded longer? With everything that's going on, I doubt Mom will have the time to think of a crueler punishment for me. I'm sure she knows by now Aurora and Saxon are mated, and that's what is stressing her out the most.

After I recite the spell while clutching the crystal, nothing happens. My heart sinks. Did I get it wrong? Or maybe I can't do it even with the extra boost. Finally, the crystal gets warmer in my hand, and slowly, fog begins to lift from the floor and spread through the hallway. Shouts of surprise sound, but I wait until the fog has engulfed the entire corridor to venture out. Lucky for me, the golden thread linking me to Rikkon's location is still visible. No one else can see that since I'm the one who cast the spell. All I have to do now is cross this area as quickly as possible and avoid bumping into anyone.

That's not an easy task, of course. I collide with a bloodsucker only after taking a few steps.

"Watch where you're going, bitch," the girl snarls, pushing me to the side.

I bite my tongue, swallowing the angry retort. Hell, no wonder Aurora hates living here.

I have no idea how close I am to finding Rikkon, but behind me, I hear the distinct voice of Solomon, the institute's headmaster.

"What the hell is going on here?"

"This is witchcraft," Mom replies.

Fuck. She's here? Why?

I break into a sprint. My time is up. The fog begins to dissipate quicker than normal, which can only mean Mom is reversing the spell. I reach a set of stairs and dash out of sight just before the fog is completely cleared. I don't stop until I reach the landing. My heart is about to burst out of my chest thanks to the adrenaline. That was close.

The golden thread continues to my right, leading me in the same direction as Aurora's apartment.

Are you kidding me? Rikkon is there? So much for trying to avoid my sister. Well, maybe I'll find out why she left the meeting with Mom in such a hurry.

With quick steps I approach my final destination, but when the thread continues past Aurora's apartment, I let out a sigh of relief. It guides me to a door not too far from my sister's place, though.

I take a deep breath before knocking on it. At first, I hear nothing, but then I can make out the sound of someone moving inside the apartment. Sweat dots my forehead, and hastily, I wipe it dry. Because tonight has offered a string of unwanted encounters, I expect one of Rikkon's vampire roommates to open the door. When he's the one who actually appears on the threshold, I suck in a breath. He's still as gorgeous as ever, but there are dark circles under his eyes, and his skin tone is definitely closer to green now.

"Mir, what are you doing here?" His eyes are wide with worry.

"I've found something. Quick, let me in." I push him back and practically force myself into his apartment. "Are you alone?"

He closes the door. "Yeah. Vaughn and Vivi just left to take a walk through the institute to see if they can hear any gossip about what's going on."

Arching my eyebrows, I turn to him. "What *is* going on? My mother is here, and so is one of the warlocks from the Ivern Guild. Aurora had a meeting with my mother earlier and she left in a hurry."

"I had another vision."

"Oh no, Rikkon. How bad was it?" I take a step closer, stopping short of touching him. We're not intimate enough for that.

"Not as bad as the previous ones." He curls his lips into a rueful smile.

"What did you see this time?"

I shiver, remembering the description of his latest one.

His expression turns into a grimace. "A dark shadow with red eyes."

"So, kind of the same of what you saw before?"

He shakes his head. "No, not the same, but equally evil."

I bite my bottom lip as my stomach twists painfully. Hugging my middle, I try to ease the ache. "Something bad is going to happen tonight. I can feel it in the air."

To my surprise, Rikkon steps into my space and pulls me into a hug. "I won't let anything happen to you, Mir."

My heart skips a beat, and then it accelerates to a hundred. I don't want to melt into his arms, but that's a fight I can't win.

"Thanks."

I wish I could stay in his arms longer, but there was a reason I risked coming here. With regret, I step back and look up. He's so damn tall.

"I found something in my mother's office that could be useful to you." I pull the small notebook from my jacket pocket.

Rikkon stares at the object for a long time without moving.

"What's wrong?"

"I don't know. What did you find out?"

When he makes no motion to take the notebook from me, I open it to the page that talks about the Nightingale warriors.

"I think the male who attacked us at the shop yesterday was one of these individuals." I point at the text.

Rikkon leans closer, brushing his shoulder with mine. He's making it super difficult to remain calm and collected.

"Does this stir anything in your memory?" I ask.

"No, but it ma—ugh!" He steps back, holding his head with both hands.

"Another vision?" I ask like a moron. What else could it be?

"Yeah," he croaks.

He doubles over, making me afraid he's going to collapse to the floor. I hurry to his side and loop my arm around his waist.

"You should sit down."

His face is twisted in pain and his eyes are shut. He doesn't speak for several beats. Only grunts escape his lips. Suddenly, his spine goes taut and his eyes pop open.

"I saw Aurora. She's in danger."

I grab him by his forearms and turn him around. "Where is she?"

"By the clearing where the dragon shifter was slain."

"I don't know where that is," I reply in a high-pitched tone.

"Solomon does. We need all the help we can get. What she's facing, none of us can fight alone."

Eight

RIKKON

Miranda's face has gone ashen, and I'm upset that I was the one who had to tell her the bad news. It seems wherever I go, bad omens follow. I'm a harbinger of doom.

"Come on, Mir. Let's find Solomon. We must hurry." I lace my fingers with hers and steer her out of the apartment.

"Who is she facing, Rik?" she asks in a small voice.

"I don't know. I only saw glimpses of the scene. She was with an elderly woman and a guy. Neither felt friendly."

We race down the corridor and stairs until we reach the main building of the institute. There's no other way to get to the headmaster's office. But it turns out, we didn't need to go that far. The familiar is standing right in the middle of the hallway in deep conversation with the High Witch.

"Oh, your mother is here. That's good," I tell Miranda, hoping to make her feel a little better.

Before they see our approach, two towering men pop out of nowhere next to them. I stop in my tracks. Those are the warlocks we met at the Nightshade Market. Solomon curses loudly, but the High Witch remains impassive. A moment later, the group's attention turns to us.

"Oh, now I know who was responsible for that fog spell," the woman says.

I don't miss when her gaze drops to my hand holding Miranda's in a firm grasp. I expect her to pull away, but when she doesn't, it fills me with hope. It's nonsense, especially considering our situation. Her sister is in mortal danger and we're under the scrutiny of not only her mother, but also the headmaster and two powerful warlocks. Things aren't looking good for us.

"Save your sermon for another time, Mom. Aurora is in danger," Miranda replies.

The High Witch's eyebrows shoot up. "What kind of danger?"

"The mortal kind, ma'am," I answer. "She's in the clearing where the dragon shifter was killed last night. I think the older lady with her was performing a black magic ritual."

The warlocks trade a troubled glance.

"We must make haste. We can't let Elena get her hands on the first grimoire."

"What's going on?" Miranda asks.

"No time to explain. You stay here and try not to get in trouble," one of the warlocks replies.

"No way in hell you're leaving us behind. Rikkon said we need all the help we can get and that includes us."

"Miranda, you're not powerful enough to be of any assistance," her mother says, making me hate her on the spot.

"Miranda is powerful, and only a blind person wouldn't see that," I retort angrily.

"Miranda and Rikkon are coming with us," Solomon chimes in, leaving no room for argument.

"If that's what you want," the second warlock says. "Be my guest." He waves his hand, and once again, his magic transports us from the institute to the outskirts of a woodsy area.

I manage to keep hold of Miranda's hand during the trip, and with my focus solely on not losing contact with her during transport, I don't have time to dwell on the effects the warlock's magic has on me.

"This is not the place," I tell them as soon as I can use my mouth.

"We know, but we can't simply drop in on them like that. It's too risky. We don't know how far things have progressed already."

Solomon turns his nose up and sniffs the air. "I smell spilled blood."

No sooner has he said that, than we hear the distinct noise of battle.

"Shit. We need to hurry," Miranda says, dashing into the darkest part of the forest.

"Mir, wait." I follow her.

"Stupid young people," I hear someone mutter, but I can't tell who spoke.

My pulse is pounding in my ears, and the wind is rushing by. Once again, I feel like I'm flying. My feet don't seem to touch the ground. But that's impossible. I catch up with Miranda soon enough and before she breaks through the cover of the forest and into the clearing, I wrap my arms around her and force her to a halt.

"Let me go, Rik," she shout-whispers.

"Wait for the others," I reply in her ear.

We don't have to wait long. The two warlocks run past us, followed by Solomon and the High Witch. Only then do I let Miranda go so we can resume our approach. The first thing I see is a massive dark cloud zooming toward Saxon and Aurora. There's no mistaking that's the evil entity I saw in my vision.

The warlocks shout words I can't understand, but whatever they are, they halt the dark smoke's progress. It rises up and then it says, "This isn't over."

It zaps in the opposite direction of our group, disappearing into the onyx sky. Saxon is holding Aurora for dear life when we approach them. I know everyone has a ton of questions, but the first to get them out is one of the warlocks.

"What the hell happened?"

Aurora glances at the man. "Elena got her hands on the first grimoire and summoned a demon called Ashmedai with it."

The warlocks curse out loud, something they seem prone to do whenever things get dicey. Solomon breaks away from the group to inspect the body of the older woman I saw in my vision. He whistles, unfazed. "I guess she didn't get what she thought she would."

"The demon killed her soon after he possessed Calvin's body," Aurora tells him.

"And who had the brilliant idea of trying to kill a demon by decapitating the host?" the High Witch asks, none too happy as she glares at Saxon.

"That fucker was about to kill us both. I have no regrets," he spits back.

"Calvin was already dead when Ashmedai took control of his body," Aurora pipes up.

They continue to argue, but my attention is no longer on the group. The familiar pain is returning, which means I'm about to have another vision, and I bet it won't be good news. I try to suffer in silence this time, not wanting to make Miranda worried about me. I bite the inside of my cheek, drawing blood as the pain intensifies. I can only make out a few words of the conversation now, but when someone questions what could Ashmedai possibly want, the answer appears as clear as day in my mind.

"He wants the Taluah Mirror," I say.

"How do you know that?" the High Witch asks.

"Rikkon has visions. It's how we knew where to find Aurora," Miranda replies.

I wince, not able to hide my reaction to the sharp pain this time. I press a closed fist against my forehead. "It's happening again. I see the demon now. He's found a new host."

My blood runs cold. I whip my face to Miranda's, hating the news I have to tell her. "It's Niko."

"No," the High Witch mutters in horror.

Miranda steps closer to me, her eyes shining with unshed tears when she asks me, "Are you sure, Rik?"

"Yeah," I reply through the lump in my throat.

I feel gutted that I have to tell her bad news. It's stupid to feel guilty about it. It's not like I'm the one causing her pain, but I can't help the emotion that's squeezing my chest in a vise hold.

"We'll find him and save Niko," Saxon declares.

"You're no match for a demon," one of the warlocks snorts. "This is warlock business now."

"Hell to the fucking no," Aurora shouts. "My sister is in danger and you're not going to keep me, or my mate, from getting her back."

Next to me, Miranda seems to shrink thanks to her sister's outburst. I don't need a vision to know she must feel responsible for what happened to Niko. She left her younger sister alone to come help me. I also share the sentiment.

"Aurora is right," the High Witch chimes in. "You're not doing this alone. Niko's life is on the line, and I know very well you don't care one ounce about killing a child in order to collect your big prize."

A shiver runs down my spine. She's not wrong about the warlocks' intentions. They will go to any lengths to lock the demon away, even if it costs Niko's life.

"You'll only be a hindrance," the second warlock retorts.

"Oh, shut up, you pompous dickwads," Solomon interrupts. "You've done nothing but sit on your asses and let Aurora fend for herself. Now quit bitching and use your magic for something useful, like getting us to the Conservatorium Hotel right the fucking now."

I don't have time to process how they know where to go before the warlocks' magic envelops us again. I reach for Miranda's hand, but I'm too slow and end up missing her entirely.

Nine

MIRANDA

This time, there's no one to stabilize me when I drop in the middle of an unfamiliar hallway. My ears are buzzing, and the world is spinning like a top. I stagger forward, aiming for the wall nearest to me, but I miss a step and end up sprawled on the floor.

"Damn it!"

"Mir, where are you?" Rikkon asks from nearby.

I don't want him to find me in this humiliating position, so I brace my hands on the floor and push myself up. But I'm still unsteady as hell, and without anything to hold on to, I sway on the spot, dangerously close to meeting the floor again.

Then he's there, holding me in his arms. *God, it feels so good.* In a moment of weakness, I lean against his chest.

"Mir, are you okay?" He turns me around and searches my face frantically, worry etched on his.

My head is still fuzzy as hell, but my dizziness isn't caused by the trip via warlock wormhole. This is the Rikkon effect.

"I'm okay. Woozy, but it will pass. And you?"

"Surprisingly, I feel fine." He breaks the connection to look around. "Where are we?"

It takes me a moment to recognize where we are. "The

warlocks brought us to the Conservatorium Hotel, but where is everybody?"

"I don't know. We need to find them." Rikkon laces his fingers with mine again and together we sprint down the corridor, heading toward the hotel lobby.

We find Aurora and Saxon in an embrace when we round the corner. Rikkon drops my hand, making me miss the contact immediately. Maybe he doesn't want anyone thinking there's more between us, like I didn't in the Nightshade Market. I know my reasons, but I wonder what his are.

"There you two are," he says.

Aurora and Saxon jump apart. While I have my sister's sole attention, Saxon has his gaze trained on Rikkon. His stare turns darker as he narrows his eyes. *Oh boy.* I wonder if there's something going on that I don't know about.

"Dude, your disguise is gone," he tells Rikkon.

"Shit. You're right," Aurora pipes up.

Damn it. I was too lost in him to notice the spell had worn off. So dumb.

"I'm sorry. I didn't realize it," he replies. "I've been having one vision after another. It's been hard to keep track of my surroundings."

Unable to contain myself, I step closer and place a hand on his back. "It's okay, Rik. I didn't notice either."

He grimaces. "And I forgot my potion."

"I don't know what's going on here, but you'd better get Rikkon off the streets," Aurora tells me. "I don't have time to worry about his cover getting blown."

I know she's been through hell and she's under a lot of stress, but her rebuff chafes me.

"What about Niko?" I ask.

Her expression softens. "We'll bring her back, Mir. I promise."

Dismissed. Just like that. I want to stomp my foot and insist on helping because Niko's gone thanks to me. But I can't let

Rikkon go back to the institute alone. What if he has another vision? I have to swallow my complaints and pride, and try not to cry out of frustration in front of everyone.

When I glance at Rikkon, he looks as pitiful as I feel. I take his arm, not caring right now what Aurora will think of my action, and steer him toward the exit. No one we meet on the way spares us a second glance, and I'm glad for it. Everyone seems in a hurry to get inside, heightening the sense of foreboding hanging in the air.

Outside, it's much cooler than before, maybe because the adrenaline has worn off. I let out a heavy sigh and fight the tears that are making my eyes burn.

"I'm sorry you couldn't stay to help," Rikkon says once we're in front of the hotel.

"Don't feel guilty about it. Aurora or my mother would find another excuse to send me home," I reply bitterly.

He pinches my chin between his thumb and forefinger and turns my face to his. Tingles run down my spine, and my stomach clenches in anticipation. My breathing becomes shallow. What is he doing?

"Don't let them bring you down. If they can't see what you're capable of, show them."

His intense blue eyes are locked on mine, which is seriously messing with my ability to breathe. I also want him to kiss me so badly, it's almost like an ache.

What am I thinking? My sister is possessed by a demon and I'm here, crushing on a boy.

I step back, freeing myself from his hold. "I have to call an Uber."

His forehead crinkles. He seems confused. *That makes two of us, buddy.*

Focusing on my phone, I try to ignore Rikkon's stare. He's burning a hole through my face, that much I can tell. I pull up the app but finding a ride seems impossible.

"Crap. It says there are no cars available."

"Maybe someone at the reception desk can find us a cab."

"I don't think so. Something big happened in town tonight."

"Bigger than a demon on the loose?"

"I don't know, but I heard sirens on my way to Bloodstone, and one of the warlocks told me it wasn't safe for my kind tonight."

He glances at the parking lot in front of the hotel. "I have an idea. Follow me."

I have no clue what he has in mind until he reaches the far end of the parking lot and stops next to an old sedan. He peers inside the vehicle, and then tries the door.

"What are you doing?" I ask.

"Probably damaging my reputation for good. Do you know any spells that can unlock a car door?"

My eyes widen. "You want to steal a car?"

He winces. "Not steal, borrow. You said finding a ride home tonight will be impossible, and it isn't safe out in the streets. I have to get you home."

I never thought I'd say this, but standing here and listening to a guy offering to steal a car in order to protect me is a major turn-on. The radioactive butterflies in my stomach agree.

"I do know how to open locks. It's child's play if they're not enchanted, which I think is the case here." I glance at the car, then at the front of the hotel. "Ah, what the hell. Desperate situations, desperate measures, right?"

I wave my hand over the keyhole, whispering the simple spell. The lock pops open, and no sound of an alarm follows. Maybe that's why Rikkon picked this older model.

"What now? I don't have a spell that can turn an engine on."

"Don't worry, I know how to hotwire a car. Go on, get in."

Once inside the vehicle, I don't say a word as I watch Rikkon pull the wires from under the steering wheel and do his thing. A moment later, the engine rumbles to life. This is it. I'm now a felon. I just have to pray the cops are too busy tonight to come after us.

"I didn't know stealing cars was also part of your rap sheet," I say after we leave the hotel's parking lot.

"When you're desperate for money to buy drugs, you try anything. It's not something I'm proud of."

"I'm sorry. I shouldn't have made that comment. I'm glad that you have those skills." I give him a tentative smile, but he doesn't glance in my direction to see it. His gaze is locked on the road ahead, just like his jaw is locked tight.

"Anyway, how is your head?" I say to break the uncomfortable silence.

"So far, no more visions coming."

"Are your visions always about bad stuff?"

He grimaces. "Yeah."

The mood has definitely shifted between us. Maybe I made it so by bringing up his rap sheet. I don't like this. I'm feeling wretched enough as it is.

"Look, I'm sorry I mentioned your past. It doesn't bother me one bit, okay?"

"It should bother you, Mir."

"Don't tell me how I should feel," I snap.

Crap. So much for trying to lighten the mood. I close my eyes and pinch the bridge of my nose. I'm so close to crying it's not even funny.

"I'm sorry," he replies.

Then he reaches for my hand and squeezes it tightly.

Butterflies go nuts in my belly.

I open my eyes and stare at my lap, fighting to control my emotions. With a shuddering breath, I look at him.

"No, I'm the one who needs to apologize. I'm a hot mess right now and it isn't your fault."

His lips curl into a crooked smile. "Let's agree then that we're both hot messes." He faces the road again, and then comments, "I need directions to your house."

"Why? I thought we were going to Bloodstone."

"My disguise is gone, and to be honest, I don't want to pretend to be a vampire any longer."

"It's safer for you there though."

He turns to me with an eyebrow raised. "Is it? I'm not so sure."

I don't have the motivation to argue with him about that. And to be fair, I'd much rather wait for news in the comfort of my own home. I'm already anxious enough as it is. I don't want to worry about vampires too. So I give Rikkon directions and within ten minutes, he's pulling up in front of my house.

He doesn't turn off the engine and I worry he won't stay.

"You're coming in with me, right?" I ask him.

I notice he's frozen like a statue, staring at the rearview mirror. The small hairs on the back of my neck stand on end. When he doesn't answer right away, I press. "What is it?"

"We're not alone. Stay in the car."

He gets out before I can ask who's outside. I unbuckle my seat belt and grab the crystal, hoping it's not completely depleted. There's no way in hell I'm staying in the car. I follow him out, ready to use the strongest offensive spell I know.

Rikkon is standing by the curb in a wide stance, ready for battle. I expect him to chastise me for following him, but he keeps his eyes glued to the house across the street. I squint, trying to see what caught his attention. Suddenly, the bushes hugging the side of the house move, and a large figure emerges from them.

The Nightingale hunter.

My blood runs cold. He's come for me. I curl my fingers tighter around the crystal, wishing I had more than an energized stone at my disposal. A katana would make me feel better, even if I can't kill the immortal warrior.

"What do you want?" Rikkon asks, his voice loud and steady.

"I came for the witch," he replies roughly.

"You can't have her."

The hunter throws his head back and laughs. "Do you think you can stop me? You have no powers, my dear prince."

He unsheathes his glowing sword and prepares to strike. From the corner of my eye, I see Rikkon is ready to block him, but all he's going to accomplish is getting impaled by the hunter's blade. Using the crystal's power, I harness the energy from all four elements. Crackling energy converges on the crystal, and right before the hunter advances, I throw a ball of energy in his direction. To my dismay, he takes the blow to his chest like he'd been hit by a water balloon.

"Your parlor tricks don't work on me, witch."

With a war cry, he lifts his glowing sword above his head with both hands. Fear paralyzes me, but Rikkon pushes me out of the way at the last second. I fall to the ground in a tuck and roll move—thank God for samurai training. There's a bright explosion of light which blinds me for a moment. I lift my arm to protect my eyes from the glow, and when it fades, Rikkon has the hunter in a choke hold, and his glowing sword is at his feet.

"I said you can't have her," Rikkon grits out.

The hunter struggles to break free, which only makes Rikkon tighten his hold on the hunter's neck. Then, out of the blue, he begins to laugh.

"What's so funny?" Rikkon asks.

"You'll soon find out."

The sword on the ground glows brighter, and then it vanishes along with its owner.

"What the hell?" Rikkon staggers forward, not expecting the male to simply evaporate into thin air.

I jump back on my feet and glance around. Maybe he will come back to attack from behind.

"Do you think he's gone for good?" I ask.

"Yeah."

"Is that a sure thing?"

He nods. "He won't be back tonight."

Still shaken by the near miss, I rub my hands on my jeans, trying to stop them from trembling. It's going to take a while to recover from this encounter though, that much I know.

Rikkon walks over, stopping just a foot from me. "Are you okay?"

"I will be in a minute."

"I'm sorry I had to push you. You didn't get hurt, did you?"

"No, I learned how to fall properly in samurai lessons. Thanks for getting me out of the sword's path. I... I froze." I look away, ashamed. So much for my training.

He places his hands on my arms. "Hey, your reaction was normal. You won't freeze the next time."

"The next time?" I squeak.

Rikkon's expression becomes darker. "I'm afraid this won't be the last instance you'll be in the path of a deadly blade and it's all because of me. I'm sorry, Mir."

I swallow the huge lump in my throat, afraid to ask if what he's saying comes from his bank of knowledge.

"Let's get inside. I think I need a drink."

Ten

RIKKON

Maybe I shouldn't have been so honest with Miranda. But my bluntness stemmed from my worry for her. She's now irrevocably embroiled in my destiny and that will come at a steep price. The memory spell only delayed the inevitable. What's coming for me is approaching fast, I can feel it in my bones.

She's too pale for my liking now, and I wish I could pull her into my arms and tell her everything will be okay. She veers for the kitchen, but instead of grabbing a beer from the fridge or any other alcoholic beverage like I thought she would, she grabs a can of coffee from a cabinet instead.

I pull up a chair and watch her move around in silence. I'm afraid that if I say anything, I'm going to fuck it up again.

"Do you want a cup?" she asks once the coffee is ready.

"Sure."

"How do you take yours?"

"Uh, black, please."

"I like mine with loads of flavored creamer, the sweeter the better."

A moment later, there's a steaming cup in front of me, and Miranda takes the seat next to mine.

"Drinking coffee won't help to calm you down, you know," I say, bringing the cup to my lips.

"I know. But I'm a lightweight when it comes to alcohol. One beer and I'll be passed out under the table." She blows on her drink, drawing my eyes to her lips. I should look away, but I'm transfixed by them.

"Besides," she continues, snapping me out of my daze, "I need to keep my head sharp until we hear news about Niko."

"They'll bring her back."

She sits straighter. "Is that a certain thing?"

I set the cup down and drop my gaze to the steamy, dark liquid inside. "No, it's not one of those certainties I have. It's just... faith." I lift my eyes to hers.

"I didn't peg you to be a religious person."

"I'm not. Faith has nothing to do with religion. Look, you have your mother, Solomon, your sister, Saxon, and two super powerful warlocks going after the demon. There's no way they'll all fail."

She takes a sip of her coffee, not meeting my eyes. She still won't look at me even after she sets the cup back on the table.

"Mir, what's the matter?"

She shakes her head. "It's nothing. Just trying to process everything that has happened today."

"Are you frightened?"

She whips her face to mine. "What? No. Do I look scared?"

"No, but it would be normal to be shaken up. A Nightingale warrior tried to kill you, and stupid me had to say that it wouldn't be the last time you would face such peril."

She curls her fingers around the mug while her shoulders sag forward. "I'm part of the supernatural community. Facing danger comes with the territory."

There's more she's not telling me. I can't pry though. She's entitled to her secrets.

"Do you still have the notebook about my kind?" I ask instead.

"Oh, man. I forgot about it." She pulls the small leather notebook from her jacket pocket. "Here."

I stare at the offering but don't make a move to take it. There's something about the little tome. It makes me reluctant to touch it.

"Is there an enchantment on that thing?" I ask.

Miranda frowns. "You feel it too?"

With a nod, I reply, "It's repelling me."

"That's odd. It worked the other way around for me. I was drawn to it, almost as if it was calling my name."

"It's a book about the Nightingales, it's been hexed to prevent my kind touching it, and it calls to you? Don't you find that a bit peculiar?"

She opens the notebook to a random page and scans the text. "For sure. Maybe the information here is not something the Nightingales wanted others to know and the mage who penned it put a protective spell on it. But so far, I haven't come across any secrets that would warrant such measures."

The front door bangs open, startling us. I push the chair back, jumping to my feet. Miranda hides the notebook inside her jacket pocket once more, and then stands as well.

"Ugh, those damn warlocks are infuriating." The High Witch's voice carries toward us.

Miranda runs to the living room with me close behind.

"Niko!" She engulfs her younger sister in a bear hug while I hang back, relieved that she's in one piece.

I watch the scene, forgetting all about the High Witch and Solomon, who also came into the house. Aurora, Saxon, and the warlocks are nowhere to be seen.

"What are you doing here?" Miranda's mother asks me accusatorily.

"I didn't want to leave Miranda alone."

She turns to her mother. "Rikkon's vampire disguise had worn off, so Aurora told me to get him off the streets. What happened? Where's Rora and Saxon?"

"Ryker took them back to the institute," Solomon replies.

"Thank you for keeping my daughter company. I can brew you a new batch of potion if you give me a moment."

I open my mouth to reply, but Solomon speaks before I can. "No need, Isadora. I have plenty back at Bloodstone. You'd better come with me now, son. Let them rest."

"Yes, of course."

I follow the familiar to the front door, but I can't take my eyes off Miranda. It's like she's pulling me into her orbit and there's nothing more I want than to let her reel me in. But I don't act upon the strange impulse. Maybe if we were alone, I might have.

"I'll talk to you soon, Mir. Have a good night."

"Yeah, you too."

Eleven

MIRANDA

A WEEK LATER

I've lost count of the number of times I've checked my phone. I haven't heard from Rikkon since the night Niko was possessed by Ashmedai and a Nightingale hunter almost cut me in two. I've sent him several texts and called almost as much, but after two days of radio silence, I stopped trying. I know nothing bad has happened to him because I would have heard about it. And yet, my heart feels heavy all the time, gripped by anxiety and fear.

It's fucking stupid to feel this way for someone who clearly doesn't give a fig about me. I thought we were friends. So much for his bodyguard services as well. Maybe he's now certain the Nightingale hunter won't come back, so he doesn't need to check on me.

He's no longer residing at the institute. He's moved into Lucca's mansion with the rest of the gang. Aurora is there too, but I haven't visited yet. I've been avoiding seeing her because I know she's going to bring up Rikkon. I can't deal with a sermon on why I shouldn't get involved with him. The talk might be wasted anyway. It's possible that all the loaded glances and fleeting touches meant nothing. It was all probably in my head.

I should get going if I'm to get to samurai training on time. I made a point of not missing a single class this past week. I don't need a knight in shining armor to defend me. I'll slay the monster myself.

There's a knock on the door, and then Niko walks in.

I toss the phone on my bed and grab a pillow to hug. Somehow, I need the protection, even if it's of the fluffy variety. Niko is too observant for her own good.

"What are you doing? You've been moping for days." She gives my room a cursory glance and then her eyes zero in on my phone. "You haven't heard from him yet, have you?"

"What?" I squeak. "I don't know what you're talking about."

"Oh, come on. I'm not stupid. I know you have a major crush on Vivienne's brother. I don't blame you. He's hot."

Heat creeps up my cheeks, and I can't even hide my embarrassment because my hair is tied in a ponytail.

"We're just friends."

"Shit. He friend-zoned you? Is it because of your major age difference?" She plops on my bed, folding her legs under her.

"He's immortal, Niko. Age is irrelevant to him."

At least I hope it is.

"Your birthday is in two weeks. Eighteen is better than seventeen for sure."

I clutch the pillow tighter. "Ugh. I don't want to talk about him with you."

"Fine." She jumps off the bed. "But can I give you a piece of advice? If you want more than friendship from him, you have to pounce. Don't just wait around for him to make the first move. Take control." She slams a closed fist against her palm.

"Okay, Love Doctor. I'll definitely do that. As a matter of fact, I'm just going to head over to his place and attack his mouth."

Ha, right. Wouldn't that be something?

Niko's lips break into a wide grin. "It seems you've been

thinking about doing that quite a lot. Stop thinking and just do it. Carpe diem."

My phone decides to ping just then, making my heart somersault to the top of my throat. Niko is still watching me with a knowing smile when I flip my phone to see who texted me. It's Rikkon. *Boom*. My heart soars. *God, I have it bad.*

"By the upturn of your lips, I guess that's a message from him?"

I level a glower at her. "Why are you still here? Get out!" I toss my pillow in her direction.

"I'm leaving. Unlike you, I do have a social life. I'm going out with Troy. Don't tell Mom."

"Who is Troy?"

"A boy in my class. He works at the movie theater, which is pretty convenient."

"And why can't Mom know about him?" I raise an eyebrow.

"Because his dad runs the guild of rogue mages in Salem." She flashes me a toothy grin, and then bails.

Of course. Niko couldn't simply date someone from a regular family. Even a human would have been more preferable to Mom than rogues. I'd worry if her boyfriends lasted more than a month. Troy is the flavor of the week, hardly worth my concern.

I switch my attention to my phone, trembling as I swipe the screen to reveal Rikkon's message. There are more than one, sent an hour ago. Somehow, there was a delay on his end. Maybe he didn't have coverage where he was. The first messages are just a bunch of random characters typed in. My heart sinks. He must have butt-typed these. But as I keep scrolling, my disappointment turns into real concern. In one of them he asks me to join him at Tuck an' Roll, a dive bar in a skeevy part of town.

Fuck. There's only one reason he'd go there: to score drugs.

I should have known. With the way visions have plagued him lately, it was just a matter of time before he relapsed.

Propelled by a sense of urgency, I get dressed in warm clothes and bolt out of my room. It's early in the evening and Mom just left the house. She won't be home until much later. I'm glad that I don't have to explain to her where I'm going in such a hurry. She's been more attentive lately, which is an improvement, but also a curse. Niko and I are too used to independence. I've had to be creative in order to sneak out to my samurai lessons.

I open the front door with a jerky movement, not prepared for the body that falls into me. A yell escapes my lips, but then I recognize Rikkon's long blond hair under his hoodie. I stagger back, straining with the weight of his body in my arms.

"What the hell, Rikkon?"

He straightens up, looking at me through glazed eyes. He reeks of cheap beer, too. *Damn it.*

"I'm sorry, Mir. I tried to resist. But I was hurting so much. It's all good now."

I pull him inside, and then shut the door. He leans against the wall, dropping his head into his hand. Niko must have just missed him. *Thank goodness.*

"What did you take?"

"It was just pot and a lot of beer." He hiccups.

I grab his hand and steer him to the kitchen. "Come on. We need to get you sobered up."

"How about some food? I'm starved."

"I bet you are."

I pull up a chair and force him to sit down. But Rikkon grabs my hand again, pulling me onto his lap. My pulse quickens while my heart drums like a hummingbird trapped in my chest.

"You're such a good friend, Mir." His eyes become clearer somehow as he stares into mine. "And so damn gorgeous. Sometimes it's hard to not let the lines blur." His gaze drops to my lips, and I'm pretty sure I stop breathing at that point.

He leans in and brushes his lips against mine. Electric sparks crackle where we touch, but a sense of wrongness also comes with it, soiling the moment. I pull back, then jump off his lap.

"You're drunk and high. Let's keep the lines sharp."

I turn around and get busy pulling stuff out of the fridge, but

I'm screaming inside. I can't believe I ran away from him. *So what if he's drunk? Doesn't alcohol make people do what they've secretly been craving for a while?*

"What do you feel like eating? I can make a grilled cheese if you like."

The screeching noise of a chair rasping against the floor draws my attention. Rikkon is standing still, his body all of a sudden tense as he stares into the hallway.

I follow his line of vision, seeing nothing out of the ordinary. "What is it?"

"Is the Taluah Mirror here?" he asks without looking at me.

"Yes. My mother brought it home from Elena's apartment. Why?"

"It's calling to me."

He leaves the kitchen, heading straight for my mother's office where the mirror is. I follow Rikkon, feeling incredibly uneasy now. That mirror turned into a portal to hell. Why is it calling him? My mother keeps it covered with a black sheet for that reason. She doesn't dare to look at it, not even by accident. But Rikkon pulls the sheet off. Right now, it's working as a mirror, not a portal—at least, the only thing I see reflected is Rikkon's image.

I stay back, not willing to chance coming any closer. Niko told me what she saw when Aurora and Saxon were trying to get back from hell. And Aurora saw something awful in it too. I don't dare risk it.

"Is everything okay?" I ask.

He neither answers nor takes his eyes off the object. Worry gnaws at my insides. *What if he's trapped in a horrifying vision?* I'm about to pull him back when he raises his arm and touches the surface. A bright flash of light illuminates the entire room, almost blinding me. I sling my arm over my face to protect my eyes. When it fades, Rikkon is sprawled on the floor, unmoving.

"Shit!" I run to him, and make sure I don't look directly into the mirror as I hook my arms under his armpits and drag him a safe distance away. Then I cover the mirror with the sheet again.

He groans, slowly coming back to the world of the living. I drop into a crouch next to him and push his long hair off his face. He blinks his eyes open, but it's another moment before he focuses on me.

"Are you okay?"

He doesn't answer right away, and I fear he has a concussion. His eyes become rounder suddenly, and at once, he sits up, grabbing me by the shoulders. "I saw Ellnesari, Mir. Through the mirror. I saw my mother's court. I remember everything. And I saw...." he trails off.

"What did you see?"

He lets go of me, turning away. "I saw the female I was supposed to marry. My fated mate."

An ice-cold hand reaches inside of me and clutches my heart, freezing it until it shatters into a thousand pieces.

"Like Aurora and Saxon," I mumble, sitting on the backs of my legs, defeated.

Rikkon lets out a shuddering breath. "Yes, but ten thousand times stronger."

I hug my middle, fighting the desperation that has crept up my throat, blocking my airway. Rikkon is mated to someone else, which means there will never be a future for him and me.

"How could you cross the veil with Vivi? I thought bonded mates couldn't be far from each other."

"The bonding didn't fall in place until the last second. When I realized what had happened, I was already on this side, and the way back to Ellnesari closed to me forever."

His expression is pinched with misery. No wonder he had it much worse than Vivi. He was pining for his mate.

"How are you feeling now?" I ask.

He furrows his eyebrows. "What do you mean?"

"Now that you remember the bond, are you in pain?"

He shakes his head. "No. I..." He looks away, running a hand through his hair. "I feel hollow inside."

A surge of hope flares in my chest. Maybe the bond was broken somehow. "Well, hollowness is better than agony."

"Maybe," he replies without conviction, deflating my optimism.

Bond or no bond, it seems he's still linked to the Nightingale female.

Twelve

RIKKON

Miranda jumps back on her feet and puts distance between us. Her face is a mask of neutrality, but her expressive eyes tell me a different story. She's hurting because of me, and that's making me feel worse than scum. I tried to kiss her, knowing I'd be dooming us both to a lifetime of misery. How can I be bonded to someone else and be so drawn to her at the same time? It makes no sense.

I get up, turning my back to the mirror. Now that I have my memories back, I know how dangerous the relic is. But I also know it can be used to open portals to different dimensions, including Ellnesari.

"Well, I'm glad you recovered your memories. Does that mean you know who that deranged hunter is?"

I widen my eyes, worried that the warrior came back for Miranda even when I knew he wouldn't. I could have made a mistake.

"Did he come back?" I ask.

"No. I haven't seen him. Thank goodness. But do you know who he is and why he was after you?"

I thread my fingers through my hair and look away. I thought recovering my memories would give me some kind of peace, but I feel more wretched than ever.

"Yes to both questions. His name is Selor Nyrk. He was my mother's most trusted knight and paramour."

"Wait? What? He's your mother's lover? What about your father?"

"What about him?"

"Uh, is he still around?"

I chuckle, now understanding her confusion. "He was when Vivi and I were banished. The rulership of Aquila's court always goes to the females, never the males. My father is a king without power. Queen Maewe rules."

"So, does that mean your mother can simply take lovers and parade them in front of your dad's face?"

"It's not considered a slight in Ellnesari if your consort is not your fated mate. But if he were, she wouldn't take a lover. They'd only have eyes for each other."

Then why is that not the case with me? At first, all I felt was a hole in my chest, but now, I can already feel the tug of the bond getting stronger, calling me to Eriel Fasanor, the princess of the Cygnus kingdom.

"Oh? So fated mates is not a common thing there?"

"I wouldn't say it's common, but it's also not that rare either. All I know is that it trumps everything, including rank and alliances."

I catch Miranda's hard swallow, and curse in my head. I shouldn't be so honest with her when I know the truth is hurting her. My low self-esteem had me blind before, but now I can see clearly that whatever I feel is not one-sided.

"Okay, so this Selor dude works or worked for your mother. What is he doing here? Was he banished too?"

"That I don't know. It's the first thing we must ask him when we catch him."

Her eyebrows shoot to the heavens. "You want to go after him? What if he tries to kill us again?"

"He won't. He's sworn an unbreakable vow to never harm any member of Queen Maewe's family."

She crosses her arms in front of her chest and glowers at me. "Oh, cool. You're protected. What about me?"

I step closer to her, ready to pull her into my arms, but I stop short. What am I thinking? I can't do this to us, to *her*.

"He won't harm you either. He has to obey my orders."

"He didn't listen to you before."

"That's because I didn't remember to use the right words. We should go look for him now."

Miranda shakes her head. "I'm sorry, Rik. I can't. I have plans."

Disappointment washes over me, and also, a spike of jealousy pierces my chest, which is absurd. Miranda can only be a friend. Nothing more.

"Oh, what kind of plans?"

"Samurai training."

Not a date then. The vise hold jealousy had on my heart eases off.

"Since I'm no longer pretending to be a vampire or bound by a ridiculous schedule, can I come?"

"You want to come to my class? Why?"

"Because I used to be an excellent fighter but I'm rusty as hell. I could use the practice."

She watches me through slits. "You don't look drunk or high anymore."

"I'm not. I think touching the mirror sobered me up."

"Okay, fine. This ought to be interesting."

My excuse is bullshit. I'm already getting plenty of combat training back at the vamp mansion. Ronan is a drill sergeant. I'm just not ready yet to part ways with Miranda. Staying away from her this past week was almost impossible.

"I'm going to change," she continues. "You'd better stay away from that mirror. We don't want to accidentally open a portal to hell again."

"Yeah. Good idea."

I wait until she walks out of the room to face the object again. The sheet is back in place, until it isn't. It's now lying in a heap next to the mirror. *Fuck.* At first, all I see is my reflection, but as I get closer, the surface ripples and then it shows me an ethereal winter garden bathed in early morning light. A fresh coat of snow has covered the leafless limbs of light gray trees and the rocky ground. Spots of bright purple appear over the exposed roots of trees as old as time. Those are the winter flowers blossoming to life. Then she appears, beautiful and cold. My fated mate, my future bride. She wears the colors of her court, white and light gray tones, which, combined with her white hair and pale skin, makes her blend in with the background. But her eyes, a striking cerulean blue color, are impossible to miss.

"Rikkon. How I've missed you," she whispers.

I should reply, as the bond commands me to do, but my tongue is stuck in my mouth, and my soul seems to be splitting in two.

She furrows her delicate eyebrows. "What's the matter? Aren't you glad to see me?"

I can't answer her without betraying a part of myself, so I do the cowardly thing and cover the mirror with the black sheet again.

White-hot pain flares in my chest, and the invisible cord that links me to Eriel becomes taut.

"Rikkon?" Miranda calls me. "Are you coming?"

"Yeah, Mir. I'm coming."

MIRANDA

Rikkon hasn't acted right since he recovered his memories. He said he was fine, and on the outside, he seems okay, but there's something off about him now. Maybe it's the bond, getting stronger by the minute and causing him pain.

Shit. I don't want to think about that. It's bad enough that I agreed to let him come to my samurai training which has been the only one thing keeping me sane. Mr. Shirogane's dojo was the only place not tainted by Rikkon's memory, and now that's going to get ruined.

While I changed, I promised myself I wouldn't ask Rikkon why he ghosted me in the past week, but not five minutes into the drive, I'm opening my big mouth.

"Why didn't you call or text me back?"

"I'm sorry, Mir. I thought it was best if I kept my distance."

"Why?"

"Why? Jesus, because I'm a disaster magnet."

I roll my eyes. "That's a lame excuse, Rik. Try again."

"I'm serious, Mir. Look at what's happened ever since we crossed paths."

"Those bad things would have happened whether we were friends or not. Don't you get it? We're on the verge of a massive war between vamps, maybe even among the entire supe community."

Rikkon doesn't speak, instead he looks out the window. Now I'm worried I was too rough in my reply. *No, Miranda. You weren't. He needs to come clean if he wants to save this friendship.*

"Hello? Aren't you going to say something? Listen, if you can't be honest with me, then we have no business being friends. I have no room in my—"

"I have an unhealthy attraction to you," he blurts out.

"What?" I turn to look at him, making the car swerve to the right. With my face burning, I get back into my lane, but I'm not seeing anything in front of me now.

"I was trying to fight it, and the only way I knew how was to keep my distance."

My heart is busy galloping at full speed while my mind is

twisting like a freaking tornado. "Why were you trying to fight it? Did Aurora or Saxon say anything to you?"

"I'm fated for someone else, Mir. Whatever is happening to me is an anomaly, something that shouldn't have occurred."

And just like that, my heart plummets. I curl my fingers tighter around the steering wheel and try not to cry.

"Are you saying that the bond didn't break?"

"No," he sounds pained. "It's back and it's getting stronger."

A rogue tear escapes the corner of my eye. I hastily wipe it away, hoping he didn't notice.

"You need to return to Ellnesari. That's why you want to find Selor. You think he knows the way back."

"I'm not sure he does, but yeah, I have a few questions for him."

"Okay. We'll find him and then discover a way to get you back to your promised."

God, I don't sound bitter at all.

"I wish things were different, Mir. For real."

"I'm glad they aren't though. You don't belong here, Rik. You have to go back."

He doesn't reply to my comment and I don't blame him. It was way too harsh, and it's so not me. I guess heartache turns us all into monsters.

I park in the same shady street as I always do, but this time, Rikkon doesn't comment about it being unsafe. And he keeps his mouth shut the entire walk to the dojo. I wish he hadn't blurted out he has a thing for me earlier. No, his actual words were "an unhealthy attraction." What the hell does that even mean? I'm regretting big time now agreeing to let him tag along. There's a cloud of turmoil hanging above us, disturbing the peace of mind required to master the ways of the samurai.

No one is on the tatami when we enter the dojo. Mr. Shirogane must be in his office and Marcello hasn't arrived yet.

"I'm going to change into my *gi*. Try not to get in trouble while I'm gone."

I veer for the changing room, but Rikkon touches my arm, halting me. "Mir, I'm so sorry."

Plastering the fakest of all smiles on my face, I reply, "Yeah, I know. Don't worry about me. I'll be fine once this class is over."

His eyes darken for a moment. What? Is he mad at me now? I want to yell and tell him he can't have his cake and eat it too, but I just swallow the angry retort and continue down the corridor.

He said what he feels for me is unhealthy. He said it was an anomaly. *Fuck that shit. He doesn't get to be angry or annoyed.* Now I'm extra motivated to get his ass back to Ellnesari so I never have to look at his stupid and gorgeous face again.

Thirteen

MIRANDA

I take my time changing so I can get my emotions under control. I'm so mad at myself for letting hope flourish inside of my chest when I knew there was zero chance anything would happen between Rikkon and me. Little did I know the major roadblock standing in our way was destiny. Aurora lucked out when she mated with Saxon, but I'm experiencing the opposite at the hands of fate, and I hate the bitch for it.

Gee, I'm not making any sense. Looking at my reflection in the small mirror above the sink, I adjust my sash, and take several steadying breaths.

"Okay, you can do this, Miranda. It's just a couple of hours."

When I return to the training room, I find Rikkon and Marcello glaring at one another, and Mr. Shirogane between them.

"What's going on here?" I ask.

"Ah, Miss Leal. Glad that you can join us. We will start." Mr. Shirogane veers for the front of the room, ignoring my question.

I turn to Rikkon. "What happened while I was in the restroom?"

"Nothing on my end. Ask your buddy."

"I didn't know he was your guest, Mir. I thought he was an intruder," Marcello replies.

Rikkon intensifies the death glare he's aiming at Marcello, making me suspect I'm not getting the full story here. But I'm too tired to get to the bottom of it. I just want to start tonight's lesson already.

"If your friend would like to participate, he needs to get rid of his shoes," Mr. Shirogane tells me.

"Yes, I'd like to join," Rikkon replies.

Marcello gives Rikkon a disdainful glance before he faces forward. "What are we doing tonight, Sensei?"

"We shall continue with the *Hyoho Niten Ichi-ryu* training. Grab your swords."

"Sweet." Marcello gives me a wicked smile and saunters to the wall where the weapons are mounted.

I suspect his glee is not one-hundred-percent linked to the training. Great. This is going to turn into a testosterone contest. Exactly what I was looking forward to tonight.

"How skilled are you with blades, son?" Mr. Shirogane asks Rikkon.

"I get by."

"I get by." Marcello snorts. "We're not training with fake weapons, buddy."

Rikkon gives him a droll look. "I won't cut my hand off if that's what you're worried about. But I might cut yours."

"Oh, shut up, you two." I take my swords from their mounts and return to my spot on the tatami.

Mr. Shirogane is watching the scene with a neutral expression save for the slight upturn of his lips. He's enjoying this and I wonder why.

Once dickwads one and two join me on the tatami, Mr. Shirogane goes through all the moves and stances again. He's not doing this for Rikkon's benefit. No matter how many times we practice this type of fighting, he does that. I try to keep my eyes solely on him, but it's hard when Rikkon stands next to me. I fight the urge to glance at him with every fiber of my being.

The introductory part of the training goes on for about twenty minutes. Now comes the fun part. We get to put into practice all the movements in actual combat.

"Since we have an odd number tonight, I'll spar with Miss Leal," Mr. Shirogane announces.

A sigh of relief whooshes out of me. I'm usually fine sparring with Marcello, but not when he seems to be trying to prove something to Rikkon. And sparring with Rikkon would be a nightmare.

But my notion that sparring with the sensei would be better flies right out of the window when I find myself under Rikkon's scrutiny. *Fucking fantastic.*

Sweat drips down my back as I take my stance. I fear I'm going to make a fool of myself in front of everyone. But when the sparring commences, it's like a fire ignites in the pit of my stomach. It's the samurai spirit taking over and helping me focus on keeping my head attached to my body. I block, I attack, and I swing my blade as if I were performing in a deadly dance. It's not easy facing off against Mr. Shirogane and he's not holding back much, I think.

Our sparring ends in a deadlock, and when he steps back and bows, I notice pride is etched on his face. *Holy shit.* I survived and I can hardly believe it. My heart might feel like it's going to burst out of my chest, and my face is burning from the exertion, but I've never felt better in my entire life. It's hard not to smile.

When I turn around, Marcello's jaw is hanging loose, but it's Rikkon's expression that does my head in. His blue eyes are fire, so intense and penetrating that it makes me feel completely bare in front of him. The yearning hits me hard, leaving me breathless. But then I remember I'm a burden to him, an inconvenience, and the heat turns into ice, my smile wilting into nothing.

"Come on, sissy boy. Let's see how hard you suck." Marcello heads to the tatami.

"Mr. Marangoni, that's not the spirit of the samurai. You're letting your ego interfere. Ego has no place in battle."

Marcello has the sense to look remorseful. "Yes, sensei. My apologies."

He whirls around and faces Rikkon, who is already positioned on the tatami, swords at the ready. But right before the sparring commences, he glances at me, and I don't know what to do with the feeling his attention evokes. The butterflies are raving mad in my belly, but my heart is being squeezed by a barbed wire. I hope the mask of indifference I'm wearing doesn't slip.

"Commence," Mr. Shirogane says.

I hold my breath, not knowing how far in his training with Ronan Rikkon has gone. Marcello is a beast, and I know he won't hold back. Immediately, I can see the difference in their styles. While Marcello puts emphasis on brutal strength, Rikkon is as nimble as a cat. The way he moves around the vampire is mesmerizing. No one can mistake him for anything but a Nightingale prince, perfect and ethereal.

Gah. What am I thinking? I sound like that Tom Mularkey dude, spewing nonsense about Rikkon's attributes.

So far, all Rikkon has done is evade and block Marcello's attacks. He's tiring his opponent, a fact that Marcello must have caught on to. He looks frustrated as hell.

"Come on, dude. Stop being a pussy and come at me already."

I catch the faint smile on Rikkon's lips right before he replies, "As you wish."

His next movements are so fast, I almost can't keep up. The swords slash the air in a blur, descending on Marcello, who barely has time to block the attack. His grunts become louder, and then both his katana and wakizashi fly out of his hands.

Instead of ending the fight by pressing the tip of his blade against Marcello's neck, Rikkon simply steps back and lowers his swords. Marcello's breathing is coming out in bursts as he braces his hands on his knees.

I've never seen him winded like that before.

"Well done, son. That was beautiful. An excellent example on how to take advantage of an enemy's lack of inner balance."

"I have inner balance," Marcello retorts. "He simply failed to disclose he was already a master." He turns to me. "Thanks for the heads-up, Mir."

"Hey! Don't go blaming me because you got your ass kicked."

"It's not Miranda's fault you lost," Rikkon says calmly, and it grates on my nerves.

"I don't need you to come to my defense," I snap.

"Mir, I didn't me—"

I raise my hand. "Save it. I have to go."

"Where are you going?" he asks.

"Anywhere but here. Don't follow me." I grab my duffel bag on the way out, but instead of veering to the restroom to change, I storm out of Mr. Shirogane's dojo. I'm so angry right now, I could break things. I acted like a child in front of the sensei and Marcello for no reason. I should have never agreed to let Rikkon tag along.

I don't sense I'm being followed, but I look over my shoulder anyway. No one came after me. Good. I don't need to keep pretending everything is fine anymore. I round the corner onto the street my car is parked and practically collide with none other than the Nightingale hunter, Selor Nyrk.

"What the hell!" I jump back, lifting my fisted hands.

He eyes my aggressive stance and lifts one eyebrow. "I'm not here to fight with you, little witch."

"Whatever. You tried to make a shish kebab out of me the last time we met."

"But I didn't."

"Only because Rikkon interfered."

The hunter chuckles. "Sure, let's pretend that was it."

"If you're not here to murder me, what do you want?"

"I'm here to help you."

It's my turn to laugh. "That's rich."

"Rikkon has recovered his memories, which means he now remembers the bond to the princess of the Cygnus kingdom."

I wince, hating how the simple mention of his bond makes me bleed. *And it had to be a princess, right? Fuck me.*

"So?"

"He needs to return to Ellnesari or he'll go mad. I can't tamper with his memories again."

"Wait? You were the one who wiped Rik's and Vivi's memories?"

The hunter waves his hands impatiently. "Unimportant details. There's a way to open a portal to Ellnesari."

My eyebrows arch. "You knew of a way and you never bothered to tell anybody? Why didn't you simply tell Rikkon instead of messing with his head?"

"It wasn't the right time. You ask too many questions, young witch."

"You bet your ass I do. If there's a way back into Ellnesari, spill it already."

"You need the Taluah Mirror, and the first familiar."

"Wait, what do you need Solomon for?"

"I'll find you in two days. Be ready."

He then disappears into thin air, leaving me with more questions than before. But if he thinks I'm going to simply wait around for him to reappear, he's sorely mistaken. It's high time I crash the king's inner circle.

Fourteen

RIKKON

"You're not going after her?" Marcello asks me.

"She told me not to follow her. I'm respecting her wishes."

He throws his hands up in the air. "Good grief. You're one clueless dude. Every time a girl says something, she means the opposite. She's probably even more furious that you didn't follow her." He looks at Mr. Shirogane. "Tell him, Sensei."

"It's better if I don't meddle. There's a reason I'm still single." He chuckles.

Heat spreads through my face, and my ears burn. They think this is a lover's quarrel. I rub my chin, torn about what to do.

"Well, if you're not going to get your head out of your ass, then I'm going after my friend."

Immediately, I bristle. "You're not following Miranda."

The vampire's eyes narrow. "Oh yeah? Who is going to stop me?"

I take a step in his direction. "I will. It seems you haven't learned your lesson."

"Enough!" Mr. Shirogane interrupts, looking pointedly at me. "I've allowed your entry in my dojo because I read good intentions in you. But now I sense much turmoil, much unbalance. That's not the way of the samurai. You must leave at once."

Shame washes over me, not because I'm being told off in front of Mr. Douche Vampire. It's because Mr. Shirogane's words apply pressure to the wound in my soul. I told Miranda what I feel for her is unhealthy, an anomaly. I almost made it sound like she's to blame for my shortcomings. *God, I need to make things right with her.*

I bow my head to Mr. Shirogane. "Thank you for the lesson, Sensei."

Without glancing in Marcello's direction, I put my shoes back on and head out. Miranda had a five-minute start, so I sprint after her, hoping she hasn't driven off yet. But as I near the side street where she parked her car, the small hairs on the back of my neck stand on end, and a small throb in my forehead makes me wince. *Shit. Am I about to have another vision?*

My steps falter, and I have to brace myself against a wall for a second. The world is spinning, making me feel sick. I prepare for the excruciating pain to come, but surprisingly, my headache slowly recedes.

A familiar presence nearby makes me look up. And there she is, standing in front of me in her *gi* and fierce ponytail. Wisps of straight hair have escaped the hairband and are now framing her lovely face. My heart skips a beat, and for a moment, I forget why I can't step into her space, hug her tight, and beg her to never let me go. Then comes the sharp tug in my chest, almost as if a hook had pierced my skin and was now pulling me in the opposite direction.

"Are you having another vision?" she asks.

I push off the wall, straightening to my full height. "No. I thought I was, but it passed. Mir, I'm so—"

"Save the apology for another time, Rikkon. Something huge just happened."

She called me Rikkon, not Rik. I really screwed up with her this time.

"What?"

"The Nightingale hunter came back. He said he knows how to use the Taluah Mirror to open a portal to Ellnesari."

"You talked to him? Just now?"

"Yeah."

I move closer, searching for any sign of a struggle in her clothes. "Did he hurt you?"

She steps back, glowering. "No. Can you please focus? He knows how to get you back to Ellnesari. Aren't you excited about that?"

The bond becomes stronger for a moment, but excitement is not the feeling swirling in my chest. Dread is. I don't want to go back.

"It could be a trap."

"Yeah, I know. He said we need the Taluah Mirror and Solomon to do it."

"Why does he need to involve Bloodstone's headmaster?"

"I don't know. I hope not to use him as a sacrifice."

I push my hair back, pulling at the strands. "What else did he say?"

"He'll be back in two days and that we need to be ready."

"I don't doubt he knows how to use the Taluah Mirror to open a portal to Ellnesari. He's here because my mother sent him. She must have given him a means to return."

"There's more. He's the one who erased your memories."

I shake my head, denying the idea. "How? I remember where I got the memory spell. It was from a druid who sold dream catchers."

"Maybe the same guy our friend had a rough talk with at the dream catcher shop?"

Son of a bitch. Now it makes sense. No magical creature here would be powerful enough to erase the memory of Nightingale royalty. Selor must have given him the spell. But why?

"Anyway, I was coming back to the dojo to get you. We're paying King Raphael a visit."

"You want to tell him what happened?"

"Of course. He needs to know about your mother's lackey's presence here."

I feel unease involving the king in this matter. The disease affecting first-generation vampires has already manifested in him. It's why Lucca is now more involved in running the show.

"I don't think it's a good idea, Mir. Maybe we should talk to Lucca first."

The furrow of her eyebrows and the pinch of her lips tell me she hates my suggestion.

"Fine. Let's head there then. I've never been to Lucca's place before." She turns around and strides away.

"Why is that?" I follow her.

"I never received an invite. I'm just the High Witch's middle child, no one of importance."

I touch her shoulder. "Don't say that. You're important."

She shrugs it off, moving away from my hand. "You don't need to say nice things to me, Rikkon. I know where I stand in the grand scheme of things."

She unlocks her car door and slides inside. This is going to be a hellish drive. I don't know what to do or say to make Miranda not mad at me anymore. Every time I open my mouth, I manage to dig myself a deeper hole.

We don't speak for a while, and the longer the silence extends, the harder it is to withstand it. I'm about to betray my sister's trust, but Miranda deserves to know why I insisted on bringing the issue of Selor to Lucca instead of the king.

"There's a reason I don't want to tell the king about my mother's minion, Mir, and it's not because I don't think you're important enough to have an audience with him. He's sick."

"What do you mean he's sick? What kind of disease?"

"He's losing his mental faculties and the only way to cure him is if the Nightingales return and bring their magic back."

"Oh my god. That's terrible."

"No one outside of his inner circle knows about it. And it has to stay that way. Imagine the chaos that would ensue if the rest of the vampire population knew their king was going mad.”

“It would be complete anarchy. And Tatiana would for sure take advantage of the situation and claim the throne for herself.”

“She’s also sick. All first-generation vampires are succumbing to the illness. King Raphael is the one who held on to his sanity the longest.”

“And the other vampires must hibernate from time to time. If nothing changes, this could very well be the end of them.”

I look out the window. “That’s the main reason I’m going back to Ellnesari. To try to convince my mother and the other rulers to restore things to normal.”

“I thought you needed to go back to your mate,” she replies in a soft voice laced with pain.

“No. If she were the only reason, I wouldn’t go.”

Miranda turns to me with eyes that are as round as saucers. “You can’t be serious. You would rather live your life in agony than go back? Why?”

I want to tell her the truth, but it won’t make things better. Headlights blind me for a moment, and suddenly, the car swerves sharply to the right while a horn buzzes loudly.

“Shit. That was close. I’d better keep my eyes on the road,” she mutters.

“Please do. I don’t want to lose you.”

Fuck. I shouldn’t have said that. She doesn’t reply for a long time. A quick peek at her face shows me she’s clenching her jaw tight.

“You are going to lose me, Rik, no matter what you wish.”

A huge lump forms in my throat. Anger and sadness mix in my chest, creating a bitter cocktail of emotions. I curl my hands into fists and stare out the window, seeing nothing.

Another five minutes on the road, and we’re approaching Lucca’s mansion. It’s hidden by a spell, but it seems Miranda can see through the glamour. Maybe all members of the Leal family can reach the place. That makes sense if there’s an emergency.

At this hour it's hard to say if they are all up yet. Now that we don't have to abide by Bloodstone's schedule, no one shows their faces until late at night, sometimes past midnight. Well, that's not true. Vaughn and I have to meet Ronan for training, usually an hour after sunset, which means I'm screwed. The towering vampire is a mean bastard when it comes to sticking to a training schedule.

Today, I was weak and succumbed to my body's cravings. I went to a dive bar with every intention of getting high out of my mind. But somehow, I held back. True, I smoked pot and drank a few too many beers, but compared to what I used to do before, it wasn't bad at all.

I think the thought of disappointing Miranda is what helped me stay strong—or not be as weak. It didn't matter in the end, I disappointed her anyway.

The front door unlocks with my touch, another enchantment put in place. Gerard Norton, the house's butler—manager, whatever—walks over wearing a pristine suit and business-mode expression.

"Good evening, Rikkon. Ronan has been looking for you. You missed your training session earlier."

"I know. On a scale of one to ten, how pissed off is he?"

"How about eleven?" the vampire in question answers, joining us in the foyer. He glances at Miranda, not hiding his surprise. "What are you wearing, kid?"

I don't understand his question for a split second, then I remember she never changed clothes.

"It's called a *gi*, and who are you calling a kid?" She glowers at the vampire, not one bit intimidated by his size.

"Mir, what are you doing here?" Aurora rushes down the grand staircase, followed by Saxon. "Is everything okay at home?"

"Will you relax? Everything is fine." She glances at me. "Well, kind of."

Saxon doesn't miss her gesture. "What's going on here? Rikkon, what did you do?"

His accusatory look snaps something in me. It finally shatters the bullshit persona the memory spell gave me. I'm not a fucking junkie, I'm not a weakling, I'm not a burden. I'm Rikkon Gael, prince of the Aquila kingdom.

"You'd better watch your tone, Saxon. I'm not your bitch, and I don't owe you any explanation."

The male's jaw drops and he watches me like I've sprouted a second head. In fact, everyone is looking at me like they're seeing me for the first time.

"Whoa. Someone finally found their balls," Vaughn laughs.

I didn't notice he had joined us.

"To answer your question, Rora, I came because Rikkon and I have huge news," Miranda chimes in.

"You're a couple," Vaughn pipes up again.

I throw him a glower. "Will you just shut up for a second? Go on Mir, continue."

"Actually, you tell the first part."

"Very well." I glance around, looking for my sister. "Where are Vivi and Lucca? They need to hear this and I don't want to repeat myself."

"Jesus, when did you acquire a douchey attitude?" Saxon asks.

I smirk. "Don't worry, pal. The title of Captain Prick of Blueblood Royal Douchery still belongs to you."

Vaugh whistles. "That escalated fast."

"Okay, you're in for it now." Saxon takes a menacing step in my direction, only to be stopped by his mate.

"Sax, quit it," Aurora scolds him.

"He started it."

"If this is a serious matter, then Manu needs to be here too," Ronan interrupts. "Let's all head to the meeting room and try to cool off."

We all follow the giant vampire down the hallway. Miranda walks next to me, but she keeps her gaze straight ahead. I wonder what she thinks of me now. Did I sound like a jerk a minute ago? Maybe, but Saxon had it coming. He's a fucking pain in the ass and loves to taunt me and Vaughn. Well, he's not using me as his punching bag anymore. There will be no more letting people judge me because of my past.

The grand room used for meetings is austere and imposing. It has the Della Morte signature. Dark wood panels cover the walls, and at one end of the room there's a fireplace and an oil painting of Lucca, Manu, and their parents above it. That was obviously commissioned centuries after both died. I always thought it was a morbid gesture, and thinking like a Nightingale now has not changed my opinion on the matter.

Ronan pulls up a chair next to the one Lucca usually occupies. The solid oak table in the middle of the room is excessively long. Twenty people can sit at it comfortably. I choose to remain standing. I'm too jittery to sit and wait for everyone to show up. I realize that all I'm doing is drawing more attention to myself. I wonder if I look different to them besides the change in attitude.

Finally, Lucca and Vivi walk in, followed by Manu, who seems like she just jumped out of bed. She's still wearing her pj's.

"Couldn't find the time to change, Manu?" Saxon asks.

"No. It's too early. I hope this impromptu meeting is worth my time."

Vivi gives me a curious glance. Can she sense I've recovered my memories?

"Okay, we're all here now," Lucca says. "What's going on?"

"The memory spell has been lifted. I know who I am. I remember everything," I reply.

"Son of a bitch," Saxon mutters. "Now things make sense."

"How? What happened?" Vivi asks.

"He touched the Taluah Mirror and that did it," Miranda answers this time.

Lucca leans back in his chair, narrowing his gaze. "That mirror seems to be capable of doing a lot of things."

Meeting his hard gaze, I say, "Yes, and it can open a portal to Ellnesari."

Fifteen

MIRANDA

No one speaks for a hot second following Rikkon's declaration, and then all hell breaks loose. Everyone starts talking at once, but Rikkon remains calm, collected, cold. His hands are clasped behind his back, and never before has he looked so much like a Nightingale prince. Something changed in him. He doesn't seem as uncertain as before. Maybe rediscovering his true self did the trick.

"All right. Can we please all be quiet for a moment?" Lucca commands.

When the chatter quiets down, he focuses on Rikkon. "Explain to me how we can use that mirror to open a portal to Ellnesari."

I expect Rikkon to answer the question, but surprisingly he turns to me. "Mir can explain."

My cheeks become warmer, and my appreciation for him grows. He could simply have answered Lucca himself, but he's letting me do it, he's giving me a voice, something no one has ever bothered doing before.

"Before Rikkon recovered his memories, while you were all dealing with Elena Montenegro, we met another Nightingale, a warrior from the Aquila court."

Vivi's eyes grow larger. "Selor is here? Why?"

"Uh, who is that?" Lucca glances at her.

"He's our mother's right hand," Rikkon replies. "I have reason to believe she sent him here after our banishment to spy on us."

"I can't believe this," Vivi murmurs. "But why?"

"To make sure Rikkon could return to Ellnesari," I say.

The blood seems to drain from Vivienne's face, and I regret my bluntness. I don't think Queen Maewe cares one bit about her daughter, that much I could gather from the Nightingale hunter. But I didn't need to be so honest in my answer.

"Why would she want Rikkon back after she banished him? And if that's the case, why wait all these centuries to bring him back?" Lucca asks.

"Selor didn't elaborate. All he said was that it wasn't the right time before."

"Don't try to make sense of my mother's capriciousness," Rikkon chimes in. "All that matters is that now I have a way into Ellnesari. I can make my case to my mother and the other rulers to bring their magic back here."

"Wait a second. You plan on going there alone?" Lucca asks. "You're out of your mind."

"Do you suggest a vampire expedition into Ellnesari? You won't make it two steps in before my mother's guards stop you. Vampires aren't allowed in our realm after the conflict between King Raphael and Tatiana started," Rikkon retorts.

Lucca opens his mouth to argue, but Vivienne cuts him off. "Rik is right, Luc. You can't go, but I can."

"No, Vivi. You're not coming with me."

"Bullshit I'm not!" She slaps the table with both hands.

"She exiled you, sister. Do you think she will be happy to see you?"

"She banished you too, brother. Or have you forgotten that detail?"

"Rikkon has a mate waiting for him," I butt in, even if it cuts me like a knife. "He has to go back no matter what."

"What? So the bond didn't break?" Vivienne arches her eyebrows, losing a bit of her anger.

"No," Rikkon replies ruefully. "It's only getting stronger."

"Let's put a pin in who gets to go on this trip for a second," Lucca chimes in. "How exactly do we turn the Taluah Mirror into a portal?"

"Unfortunately, we don't have all the details yet," I reply. "Selor said he'd be back in two days. We need the mirror and Solomon to make it happen."

"Why would we need Solomon?" Aurora asks. "Oh God. Please don't say to sacrifice him."

"Don't worry. He won't be used as a sacrifice," Rikkon pipes up.

I want to ask if it's one of his know-for-sure things, but maybe he doesn't want people to know about that peculiar gift of his.

"That's great. Rikkon gets to go back to the land of assholes. Can I go now?" Manu stands. "I was dragged out of bed and I didn't have time to eat."

"If you want a warm snack, you'll have to wait," Lucca tells her.

"Why?" Her eyebrows arch, enhancing her arrogant expression.

"Because I suspended the influx of blood donors for the time being," Ronan replies.

Manu stares daggers at him. "What the hell for?"

"I don't want to risk any of the humans coming here to spy on us. We're at war, Manu."

"You suck." She whirls around and storms out of the room in a dramatic fashion.

"So much for wanting Manu to be present," Saxon says under his breath.

"I'll deal with her later," Lucca replies. "Let's return to the problem at hand. What are we going to do about this Selor guy?"

"He can't be trusted," Vivienne pipes up. "We can't let him get his hands on the Taluah Mirror."

"Agreed." Lucca nods.

From the corner of my eye, I watch Rikkon become tenser. "That's not your decision to make."

"Excuse me?" Lucca glares at him.

"You heard me. No one here knows Selor more than I. You never spent time with the male, Vivi. I've trained with him. He wants to return to Ellnesari as badly as I do."

A steely punch hits my chest. I wasn't prepared for that declaration. No one could blame me when Rikkon keeps spewing contradictory statements left and right. Didn't he say on the way here he didn't want to go back?

"You can't possibly be thinking of bringing him the mirror, Rik."

"He could have gotten the mirror already if he wanted to. He knows the High Witch has it."

Lucca and Ronan trade a meaningful glance.

"The mirror can't stay at my mother's," Aurora butts in.

"Good luck prying that relic from her hands," I rebuff. "But I agree that we need to move the mirror. My vote is to bring it to Solomon."

I expect my idea to be rejected on the spot. I'm surprised when it doesn't happen.

"That's actually the perfect solution," Rikkon agrees. "Not that the wards at Bloodstone can keep a Nightingale warrior from breaking in, but Selor doesn't want to risk exposure."

"Then it's decided. The mirror goes to Bloodstone. That is, if Solomon agrees," Lucca announces.

"I'll talk to him. He needs to be made aware of his role in all this," Aurora adds.

"I'm coming with you," I say.

"Why? I don't think it's ne—"

"It's nonnegotiable, Rora. Selor reached out to *me* about the mirror, not you."

"Maybe because he figured you would be easier to manipulate. We don't really know what his endgame is," she argues.

My blood begins to boil. I'm sick and tired of being dismissed. "I'm not gullible. Stop treating me like I'm a child!"

"I see no harm in letting Miranda speak to Solomon," Lucca interjects.

I fight the urge to roll my eyes. Talk about backhanded support. But I won't complain. I'm getting what I want after all.

"We should go now," Rikkon pipes up.

"You have to drink the potion if you want to come," Lucca replies. "We can't let people know you're a Nightingale."

"I'm not taking any potion, and you can't stop me from coming."

"Rik, it's too dangerous otherwise," Vivienne protests.

"Don't you get it? It has always been dangerous for us, and yet we survived all these centuries without having to rely on stupid potions and vampire protection. I'm done hiding."

"Bold words for a dude without powers," Saxon butts in.

Rikkon flares his nostrils as his spine becomes rigid. "I don't need my Nightingale powers to hold my own in a fight. Get your ass out of that chair and I'll prove it to you."

Saxon jumps from his seat and prepares to pounce, but Aurora grabs his arm, stopping him. "You're not fighting. Stop with this nonsense." She glares at Rikkon. "Both of you."

"If Rikkon doesn't want to wear a disguise, we can't force him," Ronan interjects.

"That will make Vivi's glamour pointless." Lucca frowns at his friend.

"Maybe it's high time Vivi picks up a blade and stops depending on others for protection," Rikkon retorts, surprising the hell out of me.

I catch the wince in Vivienne's face and the hurt in her gaze. Summoning icy poise, she stands and walks out of the room without saying another word. Meanwhile, Lucca is giving Rikkon the mother of death glares.

"That was uncalled for," he says before following his girl-friend out of the room.

"Who is the Captain Prick of Royal Douchery now?" Saxon asks.

I stare at Rikkon, trying to understand where all this sudden aggression is coming from. Is that his true self? If it is, I don't think I like him that much.

Sixteen

RIKKON

I ignore Saxon's comment because my attention is focused on someone else. Miranda is staring at me as if she agrees with the blond vampire's comment. Maybe I am acting like a jerk. It's hard to tell. After years of abuse and beatdowns all thanks to Selor and his memory spell, I'm now on edge, in defensive mode.

"I'll wait outside," she gets up from her chair. "The air is suddenly too stifling here."

I make a motion to follow her, but Aurora gives me a warning glance. "Don't even think about it. I don't know what happened between you two, but it's clear to me Miranda doesn't want your company now."

"And what makes you think she wants yours?" I retort.

She winces, but I don't regret my latest outburst.

Saxon jumps in front of me, pulling me closer by the lapels of my jacket. "I've had it with your attitude. Apologize to Rora."

Calmly, I reply, "I'm not going to apologize for speaking the truth. Time and time again I've seen you lot treat Miranda as if her opinions don't matter, as if she were a hindrance. She's stronger and more powerful than you could possibly know."

"I never meant to make her feel like she's a nuisance. I'm just trying to protect her," Aurora argues.

"She doesn't need your protection. Now, are you going to tell your guard dog here to let me go or do I need to break his arm?"

Saxon growls. "You wish, pal."

"I've had it with this nonsense," Ronan butts in. "Let go of him already, Sax."

He does so with a shove, which only adds fuel to the anger already simmering in my gut. But I don't want to cause a scene here and fight Saxon. It'd be a waste of time.

He gives his friend a murderous stare before he strides out of the door.

Vaughn steps closer. "Boy, you sure know how to clear a room."

"It's not my fault no one here is used to hearing the truth."

"So being brutally honest is a Nightingale thing?"

I open my mouth to reply but pause to think about it for a second. Maybe it's a trait of my kind, even though Vivi didn't change her attitude once she regained her memories. But she's always been kinder than the rest of us.

"Perhaps," I say.

"Maybe you're right," Aurora chimes in. "Maybe I've been pushing Miranda aside and not giving her the chance to feel useful, wanted. It wasn't my intention."

"You should tell her that," I say.

"Well, you can do that after we speak with Solomon," Ronan interrupts. "Now that we know what the Taluah Mirror is capable of, I want that relic out of your mother's house ASAP."

"Yeah, me too." Aurora's eyes widen. "And Niko is alone right now with that thing."

"I'm not so sure about that," I say.

"What do you mean? She should be home."

"She wasn't when I came by earlier."

Aurora furrows her eyebrows, and then pulls out her cell

phone from her pocket as she walks out of the room. Vaughn follows her, but Ronan puts a hand on my shoulder, halting me.

"I'd like a word with you, please."

"We should be heading to the institute now."

"This won't take long."

"Okay."

"What I'm about to tell you can't leave this room."

I'm on high alert in an instant. What could Ronan possibly want to tell me in secret?

"Go on. You have my word I won't repeat what I hear."

He releases my shoulder, stepping back. "King Raphael has confided in me the true reason behind this conflict between vampires and Nightingales."

"It wasn't the war between his supporters and Tatiana's, then?"

Ronan shakes his head. "No. That was the excuse. The real reason is King Raphael rebuffed your mother."

"I don't follow."

"Your mother wanted King Raphael as her lover. She wanted him by her side as one of her consorts. He refused."

"That's impossible. She thinks vampires are nothing more than savages, a sentiment shared by most of the courts."

"I'd bet my life on the king's words. Would you do the same for your mother's?"

I stare at Ronan in silence as I process this new information. My mother is mercurial, that much I know. And cruel. Once I accept the possibility that this is true, then it's easy to guess how everything unfolded.

"She created the conflict between King Raphael and Tatiana when she promised her to him, knowing he'd refuse the vampire as well," I say.

"Precisely."

I pass a hand over my face, knowing it's going to be ten thousand times more difficult to convince my mother to relent. She created the perfect reason to turn the other courts against the vampires.

"And here I thought the hardest part would be to convince her to change her mind. Knowing what I know now, I have to rethink my strategy completely."

"What do you mean?"

"The Aquila kingdom is the strongest, but they're not stronger than all the other kingdoms combined. If I reveal my mother's deception to them, they might reverse their decision to leave the mortal lands."

"That's good, right?"

"No. The knowledge will lead to war, which won't help save the vampire race. A war between Nightingales could last millennia, and they'd worry about the vampires only after it was over. It would be too late."

Ronan rests his hands on his hips. "Son of a bitch."

"There might be another solution," I say.

"What?"

"King Raphael accepts my mother's offer."

Ronan's eyebrows rise up. "Are you out of your mind? We need him."

"You're losing him. How long until he goes insane, and Lucca has to end him?"

Ronan grimaces before looking away. "The king tried that route before when he saw what your mother's revenge was. She didn't want him then."

"She will now. I'll make sure of it."

He glances at me, leveling me with his signature intense stare. "You have that much influence over your mother, even after your banishment?"

"Yes, I do."

And that's one of my undeniable certainties, but I don't share that with Ronan.

MIRANDA

I'm pacing in front of Lucca's mansion when Aurora finds me. I stop moving and wait for her to chastise me for my impulsive behavior. Instead, she gives me an elevator glance and points at my outfit.

"When did you start taking martial arts?"

"It's been a while. And it's not simply martial arts. I'm training to become a samurai."

It's amusing to see the surprise in her eyes. "You are? I didn't realize there was a sensei in town."

"It's an old friend of Grandpa's, Mr. Shirogane."

"Oh, yeah. I remember him. If I'd known, I'd have joined you instead of taking self-defense lessons at the YMCA."

"Mom forbade me to do it, and you were too busy with your training to become the next High Witch. I felt it was best to keep it a secret from everyone."

"I'm sorry I haven't been a better sister to you."

I shrug, my go-to reaction. "You had a lot on your plate."

The entire gang besides Manu exits the house, ending this uncomfortable conversation. I've always wanted to be heard by my sister, but tonight, I'm dealing with too many emotions and the last thing I want is to have a heart-to-heart chat.

"Are you all coming?" I ask.

Aurora says "Yes" and Lucca says "No."

"What do you mean we aren't all going?" She turns to him.

"We don't reside at Bloodstone anymore. Arriving with a big group will only draw unnecessary attention. Only Rikkon, Miranda, Vivi, and I are going."

"What? That's crazy," Saxon complains.

"You can't stop me from going," Aurora retorts.

Lucca levels her with such a glare that it affects even me. "I'm the prince of vampires, you live under my roof, you *will* respect my decision."

"It's okay, Rora. I'm more than capable of representing the

family," I tell her, trying my hardest not to show my glee over this turn of events.

For the first time, I get to take part in something important.

Aurora is still fuming when she looks at me. "I want a full report, Mir."

"Of course."

I give her the answer she expects from me, but whether or not I follow through is a different matter. It depends on what transpires in this meeting and what Solomon has to say.

Seventeen

MIRANDA

"Are you out of your fucking minds?" Solomon yells at us after we tell him about Selor and what he wants to do with the Taluah Mirror.

"About what part?" Lucca asks.

"Everything."

The small male begins to pace back and forth in front of his desk, burning a hole through the wooden floor. I've only met him a few times, and he's always given me the impression that he's a mad scientist. Tonight it isn't any different.

"That's a pretty generic comment," Rikkon says. "In any case, it matters not what you think about our plan. I need to cross into Ellnesari, and using the mirror is our only way."

"Oh yeah? Have you ever considered what your Nightingale buddy wants from me?"

"We figured you would know," I say.

He gives me a droll look. "And why would you think that?"

"Because you're the first familiar."

"He should know," Rikkon mutters, almost to himself. "If he doesn't, it means his memories have also been messed with."

"Excuse me?" Solomon straightens to his full five-foot-nothing height.

"Rik is right. If the Taluah Mirror can be used as a gateway to Ellnesari, you would know why he wants you," Vivienne chimes in. "But it makes sense if my mother erased that knowledge from your mind."

"That's really comforting," Solomon grumbles.

"We won't know what exactly Selor wants until he returns in two days. Meanwhile, we believe the mirror will be safer with you," Lucca pipes up.

"That's what I said, but Isadora made a big stink about keeping the mirror in her house. And look at what happened." He throws a meaningful glance in Rikkon's direction.

"Nothing bad happened besides me regaining my memories. Stop being such an old grump," Rikkon retorts.

"I *am* an old grump!" He throws his hands up in the air.

"So, do you agree to keep the mirror here?" Vivienne asks.

"Sure. Good luck convincing Isadora to let go of that thing though."

"She has no choice. The mirror doesn't belong to her," Rikkon replies in an arrogant way, grating on my nerves.

What's up with him?

"She's still the High Witch, you can't simply order her about," I retort, annoyed.

Rikkon raises an eyebrow. "I thought you wanted that thing gone from your house. Why are you taking her side?"

"I'm not taking her side. You know what? Never mind." I cross my arms and look at everything but him.

"It's better if I speak with the High Witch," Lucca butts in. "She answers to my uncle, which means she answers to me during his absence."

"Glad to know someone is thinking." The headmaster taps the side of his head.

"That goes for you as well, Solomon. I want you to be ready when Queen Maewe's lackey returns. He could very well have been banished too and is just trying to find a one-way ticket home, leaving Rikkon behind."

"It's very unlikely that's the case," Vivienne pipes up.

"Why is that?" Lucca turns to her.

"She wouldn't banish Selor. He's her favorite pet."

"Better to be prepared for anything."

"I'd like to speak with Selor when he comes back," Vivienne tells Rikkon.

Lucca furrows his eyebrows. "What for? Please don't tell me you're thinking about crossing into Ellnesari, my love."

I can see then by the guilt shining in Vivienne's eyes that's exactly what she was planning to do.

"Vivi won't come with me, Lucca. You have my word," Rikkon says.

"You can't make that decision for me!" she snaps.

"If you tag along, Lucca will follow. Do you want to be responsible for his death? I can't cause you more pain, sister. I've done enough."

"What makes you think I'd die?" Lucca glowers at Rikkon.

"You would, so save the butt-hurt feelings for another occasion," Solomon chimes in. "No vampire is a match for a Nightingale, even the common folk ones."

"If they're that powerful, why did they use King Raphael and his soldiers to win the war against their enemies?" I ask.

"Because their enemies had a very peculiar weakness. Humans," Solomon replies.

"I don't get it. Were they allergic to humans?"

Rikkon and Vivienne both stare at me, but it's Vivienne who answers. "No, humans could see them."

"Our enemies were invisible to us until they bled. For every enemy we managed to wound, we lost ten of our soldiers. When we discovered humans could see them, we convinced them to assist us," Rikkon continues.

"And made them vampires as a reward," I say. "Only to fuck them over later. Good times. I'm glad I'm not bound to Ellnesari."

Rikkon gives me a loaded glance, which I try my best to

ignore. He can spew whatever lies benefit him, but we all know he's going back to his mate. Ellnesari is the last place in the universe I want to be.

Solomon pulls out his pocket watch and curses under his breath. "Well, it seems I'm late for a meeting with your illustrious mother. You know how she hates tardiness. I'd better leave. Make sure you lock the door on your way out."

He disappears in a puff of white smoke, which I make the mistake of inhaling. It causes a fit of coughing, which prompts Rikkon to tap me on my back. I jump away from him, hating how I crave his touch.

"I'm fine," I say.

Way to be obvious that something is going on between you and Rikkon, Miranda. But thankfully, Vivienne and Lucca aren't paying attention to us.

"Were you seriously thinking of going with Rikkon?" Lucca asks Vivienne.

"Yes."

"Why?"

"I want my powers back."

"I can protect you, Vivi."

"You're missing the point." She gestures wildly with her hands. "I don't want to depend on your protection. If I have my powers back, I can help in the war with Jacques."

"I understand that, but it's not worth risking your life." He takes a step closer to her, arms outstretched, but she moves away from him.

"Vivi wouldn't die if she came with me, but there are worse things than death in Ellnesari."

Vivienne grows visibly paler. She knows what Rikkon speaks of. I don't, and yet, I still get chills down my spine.

"I have to go home. Unlike you guys, I'm not on a nocturnal schedule." I fix my sash, and then pull my *gi* down, straightening the jacket.

It's funny how I went to great lengths to hide my training

outfit from everyone before, and now, here I am, wearing it with pride. Even if I were to meet my mother, I wouldn't care. I'll be eighteen in only a couple of weeks. She won't have a say anymore on what I can and cannot do.

"I'll go with you, Mir," Rikkon is quick to offer.

"How does that make sense? Lucca's mansion is in the opposite direction of my house."

"You can drive straight home. We'll follow you and then Rik comes home with us," Vivienne suggests.

Damn it. If I insist on going solo, it's going to look suspicious.

"Fine. I still think it's a waste of time."

Just like when we came into Bloodstone tonight, we use the secret passageway that leads straight to Solomon's office wing. I wish I had known about that before. It's pretty handy to be able to meet him and not having anyone know about it. God knows how gossipy bloodsuckers are. Since Rikkon refuses to take the potion that makes him look like a vampire, it's pointless for Vivienne to keep pretending too, a fact that Lucca is more than mad about.

They walk ahead of us in silence, but judging by how stiff their shoulders are, I'd say further arguing is in their future. Rikkon is next to me, too close for my liking in this narrow corridor. At one point, our hands touch. It sends a jolt of electricity up my arm—not the phantom kind, the real deal. It startles me. I pull away quickly and glance at him. He meets my eyes, but I can't tell from his stare if he felt the shock as well or not.

When we finally emerge outside of the stony walls of the institute, I inhale deeply. But the fresh air does nothing to bring my heartbeat to a normal pace. Lucca and Vivienne head to their car, leaving me alone with Rikkon in awkward silence.

"Well, let's go." I walk over to my car, and just then, a yawn hits me.

"If you're too tired to drive, I can," he offers.

"I can manage."

I'm being stubborn on purpose. It would be nice not having

to drive right now. But I know my body. I won't fall asleep behind the wheel. Besides, I wouldn't be able to sleep with Rikkon next to me anyway. At least driving gives me something to do.

Rikkon doesn't say another word until we put a good distance between us and Bloodstone. The streets are deserted at this hour, so we should make it to my place in no time. Behind me, Lucca's headlights keep us company.

"Mir, I think we should clear the air between us. You're angry with me."

I snort. "I'm not angry."

"Don't lie. It doesn't suit you."

Ugh. That's it.

"Fine. I *am* mad at you. You've been nothing but aggravating since we stepped foot in Lucca's mansion. It's like you've developed a new personality, and not a nice one."

"I didn't develop a new personality. This is who I am. I just remembered."

"Well, I liked the other version better."

"You mean the pathetic human junkie? Why? He was a loser. Unless that's your type."

"He was not a loser. He was kind and caring. He didn't say shit without thinking about people's feelings. He wasn't an arrogant ass either."

"Everything you described are human traits. I'm not human. I'm a Nightingale."

"Don't use that as an excuse. Vivienne remembers who she is and she's still a nice person."

"She's a different breed, and that's why she had a hard time at court. That's why I told her she should stand up for herself."

"She wants to. You heard her, but you were just too happy to agree with Lucca that she shouldn't go with you to Ellnesari."

"Because Lucca would follow her and that would end badly."

"Riiight. That's what you say. You know what I think?"

"Go ahead. You're clearly in the mood to share."

"You're a hypocrite. That's what I think. You want her to

fight, to not depend on others, but you're the first to shoot down her ideas when she tries to be independent."

My house looms straight ahead, surprising me. I was so incensed by this conversation that I didn't even notice the ride. I park in the driveway and practically fly out of my car.

"Miranda, wait."

I whirl around, dying to know what half-baked excuse he's going to give me now.

"What?"

I expect his expression to match mine. But he's not angry at all.

"You're right. I was an ass at Lucca's house. It was an instinct. They've only known the fucked-up Rikkon, the one who had to be bailed out by his sister countless times before. That's not who I am, and they needed to know that."

"So you thought acting like a douche was the answer?"

"Yes! I had to put Saxon back in his place. He's an alpha male; he needs to be challenged to understand."

"What nonsense is that? You're not wolves!"

"God, do you think only wolf shifters have alphas?"

"Ugh! You're doing it again."

"Doing what?" he shouts.

"Acting like a condescending ass. I'm out of here."

I turn around and head for the front door, but Rikkon grabs my arm and spins me around, trapping me in his embrace.

"Tell me the real reason you're angry with me, Mir." His voice is much softer now, and it unravels me.

Damn it. It was so much easier to fight my attraction to him while we were arguing. Now, with his mouth inches from mine, with my chest pressed to his, all I want to do is rise on my tiptoes and kiss him.

"You know why," I answer through the sudden choking feeling in my throat. "You're leaving in two days."

You're leaving me.

He cups my cheek tenderly. "I wish I weren't. You have to believe me. If it were up to me, I'd stay. *For you.*"

My breath catches. He just didn't say that. He couldn't have possibly said that. He has a fated mate. He wouldn't have developed feelings for me. It's impossible.

I'm still processing his words when he leans down and presses his lips to mine, short-circuiting any thinking cell in my brain. I practically melt in his arms, giving into him, into his kiss completely. His tongue pries my lips open tentatively, but I've been craving this moment for too long to take things slowly now. This will probably be our only kiss, so we'd better make it count.

I throw my arms around his neck, pulling him closer to me, trying to meld myself to his frame. Rikkon groans, matching my enthusiasm. His fingers curl around the back of my *gi* in a possessive way. His touch is like sparks, turning me into flames. My very bones are on fire, and I've never wanted anything more in my life than to freeze time so this moment would never end.

He hisses suddenly, releasing me as he steps back. His hand is now curled into his chest, and he's doubled over.

"Oh my god. What's happening? Is that a vision?"

"No," he grunts, looking up. "It's the bond. It doesn't agree with what I just did."

The truth feels like I've been sucker punched in the gut. Somehow, Rikkon developed feelings for me despite the bond. I want to cry, to shout at the gods for such a cruel fate. But I get to do none of those things. The headlights of an approaching vehicle distract me from my impending inner meltdown. It takes me a couple of seconds to recognize Lucca's car. And then it hits me. *Why the delay?*

Lucca parks by the curb and rolls down his window. "Are you two okay?"

Rikkon straightens to his full height, no longer looking like he's in deep agony. "Yeah, where have you been? I thought you were right behind us."

"We were, and then I blanked for a second and you guys were gone."

That's strange as hell, but I don't have the motivation to ask more questions. I just want to disappear in my room.

His eyes land on me and narrow. *Shit.* Does it look like I was just making out with Rikkon? I fix my *gi*, pulling the lapels closer together.

"I'm going in. Thanks for following me home, guys. Good night."

Rikkon turns to me, and I read a myriad of emotions in his eyes. I know he wants to talk, explain things, but I can't hear any of that. It doesn't matter what he feels or what he wishes. The truth is, he has to return to his homeland, and I have to learn to live without him.

I close the front door, and leaning against it, I finally let my tears fall. I'm probably being overdramatic. I'm only seventeen, and I just met Rikkon. But my heart doesn't care about logic. It's bleeding, and it's in agony.

With heavy steps, I trudge down the hallway. I check on Niko first to make sure she's home. She's snoring up a storm and doesn't even twitch at the sound of the door opening. I continue to my room, and after I change into my pj's and get under the blankets, I reach over to my nightstand and take the old notebook about the Nightingales from inside a magazine. Maybe I'm being a glutton for punishment, but tonight, it seems appropriate to fall asleep reading about the beautiful and cold people of Ellnesari. Maybe tomorrow I'll wake up and not have this hole in my chest anymore.

Eighteen

MIRANDA

TWO DAYS LATER

Rikkon called and texted me several times, but I ignored all his attempts at contact. At least he didn't come knocking on my door. He had that much sense. Or maybe the bond didn't allow him to come near me. Either way, it's better this way.

It's been two days since Selor cornered me to deliver his message. That means he will be making an appearance today, and that has given me major anxiety. My stomach is twisted in nautical knots, impossible to untie.

I can't bear the thought of seeing anyone while my head is miles and miles away, in a land I know nothing of. Perversely, my mind keeps conjuring up images of Rikkon's future bride, and each time she's more beautiful and more perfect. Curled into a ball, I told my mother I was sick. Since I'm such a dependable and responsible child, she didn't suspect it was a lie. At least she asked me if I needed anything.

Niko, on the other hand, knew right away I was pretending, but she didn't rat me out. She wants me to return the favor in the near future. Today, I'd agree to anything she wanted just to be left alone.

When everyone is gone, I get out of bed and go make myself some coffee. But my steps are heavy and my head is throbbing as if there were a little man inside, pounding my skull with a miniature hammer. On top of that, my throat feels scratchy. Maybe I *am* getting sick.

"Wouldn't that be ironic?" I mumble to myself.

I forgo coffee and put water in a mug to microwave it. A cup of mint and honey tea will make me feel better, I hope. I should eat, but my appetite has deserted me. The microwave beeps, telling me the water is ready. Absentmindedly I reach for the mint plant that Mom keeps on the counter. It's gone. Great. I hope there's regular mint in the cupboard.

"You look absolutely dreadful," a male voice tells me.

I yell, turning around, while my heart lodges itself in my throat.

Selor Nyrk, Queen Maewe's warrior, is sitting leisurely at my kitchen table as if he didn't have a care in the world.

"What the hell! How did you get in?"

"Don't bore me with inane questions, little witch. I said I'd be back in two days. It's been two days."

Still rattled, I run a shaky hand through my hair. "I thought you would be back after dark."

"And risk having your vampire friends interrupt our party? I don't think so. Come on. Get ready so we can leave."

I take a step back, but there's nowhere to go. I'm cornered in my own kitchen. *Son of a bitch.*

"I'm not going anywhere with you. You don't need me. You said you needed the Taluah Mirror and Solomon."

"Oh, but I do need you, little witch. You're the final ingredient. That's why I left you a little gift."

He snaps his fingers, and the notebook I'd been reading about the Nightingales appears in his hand.

"That belonged to my dad," I say.

He cocks his head, and smirks. "Are you sure?"

My blood runs cold. "Are you saying you planted that notebook among my dad's things? What for? The notebook has no useful information."

"Oh, be assured it does, you just don't know how to read it yet. You will though, when the time is right."

I shake my head, refusing to accept I've been played by this horrible male.

"Stop saying vague shit like that. And now that I know you're Tom Mularkey, I have zero interest in that notebook."

His eyebrows shoot to the heavens. "I'm not Tom Mularkey, child. Don't offend me."

"Whatever. Just leave already. I'm not going anywhere with you."

He glances at the ceiling, letting out an exasperated exhale. "The things I do for my queen."

When he locks eyes with me again, they're different. Magnetic. I can't look away. Slowly, the fight in me begins to ebb away, and my will to resist Selor goes with it.

"Now go change, little witch. I have no desire to go through the wardrobe of a teenage human. And please pick sensible clothes for a long voyage."

"Yes, of course."

My feet drag me back to my room, and moving like a robot now, I take a shower, then get dressed in my favorite pair of jeans, and a T-shirt. An oversized hoodie comes next and then my leather jacket. Since Selor mentioned a long journey, I opt for my old leather boots. Then I finally look at my reflection in the mirror. Selor is right. I do look awful. The dark circles under my eyes make it seem I've been punched. And my lips are dry and chapped. But what does it matter? I'm not going to be kissing anyone anytime soon.

My hair is another matter. If I don't pull it back in a ponytail, it will get in the way. Maybe I should chop it all off.

Before I return to the kitchen, I grab my leather bag and stuff my grimoire inside, plus some crystals and river stones that I energized earlier. Nothing with a lot of juice. Once again, I regret having lost my dagger.

I find Selor rapping his fingers impatiently on the table. He turns to me, gives me a scrutinizing glance, and flattens his lips in a disapproving way. *Fuck.* He's acting like he's fucking Tim Gunn appraising a horrendous gown.

"God, couldn't you even try to look, what's the word... cute?"

"Fuck off, buddy. I'm not trying to impress anyone."

He rolls his eyes. "Clearly. It's my fault. I should have been more precise in my instructions. It matters not. We're already late."

"Late for what? I didn't realize we were on a schedule."

"Enough talking. You've given me a headache already." He snaps his fingers, and my ability to speak is gone.

What the hell?

He stands up and walks over. I remain rooted to the spot, frozen, and it's not my choice. He's doing this. Even my heart, which should be galloping at full speed, doesn't change its pace. Selor stops in front of me and places a hand on my shoulder.

My kitchen disappears, and in the blink of an eye, I'm standing in the middle of a clearing. Soft grass peppered with yellow flowers spread before me. A crystalline lake to my right looks like glass, and the trees surrounding the meadow are as tall as a three-story building.

"Where are we?" I ask, forgetting that he had cut off my ability to speak a minute ago. I guess the gag spell is off again.

"A special place. Now grab your phone. You did bring your phone, right?"

I furrow my eyebrows. This dude is not making a lick of sense. "I think so. Why do you need my phone?"

"If you don't stop asking stupid questions, I'm going to catch your tongue again."

"That's not how you use that idiom." I fish my phone out, and it flies right out of my hand and into Selor's. "Hey!"

He steps closer, points the camera at us, and says, "Cheese!"

"Did you just take a selfie with me?" I ask in disbelief as I put my hands on my hips, glaring at the guy.

So far, this is the most bizarre interaction I've had with this male to date. He ignores me and types something on my phone.

"There. We're all set." He throws my phone back at me, but I wasn't expecting that, so it hits my chest and falls on the ground.

"Son of a bitch. Look at what you've done."

"It's not my fault you have poor reflexes. I thought you were training to become a samurai."

I don't bother replying with words, I simply flip him off, and then read the text he sent to none other than Rikkon.

> **Selor: Got your girlie. If you don't want to see the little witch cut up in pieces, bring the Taluah Mirror and Solomon. Don't tell anyone else or the girl pays.**

"You sent Rikkon a ransom text?" I look at the Nightingale hunter, stupefied.

"I figured he would need motivation to come."

"No, he wouldn't. He wants to go back to Ellnesari. He'd bring the mirror and Solomon. You didn't need to kidnap me!"

He shrugs. "Nah, what's the fun in that? Kidnapping is more entertaining."

"Well, you forgot one tiny detail. You didn't tell him our location."

The surprised look on his face would have been comical in a different situation.

"Oh, that's right. Totally forgot." He steals my phone again, pissing me off even more. "There, now we're all set."

I expect him to send my phone flying back in my direction again, but when he tosses it into the lake, my jaw drops.

"My phone! What did you do that for?"

"We won't be needing it anymore."

"What the actual fuck!"

Selor ignores me. He throws a pebble at the lake, and then sits on a rock near the shore. If there were even a tiny possibility that I could hex the warrior and flee, I'd risk it. But I have no clue where we are, and the crystals in my bag are only good for small spells.

"That's it. I got it. You're crazy."

"I'm not crazy." He glares at me.

"Yes, you are. How long have you been living on this side of the fence? Since your queen banished Rikkon and Vivi, right? I bet you haven't set foot in Ellnesari once in all this time. It must have affected you the same way it affected them."

"You're forgetting one small detail, little witch. I still have my powers. Rikkon and Vryenn don't."

"That means nothing. I'd still say you have one or two screws loose in your head. In any case, you already sent that bait text. You don't need me for anything. I'm out of here."

I stride toward the trees hugging the meadow, glancing over my shoulder every two steps. Selor remains where he is seated. He's not even looking in my direction. He must know something I don't. That doesn't stop me from breaking into a sprint, which is a terrible idea. I hit an invisible wall face-first and fall on my back. My nose throbs and when I touch it, my fingers come away smeared in blood.

"What the hell! I'd better not have broken my nose, asshole."

"It's not my fault you decided to act foolishly."

I get back on my feet, fed up by this whole situation. When I spot a rock on the ground, peeking through the tall grass, I pick it up, and without stopping to think, throw it with all my strength at the back of Selor's head. It hits the mark.

"Ouch," he blurts out.

"Bullseye!" I yell.

He stands to his full height and turns slowly in my direction. My victorious smile vanishes when I'm leveled by his murderous stare. It's the same look he gave me when he tried to cut me in two.

He points at me. "You're dead meat."

"Ah, fuck."

He breaks into a run, and I do the only thing I can; I head in the opposite direction. But if this meadow is enchanted and I can't get out, there's nothing left for me to do but run in circles and hope he tires first.

Yeah, that's likely to happen. What were you thinking, Miranda? You don't mess with crazy, especially the immortal kind.

"There's nowhere to go, little witch," he taunts me.

He's right—well, there's one place I can go. I change course and run toward the lake.

"Hey, what do you think you're doing?" he yells, too close to me already.

"Going for a swim."

"No, stop it!"

I sense his magic at work, but it doesn't reach me before I break through the ice-cold water. It's only at my calves, but somehow, it's freezing my entire body already. I stop moving at once and turn around.

"I told you not to get in there." Selor watches me like a parent watches their small children: frustrated as hell.

"Why is this lake so fucking cold?"

"Get out of there before you freeze to death."

I try to take a step forward, but my feet are numb already and I end up falling to my knees, getting even wetter. Okay, there's definitely something fishy going on with this lake.

"I can't move. Why don't you use your magic and get me out?"

"I can't use my magic," he grits out.

"Miranda!" Rikkon calls my name, and my heart soars.

He's at the edge of the clearing with Solomon next to him. The Taluah Mirror floats behind the headmaster. Rikkon takes off, running faster than a human could. It's almost like he got his powers back.

"Don't get into that lake, fool!" Solomon follows him at a much slower pace, huffing and puffing.

Why is he not using his magic to move faster? Nothing is making any sense.

Rikkon doesn't seem to be inclined to heed the headmaster's advice, but Selor stops him from setting foot in the lake.

"Are you daft? You can't get in there," he tells him.

He shoves Selor off. "Why did you let her get in there?"

"She's a willful child. I couldn't stop her."

While they argue, I'm slowly turning into a popsicle. My teeth are chattering together. I really didn't think this is how I'd die, frozen by magic in shallow water.

Solomon is now standing at the edge of the lake as well. He sets the mirror down, and that gets Selor's full attention. *Asshole.*

"A-a little help here," I manage to say through the shaking of my jaw.

Solomon closes his eyes and points two fingers in my direction. He begins to chant something I can't quite hear, but whatever it is, it's helping me. The water is getting warmer, and my body is no longer freezing. When I regain the feeling in my legs, I stagger to my feet and walk out of the lake, collapsing into Rikkon's arms.

And it feels so damn nice.

No! Not nice. I jump back, almost falling back into the deadly lake. Solomon reaches out and grabs my arm.

"Do not fall in there again. My magic only goes so far."

"Mir, are you okay?" Rikkon asks.

"I'm okay now."

"She's fine," Selor pipes up, without glancing in our direction. He's transfixed by the mirror.

Rikkon keeps looking at me like he doesn't believe my words.

"Truly, I'm fine. Whatever Solomon did, it helped."

"And thank goodness I still have clout with some of the elementals."

"Who?" I ask.

"Never mind." He switches his attention to Selor. "We're here. Let's get this going so I can take Miranda back before her mother notices she's missing."

The Nightingale warrior peels his eyes away from the mirror to reward us with one of his most maniacal grins yet.

"Take her back? She's not going back."

Nineteen

RIKKON

"You foul creature! What are you saying?" I shout.

"Miranda can't go anywhere but forward. There's nothing I can do about it. The spell has been cast. Either she goes through the mirror into Ellnesari, or she will die here in this meadow," Selor replies calmly.

"So that was the magic I sensed when we crossed into this clearing," Solomon mutters.

"You're joking, right? I'm not going to Ellnesari. There's nothing for me there!" Miranda shouts, making me wince.

There's nothing for her there. What about me? I want to ask, but it's a selfish sentiment.

"I don't make the decisions. I just follow orders." Selor raises his hands, palms facing forward as if he's not a culprit in all this.

"Is my mother behind this wicked trick?" I ask through clenched teeth. "Is this how she plans to punish me for choosing Vryenn over her?"

He gives me a droll look. "You know I'm bound to not reveal her secrets to anyone."

"I can't go to Ellnesari," Miranda breaks down into sobs, making my guilt grow.

She's in this mess because of me. I should have stayed away. I knew there would be a high price to pay for indulging my attraction for her. But I didn't know she would be the one suffering the worst of it. Even with the guilt, I want to pull her into my arms and tell her I'll find a way to get her out of this mess. However, that will only make matters worse, and we all know I can't make such a promise. I might be going back, but I'm still without my powers.

I turn to Solomon. "Can't you break the spell this idiot put in place?"

"Of course I can't. He's a Nightingale."

"Why do you want me to go to Ellnesari?" Miranda asks Selor.

"I can't answer that. It's going to be fine, little witch." He smiles as if he actually cares about her welfare. "You'll see."

"Stop calling her little witch!" I snap.

The warrior widens his eyes. "Ooh, someone is jealous."

"It seems I can't escape idiots no matter where I go." Solomon looks at Miranda. "Listen, kid. There's nothing we can do besides opening the portal to Ellnesari. You have my word that I will find a way to bring you back."

Miranda's eyes are round and bright, but no more tears fall down her cheeks. She nods, resolute. "I know you will. Tell Niko and Aurora I'll see them soon."

"And your mother? No message for her?" Solomon asks.

"Tell her not to stress about me. I can handle myself."

Solomon furrows his bushy brows. That's clearly not the message he was expecting from her. But I get it. With the way everyone in her family overlooked Miranda, it's easy to guess how worried everyone will be about her well-being. They think she doesn't have what it takes to survive in Ellnesari, when in fact, she's the only one in her family who can. That's a certainty I know deep in my bones.

"Now that everyone is on board with the plan, let's get the show on the road, shall we?" Selor says, right before he pulls his sword from its invisible sheath. It's not glowing now.

I step between him and the others. "What do you think you're doing?"

"I knew it. He's going to kill me to make that damn mirror work," Solomon pipes up.

"I'm not going to kill you," Selor grumbles. "I just need a little bit of your blood."

"But do you need to use that huge sword to do it?" Miranda asks.

"Yes. The starfire blade has special properties. If it were that easy to open a portal to Ellnesari, that old hag who had the mirror prior would have done it already. She did try though," the idiot chuckles.

Solomon takes a step forward and offers his arm to Selor. "If you need to cut me, do it already."

"Actually, I need Miranda's and Rikkon's blood too."

Unease takes hold of me. Lots of wicked magic can be unleashed by using blood, especially blood from a royal Nightingale. But despite my apprehension, there's nothing I can do. We're all at Selor's mercy here.

Miranda sticks out her arm, pulling the sleeve of her jacket up. She looks at me, holding my stare even when Selor cuts the soft skin of her underarm and blood wells from the wound. The only sign of her discomfort is a slight flinch. If the sword had been glowing, it would burn as well. Selor collects her blood in a small bowl and then repeats the same task on Solomon.

When it's my turn, I warn under my breath, "If this turns out to be another grand scheme by my mother, I'll come for your head first."

Selor sneers. "Do you think your threats scare me?"

He grabs my arm roughly, and when he presses his blade against my skin, he means to inflict as much pain as possible. The cut is deep, almost to the bone. But I don't show discomfort. He won't see any weakness from me, not anymore.

He steps back, and begins to hum an old ballad that my mother used to sing to me when I was younger. It's strange that

Selor would pick that particular song in this moment, but again, he was never a stable male back in Ellnesari. I can't imagine staying in the mortal lands for all these centuries did him any favors.

He dips his fingers in the bowl and paints characters on the mirror's surface. He's blocking my view, which is probably deliberate. I move closer, but he won't let me see what he's writing until he's done.

"Now, Rikkon and Miranda, hold hands. You do not want to get separated during the crossing."

Miranda steps next to me, but makes no move to take my hand. I'm distracted, trying to read the mess of Selor's handwriting. I can barely make out the first symbol.

Suddenly, the writing begins to glow, and I can read the spell clearly. My blood freezes in my veins.

"No," I whisper.

"What is it?" Miranda asks me.

"I said hold her hand, damn it!" Selor hollers in my ear.

The writing vanishes when the glow takes over the entire mirror's surface. In the end, Miranda grabs my hand and with a shove, Selor sends us both through the mirror. The trip is similar to traveling through the warlocks' wormhole, but for Miranda that is clearly not the case. She screams through the entire journey, making me hate myself ten thousand times more.

MIRANDA

The trip through the Taluah Mirror is the longest ten seconds of my entire life. Now I know how the witches who burned at the stake felt. When I land on my back on an unknown soft surface, I'm still shaking from the experience. Rikkon's hand is no longer in mine, and for a moment I panic. Selor was adamant that we hold on to each other. What if I'm lost in Ellnesari?

I sit up too fast and become woozy in a flash. Then Rikkon is pulling me into his arms, speaking a lot of words that don't make sense to me. Maybe I hit my head. He kisses my forehead, then pushes me back to search my face. His lips are moving but I can't hear him. There's a terrible noise in my ears, blocking any other sound.

"What?" I yell.

"Are you okay?" he asks.

His voice is still muffled but at least I could read his lips.

"Yeah. Shit, that trip was hellish."

I press my fingers on my tragi, moving them back and forth to try to get rid of the buzzing in my ears. It helps.

"I'm so sorry, Mir."

"Why? It wasn't your fault the journey through the mirror was akin to taking a dive into a churning volcano."

"It's my fault you're away from your family."

"Well, only for a little bit. I'm sure I'll find a way back home in no time."

I try to sound optimistic, even knowing it is not going to be an easy task. But remaining trapped in this land of cold and ruthless immortals and watching Rikkon shack up with a random princess is a much worse fate. Talk about motivation to get the hell out of here.

Rikkon grimaces, and glances away. That looked super guilty and I want to know why.

"What is it?"

He shakes his head. "It's nothing."

When he looks at me again, he has a small smile on his lips, but it doesn't reach his eyes. He should be happy to finally be back home.

"Come on." He offers me his hand. "Let's see where the Taluah Mirror brought us."

I let him help me to my feet only because I'm a little unsteady on my legs. He doesn't let go of me right away. It feels nice to touch him, even if it's innocent handholding, but I can't get used to it. I pull away, crossing my arms in front of my chest and regretting it in the next second.

"Shit." I check the cut on my arm.

"Let me see that." Rikkon steps into my space again under the pretense of examining my wound.

I try not to breathe or look at his face. "It's fine. I just forgot about it for a hot second."

"We should bandage it anyway. Do you have anything in your bag that we can use?"

"Yeah, there should be a first aid kit here somewhere." I look inside the black hole that is my bag. I brought my usual giant one because Selor told me to pack for a trip and my puppet-self figured this one would be the ideal accessory.

"Do you need any help?"

"No, it's okay."

He could hold my bag open for me while I search, but that would mean him getting too close again. I finally locate the small plastic box. *Let's hope it's not completely empty of supplies.*

"I got it." I lift my eyes and finally take in our surroundings. My jaw drops to the floor. "Holy smoke. What is this place?"

Thick moss-covered trees rise up to the sky in unique spiraling formations that defy logic. The moss is yellow in most of them, giving the illusion that they're covered in pollen or gold dust. The leaves on those trees are the same shade of rich yellow, and the size of a grown man.

Rikkon is looking up as well, but instead of staring in awe like me, he's frowning. "We're in Hornet's Gardens. Not far from my mother's palace. We shouldn't linger."

"Why is that?" I ask in a lower voice, noticing the hint of alarm in Rikkon's reply.

"Dangerous creatures like to come here to mate. We can't be around then."

My cheeks become warmer, and to hide my embarrassment, I joke, "So, they're not into voyeurism, huh?"

"You shouldn't take my comments lightly, Mir. Ellnesari is a dangerous place, especially for a human."

"I'm a witch," I argue.

He flattens his lips. "Fine. It's dangerous for you."

"Well, if it's dangerous, let's get the hell out of here. Where's that douchebag Selor, by the way?"

"No doubt already at the palace."

"He couldn't wait for us?"

"Of course not. He needs to reach the court first to alert the queen of our imminent arrival."

"Do you think she's going to receive you with open arms?"

"Yeah, she will. She wants me back. For what purpose, I don't know."

"Well, to marry the princess of the Cygnus court, of course." My comment makes Rikkon grimace. "Stop frowning or you *will* get premature expression lines," I tell him.

"We don't get those."

"Lucky you. I guess cosmetic companies are unheard of here."

"Not likely. We don't age, but Nightingales are vain as fuck. You'll see."

Great. That's exactly what I need, to be surrounded by gorgeous beings who love to preen. I glance at my practical attire, and wonder what they will think about me. My jeans are caked in mud thanks to my idiotic dive into the lake. Part of my hair has escaped the hairband, and my ponytail is most definitely looking sad now. I run my fingers through my hair and pick up pieces of yellow strings that are a cross between twigs and grass.

"What is this?" I ask.

He looks over his shoulder, still frowning, but when he sees what I'm holding, his eyes widen, and then he chuckles.

"What's so funny? Do I have this crap all over my hair?"

"Yeah, you do, but I'm not laughing because of that."

"Then why?"

"Well, you know how I said the Hornet's Gardens are used as a mating place?"

"Right."

"Well, what you're holding is the result."

"Yew." I drop the golden string and then undo my ponytail to shake my head. "I can't believe I have fucking dry semen in my hair."

Rikkon has the audacity to laugh harder.

I toss my head back and then hit his arm. "Not funny, jackass. You knew I had this shit all over me and you didn't say anything."

"I was more concerned with making sure you didn't have any broken bones."

The smirk is still etched on his face and his eyes dance with glee, reminding me of what made me like him in the first place. My amusement vanishes in an instant as yearning takes its place. He seems to notice my change in demeanor, losing his humor too. Now he's staring at me like he wants a repeat of the other night.

The silence in the gardens is broken by an approaching buzzing noise. I whirl around and stare in the distance. "What's that?"

"Shit, we have to go. Now."

He takes my hand and drags me through the maze of twisted tree limbs and exposed tree roots. The buzzing is getting louder and more annoying. It's like flies on steroids. I don't dare to ask what's coming after us for fear of slowing us down. My enormous bag is once again a hindrance, snagging on branches, and bouncing against my hip hard. I'll probably bruise.

Suddenly, Rikkon veers to the right, pulling me off balance. I stagger forward, almost falling on my face. I would have if he wasn't holding my hand.

"What are you doing?" I hiss.

"We're not going to make it out of here before they spot us. We need to hide."

He stops in front of a giant tree—the biggest one I've seen so far—and pushes me forward. "Get in there."

"Where?"

"Underneath that root."

I hesitate, there's barely any space for one person to fit in, much less two. But the buzzing is super loud now, to the point I have to cover my ears or they might start bleeding. I dive forward in an awkward fashion, forgetting my samurai training. I try not to think of the foreign things that are now rubbing my back and getting into my hair as I scooch as far back into the hole underneath the tree trunk as possible. Hopefully, there aren't any spiders in Ellnesari.

Rikkon joins me, and we're now pressed together in the semi-darkness. My heart is thumping loudly inside of my chest, and it's not only because of the danger that's hovering above us. The proximity to him is once again doing my head in. It's like my attraction, crush, whatever, was heightened when I crossed into his homeland. I want to bring my nose to his neck and take a deep breath. *How crazy is that?*

Of course, I don't act on my irrational impulse, not even when he laces his fingers with mine.

Wait? Why is he grabbing my hand?

The buzzing finally begins to move away, but it's another five minutes before the forest is silent again.

"That was close," I whisper.

Rikkon turns, and now I sense him staring at my face. *Don't look. Don't look. You're far too close.* I look, almost bumping my nose with his.

"What is it? Why are you staring at me like that?"

"I don't know. I just want to."

His eyes drop to my lips, and like an idiot, I decide to lick them. Hell if that's not an invitation to be kissed. He leans in, bringing his lips an inch from mine, but somehow, I manage to wake up from my lust-infused daze and push him back.

"We can't."

He clamps his jaw shut and then looks away.

"You're right. I'm sorry."

"Let's get out of here, I'm beginning to feel claustrophobic."

I get on my hands and knees, making my jeans even dirtier,

and crawl out of the hole. In hindsight, maybe I should have let Rikkon go first instead of giving him a nice display of my ass. *Oh well.* I curl my fingers around a skinny root to gain leverage and push myself out, when rough hands grab my arms and yank me up. I don't even have a chance to scream before a gag is shoved in my mouth and a burlap sack is thrown over my head.

Twenty

RIKKON

Miranda is yanked forward, disappearing from view before I can reach her. I follow her, disregarding the danger to myself, only to be apprehended as well. I don't offer resistance when I'm pulled out of the hole, but the moment I'm vertical again, I free my right arm, and hit the male to my left on his throat. He releases me at once, coughing and covering his neck.

The second hooded male draws his sword, revealing the insignia on his breastplate. They're Aquila patrol guards.

"*Nopaew ruoy pord, reidlos,*" I command in the native language only royals of the house of Aquila can speak, but all its subjects can understand and must obey.

I didn't know I was still able to utter those words without my powers.

The guard immediately lowers his sword and stares at me with wide eyes. "Your Highness?"

Ignoring the male, I look for Miranda. A third guard has her in his grasp, gagged and blindfolded. She's struggling, trying to break free. Fury erupts in the pit of my stomach, spreading like wildfire through my body. If I had my powers, he'd be nothing but dust right now.

"Release her," I grit out.

I didn't speak in the royal tongue, but I didn't have to this time. They know who I am, and they're cowering in their boots. Banished or not, I'm still their prince. The third guard drops her arm and steps aside. Free from his hold, Miranda removes the burlap sack from over her head and spits out the gag from her mouth.

"Son of a bitch. Talk about a welcoming committee." She glowers at the guard closest to her before stepping away from him.

I wish she'd come to stand next to me, but I'm still surrounded by the other guards, so I understand her hesitation.

Or maybe she doesn't want to come near you since every time she does, you try to kiss her, dumbass.

"Your Highness, we didn't recognize you. It's been so long," the guard with the sword apologizes.

"Save your excuses, soldier. What are you doing patrolling Hornet's Gardens? Did my mother send you to find me?"

The guards trade a confused glance and I have my answer.

"No, Your Highness. We didn't know you were coming."

"So why are you here? You just missed a group of hellionflares. You must have heard them."

"Yes, but they can't sense us when we are wearing these." He points at his cape.

I see nothing special about the attire that would offer protection, but I've been gone for centuries. A lot has changed, no doubt.

"You didn't answer my first question. Why are you patrolling this area?"

"There's been trouble at the borders, Your Highness," the second guard replies, pulling his hood down. "The marsh people found a way to break through the protective wards."

"The marsh people have always kept to themselves."

"Not anymore."

I want to ask more questions, but I don't want to remind them I've been gone for so long. Besides, they only know what they've been told, which doesn't mean they know the truth. A ray of sunshine pierces through the canopy, hitting the male straight on. It turns his fiery hair even brighter, and it hurts my eyes. I know exactly where he's from now.

"You must be part of the Mularkey clan."

"Yes, Your Highness."

"Wait? Mularkey?" Miranda's eyebrows arch, and then she turns to me.

I don't understand her look of astonishment, until I remember the notebook she found about the Nightingales. It was penned by someone with that same last name. I didn't think much about it. I've met countless humans with that same last name, and they didn't have any affiliation with the Nightingales. And by the way the author idolized his subjects, I was sure the notebook had been written by a human. It never occurred to me that the author could have been a Nightingale too.

The soldier frowns at Miranda, and it occurs to me he might never have seen a human before. "Yes. My name is Ronwen Mularkey."

Her jaw drops. "You're kidding. Does everyone in your family have that flaming red hair?"

"Yeah. Why?" He narrows his eyes, scrutinizing Miranda.

Now all the guards are staring at her with suspicion. To be honest, I'm not sure what she finds so fascinating about his name or the fact the Mularkey clan has red hair.

"Oh my god. This is too much." She throws her hands up in the air.

"What is? Mir, you're not making any sense."

"I can't believe one of the first people I meet when I cross into Ellnesari is the Nightingale version of Ron Weasley."

"Who is this Weasley person?" the first guard asks.

I wave my hand impatiently. "No one of importance. You are to escort us to the palace at once."

Miranda flattens her lips, giving me a death glare. I'm not sure why she's angry now. It can't be because of a fictional character.

"But we haven't finished our pat—" Ronwen starts, only to be cut off by the angry stare of the first soldier. "Of course, Your Highness."

"Wait, I want to know what the other two Stooges' names are," Miranda chimes in.

"Stooges?" Ronwen scratches his head. "I've never heard of such a thing."

"My name is Finnick Ballard," the patrol guard who seems to be in charge replies. "And that's Sora Solano."

"Okay, now you know their names. Let's get going," I say.

Finnick takes the lead, and the other two soldiers position themselves at the rear. I glance at Miranda, offering my hand.

"Come on. We have a bit of a walk back, and we don't want to be caught outside after nightfall."

She twists her face into a grimace. "Why? More gruesome creatures roaming around?"

"Naturally. This is Ellnesari. I could protect you, but why go through the trouble if we can avoid it?"

She gives me a quizzical look, probably wondering why I'm lying like that. I couldn't protect her from anything here, not in my current powerless state. But I'm betting those soldiers don't know my mother took away my powers, and I'd like them to stay in the dark.

"You could walk the wind, Your Highness," Ronwen offers diffidently.

"Walk the wind? What's that?" Miranda asks.

"It's the ability to travel fast, going from A to B in the blink of an eye," I say.

"Oh, that type of travel. Yeah, hard pass." She turns to Ronwen. "It makes me incredibly ill. I'd be puking my guts out before we arrived at the castle, and no one wants that."

Since Miranda has never walked the wind with me, she must be referring to when Selor kidnapped her. Now that I'm back home, the next time I see that smug son of a bitch, I'll punch him in the throat. Not only for making Miranda sick, but for what he wrote on the Taluah Mirror. Even though I knew giving him my blood was a bad idea, I couldn't have foreseen he'd do something like that. That spell has my mother's fingerprints all over it, and I want to know why she bound Miranda's fate with mine, trapping her in Ellnesari forever.

MIRANDA

Rikkon is back to acting like an arrogant ass, and even though I hate it, I can see the necessity this time. He's been gone for too long, and if the soldiers sense weakness, they might turn against him. He lied about his ability to protect me, that much I know. If he could protect me against the strange creatures in this place, he wouldn't have hidden from the hellionflares. I had to come up with an excuse for why he can't walk the wind.

It takes around ten minutes for the landscape to change. The spiraling golden trees give way to trees closer in appearance to the ones back home. Well, they grow straight and that's how far the likeness goes. There aren't trees as large as these ones anywhere in the human world. Some of the tree trunks are the width of a house, and they're so tall I can't even see the top. They vanish in the clouds.

I'm staring up in awe when Rikkon nudges me. "We're in the Sacred Forest now. The Aquila castle is on the other side."

"How big is this forest?"

"It extends for miles. We should be able to cross it in four hours."

"Four hours?" I squeak, and then look at my mud-caked boots. "I'll wear a hole through my soles."

One of the soldiers behind us clears his throat. When I look, it's the Mularkey boy again.

"Do you have something on your mind, soldier?" Rikkon asks.

"Yes, Your Highness. If your friend can't handle the long walk, we can use the cargo system."

Finnick turns around. "Don't be ridiculous, Ronwen. The prince of Aquila can't travel with the cargo." He glances at Rikkon, apologetically. "Forgive Mularkey, Your Highness. He's a new recruit."

If there's another way to reach the castle that doesn't involve walking for four hours, I want to know more about it.

"How bad is the cargo system? I mean, if it's like traveling on the back of a truck, it can't be that demeaning."

Rikkon laughs. "I'd say it's better than traveling on the back of a truck. I can't believe the palace finally approved its construction."

"It's a new implementation, Your Highness, only four hundred years old," Ronwen replies and then turns to me. "If the prince says it's better than a truck, milady, then it is."

"Milady?" I chuckle, and poor Ronwen turns all shades of red.

Rikkon places a hand on my lower back, sucking away all my amusement in a flash. His touch is electrifying, and it ignites all the illicit feelings in me that I have to suppress. I can't let anyone know I have the hots for the prince. I'm certain his mate won't appreciate it, and I can only imagine what a jealous Nightingale princess would do to me.

Like the pest that he is—a very wicked and delicious pest—Rikkon leans close to my ear and whispers, "You're in my company, therefore, you've earned the title. Go along with it."

Goose bumps break out on my skin, and desire skitters down my spine. When I think things couldn't get any worse, Rikkon takes a whiff of my neck. My eyes roll back in their sockets, and I sway on the spot.

"Is she getting ill?" one of the soldiers asks and I can't tell who spoke, but it's enough to make me aware of my surroundings.

I jump forward and away from Rikkon, glad that I haven't

lost all my reflexes yet. "I'm fine, but I really would like to check the cargo system."

"And that's what we'll do." He turns to the soldier in charge. "Take us there."

The dark male is not happy about the change of plans, which makes me dislike him even more. Actually, the only one of the trio who doesn't give me bad vibes is Ronwen. Maybe it's the flaming red hair and his resemblance to Ron Weasley that make me feel this way. It's stupid though. He's a Nightingale, therefore he can't be trusted.

The cargo system is only a minute away from where we were. I was expecting a rough wooden carriage pulled by an enormous and smelly beast, not the intricate system of lifts going up one of the largest trees and disappearing from view at the top. I suspect cables must link the trees so the lifts can move back and forth.

The perimeter is protected by more guards, and potent magic. I haven't been able to feel anything of the sort since I arrived here, but as we approach the lifts, it's all I can sense. It wraps around my body in a seductive way, making me lightheaded for a second.

I glance at Rikkon, trying to catch his attention so I can ask about it, but his gaze is riveted on the cargo system. His expression reveals nothing, yet I wonder how he's taking everything in. I can't imagine how he must be feeling to return to Ellnesari after hundreds of years. How much has his homeland changed?

The guards manning the entrance to the cargo system are now staring at us. *Correction, they're all staring at Rikkon.* One finally breaks away from the group and walks over. He's as tall as Rikkon, but built like a mountain, with wide shoulders and arms that would translate as trees back home. His short hair is the color of the Mediterranean Sea, and his skin is as dark as a moonless sky, except for the freckles on his face that resemble stars. Not counting Rikkon, he's the most beautiful male I've ever seen in my entire life.

"Prince Rikkon of Aquila, I never thought I'd ever see you again," he says, trying to hide his smirk.

The magic surrounding us seems to grow with his proximity, and belatedly I realize it's coming from him. He's not an ordinary Nightingale. He feels powerful, royal.

"Sorry to disappoint you, Castiel of Lynx," Rikkon replies.

"It's Prince Castiel now," he says, more serious this time.

"What happened to your brother?"

"The same thing that happened to you."

Rikkon swallows hard. "I see. I'm sorry to hear that."

The same thing how? Banishment to the human world, or losing his powers? I'd love to ask, but I suspect I should keep my mouth shut for now.

"I'm not. He was a jerk. I don't miss him. You, my friend, are another story. It's good to have you back." He turns to me, dropping his eyes to my feet to let them slowly travel the length of my body. "You brought a friend, a *special* friend."

Oh, that doesn't sound good. I bristle in an instant. "What do you mean by that?"

Castiel arches his eyebrows and glances at Rikkon, amused. "Feisty. That's good, considering the—"

"She can't handle walking the wind, so we need to use the cargo system to reach the palace," Rikkon interrupts and I wonder what his friend was going to say.

My guess is he was going to bring up Rikkon's bond with the princess of whatever. I'm bitter and sad in an instant. What good is not being a doormat in this situation? I can't fight fate.

"A prince using the cargo system to travel?" Castiel presses his hand against his chest, faking outrage. "That's unheard of."

The annoying escort mumbles something under his breath, and I'm betting it goes along the lines of "that's what I said."

"It's my design, I'd love to test it out. Besides, you know I love to make an entrance," Rikkon chuckles, making me even more confused.

He didn't seem like the kind of guy who likes attention, even after he regained his memories and started to act like a royal pain in the ass. Also, he designed the cargo system? I had no idea he was a Nightingale engineer.

"Sure you do," Castiel pipes up.

Duh, sarcasm, Miranda. God, I must have hit my head when I fell into Ellnesari.

"Well, unfortunately, you can't use the cargo system right now. We're transporting something very valuable to your mother and it will take a while before we're done."

"How long?" Rikkon frowns, clearly not happy with the news.

"Longer than it will take to complete the journey on foot."

"Great," I mumble.

Castiel raises an eyebrow at me while the phantom of a smirk appears on his lips. "Not a fan of a good hike?"

"No, I can't say that I am. I guess there aren't any cars here?"

"I'm afraid not. The portals were sealed before all of the wonderful technological advances from humans," Rikkon replies. "Besides, my mother would most likely refuse to explore the possibility."

His expression becomes serious again, and I guess there's more to that story. I wonder if I'll get to hear about it before I find a way home.

Better not, Miranda. The more time you spend with Rikkon, the harder you will fall for him.

"But fret not, milady. I have a solution," Castiel chimes in.

"Heavens. What now?" Rikkon grumbles.

Castiel sticks two fingers in his mouth and whistles so loudly it hurts my ears. The noise seems to go on forever, but it's just the echo bouncing off the trees. A moment later, the sound of giant wings flapping in the distance makes me look up. At first, all I see is a great shadow, getting bigger by the second. And then a beautiful blue bird with iridescent feathers appears. It looks like a cross between an oversized peacock and an eagle.

It hovers in circles above us before it lands next to Castiel.

"Fili?" Rikkon walks over and the bird lowers its beaked head.

"I can't believe you're still around." He pats the bird's cheek affectionately, and like an idiot, I watch the scene with a lovesick puppy expression.

"I found a way to circumvent that whole mortal thing," Castiel chimes in.

"You made Fili immortal without changing her essence? How? I thought we had hit a dead end."

He must be referring to how the Nightingales turned humans into vampires. They made them immortals, yes, but changed them into beings allergic to sunlight and dependent on drinking blood to survive.

"Not just Fili, Your Highness, but all the winged beasts in the land," Ronwen butts in.

I was wondering when the rebel soldier would open his piehole. His surly friend elbows Ronwen's ribs in warning, and I can't help the chuckle that escapes my lips when his face turns beet red again.

"So much to tell you, my friend," Castiel adds.

Rikkon seems stunned by all those revelations. I'm still watching him when Castiel offers me his hand. "Milady."

"What?" I step back.

"He wants to help you get on Fili," Rikkon explains.

I eye the bird, feeling droplets of dread roll down my spine. "You expect me to ride on the back of that? She's not even wearing a harness. Where am I supposed to hold?"

"You grab on to her feathers. Don't worry, you won't fall. Rikkon won't let you." Castiel gives his friend a meaningful glance.

It almost seems like he suspects there's something going on between Rikkon and me. *Am I that transparent? Ugh.*

"Come on, Mir. It's either flying or walking for four hours. Your choice," Rikkon tells me.

"Fine. Let's do this."

MIRANDA

"Will you relax? I'm not going to let you fall." Rikkon screams in my ear as we soar high up in the sky.

I curl my fingers tighter around Fili's feathers, yanking them a little. The bird complains with a loud shriek and a sharp angle to the right. I close my eyes and yell.

Rikkon has the audacity to laugh.

"Shut up, jerkface. This is not funny."

He pulls me closer to him and brings his lips to my ears. "Oh, but it is."

Fear was obscuring the fact we're awfully close. But his seductive voice whispering in my ear reminds me of how we're making a witch and prince sandwich right now. My back is pressed against his chest, and his legs are flush with mine. And now his damn lips are inches from my neck. I'm beginning to feel things that I really shouldn't, like the sudden ache between my legs. I think if I swayed my hips back and forth, I'd probably climax like Selma Blair's character did in *Cruel Intentions*. My body starts to melt into his as I relax my stance, and the prospect of plunging to my death is no longer relevant.

"Mir?" he says in the huskiest tone I've heard from him.

"Yes?"

"You smell really good."

I jerk forward, sliding to the side a little. "Shit!"

Rikkon tightens his hold on me. "Easy there."

My heart is hammering wildly against my ribcage now, wanting to soar but bound by the harsh chains of reality.

"Stop saying things like that to me, Rik. It's not fair."

He sighs so loudly that I can hear it over the sound of the wind rushing by.

"I know. I'm sorry."

His reply is pained, almost as if he's fallen as hard as I have. It's obviously nonsense, nothing more than a figment of my imagination. No bonded male would have his heart torn in two.

Fili has taken us so high that I see nothing but clouds. I wish we were flying lower so I could at least have the view to distract me from Rikkon and my stupid feelings for him.

"I take it Castiel was your friend before your banishment," I say to change the subject.

"Yes, he was my best friend."

"He looks so different from all the other Nightingales I've met so far."

"He's from the Lynx court, but he was sent to Aquila for his training when he was young."

"Why?"

"Because he was the king's second son, and therefore, had no right to the throne. It's common for rulers to send their offspring to other kingdoms when they aren't the direct heirs."

"To avoid fratricide or sororicide, right?"

"Yeah, that's one of the reasons in some kingdoms, but mostly, it's to cultivate relationships."

"But Castiel said he's a prince now, so shouldn't he have returned to his homeland?"

"In theory. I'm sure I'll learn the reason for his presence here in good time."

There's a sudden dip, and I let out a little yelp. "What's Fili doing?"

"We're approaching the castle."

We break through the clouds that were blocking our view a second ago, and the vision that appears before my eyes is breathtaking.

"Oh my god."

A magnificent white castle shining under the sun rises from its own private island. Hogwarts has nothing on it. The bricks seem to be made out of mother of pearl, judging by the way they reflect the light in a prism of colors. I lose count of the number of turrets, there are so many.

Gardens that would put to shame the ones in the Versailles surround the castle. The patterns they make are intricate and beautiful. Some look like birds, others like flowers, but most are abstract symbols that don't mean much to me. I guess they must have some significance to the Nightingales. I even spot a large maze with a fountain at its center. It's probably enchanted, so I make a mental note to not venture there.

"It's quite the sight, isn't it?" Rikkon says.

"It's amazing. You must have missed this."

He doesn't reply right away, but his fingers curl a little tighter around my jacket.

"I missed the place, for sure."

A gust of strong wind comes out of nowhere and pushes Fili off course. She shrieks, trying to keep herself leveled so we don't fall, but we're hanging at a perilous angle now. Rikkon shouts something in a foreign language to try to calm down our ride. I'm not sure it's working. I can sense Fili's panic growing at an alarming pace. *Holy shit. How am I doing this?* I was never able to sense the moods of animals before.

The sky darkens as stormy clouds gather above us.

"What the hell is going on?" I ask.

"I don't know. This doesn't feel natural. Hold tight, Mir."

"I'm try—"

Lightning strikes right in front of us, spooking poor Fili even more. She zooms upward suddenly in an almost vertical ascension, making it impossible to hold on to her. I lose my grip, sending me and Rikkon spiraling down to our deaths.

"Miranda!" he shouts, trying to reach me, but free-falling when there's a windstorm blasting at full force doesn't help. He keeps getting farther and farther away from me.

I have to do something. I don't know if he will die from the fall, but I certainly will. Somehow, I manage to stick my hand in my bag and find a crystal, the largest I had in there. Closing my eyes, I concentrate on a spell I recently learned at the institute. It's supposed to levitate feathers, not give people the ability to fly, but maybe if I change the words around, I can levitate Rikkon and me.

The crystal becomes warm in my hand, which means the magic is working. But then, the stone turns piping hot, burning my palm. I cry out from the pain, but I can't let go. The magic is also getting stronger. The wind is still howling, but it's no longer rushing by. I finally open my eyes again and notice I'm descending slowly, like a feather does. I search for Rikkon and when I don't see him right away, I fear the spell only worked for me. But then his fingers brush the back of my wrist before he takes my hand and turns me around

"Are you doing this?" he asks.

"Yes."

He pulls me fully into his arms and links his legs with mine. I get why he's doing it. He doesn't want to get separated again, but now I'm back to wanting to jump his bones. Why am I getting so turned on by him when he's probably days away from marrying someone else?

"That's amazing. *You* are amazing, Mir."

His eyes are earnest and intense, and the way he's staring at me with so much admiration is creating havoc in my body and my mind. Maybe it's the adrenaline still pumping in my veins, or the close brush with death that says the hell with consequences. I kiss him this time, furiously and hungrily. Rikkon not only matches my eagerness, but he also brings it up several notches. I'm now on fire, needing to soak up as much of his passion into me as possible.

I barely notice when our feet touch the ground, or when the crystal in my hand finally cools off. We remain tangled, devouring each other's mouths like there's no tomorrow because for us, there isn't. I could have stayed in his embrace forever, but alarming shouts force us apart. Rikkon spins us around, pushing me behind him.

We landed in the middle of one of the gardens, and the smell of flowers is suddenly all I can sense. It's sweetly intoxicating and it's making me dizzy. I shake my head in an attempt to keep my mind sharp.

"Who's coming?" I ask.

"The castle guards."

When they come into view, they seem to shine with splendor even though the sun is still hidden behind the dark clouds. They're all fair like Rikkon, and their armor is the color of white gold. I count seven at least, fast approaching in a spearhead formation, all carrying glowing swords like the one Selor had.

"They don't look friendly. I thought Selor came ahead to tell your mother you were coming," I reply.

"That means nothing," he grumbles under his breath. "Don't worry, I—"

The ground beneath our feet begins to shake and split in patches. "What the hell!" I shout.

Tree roots sprout from the fissures, wrapping around our limbs before either of us can jump away.

"*Su esaeler!*" Rikkon commands in that strange language again, but this time, the guards don't heed his words.

Shit. We're in trouble, big trouble.

RIKKON

The soldier leading the group advances, keeping his weapon at the ready. Even after all these years, and his change in appearance, I still recognize him. When I was banished, he was just a scrawny boy with big dreams. Now he's as big as his brother.

"So, it is true. You're back. I thought Selor was raving mad. He's been gone for so long."

"Telar Nyrk, I see you've passed the rites." I eye his starfire sword.

He furrows his eyebrows, clenching his jaw as well. "Yes. Many years ago."

"Then you should know better. Is this how you treat your prince?"

Never mind that my command should have worked on him as it did with the other soldiers.

"I'm under orders from Queen Maewe to imprison anyone who disrupts the storm wards."

"The what now?" Miranda asks.

Unlike the patrol guards, Telar doesn't even glance in her direction. As a matter of fact, none of the males with him do. It seems they're ignoring her on purpose. I hate not knowing what the hell is going on. It leaves me vulnerable and weak. I have been gone for far too long and I feel way out of my depth.

Fili's shrieks pierce the air, followed by the loud flapping of her wings. Telar and his soldiers retreat as she approaches, eyeing the giant bird with apprehension. Lightshadow Wings are known to be quite savage when provoked; their beaks and talons can decapitate a Nightingale in the blink of an eye. They're also extremely docile and loyal animals when won over.

Fili lands right in front of us, opening her wings to their full span and thus creating a shield.

"Tell your bird to back down, Rikkon, or I'll be forced to cut her in two," Telar warns.

"I don't think so. Undo these roots and I'll try to convince her to leave the lot of you in one piece."

I'm hoping my bluff works. Fili could handle one soldier, but seven is pushing her luck. I'm also banking that with her distraction, Telar won't realize I could have freed myself if I had my powers.

Grumbling, he signals for his companions to lower their weapons, and then he sheathes his sword out of sight. The roots keeping Miranda and me trapped slacken and withdraw until they disappear into the ground.

Free to move, I stop next to Fili, placing a hand on her neck to calm her down. She folds her wings and leans into my caress.

"I can't believe that bird still remembers you," Telar pipes up.

"I've earned her loyalty." I glance fleetingly at Miranda, hoping not to lose hers when she learns the truth.

Telar snorts. "Come on now. I'd better escort you inside before you trigger another ward."

"How many wards are there?" Miranda asks, but once again Telar ignores her.

He simply whirls around and strides toward the castle, followed by his companions.

"What's up with your friend? Am I invisible to him?"

"I don't know, Mir. I've been gone for centuries, remember?"

"Right. Sorry. It's really hard to reconcile that you're ancient."

I scowl. "Gee, thanks."

Miranda rolls her eyes, reminding me of how young she is. When my memories were gone, I felt and acted like the twentysomething-year-old that I appeared to be in the human realm. But now, all my years of immortality are a great weight on my shoulders. The things I've witnessed and endured have scarred me permanently. It's one more reason—maybe the main reason—to find a way to unbind myself from her and send her back home. Even if I weren't bonded to someone else, it would be vile to pursue her. I have no right to ruin Miranda's life.

"Why are you looking at me like that?" She frowns.

I shake my head. "It's nothing. Let's go before they leave us behind."

Twenty-Two

MIRANDA

My apprehension grows by leaps and bounds on the trek from the gardens to the palace. I'm wriggling my fingers together when Telar leads us to a set of double doors manned by two guards who I thought were marble statues at first. Their uniforms are white, matching their skin and hair color. When they move, I get a little spooked and gasp.

Heat spreads through my cheeks. I can't let little things get to me like that. Rikkon warned me Ellnesari is not a place where you can show weakness. It's not that much different than the Witchcraft Institute to be honest. It's eat or be eaten there too.

The marble-like guards step aside as the doors open inward. The one to my right glances at me with eyes that are pale gray save for his black pupils. In a way, he reminds me of Manu, Lucca's sister. She was cursed by Queen Maewe. *Were these guys cursed too?*

The suspicion doesn't give me comfort. What if she doesn't like me and decides to do the same or worse? Rikkon can't protect me. No one can.

You're on your own, Miranda. You can't count on Prince Charming to rescue you. In this story, the witch saves herself.

The double doors lead to a wide and long corridor. Frescoes

on the high vaulted ceiling depict a glorious sky with fluffy white clouds and giant birds like Fili. By the bits of conversation I gathered concerning the giant bird, I get the sense they're almost sacred animals here. It makes perfect sense. Aquila means eagle in Latin, and in Greek mythology Aquila was the name of the bird that carried Zeus's thunderbolts.

We move in silence so complete not even our footsteps can be heard clanking against the marble floor. Some kind of magic must be at work. The walls on each side are painfully bare at first, but halfway down the corridor, they change into a seamless mirrored surface. I wince when I catch my reflection. My clothes are filthy, I have soot on my face, and my hair is a disaster. I can't believe Rikkon wanted to kiss me.

No, don't think about that when you're moments away from meeting his mother.

I should keep my eyes glued to the back of the soldiers ahead of us, but I'm a rebel and glutton for punishment. Naturally, I have to glance at Rikkon, who looks like a rock star even with a bit of mud smeared on his cheek. My fingers itch to wipe his face clean, almost like a compulsion I can't fight. I have to curl my hands into fists and dig my nails into my palms until they hurt.

Rikkon glances at me then, catching me ogling. *Busted.*

"That's it, Mir," he says.

"What?" I ask like a moron.

"My mother and her court of sycophants are on the other side of those doors."

It's then that I notice Telar and the other guards have stood to the side, and in front of us stand a set of silvery double doors that go all the way up to the ceiling. A giant could step through them without a problem.

Dots of sweat break out on my forehead and no matter how hard I try to calm down, I can't stop my body from trembling from head to toe.

"What should I do? Is there a protocol I should follow?" I ask.

It's a little late to worry about that now. The doors open

inward, and if there was any knowledge Rikkon should have shared with me, he can't do it now.

"Don't say anything and let me handle my mother. Stay close to me, though."

"Okay."

We walk through the doors together. I pretend we're just entering an ordinary room, not the receiving chamber of one of the most powerful beings in this strange land. Courtiers are standing, gathered on each side of the room as they watch Rikkon stride with purpose toward the throne at the end. I follow his lead and don't take my eyes off his mother even though I'm dying to look around.

She sits regally on a throne made of glass, and her cold face matches her fancy chair. Her white-blonde hair is braided at the front, and peeking from the strands, a small but sparkly tiara adorns her head. She's the real-life version of Elsa.

Miranda, you really have to stop drawing comparisons between Nightingales and cute fictional characters.

Next to her is a beautiful male, who I guess is Rikkon's father. He's also fair, but his hair is strawberry blond and wavy, touching his shoulders. Neither show any emotion despite seeing their son after all these years. Talk about heartless people.

They're not people, Miranda. They're Nightingales.

I expect Rikkon to bow when he stops a few feet away from the dais, but he remains standing upright with his chin held high. From the corner of my eye, I spot Selor, standing in the shadows but close enough to his queen. I turn to fully look at him just in case he's plotting another ambush. He catches me staring and winks at me. *Asshole.*

An entire minute goes by yet no one speaks. Rikkon is currently locked in a staring contest with his mother and it's giving me anxiety. I feel like I should say something, break the ice, but Rikkon asked me to let him handle things, so I heed his words. I know nothing about the customs of this place. Maybe staring contests are the protocol around here.

"So," the queen finally opens her mouth. "This is the witch."

Wait? What? That's what she has to say to her son after his long-ass banishment?

"Uh," I start, an involuntary reaction.

"Good to see you too, Your Majesty," Rikkon cuts me off.

She waves her hand impatiently. "Yes, yes, I'll get to you in a moment." She turns her icy stare on me. "Come here, child. Let me have a good look at you."

Oh my god. What's happening? Why is she singling me out like that? I throw a panicked look at Rikkon, begging him to help me, but he just stares at me in the same detached manner as everyone else. I want to fucking scream.

Since assistance is not coming from him, I do as the queen says and approach the dais, feeling like a horse on display.

"Your Majesty," I curtsy, making the female chuckle.

My ears and face burn, and now I'm glad I'm covered in soot. Maybe she won't notice my reaction.

"Glad to see you're not as wild as I feared," she says.

"I'm not an animal," I retort, forgetting for a second who I'm speaking to.

The queen frowns, and I'm blasted by magic so strong, it almost sends me to my knees.

"Mother, stop it," Rikkon finally intervenes.

The magic recedes, and I can breathe easily again.

She tsks. "You clearly don't know what you've found, Rik. But it matters not. I'm satisfied. We shall have a ball to celebrate this joyous occasion."

The courtiers, who had been silent until that moment, erupt in animated chatter. I don't know what just happened, but I have the distinct notion that I was tested, and somehow passed the test. I wonder what would have happened to me if Queen Maewe had found me lacking.

She stands from her throne and walks over to Rikkon. He becomes even tenser than before, especially when she captures his face between her hands.

"It's good to see you, my son. You haven't changed a bit."

"But I have, Mother, in more ways than you can imagine."

She steps back, not pleased with his answer if I'm to judge by the furrow of her blonde eyebrows.

"We'll talk about that later. Now go to your chambers to freshen up. Festivities will commence in an hour."

She makes a motion to walk away, but Rikkon grabs her arm. "I need to speak with you in private."

The queen drops her gaze to Rikkon's hand, and then slowly lifts her eyes to his. "I know what burdens your mind. You'll have the answers you seek, but not now. Go. We don't have much time."

Rikkon steps away, releasing her arm. As for me, I'm as lost as a chicken in the North Pole. She's acting as if she didn't banish her son for hundreds of years. She seemed more pleased to see me, a complete stranger, than her own flesh and blood.

I'm beginning to suspect my presence here wasn't a simple whim of the queen or a way to punish Rikkon. She has a much bigger purpose for me, which is even more terrifying.

He turns to me, extending his hand. "Come on, Mir. You heard the queen; we must get ready for the ball."

"Don't worry about Miranda. You go on. Your chambers are ready for you." She places a hand on my shoulder, and I feel a jolt of electricity go through my body. It's not painful, but it's uncomfortable just the same.

"I'd rather—" Rikkon begins.

"You *will* go to your chambers now. That's not a request."

I sense the magic in her words, and how Rikkon reacts to them. His spine becomes taut, and the muscles around his mouth tense.

Pitifully, he glances at me. I read the apology in his eyes, but unfortunately, it doesn't help me one bit.

"Very well," he replies tersely, and then turns to me. "I'll see you soon, Mir."

I watch him walk away, and with each step he takes, my

desperation and fear grow. He just left me alone with his psychotic mother. *Fuck!*

The queen turns to me with a cold smile plastered on her annoyingly beautiful face. "Now, come with me, child. I want to know everything about you."

Twenty-Three

MIRANDA

The queen laces her arm with mine and leads me to the shadowy alcove where I spotted Selor earlier. The warrior isn't there anymore, but that doesn't mean he's gone. I have no idea where she's taking me, for there's nothing but a smooth wall in front of us. That is, until she waves her hand in front of it and a door appears.

"That's a neat trick," I say, and immediately berate myself for it.

She simply chuckles and nudges me to go through the door first. I don't want to. It's pitch black on the other side and I half expect Selor to appear with his glowing sword to chop my head off. But it's not like I can plant my feet on the floor and refuse to move.

So with my heart stuck in my throat, I cross the threshold. The darkness gives way to reveal a sunny private garden that looks like it sprang from a Disney fairy tale movie. It's an explosion of colors and smells and honestly, I don't know where to look first. Little colorful birds fly in circles above me, tweeting happily. All we're missing now is for Queen Maewe to burst into song.

She laces her arm with mine again and steers me down the cobblestone path that cuts through the garden.

"This is my secret place away from all the politics of court. My sanctuary."

"It's beautiful."

"Yes, it was a gift from Ruel after Rikkon was born."

"Ruel?" I ask.

"The king, my dear."

"Oh, of course."

Not one of her lovers then.

"You've become very close to my son in a short period of time," she continues.

"Yes. How do you know?"

"Oh, I know many things, child."

"So you know how bad off Rikkon and Vivienne have been since you banished them?"

Her arm tenses in mine, and I brace for the strike of a blast of magic. I have to remember who I'm talking to here. It seems my survival instincts have deserted me.

"Yes, naturally."

"And you don't care?"

She doesn't reply, but I notice her grip on me becomes stronger, almost like a vise. *Shit*. Not only do I not have any survival instincts left, but I also took a nosedive in the lake of stupid.

We stop by a stone well, and finally the queen releases me. She lowers the bucket, humming the same song that Selor did when he was prepping the Taluah Mirror for our travel. When the bucket returns filled to the brim, she turns to me.

"Tell me, Miranda, how does it feel to be the most powerful witch in your family and be overlooked because you weren't born first?"

Whoa, talk about a one-eighty in this conversation.

"I'm not the most powerful witch in my family."

"Hmm." She gives me an amused glance before she returns her attention to the bucket.

Out of nowhere, a golden goblet appears in her hand, which she proceeds to fill.

"You must be parched after your journey. Here, have a drink." She offers me the cup.

I eye the offering suspiciously, but take the goblet, not wanting to dig a bigger hole. I've already said too many things I shouldn't. I'm tempted to take a whiff of the liquid, but that would probably offend the queen.

Slowly, I bring the cup to my lips and take a sip. *Holy shit.* It's plain water, but somehow it tastes a million times better than any I've had back home. I toss my head back and drink the rest with gusto. *Who knew, I was indeed thirsty.* Some of it sloshes down my chin, which I wipe off with the back of my arm like an unrefined swine.

The queen is watching me almost too eagerly.

"What is it?" I ask.

"What did you think?"

"About the water? Honestly, it's the best damn water I've ever had in my life."

Wait, why am I talking to the queen in this familiar tone? What was in this fucking water?

"This well is very special. Those who drink from it experience different things."

"I definitely feel fine now. Actually, I feel great, like I could take over the world."

The queen smiles from ear to ear. "I'm glad to hear that, Miranda. Most who drink from it die after a few sips."

My amusement jumps off a cliff and perishes. "What? You poisoned me?"

She shakes her head. "Oh no, my dear. I have no intention of poisoning you. I had to make sure you were the one."

I set the cup on the ledge of the well. "I don't get it. The one for what?"

"To save my son."

My entire body becomes tense in an instant. "From what?"

She turns around, lacing her hands behind her back, and gazes at the sky. "I have the same gift Rikkon has. I have the sight."

"What did you see?" I step next to her, all fear of the woman suddenly falling to the wayside. I'm sure this sense of familiarity and lack of fear of her will vanish soon enough.

"I saw Rikkon's bond to the princess of the Cygnus court."

My heart shrivels. "He came back for her."

"I could only keep him away for so long."

"Wait. You banished him on purpose?"

She turns to me, revealing red-rimmed eyes. "I saw his death. If he marries the princess, he dies. I can't allow that to happen."

She might as well have reached inside my chest and pulled my heart out.

"Can't you break the bond?"

"No, nothing can break the bond but Rikkon's own will."

"He said he doesn't want the bond, so he has to simply deny it and poof, it's gone?" I ask, but it's a silly question. Of course it's not that simple.

"I wish that were the case. But there's another way to avoid his demise."

"What is it?"

"The princess must die."

Ah hell. Now I get where she's going with this conversation.

"And you want me to kill her, right? That's what this little tete-a-tete is all about."

"Yes."

"Why can't you send Selor to do your dirty work? He's blood-thirsty enough, plus he has that glowing sword of his. I'm just a witch. A *human* witch."

"I've seen many scenarios, Miranda, and in all of them, Rikkon dies. The only future where he lives is where you are. It has to be you, child. There's no other choice."

"How am I supposed to kill a royal Nightingale?"

The queen looks away again. "That I cannot see. You have the ability to do it, though. I made sure of it."

"What do you mean you made sure?"

"You survived the trip through the Taluah Mirror. That was your first test. And you drank from my well and didn't die."

"Are you kidding me?" I pull my hair back, yanking at the strands. "That hellish burning was a test?"

"You've also felt the change inside of you since you arrived in Ellnesari, don't try to deny it. You feel stronger, more connected to your inner power, yes? It's not by chance, Miranda. You were meant to come here. You were meant to save my son."

A suspicion sprouts in my head. "Are my feelings for Rikkon real then, or is that part of your plot to convince me to help?"

Her eyes widen. "I can't make people fall in or out of love, child. If I could, Vryenn would still be here, ready to be the next queen of Aquila. Instead, she's with that beast."

"Why do you hate the vampires so much? They helped you win a war."

She looks away hastily. "We've lingered here too long. You must get ready for the ball. You're the guest of honor, after all."

"You don't want my answer?"

She glances over her shoulder, smiling in a chilling way. "You have until after the ball. I know you'll make the right decision."

Twenty-Four

RIKKON

I find my chambers identical to when I left. Even the items on my desk are in the same position. The notebook opened to a blank page, the quill lying across from it. My starfire sword sheathed and hanging from the peg on the wall. But not a speck of dust. Clearly, my mother instructed that my room be kept clean but undisturbed.

I don't remember what I planned to write when I heard the commotion outside of my apartment. I left to investigate and found Vivi having a heated argument with our mother in the throne room over Lucca Della Morte. I never came back.

When Miranda asked me if I missed Ellnesari, I didn't know what to say. I did miss my life here, my work, Fili and Castiel. The court and the intrigue not so much. It's definitely better than living in the human lands, yet I hesitated to tell her the truth, and I don't know why. Most of my existence in the human realm had been hellish. The first few hundred years were torture. I had to learn to survive in a strange land without my powers and take care of Vivi. Plus, the bond had just taken root and the separation nearly drove me insane. The pain was excruciating. It's not as acute now; it only flares up when I'm acting against it.

Miranda. Thinking about our last kiss injects me with that heady feeling again. She was the only bright spot of my miserable existence in the human realm. Even when I didn't remember all the awful things that had happened to me in the years of banishment, or remember that I had a fated mate, she made me feel alive. I didn't know what I was missing until I found her.

The tug comes, making me hiss. I massage my chest, trying to get rid of the ache. It's unheard of for a bonded male to be attracted to anyone else besides his mate, but maybe after all these years of separation, the bond is not as strong as before. What's going to happen when I see Eriel Fasanor face-to-face? Will I forget Miranda then?

No. I don't want to give her up. It's selfish and awful to think this way, but I need her.

Maybe I can break the bond. There has to be a way. The first order of business is to get my powers back and for that, I need to speak with the person who took them away. My mother.

Worry about Miranda gnaws at my insides. What could my mother possibly want with her? Nothing good, that's for sure.

A knock on the door pulls me back from my inner thoughts. Without my powers, there's no way to know who is outside, but if I ask, I might as well announce to the entire court I'm a shell of the male I used to be. I make a beeline for my sword, pulling it from its sheath. It doesn't resonate with my touch; it doesn't sing as it should. But I don't need it to react to me, I just need a blade in my hand before I allow whoever is outside into my chambers.

"Come in," I say.

Two males wearing palace uniforms enter. One of them is pushing a cart with fresh towels, crystal bottles, ointments, and a bunch of other things I don't care to inspect. They're here to assist me in getting ready for the ball.

I sigh out loud, resigned. The quicker I become presentable for court, the faster I can check on Miranda. I set my sword on the desk, and then face the servants.

"Where do you want to start?"

They trade glances, and then the one wearing the darker

jacket, which means he has a senior position, replies, "Whatever you wish, Your Highness."

I glance down at my filthy clothes. Funny how no one batted an eyelash at my jeans and hoodie. To be honest, I'll miss their simplicity and comfort.

"Bath. I definitely need a bath."

The servants take their time getting rid of all the grime I accumulated during my journey here. No matter how many times I tell them I'm clean enough, they insist it isn't so. I suspect they're under orders from my mother to stall for as long as possible because not even using my most commanding voice works on them. Blast hierarchy and my mother's conniving ways.

Only after I threaten to cut their hands off do they back off. I dismiss them after the longest bath ever and get dressed by myself. A behavior like that from a royal is strange, but I was never one to follow the rules, and it wasn't uncommon for me to dismiss help. But as I spend ten minutes staring at the endless array of options in my closet, I regret sending those males away. I don't know how to dress for a Nightingale ball anymore. *Shit.*

What the hell. Who cares what I'm wearing? The court will behave however my mother commands. I could be wearing a burlap sack and they'd fawn all over me if the queen approved of my appearance. I pick the first outfit within reach, get dressed, and head out with only one destination in my mind: my mother's quarters.

Her wing is the next one to mine and walking at a normal speed, it takes me ten minutes to reach. There are no guards stationed at her door, which means she's expecting my visit and doesn't want anyone to know about it. I don't bother knocking. I'd find the door barred to me if she didn't want my company.

She's in the receiving room with a glass of limilla liqueur in her hand, staring at her reflection in the three-way mirror. She's already dressed for the ball in a blindingly sparkly silver gown. Gems similar to diamonds adorn the bodice and skirt. Some of them are as big as chicken eggs. Her white-blonde hair is divided into sections and braided into intricate designs. She's a stunning female and I'm a little surprised that King Raphael refused her offer. Very few males would.

"I was wondering when you would show up. Care for a glass of limilla? I remember it used to be your favorite."

"I'm surprised you remember anything about me. I didn't think you cared enough."

She furrows her eyebrows. "Don't say that. Everything I've ever done was to protect you."

"Right. That's why you banished me to the mortal lands and stripped me of my powers."

"I sent Selor after you. He was instructed to keep an eye on you and your sister."

I snort. "Some protector he was."

"If you came here to try to make me feel guilty about my choices, you're wasting your time. Shouldn't you be going after Miranda?"

"I came here to talk about her. Why did you have Selor bind her fate to mine? You know I'll have to depart for the Cygnus court soon. You know about my fated mate."

Her eyes darken. "Yes, I know. Why do you think I took away your powers? I was hoping without them you wouldn't feel the effects of the bond."

"Really? And what's your excuse for taking away Vryenn's powers?"

"Excuse? I don't need one. She defied me. That was her punishment."

I shake my head, trying to get my thoughts in order. I want to find a way to help my sister, but Miranda is who needs my immediate attention now. She's the one stuck in Ellnesari without the means to return to her family.

"Why did you bring Miranda here?"

"I know how you feel about her. She calls to your heart and soul despite the bond. That's never happened before, Rikkon. No bonded male has ever had any eyes for anyone else besides their mate. You're torn, and if Miranda goes away, you'll always feel empty."

"So your solution is to force her to stay to watch me marry another?" My voice rises. "Do you think I want that future for her?"

My mother waves her hand dismissively. "She can be your lover, your friend, whatever you desire her to be. You'll need someone you can trust at the Cygnus court. You know there's no lost love between Titus and me. You won't find allies there, not even in your fated mate."

"Miranda will never agree to that, nor will I ever ask her to be my mistress."

Even if I crave her touch with every fiber of my being, I won't mistreat her that way. She deserves a male who can give her the world, who treats her like a queen. I'll never be able to offer her that.

"I wouldn't be so sure about that," my mother replies.

Since I won't be able to persuade her to send Miranda back, I have to recover my powers at all costs.

"I'm back now, and even without powers, I can still feel the effects of the bond. I can't live at the Cygnus court without them. I'll be slaughtered."

She sets her glass down at a nearby table and adjusts her dress. "I can't give you your powers back."

"Bullshit. Of course you can. You're the one who took them away!"

"Yes, and it pained me to do so. I made sure I wouldn't be weak and reverse the spell in case it did succeed in making you forget the bond."

"What does that mean? Is it irreversible?"

"Of course not. There's a trigger that will break the spell. I have a feeling it will happen soon enough." She cocks her head to the side and seems to daydream for a second. "If you leave now, you can catch Miranda before she reaches the ballroom. You really don't want her roaming alone in the palace. My courtiers are curious about the young witch now that I bestowed my attention upon her, and you know some of them can't be trusted around a pretty thing like her."

Fuck. I know my mother is manipulating me, but I hastily leave her chambers anyway. She's not lying about her courtiers. I should have asked where she placed Miranda before I left though. I return to my wing of the palace, and color me surprised, I find her stepping out of the apartment next to mine. I should have known.

Miranda turns in my direction and I slow my pace. My heart, though, is another matter. It takes off at warp speed, clamoring against my ribcage, trying to break free. She's a vision in silver flames and moonlight. My mother dressed her in the Aquila colors, another sign that Miranda is her favorite. Regardless of her motives, the colors suit her. It contrasts nicely with her tan and dark hair.

I stop a breath away from her, fighting to keep the distance.

"Hi," I say, though my voice sounds choked.

"Hey. You look nice, like a real fairy tale prince."

"You... God, I have no words."

She scrunches up her nose and glances down. "What's wrong? You don't like my dress. I know it's a bit much, but—"

"I love your dress, Mir. You look stunning."

She looks up, beaming. "Thanks. So, what shall we do?"

The ball is about to start, but I want—*need*—a moment alone with Miranda. I know that news of my return must have spread across Ellnesari already. Not to mention Eriel must have felt my presence as well. I won't be able to linger in Aquila for much longer.

"We have a few more minutes before the ball. Let's go for a walk." I offer her my elbow, hoping she'll take it.

"Okay."

I try not to show my reaction when she hooks her arm with mine, but my entire body tingles at the contact. We walk in silence until we exit through one of the side doors onto a veranda that faces the main garden, which is appropriately named the Lovers' Garden. I don't dare speak, afraid that I'll say something unfortunate. I don't want to take advantage of Miranda again.

We stop at the bottom of the steps and Miranda takes a deep breath in. "The flowers in this place have such a strong scent, it does my head in."

"Does it bother you? We can go back inside."

She shakes her head and smiles at me. "No. It's not too bad now, and the fresh air is nice. What season is it here? Surely not winter."

"Ellnesari weather doesn't behave in seasonal patterns. Here in Aquila, it always feels like springtime."

"Wow, no change ever? As much as I complain about the winter's bite, I think I'd go a little nuts if the weather always remained the same."

"Castiel and I used to travel to Cygnus whenever we missed snow. It's a winterland over there all year around."

Miranda tenses in my arm, and I curse in my head for mentioning my trips to Eriel's homeland.

"That will be your new home soon," she replies quietly.

The notion should make me ecstatic. As a matter of fact, I should be on my way to Cygnus right now, eager to finally be reunited with my fated mate. But I'm dreading it. I opt for silence once more because nothing I can say will change my reality.

We continue down the path toward the middle of the garden. The design hasn't changed since the last time I was here. I hope the old gazebo is still there.

"I want to take you to a special place of mine," I say finally.

"Oh, like the queen took me to her secret garden?"

Alarms sound in my head. Very few of the guests my mother takes to her sanctuary come out alive.

"What happened there, Mir?"

I can't hide the tension in my voice and Miranda notices it.

"Nothing. I'm fine."

"You didn't answer my question. Did my mother make you drink from the well?"

Miranda clenches her jaw. She doesn't answer for a couple of beats, and it takes everything in me to bite my tongue and give her the chance to reply instead of pressuring her into doing so.

"Yes, she did. She said it was a test."

The gazebo looms in the distance, but I halt suddenly and turn Miranda around. "A test for what, Mir?"

Her eyes become rounder, and I can read fear and guilt in them. "I don't know. I guess she wanted to make sure I was worthy of your company." She looks away—a guilty gesture—and points ahead. "Is that your special place?"

Miranda is hiding something from me, but if my mother is forcing her to keep a secret, that means I won't get to know the truth. I know how Queen Maewe operates.

Trying my best to contain my anger, I reply, "Yeah."

She tugs my hand. "Well, let's go then."

I let her steer me toward my childhood hiding place, but my mind is racing at the speed of light, running through endless scenarios and scheme possibilities that could have sprung from my mother's devious mind. More than ever, I must find a way to send Miranda back. She's not safe here.

The gazebo was my miniature fortress of solitude. I didn't know about Superman then, nor had he been created yet when I was a youngster. But it's a fitting name for the gazebo, even if it's not an icy cave in a faraway mountain.

The old construction is rusty in places and covered in unappealing vines and shrubs, which made it an undesirable place for everyone save me. Once Vivienne asked my mother why she didn't tear it down and build something prettier, but she said the gazebo was a reminder that eventually even the prettiest things will rot. I used to come here all the time when I wanted a break from my tutors or the constant chatter from the court.

We race up the steps before Miranda finally lets go of my hand to look around. "This reminds me of the gazebo at the Salem grounds."

"Perhaps when this was built," I say.

She cocks her head, smirking. "I like the building's condemned-chic look."

Warmth spreads through my chest while my heart beats a staccato rhythm. The jagged pain from the bond is also there, but subdued by a much more potent feeling.

Miranda breaks away from our locked gazes and continues to inspect the area. While she's busy staring at the structure, my eyes remain glued to her, following all her movements like a stalker, dying to move into her orbit. Then there's music, and my feet move of their own volition. I pull her into my arms, bringing her flush with my body.

"Dance with me."

I don't wait for a response and lead her to the beat of the waltz playing somewhere inside the palace. The ball has commenced, and I don't care.

"I've never waltzed before. It feels like I'm floating on air," she says.

"I'm a good partner," I reply through a cheeky smile.

Miranda drops her face to the hollow of my neck and sighs loudly. "I wish you were mine."

I stop moving at once, and with my forefinger, I bring her chin up. "I am, Mir. I am yours."

My lips find hers and I forget all the reasons I shouldn't be doing this, or the fact that I just lied to her. I can't be hers when fate has given me to someone else, but tonight I'll pretend I'm free to love whoever I want.

Twenty-Five

MIRANDA

I'm kissing Rikkon again, and it feels amazing, more so than all the previous times. It seems we can't be alone together and keep our hands to ourselves. He tastes like rain and kisses like a summer storm, wild and unpredictable. I let go of all my worries and pour every ounce of my being, of my soul, in that kiss. I want it to last forever.

My hands are locked behind his neck when his go on an exploratory trip down my body. When his fingers graze the underside of my breast, I sigh into his mouth as desire curls around the base of my spine. I step closer to him, trying to imprint myself on him.

The waltz in the background reaches a crescendo, and our tongues begin to move with more urgency, almost in sync with the music. Rikkon cups my breasts over the dress's corset, making me hate the garment I fell in love with not even an hour ago. *Is it crazy that I want it gone?*

Rikkon pushes me against one of the gazebo's columns and abandons my lips to pepper open kisses down my neck. I arch my back, burning for him and his touch. My head is currently stuck in the clouds, light and free.

When Rikkon runs a lazy tongue across my cleavage, I almost die. I'm burning up and all I want is his mouth and hands everywhere on my body. The ache between my legs becomes unbearable. I need relief. As if reading my mind, Rikkon finds the slit in my skirt and his fingers draw a path of heat up my leg until they reach their final destination.

He stops when he realizes I'm not wearing any underwear and leans back, frowning.

"Mir?"

"What?" I stare at him through hooded eyes. "I thought going commando was a custom here in Ellnesari."

"It isn't," he replies in a tight voice, still not moving his hand to where I desperately need it.

"The folks who came to help me didn't provide panties."

Unable to withstand this torture, I help Rikkon out by nudging his hand to my center. No man has ever touched me there before, so I don't know what to expect. The bolt of pleasure that shoots up to my belly button makes me gasp, and my knees go weak. I throw my head back and close my eyes.

"Is this okay, Mir?" Rikkon asks, inches from my mouth.

I open my eyes and thread my fingers through his long strands. He doesn't break eye contact as he swipes a finger over my clit.

"Yes," I hiss.

Grabbing a fistful of his hair, I seal my lips to his again. Rikkon keeps playing with my bundle of nerves, moving his finger back and forth, building the pressure. I'm on the verge of reaching for his pants and freeing his dick when he changes his ministrations. Now his thumb is pressing against my clit while his other fingers find my opening. I tense a little and he notices.

He leans back to ask, "Too far? Should I stop?"

My breathing is coming out in bursts, and I'm sure my face is flushed. I don't know how he can ask me that when it's clear how much I want him to continue.

"If you stop now, I'll hex you."

His lips curl into a crooked grin as he slides a finger inside of me. A gasp escapes my lips.

"How is this, Mir?"

"It's good. Go on, don't stop."

He inserts another finger and pushes all the way in. It hurts a little, but the pleasure is greater. I close my eyes again.

"No, keep them open, Mir. I want to see the fire in your eyes when you shatter."

He pulls his fingers out a little and plunges them in again, back and forth while his thumb does crazy things to my clit. His gaze is filled with desire as he stares at me. Even though there's no denying what's happening to me, I still can't believe Rikkon is finger fucking me in the middle of his mother's gardens. This moment is too surreal and so unlike me.

I climax just as the music hits its highest note. I'd close my eyes but I want to see Rikkon's expression as he watches me break into a million pieces. It's hard to keep my moans quiet, but halfway through the wave of pleasure, he kisses me, muffling the sounds coming out of my mouth. His tongue mingling with mine only heightens my release.

When the tremors finally recede and I'm putty against his body, Rikkon pulls his hand back and then pinches my ass.

"Ouch. What did you do that for?"

He chuckles. "Sorry, I couldn't resist. You're even more beautiful when you come."

Fire burns my face and ears, and I'm glad for the cover of the shadows. Then Rikkon has to lick his fingers as if he were sucking on a lollipop to make me even more embarrassed.

"You taste divine too, Mir."

I swallow the awkwardness. This is all new to me. But I also know I want much more. Ignoring the fact that I am an inexperienced girl, I brush my hand against the front of his pants, finding a veritable bulge there.

"How about you?"

"What about me?" he asks in a tight voice.

Oh God. He's going to make me say it.

"Can I return the favor?"

He smiles from ear to ear while his eyes dance with amusement. "As much as I'm burning for you, Mir, I think we should return inside before my mother sends a search party for us. You're the guest of honor, after all."

No sooner does he say that than I hear hard footsteps on the cobblestone path, fast approaching. Rikkon steps back from me but positions himself to block whoever is coming from seeing me. I hastily fix my dress, hoping there aren't any visible wrinkles.

"There you are. I've been looking all over for you."

I recognize the male voice, so I stick my head out from behind Rikkon's wide back, and there he is, Prince Castiel of Lynx.

"Oh hi, Miranda. I knew I'd find you here too." He beams at me, and I swear, the freckles on his face sparkle like real stars.

"Why were you looking for me? Don't tell me you've become one of my mother's lackeys."

The good humor vanishes from Castiel's face. "Don't insult me, my friend. I'm at the Aquila court as a personal favor to King Ruel."

"Why would my father ask you to stay? To what purpose?"

Castiel glances at me fleetingly, and I wonder if he doesn't want to answer the question because of me.

"Maybe I should return to the palace and let you two catch up." I walk around Rikkon, but he shoots his arm out, blocking my path.

"No, Mir. You shouldn't roam alone. It's not safe."

My spine becomes taut. "I can defend myself."

"Rikkon is right, dear. The palace is crawling with all kinds of individuals tonight, many who wouldn't think twice about kidnapping the queen's guest of honor."

"First of all, I'm not your dear. And second, let them try." I pull a crystal from my skirt's pocket.

"What am I supposed to be looking at?" Castiel squints.

Rikkon drops his eyes to my hand and then back to my face, sporting a frown. "Mir, the magic you can wield from that crystal won't be enough to deter a Nightingale."

I almost tell him that my powers seem to have increased tenfold since I arrived here, but maybe being cocky is not a smart move. Besides, I don't know Castiel. He used to be Rikkon's best friend, but that was many lifetimes ago.

"Okay, fine," I grumble, shoving my crystal into my pocket again.

"Go on, Castiel. You can speak freely in front of Miranda," Rikkon continues.

"Your father asked me to return to continue the work we started."

I sense a shift in Rikkon and with one glance at his expression, I know the news isn't welcome. That makes me even more curious. *What kind of work was he doing before?* It dawns on me then that this Rikkon, the Nightingale prince, is a complete stranger to me, more so than his recovering addict version.

And I'm willing to kill someone to save his life.

There's never been a question whether I would agree to the queen's request and she damn well knew that. I still don't know how I'm going to pull it off though. I'll worry about that later.

"Have you made any progress?" Rikkon asks, bringing me back from my thoughts.

"Some. But let's not talk work now. Tonight, we shall celebrate your return in grand style."

"Yes, we'd better continue this conversation later."

He turns to me, offering me his elbow. "Shall we, milady?"

A small smile has returned to his face, but his eyes remain serious and troubled. As if in response, my heart constricts tightly, but I'm not sure if it's a reaction to the turmoil I see reflected in his gaze, or if it's the anxiety about an uncertain future that makes my chest so damn heavy.

I force a grin to my lips, not wanting him to worry about me. "Of course. I love a good party."

Castiel chuckles and strides ahead of us.

"I'm not sure a Nightingale ball qualifies as a party by your standards, but we'll make the best of it." Rikkon leans over and kisses my cheek, sending the butterflies in my stomach soaring high.

Twenty-Six

Pleasuring Miranda was one of the greatest highs of my existence, but now the mood is sullied by the news Castiel provided. I had misgivings about the project I had been working on before my banishment, and knowing Castiel was asked to continue the research while I was gone doesn't sit well with me. I love the male as if he were my brother, but our work ethics vary greatly. There's nothing he won't do for science; I have lines I won't dare cross.

Hell. I can't go to Cygnus and leave him alone with that experiment. It's my duty to see how far he has progressed and whether or not I ought to shut down the whole thing. My father is the king, but he has no power over me. Only the queen can make me bend to her will.

She'd probably approve if it's proven successful. It would definitely give Aquila and Lynx a huge advantage over the other kingdoms. We're at peace now, all thanks to a common enemy. But the vampires won the war for us over a thousand years ago. It's a miracle the truce still stands.

And if I break the bond with Eriel, that might nudge the Cygnus kingdom to finally declare war against us. Maybe that's why fate made her my mate: not because she's my perfect match, but to avoid the destruction of our world.

Consumed by my disturbing thoughts, I barely notice the walk back to the palace. Miranda is also quiet and I fear that perhaps she thinks my sudden surly disposition has to do with her. I want to make sure she knows that isn't the case. We're approaching the main hallway that leads to the ballroom. I let Castiel go ahead of us, and when the opportunity presents itself, I stop next to a shadowy alcove, pulling Miranda in with me and away from prying eyes.

"What is it?" she asks, startled.

"I want to make sure you're okay."

She blinks a couple of times while a blush spreads through her cheeks. "About what?"

I let out a humorless laugh. "Everything."

"I'm not okay with being dragged to Ellnesari by Selor, but at the same time, I'm glad that I'm with you." She steps closer to me, wrapping her arms around my waist and kissing me on my chin. "And I'm more than okay about our little waltz in the gazebo."

I twist my fingers in the strands of her hair and kiss her hard and fast. Miranda melts into me like she's always belonged in my arms. But the hook of the bond yanks me in the opposite direction, reminding me that I'm powerless to stop what has been put in motion. *Strange how I didn't feel the effects of the bond back in the gazebo.*

I pull back, trying to hide my discomfort from her through a forced smile. "Good. Let's go before the urge to dance strikes us again."

With a giggle, she steps back and fixes her skirt. I have to do some fixing in my pants too. It won't do to show up at the ball sporting a major boner. It's bad enough that anyone who comes near us will be able to smell Miranda's scent all over me.

It wasn't smart in the least to act recklessly tonight. As if my mother singling Miranda out didn't already put a target on her back, I had to mark her as my lover too.

You're an idiot, Rikkon.

"It's best if we keep pretending to be only friends," I tell her. She doesn't reply, so I glance at her. "Mir?"

She looks at me, sporting a tight smile now. "Yes, that's the smart thing to do."

"I hate this," I confess.

"Me too." She breaks eye contact first. "Don't worry, Rik. I'm not a breakable porcelain doll. I'm a samurai."

The line of courtiers who were waiting for their turn to enter the ballroom stop and stare when they notice our approach. I ignore their attention, cutting in front of them and not bothering to wait for the herald to announce our names.

The guests that have already arrived all turn to gawk at us and even with the music in the background, I can hear their gossipy murmurs. *Fuck.* They know about Miranda and me, just like I feared. When I finally reach the royal dais, my mother is smirking in a pleased way. I don't know why she's adamant that I take Miranda as my lover, but I know that it's not out of concern for me. Everything she does is self-serving.

I bow my head slightly. "Your Majesties."

"You look dashing, my son. Nothing like a good scrub and appropriate clothing to reveal your true identity."

"And what is my true identity, Mother?" I drop the title, knowing she hates when I don't follow protocol in public.

My slight doesn't seem to faze her tonight, though. Clearly, my visit to the Lovers' Garden and what transpired there has pleased her greatly.

"You're a prince of the House of Gael, of course. Never forget that." Her reply comes with an edge, a hint of warning.

My father stands suddenly, drawing my mother's attention. "Where are you going?" she asks.

"I'm starving and thirsty. It seems the servants are too afraid to approach you, my dear."

He takes the steps down the dais, and I know that now will be my best chance to talk to him without my mother prying. But there's Miranda, and I don't want to leave her alone.

"You should join your father, Rik, lest he gets lost on the way to the buffet," my mother chimes in. "I'll look after Miranda."

Yeah, like I believe a word that comes out of her mouth. I turn to Miranda, the only feedback that matters.

"You can go. I'll be fine." She waves in a nonchalant way.

She's more than capable of handling dangerous situations in the mortal lands, but here, she's as defenseless as a toddler. But I know my mother won't let anything happen to Miranda, not before she gets whatever it is she desires from her.

"I'll be right back."

I have to jog to catch up with my father, who has walked the wind to reach the buffet on the other side of the room. Only the queen and king are allowed to move in such a way inside the royal palace. Not even I could have done it during an official function. The stupid protocol used to irritate the hell out of me, but now, it gives me a solid reason not to use the powers I don't have.

The courtiers give my father a wide berth, mainly because he has the social skills of a shark during a feeding frenzy. Also, he has no true political power, so there's no reason to kiss his ass in exchange for favors.

"I heard Castiel is still here because you asked him to continue my project," I say straight away. I was never a fan of beating around the bush.

Dad shoves a piece of pie in his mouth, and then washes it down with wine before replying. "I did, and he has made remarkable progress."

I flare my nostrils, responding to the sudden anger that rises up my throat. "Is that so?" I say through clenched teeth.

"You don't sound pleased. Are you jealous that your friend was able to achieve what you couldn't?"

"No, I'm pissed that you continued with my research without my consent."

He gives me a droll look. "And how was I supposed to ask for your consent? You got yourself banished."

There's no point trying to argue with him. In some ways, he's worse than my mother. At least she conveys something akin to emotions. The male in front of me has the emotional range of a rock.

I open my mouth to ask what progress Castiel has made when the power of the bond flares up in my chest, making every muscle in my body turn rigid like a frozen lake. In the next second, the herald announces the arrival of Eriel Fasanor, princess of the Cygnus kingdom. My mate.

MIRANDA

"What did you think of my gardens, Miranda?" the queen asks as soon as Rikkon disappears in the crowd.

My cheeks become warmer again. *Crap.*

"They're lovely." I don't make eye contact and pretend to watch the crowd.

I'd be doing it for real if I wasn't in the company of Queen Maewe. The courtiers dressed in their finest are definitely a sight to behold. The females wear dresses that belong in a haute couture fashion show, each creation more extravagant than the next. One in particular has a live animal draped around her shoulder, a medium-size furry creature that reminds me of an oversized squirrel. But I can't ignore that the most powerful being in this room is standing next to me, no doubt thinking of ways to punish me if I refuse her offer.

"Do you know what that particular garden is called?" she continues.

"No, Rikkon didn't say."

"Lovers' Garden. Appropriate, don't you think?"

Now my face is in flames. She must know what happened in

the gazebo. If there was ever a time to come up with an invisibility spell, now would be it. Or maybe I could create a hole on the floor to swallow me.

"If you say so," I mumble.

She chuckles, a sound that's completely at odds with what she represents.

"You don't need to be embarrassed for succumbing to your deepest desires, child."

"I'm not embarrassed about anything. Can we please change the subject?"

When she doesn't answer, I dare a quick glimpse of her. She's staring straight ahead, her face solemn and hard now.

"You'd better brace yourself, dear," she finally murmurs.

"Why?"

No sooner have I asked the question, than the background music cuts off suddenly and the herald announces the arrival of a new guest. All I have to hear is the word Cygnus to understand the queen's comment. Rikkon's mate is here.

A pain more than sharp pierces my chest, and it feels like a real dagger is doing the damage. I hug my middle, trying to create a shield around me, but nothing can protect me from the agony of this moment. The crowd parts, creating a direct path for the princess to reach the queen. *Shit*. I'm standing right next to her, so it means there's no escaping the room now.

"Did you know she was coming tonight?" I ask in a low tone.

"Yes, naturally."

"Couldn't you have warned me at least?"

"And ruin the surprise?" She tsks disapprovingly. "Don't worry, dear. Despite your rudimentary human appearance, tonight you look almost as pretty as the Cygnus princess."

Rudimentary looks? What the hell.

I have to ball my hands into fists and bite the inside of my cheek to keep the angry retort bottled in. *Who does this bitch think she is?*

The most powerful she-devil in all the land, duh.

I'm raving mad now, so when the princess finally stops a few feet from us and bows to the queen, I couldn't give a rat's ass about her looks. She is stunning, no doubt. Her hair is silver, almost white, and it matches her dress. *Ugh, she had to look like a fucking bride.* She's pale though, almost to the point of looking sickly, a fact that her bony structure emphasizes. *Ha! At least I have my tan and curves, bitch.*

"Your Majesty," she says in a melodic tone.

Sure, Universe, give me more reasons to hate the female.

"Princess Eriel, so glad you could make it to my little soiree with such short notice," the queen replies in the fakest voice. Surely everyone noticed that.

The princess's expression remains neutral until she switches her attention to me. "And who is this peculiar being?"

I narrow my eyes as she gives me an overall glance and wrinkles her too-delicate nose as if she found me revolting.

The queen places a hand on my shoulder and squeezes it lightly. My skin tingles at the touch, a reaction to the magic that just whooshed out of her hands into me. *Hell and damn. What did she do to me now?*

"This is Miranda Leal, my guest of honor."

Eriel's nostrils flare, reminding me of dogs when they catch the scent of their prey. Her eyes narrow, their blue color darkening. "What's that awful smell?"

"I don't know, maybe your bad breath?" I reply before stopping to think.

Her eyes widen in surprise and then her brows furrow in outrage. But all she can do is stare daggers at me. I don't know much about royal protocol, but I'm going out on a limb here in assuming that attacking Queen Maewe's honored guest in front of her would be considered a terrible offense.

It takes a couple of seconds for her to school her expression into one of neutrality again. She seems tense all of a sudden, as if her body were being pulled tight by an invisible cord. I can sense she wants to stretch her neck and look around. She wants to search for Rikkon, but until the queen dismisses her, she must stay rooted to the spot.

I would appreciate watching her discomfort more if I didn't know what's going to happen eventually. Rikkon will find her, and they will run off into the sunset. I'm back to feeling miserable.

The air becomes heavy with tension, but the queen remains silent, perhaps daring Eriel to put her foot in her mouth like I did, or cave and ask where her fated mate is. If he were truly eager for the bond, he'd be by her side by now.

As a matter of fact, where the hell is he?

Twenty-Seven

RIKKON

The bond is calling to me, demanding that I run to Eriel's side, but stubbornly, I plant my feet on the ground and don't move.

"You really aren't happy with what fate bestowed upon you, are you, my son?" my father points out the obvious. "It's pointless to fight it, though. You might as well get it over with. It will be a good thing for you to marry the Cygnus princess. We're not quite ready to start a war with anyone yet."

"Not quite ready? What's that supposed to mean?" I grit out.

It's getting difficult to carry on the conversation and resist the compulsion to find Eriel. My body is beginning to shake from the strain.

"Rikkon, there you are," Castiel appears suddenly, making me suspect he walked the wind. "May I borrow your son for a moment, Your Majesty?"

My father shrugs. "Sure."

Castiel grabs my arm in an iron grip and steers me farther away from where Eriel is. The compulsion to find her turns into a piercing pain in my chest, making me hiss.

"Let me go, Castiel. I need to—"

"I know what you need to do, Rik. But you can't meet your fated mate reeking of another female's pussy."

Shit. He's right. It was bad enough that the courtiers could smell Miranda on me, but if Eriel gets a whiff of that, she's probably going to kill Miranda on the spot.

"Where are you taking me? I don't think I have time for another bath."

"I know that." He drags me to a shadowy spot behind a large column and pulls a glass vial from his breast pocket.

"What the hell is that?"

"I knew when I found you with Miranda in the gazebo that your dear mother was plotting something. Why else would she enchant the flowers to release an aphrodisiac scent?"

"What? I would have been able to notice it."

"Not without your powers. Give me your hands, palms facing up."

I do as he says, but my mind is reeling. My mother wants Eriel to know I was with Miranda earlier. *What the fuck?* Now it makes sense why I couldn't feel the effect of the bond. Those flowers blocked it somehow.

Castiel pours a cold, pungent liquid over my hands, and then he tells me to rub some on my face too. It burns my skin a little, like rubbing alcohol does.

"What is this?"

"A quick potion I put together. It's nothing fancy, it just has a scent strong enough that I hope will overpower the smell of sex."

"Seriously? You're the most talented alchemist in the land and this is the solution you came up with?"

He glowers at me. "I've never had to create a potion that masked the vestiges of postcoital bliss. Nobody cares about infidelity, unless you're bonded, but then again, bonded individuals don't sniff around someone else's bushes."

"Maybe it's because this fucking bond is not really meant to be."

Castiel's shrewd eyes widen a fraction as if the idea had never occurred to him. "Or maybe it has been tampered with for far too long and it has lost its power."

I double over when the pain in my chest intensifies. *Lost its power, my ass.*

"Fuck, are you all right?" Castiel asks.

I give him my most potent death glare. "Does it look like I'm all right?"

"No, you look like shit. Go on to your mate now. I did my best to help you. Let's hope Eriel will be so pleased to finally see you face-to-face that she won't notice Miranda's scent all over you."

I'm in so much pain now that I can't even tell him to go to hell. So I flip him off and stride back into the busy ballroom. As I move closer to Eriel, the discomfort lessens, but when I see her standing only a few feet away from Miranda, a new kind of pain spreads through my chest. It's despair. I'm about to break her heart and there's nothing I can do to stop it.

The princess turns when she senses my approach. Her face splits into a wide smile and her eyes shine with emotion. I know she wants to come running to me, but she can't move until the queen dismisses her. Knowing my mother, she's enjoying torturing Eriel.

Like a coward, I don't let my eyes stray to Miranda. I don't want to see the hurt in her expression. If I'm hating this moment that's beyond my control, this can't be easy for her. But she must stand next to my mother. She's the guest of honor after all.

When I finally stop in front of Eriel, the compulsion to pull her into my arms and kiss her is almost overwhelming. The only reason I don't succumb to the power of the bond is the presence of my fierce samurai girl, standing there and watching every move I make.

I wish I could speak to her mind to mind and tell her I don't want to be doing this, but the gift to communicate telepathically wasn't an ability I ever possessed.

"Eriel, you look well." I force the words out.

"You too, my prince."

I loathe the way she stares at me as if I'm her kingdom come and how a part of me is relishing her devotion.

"Oh, for crying out loud, just get on with it already." My mother makes a flourishing gesture with her hand.

I break eye contact with Eriel for a fleeting moment to glare at my mother, but then my mate throws herself at me and before I can stop her, she plants her lips on mine. Then it's game over—I can't fight the bond's compulsion anymore. My body takes control and I kiss her back passionately, but all the while, a part of me is dying.

I'm not sure how long the kiss lasts, only that Eriel ends it abruptly, stepping back. She's staring at me in surprise, and then, in a split second, something changes. A storm of bad emotions gathers in her blue eyes, turning them darker, almost black.

Fuck. Castiel's plan didn't work.

"I can't believe this," she hisses. "She's the reason you didn't come for me right away?"

"Eriel, my love. Calm down. It's not what you think."

My love? What the hell am I saying? I don't love her. This fucking bond is messing with my head.

"I can smell her on you," she spits back and whirls around to face Miranda. "You wretched creature."

She raises her arm, and I see it before it happens, the Cygnus power to freeze anything forever shoots from her outstretched hand in Miranda's direction. It's irreversible. In the blink of an eye, I move. I walk the wind and push Miranda out of Eriel's blow. My powers have returned and suddenly my mother's words click into place. Protecting Miranda from my mate's fury was the trigger to unlock them.

"What the hell!" Miranda shouts.

Furious, Eriel prepares to strike again, but my mother snaps her fingers and binds the princess, ceasing her movements with vises made out of a golden lasso.

"Enough, my dear. You're causing a scene," the queen says coolly.

"Rikkon is my mate. She dared to interfere."

"She's the reason your mate is back. You should be kissing the ground beneath her feet. Her blood brought him to us. Surely you can forgive the carnal part of the spell."

She glances at my mother, and then at me, confused. "Are you saying this was a maidenhead ritual?"

Curse my mother to hell. What is she doing lying to Eriel like that? But if I don't follow along with whatever she's planning, then Miranda will pay the ultimate price. Eriel will unleash her wrath on her the moment we turn our backs.

"Yes, that's exactly it." Miranda is the one who answers. Her chin is held high, and in her gaze I find nothing but courage and defiance. "I laid with your *mate*"—she makes a face of disgust—"solely for magical purposes. You don't have to worry, he's all yours." She turns to my mother. "Your Majesty, may I ask permission to retire? It seems the journey tired me more than I imagined."

"Pity, but I won't keep you hostage when you've done so much for my family already. You may leave."

No, I can't let her leave alone. But if I offer to escort her instead of staying with my mate, then all these lies were for nothing.

"I'll escort the guest of honor to her quarters," Castiel offers, saving me from making another mistake.

I catch his gaze, trying to convey to him how thankful I am. There's no indication from him he understood my silent message, but he's a master of discretion.

Miranda beams at him, giving my friend the same smile that she bestowed upon me not too long ago. My vision tinges in crimson as the cold dagger of jealousy pierces my chest. When she accepts his elbow, I want to push him off and separate them. I do nothing because even if acting on my jealousy posed no risk to Miranda, the bond has my body locked tight. My free will is gone.

Twenty-Eight

MIRANDA

Of all the trials I've gone through in this godforsaken place, watching Rikkon make out with his mate was the hardest and the most agonizing ordeal of all. It took everything in me to remain stoic, to not show how the sight was destroying my soul and obliterating my heart.

And then he called her his love. Talk about adding insult to injury.

I should have known. I've seen how crazy Saxon and Aurora acted around each other. Sure, Rikkon has feelings for me, but it doesn't compare to his connection to Princess fucking Eriel. I hate her so damn much I could choke on the feeling.

I barely notice all the faces that are staring at me while I do my walk of shame. Thanks to Queen Maewe's ridiculous lie, now everyone thinks I lost my virginity to Rikkon in order to bring his sorry ass back to his fated mate. The worst of all is that if Castiel hadn't interrupted us, it could have happened in that gazebo.

God, I'm such a fool.

As soon as we exit the ballroom, Castiel opens his piehole. "It was great what you did back there."

"What exactly did I do?" I ask with a bite.

"You went along with Queen Maewe's story."

I snort. "Don't try to praise me for lying. I only did it to save my ass."

"You were quick on your feet. You didn't cower in the presence of the Cygnus princess. That was impressive."

"Yeah, anger is a great boost of courage."

Castiel laughs softly. "You're really not used to receiving compliments, are you?"

"I can't say that's something that happens to me very often."

Rikkon was the only one who showered me with them since our first meeting, but now all those moments are soiled.

Castiel and I don't speak for a moment. I'm still stewing in my disappointment over Rikkon, but then I feel the need to speak up. "Thank you for offering to be my escort. To be honest, I don't think I'd be able to find my way back to my apartment."

"It's not a problem. Between you and me, I hate social functions. I'd much rather spend all my time in the lab."

"What do you do exactly?"

I try to keep Rikkon out of the conversation, but my question to his friend stems from my curiosity about his life prior to banishment. I know Rikkon and Castiel worked together.

"I'm an alchemist, among other things."

Okay, that doesn't really satisfy my curiosity.

"Is that what Rikkon is as well?"

"I don't think I could pigeonhole Rikkon into one category. He excels in so many things, alchemy, engineering. Honestly, the male is a genius."

My heart constricts painfully in my chest, remembering how low Rikkon had fallen when he crossed into the human realm. Despite his betrayal, I can't help but feel heartbroken about what happened to him.

"Don't hate him for what the bond is forcing him to do. He tried to resist going to her, but the compulsion was just too strong."

"I don't hate him," I say too quickly.

"You're angry with him though."

I ignore his remark, knowing that anything I tell Castiel he'll report to Rikkon. Besides, it's pretty obvious that I'm angry, considering what I had been doing prior to the ball with his friend.

I recognize the hallway we're in now and relief washes over me. My apartment's door is only a few steps away. I'm glad that this trip is coming to an end. I don't really feel like discussing my relationship issues with Castiel, a male I know nothing about.

I put my hand on the magical doorknob that has been enchanted to only work for me—at least according to Queen Maewe who brought me here herself earlier. My palm tingles as the magic wraps around my hand and wrist. The sensation only lasts a few seconds and then, there's the distinct click of a lock releasing.

"This is me," I tell Castiel. "Thanks for keeping me safe."

"My pleasure. One more thing before you go. Whatever it is that the queen wants you to do, think very carefully before you agree to it."

Every muscle in my body becomes rigid. Does Castiel suspect the queen asked me to kill the Cygnus princess? Or is he just pretending to be concerned to gain intel?

"I have no idea what you're talking about. The queen is only happy that I brought Rikkon back."

"A son who she banished herself." He raises an eyebrow, curling his lips into a knowing grin.

"Whatever, dude. Don't try to involve me in court politics. I'm not interested. All I want is to go back home."

He takes a step back, raising both hands, palms facing me. "I'm not trying to get you into trouble. Rikkon is my best friend, and he cares about you. It's my duty to help you when he can't."

"Do you have a one-way ticket to the mortal lands?"

"Unfortunately, no. I'll leave you in peace, you must be weary from your travels. Take care, Miranda."

He waits until I enter my apartment to walk away. I lock the door, but I don't move from my spot until I no longer can hear the sound of his footsteps rapping on the hardwood floor. The soft glow of lights powered by magic gives the spacious living room a cozy atmosphere that unfortunately does nothing to make me feel better.

Finally alone, the weight of my new reality sits heavily on my shoulders. Anxiety, insecurity, and fear take hold of me, wrapping my heart in barbed wire. I'm trapped in a foreign world where the natives think I'm no better than a bug, I'm in love with someone bound to another female, and the queen wants me to become a murderer.

A sob escapes my lips, but I swallow anything else that may follow. I will not crumble and become a mess, crying my eyes out. I'm training to become a samurai, for crying out loud, one of the toughest warriors in the history of mankind.

Instead of succumbing to despair, I take a deep breath and make a beeline to my bedroom where I left my bag with my only possessions. My grimoire, a change of clothing, a few river stones and crystals, and a pen. I wish I still had my phone so I could at least look at pictures of my old life. I'm not sure if I will ever go back.

No, Miranda. You will return home.

The magical lights turn on automatically when I step foot in the room, revealing a figure clad in black lying on my bed.

I scream, jumping out of my skin, and then I run for the desk where I left my bag.

"Relax, little witch. It's just me," Selor pipes up.

Yeah, like that's comforting. I pull a river stone out of my bag and whirl around, ready to do… nothing. I can't do anything that will stop the Nightingale from harming me if that's what he wishes to do.

"What are you doing in my bedroom?" I ask.

He throws his long legs over the side of the bed and sits up. "I came to give you something."

"If that something is what you have between your legs, I'll pass."

He twists his face into a grimace. "Ew. Do you think I came here to seduce you?"

Ew? Seriously? What's up with these assholes trying to make me feel like shit?

"You were in my bed. What was I supposed to think?"

"You took too long, and I decided to take a nap. Don't look so offended, little witch. It's not that I find you repugnant. You just don't have the right... *equipment*."

"Oh? Ooooh... You like guys."

"I prefer Nightingale males, but I learned to appreciate humans too." He laughs with derision, shaking his head. "I had to or go celibate for centuries."

"You didn't come here to share your sad past with me. What do you want?"

Selor stands, reminding me of his giant size. *Crap.* I preferred when he was sitting.

"You should be nicer to me. I came bearing a gift."

A short sheathed sword appears on his hand. It even has a red bow on it.

"Is that for me?" I arch my eyebrows.

"No, it's for the other goblin standing next to you."

Like an idiot, I actually look to my side. Then I shake my head, trying to kick-start my brain into actually working.

"Ha ha. You're hilarious. You can't blame me for asking," I say. "We don't have a good history. You tried to kill me, and you kidnapped me."

He squints. "You stabbed me, witch. Be glad that I was under strict orders to not harm you."

"Well, you kept my dagger. It was my favorite," I retort, unable to stop goading the warrior.

"Sure. That piece-of-shit blade turned into dust simply by coming into contact with my blood."

Hell. That's new and important information.

"Does that happen all the time? I mean, do our weapons always crumble like that when used against you?"

Selor glances at the ceiling, muttering a string of curses.

"Why must you take everything I say literally? No, little witch. I destroyed that dagger with my thoughts. Now will you just shut up and accept your birthday gift already?" He extends the sword toward me.

I grab the offering quickly because having a weapon in this place is a necessity. I couldn't care less about the dagger Selor destroyed. The moment his gift touches my hand, I sense the power coming from it.

"Thanks. But my birthday is not for another two weeks."

"You're wrong again. Today is your birthday. Didn't Prince Rikkon tell you?"

"What? That's impossible."

Selor rubs his chin. "He didn't tell you. He probably didn't realize it then. Travel through the Taluah Mirror doesn't happen instantly, even though it might appear so to humans. Two weeks have already passed in the mortal lands."

"Son of a bitch. Are you saying that for all my loved ones I've been missing for two weeks?" My voice rises to a shrill.

"Yeah." He shrugs.

"Does that mean that time also moves differently here?"

"Probably."

"How differently? If I return a week from now, will I find out that centuries have passed?"

"I don't know, little witch. You should ask Prince Rikkon that. Why are you concerning yourself with such an unimportant detail? It's unlikely you will ever return to the mortal lands."

"I wouldn't count on that," I grit out.

Selor lifts his shoulders and snorts in derision. "Don't care either way. Go on, take a peek at your gift."

I unsheathe the sword slowly and then switch it from hand to hand, testing its weight. It feels like an extension of my arm. Looking closely, I notice symbols etched on the blade.

"What are these?" I run my finger over them, and somehow end up nicking the tip on the sharp edge.

The little blood disappears into the metal, and a second later, the sword glows from within, and the magic I felt from the object earlier increases by tenfold. "What the hell?"

"Ah, it sings to you. That's a relief."

"What do you mean it sings to me?"

"What you have in your hands is a starfire sword, little witch. Only the greatest warriors in our nation receive the honor of carrying one of those. The queen felt you deserved it thanks to your services to the crown."

"Does it become invisible as well?" I look at the weapon, perplexed.

"Yes, but you have to learn how to wield the sword first before you can make it vanish from prying eyes."

"Does that involve weeks of training with you?" I dread the thought.

He shakes his head. "No one can teach you how to master a starfire sword. You'll have to learn on your own. But I'd continue reading Tom Mularkey's notebook. You might find something there worthwhile."

Unlikely. I've read the whole thing already and there isn't an instruction manual for this magical weapon.

"Great. Well, it still works like a regular sword, right?" I slash the air a couple of times.

"Naturally." Selor yawns, stretching his arms over his head. "See you later, little witch."

He strides toward the bedroom door.

"What? You can't poof out of here?"

He looks over his shoulder. "There are wards protecting your quarters. I can't walk the wind."

"How did you get in then?"

"I have the magical touch." He winks at me before he walks out.

Twenty-Nine

Even with Miranda gone, I fight against the bond as I twirl Eriel around in the ballroom to the beat of the music while the courtiers stare and gossip. It's hard to resist the pull, the need to consummate the bond, especially with the princess pressed against my body.

"I can't believe you're finally here, my love. These centuries apart have been torture. They almost drove me insane," she says.

"I know." My reply comes clipped, pained.

"Well, it's over now. We'll never be apart again." She leans against my chest, resting her cheek against it.

The smell of fresh snow in the forest and pine trees reaches my nose. Eriel's scent should be driving me wild with need, but all I can remember is how sweet Miranda smelled and tasted when I ran my tongue across her cleavage. My cock becomes hard, straining against my pants.

Eriel pulls back and glances at me with a knowing smile. *Shit.* She can feel my erection, pushing against her belly. I know what she wants, I can read the desire and yearning in her eyes. If she only knew she isn't the one making me burn. My heart is rebelling; it won't let me surrender completely to the bond magic that rips me apart instead of making me whole. If I sleep with Eriel, I'll be betraying Miranda.

How in the world am I going to refuse my fated mate though? Bonded males and females are like animals in heat. By all rights, I shouldn't be in this ballroom dancing with her. I should have already dragged her out of here and taken her to my quarters.

I'm stalling in order to think of a solution. Swirling us around in the grand ballroom, I break eye contact with Eriel to search for my mother. If there's anyone who can create a diversion to prevent the worst from happening, she's the one. But she made herself scarce soon after Castiel escorted Miranda out.

"What's the matter, my love?" Eriel asks, drawing my attention back to her.

"My apologies. I've still not adjusted to being back in Ellnesari."

Her eyebrows furrow. "I can't imagine what it must have been like for you in the mortal lands. And Vryenn. Poor thing."

Eriel's poorly executed attempt to show concern for my sister grates on my nerves. She didn't even try to make her comment sound believable.

"Vryenn is well now. She doesn't miss Ellnesari."

A spark of interest appears in her eyes. "Oh, so she's with her vampire lover at last?"

"Yes."

"I'm proud that you volunteered to join Vryenn in her banishment. It tells me you're a male of honor. But I thought you would find a way back to me sooner."

"I'm sorry, Eriel. I tried," I lie.

I didn't really try, not even when the pain of the bond denied had me crippled in bed for months. I couldn't leave Vivi behind. So all my efforts were half-assed. It wouldn't have mattered anyway, my mother would only allow me back when the time was right, and that's why I'm here now.

"I still don't understand how you managed to return," Eriel continues.

"My mother deemed me punished enough."

Her eyes darken again, matching her scowl. "Didn't she stop to consider she was also punishing me?"

"I don't think she cared."

She tenses in my arms. Perhaps I shouldn't have answered so bluntly. I was never one to beat around the bush, and my directness was sometimes perceived as arrogance and cruelty. Not a terrible reputation to have in any court. But antagonizing Eriel won't work in my favor. I need to find a way to break the bond without starting a war.

Yeah, right. Wishful thinking, Rikkon.

"My father wanted to wage war on Aquila because of it. It took great effort on my part to convince him to wait for your return."

I stiffen, knowing that Eriel isn't lying. Is that my mother's endgame? To start a war with the Cygnus kingdom. But to what purpose?

Eriel touches the frown in my forehead with the tips of her fingers. "You don't need to worry, my love. His sour disposition toward Aquila will cease the moment we put a grandson in his arms."

My steps falter, and my airways constrict to the point it's hard to breathe. I see the vision Eriel just painted as clearly as day in my mind. Me taking our newborn son from her tired arms, and then striding into the Cygnus throne room with the squealing baby in order to present the new heir to the crown.

"Rikkon? Are you well?" Eriel's voice sounds far away.

It takes me a moment to drown out the noise of my pulse beating in my ears. *A vision, I just had a vision.* It didn't come preceded by a blinding pain. It's the first time I've had one while in possession of my powers. No pain, but it made me sick to my stomach. Every single one of the visions I had in the human world came to pass. I have no reason to believe it won't be the case now.

This means I'll fail to break the bond. I'll fail Miranda.

Bile pools in my mouth, but I force it down. I can't show weakness in front of Eriel or anyone else here in Ellnesari.

When I believe I can keep the contents of my stomach where they belong, I reply, "Yes. Of course. I could use refreshments though. Let's get a drink."

Automatically, I offer her my elbow, but she opts for lacing her fingers with mine—a much more intimate gesture. I see the child again—*my* child with her—and the nausea returns. My reaction doesn't bode well for our future. I should be over the moon with excitement. Instead, all I want to do is run outside and scream into the wind.

"You know, the guest quarters have plenty of liquor," Eriel says when we stop next to the long table of refreshments.

I freeze for a second. After seeing what I saw, there's no point in fighting the inevitable. Yet, a part of me refuses to give up on Miranda, on the future we could have together. I want her to be the mother of my children, and that's one of my absolute certainties.

Eriel is staring at me, waiting for an answer, and the longer I remain silent, the harder it will be to pretend I'm happy about our union.

The sudden flicker of lights in the ballroom saves me from revealing the truth to her. The courtiers murmur in surprise, with good reason. Something powerful is disturbing the magic that controls them. I'm on high alert now as I scan the room, looking for trouble.

"What's going on, Rikkon?"

"I'm not sure."

A loud boom at the entrance draws screams from the crowd, and a second later, darkness descends in the room. It takes only a few seconds for my vision to adjust to the gloom, in time to watch all the panicked guests trying to find a way out. Shadows alone wouldn't cause that. Something else is driving fear into their hearts.

Eriel gasps, and then she clutches my arm. "No. They were supposed to be gone forever."

I keep searching for the source of her fear, finding nothing out of the ordinary. "What do you see?"

"Not see, *feel*. The shadowbeasts. They've returned."

The hairs on the back of my neck stand on end. I sense the vile monsters then. They're invisible to us, but we always knew when they were near and ready to strike.

Eriel lets out a piercing shriek as she sends icy blasts aleatorily, not caring who she hits. One of them finds a mark, a guest who was running for the exit. She doesn't stop. Fear is controlling her actions.

I grab her wrist, impeding her from blasting another unfortunate soul. "Quit it. You'll freeze the entire party."

She pulls her arm free from my grasp. "I don't care. At least I'm doing something. Where's your sword?"

Fuck. My starfire sword. I left it in my room since it didn't sing to me because I didn't have my powers. I couldn't keep it hidden. Then another worry consumes my thoughts. *Miranda*. She's alone. I have to get her out of here.

"Come on. We can't stay here!" I yell at Eriel to be heard through the noise.

She nods, but before we can break into a run, I'm shoved to the side and crash against the refreshment table. Eriel screams again, and a second later, the freezing cold of winter washes over me. She managed to freeze a shadowbeast this time. I jump back onto my feet and join her side in the blink of an eye, ready to drag her out of here before another monster finds us.

The lights return then, revealing a grotesque scene of mangled bodies, torn gowns, and blood. The courtiers who survived the attack are huddled together in clusters. They might not be as powerful as royals, but they're not commoners, damn it. Maybe the long period of peace made them soft.

Eriel is looking at the creature she froze, frowning. The fear is gone from her scent. Now she's just curious. I'm about to inspect the monster myself when I catch sight of Miranda across the room holding a starfire sword. Her dress is torn at the bottom, and she has blood on her face. I don't stop to think about the consequences. I walk the wind and then crush her into my arms.

Thirty

MIRANDA

I think I must have spent five minutes staring at the starfire sword in my lap, trying to process that today is actually my birthday. I'm eighteen and I didn't even know. My eyes prickle, burning with the tears that are ready to spill.

I had plans for my birthday. Nothing grand. I was going to spend the day with my friends from high school—no supes—maybe even go to Boston and play tourist in the big city. No magic or vampires involved. I just wanted a day where I could pretend to be a carefree teenager for a change, not the second daughter of a powerful witch.

Instead, I'm in a foreign—albeit luxurious—room, alone and heartbroken. And the only person who actually came to wish me happy birthday was a bipolar warrior who I'm sure wishes me dead fifty percent of the time.

A tear rolls down my cheek and drops on the sword's sheath. The blade glows from within for a split second.

"What the hell."

I draw the sword and stand up. The metal is back to its dull gray color, and no matter how many times I pierce and slash the air, it doesn't glow again.

"So, you only want my blood and tears, huh?"

I pause, expecting the damn sword to reply. I must be losing my mind.

"Well, you're in luck. Tears are the only thing I'm doling out today."

I move to sheathe the sword once more when the lights in the room begin to flicker. *Okay, that's not a good sign.*

I keep the sword in my hand and at the ready while I move closer to my bag to retrieve the last energized crystal I had in there. I shove it in my pocket with the other stone I put in there earlier. It feels more powerful now, as if it received a boost. Maybe it did when Queen Maewe touched me.

No time to worry about it. I'm glad that I have the sword in my arsenal as well.

I get chills suddenly, as if the window in my room had opened to let the winter air in. But Rikkon told me Aquila is forever in spring. Also, my window remains shut.

No, this isn't a natural occurrence. This bone-deep cold is caused by magic, ancient and wicked. I spread my legs, preparing my stance for an attack. It doesn't come. Instead, a distant blast reverberates through the walls and shakes the floor. It sounded like a bomb went off somewhere in the castle.

Oh my god. The ballroom. Rikkon.

The lights go out completely, sending me into action. I run out of my bedroom, not pausing to check if any danger lurks in my apartment. There's no need to be cautious here. This attack wasn't aimed at me. If someone wanted me dead, they'd have blown up my quarters. I do, however, open the door to the hallway slowly. My eyes take a while to adjust, but I'm not picking up the presence of anyone or anything. The enemy is not here yet.

I finally head out, going in the direction of the ballroom. I want to rush to Rikkon, but my samurai training kicks in. I find the steely calmness of a warrior in the roaring of my heart. Adrenaline surges through my veins freely, making my senses extra sharp.

The sound of someone running puts me on high alert. I raise

the sword, ready to strike. My heart is thundering in my chest, and my hands are sweaty around the hilt of the sword. I curl my fingers tighter, not wanting to lose my grip.

I can hear the panting of whatever is coming. The sound is ragged and almost beastly. *Shit.* My arms tense, ready for the swing, when I sense a new presence behind me. Steely arms wrap around my body, locking me in place.

"Let go." I struggle.

"Shh. It's me. Castiel," he whispers in my ear.

I relax, but only a fraction. The creature I was about to cut in two rushes past us.

"Run, you fools. They're back." His voice sounds distorted, but he's definitely not a beast like I believed at first.

Castiel releases me, and I ask, "What was wrong with his voice?"

"He partially morphed into his beast form. Some Nightingales can do that."

"I almost killed him."

"I know."

"What was he talking about? Who is back?"

"No time to explain. Let's go."

He reaches for my arm in the darkness, curling his fingers around me firmly. Before I can pull free from his hold, we're moving so fast, I can't feel my body. The trip only lasts the blink of an eye. When the world returns to a normal pace, I'm disoriented and a little nauseated.

"What the hell was that?" I shout-whisper.

"Walking the wind. You'll get used to it."

We're still plunged in darkness, but I can make out the outline of the wall next to me. I brace my hand against it, trying to recover from the trip. Besides the lack of light, we still have to contend with the thick smoke that has taken over this area. But I know we're near the ballroom's entrance, or what is left of it. It's impossible not to hear the screams coming from inside, or not to feel the malignant presence of whatever is responsible for this.

"Are they trapped?" I ask.

As if in answer, a huge portion of the wall crumbles forward, falling over the mountain of rubble that was blocking the ballroom's exit and creating a hole. Guests begin to crawl out and even in the gloom, I can see their desperation to escape.

A series of shrieks coming from the far end of the hallway sends the courtiers fleeing the ballroom into renewed panic. I retrieve one of the crystals from my pocket—the one that's supercharged—with the intention of using a levitation spell to move the rocks blocking their way.

"Miranda, watch out!" Castiel warns.

I'm jolted into action and in my hurry to grab the sword with both hands, I drop the crystal. There's no time to mourn its loss. A monster with red eyes and an oversized mouth is upon me, and I'm lucky to have enough time to chop his grotesque head off.

More crimson eyes appear in the darkness. I change my stance, shifting back a little to be near Castiel, but he's no longer by my side. I hear grunts and hisses nearby, which means he's busy fighting a monster too.

"You're on your own, Miranda," I say under my breath.

It works like a mantra to keep me focused on the task at hand, and not the fear that's quickly spreading through my veins like icy fire, threatening to freeze me in place.

My sword hums in my hands. It's singing to me. I feel the connection between the weapon and myself take place. It also becomes much lighter and easy to use. I'm not surprised when it glows in the next second, revealing the atrocity that's coming my way. Tall and gangly creatures with gray skin, red eyes, and razor-sharp teeth are running down the hallway, using their long arms as extra legs. The sight is horrifying and it fills me with so much dread, it almost paralyzes me.

If they all come for me, I'm dead meat. Luckily, only one breaks from the group and veers in my direction. I brace for it, and when it leaps with its distorted jaw extended, revealing jagged teeth that could shred me in seconds, I say, "Not today, Satan."

I swing my glowing starfire sword hard, cutting through the monster's long neck as if it were made out of butter. I try to step out of the way, but its claw gets me on my forehead, slicing it open. Blood immediately pours from the cut, dripping into my eyes.

It's a distraction I don't need. It leaves me vulnerable for the second creature coming from my left. I don't have time to raise my sword before it body-slams me into the ground. The impact sends the sword flying out of my hand. I'm now pinned beneath the monster's weight, easy prey.

I close my eyes, refusing to allow my last memory to be of its teeth coming for me. Seconds pass, and I'm still alive and in one piece. I sense the monster's putrid breath on my skin though. It has come closer and it's now... sniffing me? *What the hell? Is it trying to decide if I'm a good meal?*

Suddenly, it jumps off me and that's when I dare to open my eyes again. The monster is gone. It spared me, but why?

"Miranda, are you okay?" Castiel appears in front of me, extending a hand.

I let him help me up, and then I search for my sword. "Yeah, and you?"

"Just a scratch. We need to get inside. The shadowbeasts are in there."

Now that I'm no longer at the mercy of the foul creature, I can hear the screams coming from inside.

"I need to find my sword."

As if answering to my call, it glows, revealing its location. I run for it, and then use its light to search for the crystal I lost.

"What are you doing? Let's go," Castiel urges.

Fuck. I'll have to make do with what I've got. I turn in time to see Castiel's shadowy form disappear through the opening in the debris. I follow him, hoping I'm not too late and Rikkon is still alive.

No sooner do I reach the other side, than I smell all the blood spilled and feel the fear hanging over our heads like a dark cloud.

It's pitch dark inside, and if it weren't for my starfire sword, I'd be walking blind.

Suddenly, the lights return, revealing the brutal carnage in front of me. Several bodies—and body parts—are spread throughout the room. The first image that catches my attention is of the female wearing the live animal on her dress. Her throat and torso have been torn open, and now, her animal accessory is eating her spilled guts. Bile rises up my throat, but I clamp my jaw hard and look away.

I need to find Rikkon. With my heart stuck in my throat, I search for him. It doesn't take long to locate him across the room, standing next to his precious mate. His eyes find mine, and then he vanishes for a split second, reappearing in front of me to crush me in his arms.

Thirty-One

Miranda doesn't hug me back. She remains stiff in my arms, and I wonder if she's hurt in other parts of her body that aren't visible. I ease off from the embrace and search her face for any signs of discomfort.

"What are you doing?" she whisper-shouts. "Your fated mate is watching."

"I don't care."

She pushes me off her, and not expecting it, I stagger back.

"Well, I do care."

"Miranda is right. You can't announce to the entire world that you have feelings for her," Castiel, who was standing next to her the entire time, chimes in.

His rebuke irritates me, but it also serves to clear my mind. Seeing Miranda covered in blood triggered a deep-rooted need in me to make sure she was okay, but it also made me careless. All I did now was put her life in danger again.

I sense Eriel's approach and do my best to school my emotions. Mercifully, she chooses to pretend I didn't zap across the room to hug another female.

"What happened to you?" she asks Miranda.

"I bumped into a couple of shadowbeasts."

"And you survived?" Eriel arches her eyebrows.

"Why are you surprised?" Castiel butts in. "Human warriors were responsible for ending the war with those savages."

"Yes, male warriors. I didn't think they allowed females to train with them." Eriel is squinting at Miranda, scrutinizing her.

"They didn't before. Times have changed," Miranda replies, not showing an ounce of emotion in her hazel eyes. "What are those shadowbeasts, and how did they get into the palace? It's heavily warded against intrusion."

"That's something I'd like to know as well," I say, staring meaningfully at Castiel.

He swallows hard, but he doesn't break eye contact. Yet, his pupils have dilated a fraction, telling me that he has an idea of how our enemies from the past came back from the dead and launched an assault in the heart of the Aquila court.

"I sensed when the inner wards broke and went to check on Miranda first," he tells me, eliciting a pang of jealousy in my chest.

I didn't notice anything amiss until the attack started. Also, I can't tell if he said that to insinuate he's interested in Miranda romantically only to get Eriel off our backs or if he's truly captivated by her. Either way, I'm seeing everything through a crimson haze. My powers ignite in the pit of my stomach and spread through the rest of my body like the wind itself. I ball my hands into fists to avoid accidentally turning my friend into ashes.

"How did you get that cut, Mir... er... Miranda?" I ask.

She touches the wound and checks her fingertips for blood. "I wasn't quick enough to move out of the way after I cut off the head of one. Its claw grazed my forehead."

"I managed to get one too. Turned it into a frozen statue." Eriel points across the room.

It reminds me I never inspected the beast. I start toward it, but it explodes suddenly, shattering into a thousand pieces. Nearby, I spot my father, his stare locked on the mountain of ice. Why would he destroy that frozen shadowbeast?

"Oh, now the king decides to help," Eriel snorts. "Where were he and the queen when the attack started?"

"Who do you think got rid of the rest of the shadowbeasts, my dear?" my mother replies, now standing not too far from us.

Her face is a mask of aloof politeness, but her blue eyes burn with intensity. She's not amused by Eriel's comment or by what happened here. If the shadowbeasts have returned, then it means we need the vampires back. No, she can't be happy about this new development when she went to great lengths to cut them off from Ellnesari and our magic.

"The shadowbeasts were supposed to be extinct. That was your biggest argument to dismiss the vampires," Eriel reminds her.

My mother's nostrils flare. "Don't test me, Eriel. You might be my son's fated mate, but you're only a princess of Cygnus. You do not want to get on my bad side."

She releases the leash she keeps on her powers, showcasing to Eriel and everyone else in the room why she's the most powerful queen in Ellnesari. Eriel's face pales even more than usual, and I detect a hint of fear in her scent. She shifts closer to me, and automatically I curl my arm around her waist. The bond at work. *Son of a bitch.* I didn't make the conscious decision to do it, but now my conscience is screaming at me.

I chance a glance at Miranda, catching her staring at my hand resting on Eriel's hip. She lifts her eyes to mine, and the sorrow I see there breaks me. But the damage is done, and if suddenly I push Eriel off me, I'd only be feeding the suspicions she must already have about Miranda and me.

"My apologies, Your Majesty. I'm distraught by these awful events," Eriel replies, then turns to me. "I think I'd like to return to my quarters now, my love, if it's safe."

"I said they're gone," my mother cuts in. "Castiel can escort you to your quarters, I need a word with my son."

Eriel stiffens next to me, and I can sense her powers gathering. She won't attack my mother. One, it wouldn't work. My mother's shields are tight; nothing can break them, not even the claws or teeth of the shadowbeasts.

The bond urges me to disregard my mother's orders, but I fight that compulsion, glad that she gave me the opportunity to escape Eriel's clutches for one more night. I turn Eriel around and kiss her forehead.

"I'll see you tomorrow." I almost let "my love" slip out but catch myself in time.

My face reveals nothing yet I'm smiling in my head. Every time that I go against the bond, it gives me hope I can break it.

You've seen the future, Rikkon. There's no hope.

I shove the pesky thought to a dark corner in my mind. When I ran to Miranda after noticing she was hurt, the bond didn't yank me back or cause me pain. That has to mean something.

"What about me, Your Majesty? Can I return to my quarters?" Miranda asks in a small voice.

Her tone usually has a spark, but it's flat now, almost as if she's given up on everything.

"No, child. You're coming with me as well."

MIRANDA

I sense the princess of Cygnus staring daggers at me. I ignore it. If she thinks I'm happy about being asked to attend a meeting with the queen and Rikkon, she's mistaken. Right now, I'd trade places with her in a heartbeat. The rush from the adrenaline has left my system, leaving me bone-tired and miserable. But I follow the queen quietly, even if my feet drag.

Rikkon walks by my side, and every few seconds, I sense his cursory glances. I ignore those too. I came back for him, but now that the danger has passed, I remember what date it is and my predicament, so all the joy I would have felt when Rikkon left his fated mate to rush to me is crushed under the gloom that has taken over my heart.

We don't go to the queen's private gardens this time. Instead, she leads us to a meeting room of sorts. The central focus of it is a long table, and at the end, there's a chair that looks more luxurious than the rest, a small throne, per se. The carvings on the white wood seem to depict a story. I see warriors brandishing swords, wolves nipping at their heels, and the very top, a beautiful lady wearing a crown. The queen, I bet.

Queen Maewe doesn't take that seat. Instead, she makes a beeline for the liquor cabinet and pours herself a very generous amount of something similar to red wine. She doesn't offer us any. *Good, the last time I drank anything from her, it could have been lethal to me.*

She turns around and leans against the counter. It's such a laid-back posture that I have a hard time reconciling it with what she represents.

"What an awful mess you've made of things, Rikkon," she says before taking a sip of her drink.

"I made a mess? Are you implying that I let those shadowbeasts into the palace? I've just regained my powers and the shadowbeasts were supposed to be extinct."

"Don't play stupid with me. It doesn't suit you. You don't think I don't know about the little experiment you started with Castiel prior to your banishment?"

I have no idea about what's going on, but whatever it is, it's serious shit. Rikkon's face drains of color and his eyes bug out.

"That experiment went nowhere. Those specimens were killed in the end."

"Can anyone clue me in?" I finally decided to butt in. "What experiment are you talking about?"

Rikkon turns to me. "When the war against the shadowbeasts ended, we took some of them prisoner. We didn't know much about them. Why they wanted to kill us all." Rikkon glances at his mother, glowering. "But we weren't the only ones who came home with spoils of war. Other kingdoms took prisoners too."

"Yes, but as far as my spies tell me, we were the only kingdom that went beyond interrogation. You wanted to know how those monsters worked, didn't you?"

"Of course I did. Any man of science would want to know how their magic worked and why humans weren't affected by it."

I glance at my sword, still coated in the shadowbeast's blood, and shiver, remembering how close I was to being torn to pieces.

"One of them had the chance to kill me, and it let me go."

Rikkon turns to me so fast, I hear something in his body crack. "What happened?"

"It had me pinned down, but all it did was sniff my blood, and then leave."

He seems frozen. He doesn't even blink whereas Queen Maewe is watching me through narrowed eyes.

"I think I know what's going on here." She stands straighter and sets her glass on the counter.

"Are you going to share your insight with us?" Rikkon asks.

"No, it's better if you know nothing about it. Your mind is unshielded. You've forgotten how to block others from prying. Anyone with a will strong enough can read your thoughts. I suggest you focus on fixing that problem before you depart for Cygnus."

She veers for the door closest to her and exits the room without another word.

"Well, that was anticlimactic," I say.

"Mir." Rikkon inches closer. "I'm so sorry for tonight."

I let out a humorless laugh. "Which part? The bit where you kissed Eriel in front of me, or me almost being killed by a horrifying beast?"

"Everything." He lifts his hand to my head. "May I?"

"May you what?" I shuffle back, not wanting him to touch me. Every time he does, I lose my ability to think straight.

"I can heal you."

"Whoa. I didn't know that was part of your repertoire. What else can you do?"

Rikkon lowers his hand, letting out a loaded sigh. "You're stalling. Don't you want me to help you?"

I bite my lower lip and think it over. I have no idea if this place has an emergency room, and if I don't get this gash stitched up, it might get infected.

"Fine. Go ahead."

He barely touches my forehead with the tips of his fingers. It's featherlight and it tingles where the magic concentrates. The discomfort vanishes as my skin knits back together. Freaky. Rikkon lowers his arm and smiles tightly.

"There. All better."

"Hardly." I let it slip, regretting it immediately.

His face twists into a grimace, and regret shines in his eyes. "Mir, what can I do to make things right?"

My damn eyes decide to betray me and produce more fucking tears. I thought I was over the worst already. But seeing the anguish in Rikkon's expression does something to my heart. I know he's suffering in this situation as well, but I can't think of anything short of accepting the queen's mission. Kill the Cygnus princess, save Rikkon's life.

I want to tell him there's nothing he can do, but instead, another truth rolls off my tongue.

"It's my birthday today."

His eyebrows shoot to the heavens. "Why didn't you tell me?"

"Because I didn't know. When we left the human lands, my birthday wasn't for two weeks, but Selor told me it took us exactly two weeks to travel through the Taluah Mirror. He gave me this as a birthday gift."

I lift the sword, and it glows a little before the light fades again.

"He gave you a starfire sword?"

"Well, the queen gave me the sword, he was just the delivery guy." I shrug.

"That's a big deal, Mir. Only the most honorable and skilled warriors receive a starfire sword, and it sometimes takes months for the swords to sing to them. You made it happen in less than an hour."

"I paid for it in blood and tears."

He shakes his head. "I don't follow."

"It doesn't matter, okay? I'm tired, and I just want to go back to my room."

"Okay, Mir. I'll take you." He offers me his arm, but I just stare at it.

"Are we walking the wind?"

"Yeah, it's the quickest and safest way to travel."

I make a face. "And super unpleasant."

"When did you... ah. Castiel."

"Yep."

Rikkon's gaze darkens. "He seems to have taken a liking to you."

I can't believe this. "Don't start with that nonsense, okay?"

"What nonsense?"

"Don't play dumb with me. You're jealous of Castiel."

Rikkon gets into my personal space, making me keenly aware of the power crackling around his frame. *Shit.* If I had issues resisting the male when he was nothing but an empty shell, now that he's back to his true form, I shouldn't even bother trying to stay away. But I do, because I'm stubborn as fuck and I'm mad as hell.

"Damn right I'm jealous." He grabs my shoulders, pulling me closer to him. I have to crane my neck to keep my eyes locked with his.

"What gives you the right? You're the one with a fated mate. I'm as free as a bird."

"Don't say that. Don't remind me of the rock hanging around my neck. I don't want her, Mir. I want you, only you."

He kisses me, and like an idiot, I let him. But then we're moving at the speed of light again, and I don't have the chance to enjoy the moment. When I can feel solid ground again beneath my feet, I step back and push him away.

"You tricked me!"

"No, I didn't."

"Then explain why we're suddenly in my apartment?"

He runs a hand through his hair. "I kissed you because I wanted to, but I also needed you safe behind wards, so I took the opportunity."

Jerk. I look at the vase decorating one of the tables and will it to fly into Rikkon. I didn't think it would actually work, I didn't recite any spell, but when the object does zoom across the room, I can't believe my eyes.

Rikkon manages to jump out of the way, and the vase crashes against the far wall. He glances at the mess on the floor, and then back at me.

"Your powers... they've increased tenfold since you got here."

"So? Maybe it's out of necessity. Mother Earth gives what we need."

This is total and utter bullshit. I know my new abilities have nothing to do with Mother Earth. This is all Queen Maewe's doing. She wants me to be her assassin, so she's giving me all the tools I need to succeed.

He watches me through slits for a moment before he replies, "I think I'd better listen to you and leave you alone. Happy birthday, Mir."

And just like that, he's gone.

Thirty-Two

MIRANDA

It takes me a while to fall asleep. I keep tossing and turning, reliving everything that happened today. Funnily enough, the part when I had to face off those shadowbeasts and almost lost my life is not what traumatized me the most, nor what my mind is fixated on. Watching Rikkon kiss Eriel is my biggest pain.

I don't know when eventually tiredness drags me into slumber, but when I find myself in the center of the palace's maze, facing the fountain, I know this is a dream. Queen Maewe's presence here is also a dead giveaway.

"Hello, Miranda."

"What are you doing here? Isn't dreamland safe anymore?"

"We have unfinished business, and I'm afraid I can't wait until tomorrow to have your answer."

"You shouldn't have left in a hurry last night then." I cross my arms.

She narrows her gaze. "Watch it, child. Dream or not, I can still hurt you."

Yeah, I'm sure she can. Why do I keep forgetting who I'm speaking to?

"Sorry. It took me forever to fall asleep, and I was hoping for oblivion, not an ambush."

Queen Maewe sighs heavily and rolls her eyes. Such a strange thing for her to do, but I'm beginning to realize I shouldn't expect her to follow any pattern of behavior. She's as unpredictable as the wind.

"Well, what is your answer?"

"Like you don't know it already."

"I need to hear the words spoken out loud."

"Why? Will that create some type of binding contract?"

"Something like that."

I should know better than to make any type of deal that uses magic as binding. Aurora almost died when she agreed to a blood vow with that bitch Elena Montenegro. Queen Maewe could be lying about Rikkon's death if he marries the Cygnus princess, but I'm not willing to call her bluff. I can't gamble Rikkon's life like that.

"Okay, I agree to kill Eriel, but I have one condition."

Her eyes flash with annoyance, but I won't back down.

"Isn't the life of Rikkon reward enough?"

"I'm doing this for him, but I also know that once the deed is done, my life will be forfeited."

"Not necessarily. Titus doesn't need to know his daughter was felled by you if you're stealthy."

"You don't understand, I don't want to be stealthy. I'm planning to kill the princess while she's still here in Aquila."

The queen arches her eyebrows. "That won't work, child. We can't be held responsible for Eriel's death. That will cause a war."

"Not if it's a crime of passion. I'll kill the princess, driven by mad jealousy. You can throw me under the bus, toss me to the wolves, I'll gladly take the blame if you send me back to the mortal lands after my mission is complete."

The queen shakes her head. "Your scenario has many flaws, my dear. For starters, King Titus wouldn't care if the crime was one of passion, he'd still use his daughter's murder to declare war against us. Also, returning to the mortal lands wouldn't keep you safe. He'd find a way to open a portal to the human realm to go after you. Besides, you can't leave Ellnesari."

"Why the hell not?"

"To make the Taluah Mirror work as a portal, I had to bind your fate to my son's. There's no magic in this world that will allow you to cross back to the mortal lands without Rikkon. And you and I know how miserable he was during his banishment."

"Are you saying that if Rikkon chooses to stay, I have to stay?" My voice rises to a shrill. What was a semi-pleasant dream has quickly become a nightmare.

"Precisely."

"Does Rikkon know about this?" I ask, trying to keep my voice leveled this time.

"Yes, he knew the moment the spell was cast."

I wince from the invisible blow her words delivered. I can't believe this. He knew I was trapped here and he didn't tell me?

"You look distraught, child. I hope this knowledge doesn't make you change your mind."

My head is spinning, and my heart is shriveling. This was such a betrayal. I thought Rikkon was different from the other Nightingales I've met, but it turns out he's just as shady as the rest of them.

"No, Your Majesty. I'm still going to do your dirty work for you. Now can I please go back to sleep without interference?"

"Of course. We'll speak tomorrow. There's much to plan for your trip to the Cygnus court."

She vanishes, and a second later, my eyes blink open and I'm staring at the canopy above my bed.

My breathing is erratic, matching the crazy beat of my heart. It's dark in the room save for the moonlight streaming through the window. I have no idea how early in the morning it is, but there's zero chance I can fall back asleep now.

I push the covers aside and get up. The lights turn on to a dim setting, but I ignore them altogether and begin pacing back and forth, shaking in anger.

I can't believe Rikkon kept that information from me. He had ample opportunity to tell me, and he chose silence. As I replay our conversations and interactions with others, things begin to make sense. As a matter of fact, I believe Castiel was going to mention that tiny detail when we met, and Rikkon interrupted him.

Ugh, if he was standing in front of me now, I'd punch him in the throat.

The next step I take doesn't meet the floor. My body becomes nothing and whole again in the span of a second. The change is so jarring that I almost fall when I can feel my legs again. Only, I'm no longer in my bedroom.

Holy shit. Did I just walk the wind?

The sound of a bedsheet being tossed aside makes me pivot on the spot. Rikkon is getting out of bed—*his* bed—shirtless and with messy hair. Desire competes with the anger swirling in my chest. *No, I can't get distracted by his "hot enough to melt ice in the freezer" look.*

"Mir, what are you doing here? How did you get in?"

"I don't know how. Your mother paid a visit to me in my dream."

"Why?" His eyes widen as he takes a step closer.

I shuffle back, not wanting to decrease the distance between us. It's too dangerous.

"Because she's the queen and can do whatever she wants."

His eyes narrow. "You're evading the question. She wouldn't just pop in your dreams to chitchat."

No, she wouldn't, but I can't tell Rikkon the reason for her visit.

"She told me about the spell that bound my fate to yours, and that you knew about it this whole time."

Guilt washes over Rikkon's handsome face. "Yes, I knew it as soon as I saw Selor's writing on the Taluah Mirror."

"Why didn't you tell me?" My voice cracks even though I tried to make it come out strong.

"Because I didn't want to upset you. I'm going to find a way to free you from this nonsense spell. I swear, Mir."

"Yes, heaven forbid you being shackled to another female against your will, right?"

I must be going crazy, because seeing the determination in his face hurts more than I thought possible. He's promising to break the spell that keeps me trapped in Ellnesari and I'm upset about it?

"Are you saying you don't want to untie your fate from mine?" He inches closer again, but I keep my feet rooted to the spot this time.

"I don't know what I want anymore."

"Do you think my desire to be free of our linked fates means I don't care about you? Is that it?"

Another step closer. His eyes are burning cold like ice, and the air between us crackles with the power emanating from him in violent waves.

I clamp my jaw shut, refusing to voice that pitiful confession.

"If that's the case, you're so, so wrong."

"Why then?" I dare to ask.

"Because I don't want you to feel like I did when I was trapped in the human world, afraid, cut off from everything I ever knew. You don't deserve that fate." His voice rises an octave. "I can't stand to see you suffer, Mir," he speaks softer now and reaches for my face, making every cell in my body yearn for more.

My heart is racing at breakneck speed and my head is not far behind. I have to stop this or I'll throw myself in his arms and beg him to never let go.

"Suffering is part of the life of a witch," I whisper softly.

"No, it doesn't have to be. I *won't* let it be like that for you even if it kills me."

He doesn't know how real that prospect is.

"Don't be absurd. I'll never let you perish in order to save me."

"That's not your call," he grits out, blasting me with his power.

It's intense and wild. It makes my head spin and fire burn in my veins. It fuels the rage I felt earlier.

"It is my call!" I shove him back with every bit of strength I have, but it's like trying to move a boulder.

He drops his hand from my face to grip my shoulders tightly. "I can't let you pay for my sins. I won't stand for it."

"They're not your sins!" I yell back, frustrated.

"They are. Every horrible thing that's happened to you is because of me. It destroys me when I see the pain in your eyes. Don't you get it, Mir? I love you."

I stop moving, stop breathing, and maybe my heart even stops beating for a second. My ears are buzzing and my entire body tingles, reacting not only to Rikkon's confession, but also his magic. It's akin to being caught unaware in the middle of a summer storm.

Then I snap and do what I wanted to since barging in here. I crash against his chest, throwing my arms around his neck and crushing my lips to his. His mouth devours mine as his tongue takes control, tasting me like I'm the only substance he needs. I bite his lower lip, then run my tongue across his teeth without rhythm or rhyme. I just want to consume and be consumed by him.

Rikkon releases my arm to slide his fingers down my back until his hands rest on the curve of my ass. His fingers press against my skin, pushing me even closer to him and his fire. Heady magic is all around us, heightening every touch, every bite. We have created an inferno in his room.

With little effort, he lifts me off the floor. My legs wrap around his hips, bringing my throbbing core flush against his erection. He spins us around and then we're on his bed, making out like lust-addled maniacs. Rikkon is half on top of me, using his hand to wreak havoc on my body. I arch my back, an offering for him to do whatever he wants to me. He abandons my mouth to pepper open kisses across my jaw and down the column of my neck, and all the while he squeezes my breast with his hand through the thin layer of my chemise.

Needing to touch him too, I let my finger trail a path down his abs until I find the band of his loose sleeping pants. With deft fingers, I make quick work of the string knot keeping his pants in place. When I touch the tip of his cock, Rikkon hisses and quickly finds another way to torture me. He pushes my chemise aside and drops his lips to my exposed breast, sucking my nipple into his mouth.

"Rik, oh God," I moan, wrapping my fingers around his shaft.

In response, he sucks my nipple harder, mixing pleasure with a little bit of pain. It's divine, it's driving me crazy with need. I need these clothes gone. I want to feel the weight of his body over mine, the thrust of his cock into my pussy.

When he cups my sex with his hand, pressing his thumb against my clit, I almost die from the pleasure. My hips buck as I try to increase the friction.

Rikkon releases my nipple with a soft pop and eases off me almost completely. I stare at him through hooded eyes for only a moment before I notice the darkness brewing in his gaze.

"What is it?"

"I can't go on before I confess everything, Mir."

His solemn expression and pained tone douse the fire that was consuming me a second ago. I release his shaft, and then lean on my elbows.

"I'm listening."

He sits up, turning away from me. There's a sudden distance between us now, a barrier he raised that left me cold and bereft. My heart becomes small and tight all of a sudden.

"I had another vision. I saw..." He pauses, dipping his chin to thread his fingers through his hair. "I saw my son, and Eriel was the mother."

The air seems to vanish from the room, or I simply lost my ability to breathe. All of Rikkon's visions have come to pass, he told me so himself. That means I will fail. I won't be able to kill the princess and save him from certain death.

No, I can't give up. Maybe this time will be different. Maybe his vision is only one possible outcome out of many.

I sit up as well and force him to turn around and look at me. "Your mother has the same gift as you."

"She told you that?"

I nod. "And not all her visions are certain, they're only possibilities."

"I want to believe that, Mir. I *have* to believe that because I can't think of a future where you're not in it." He cups my face and rubs his thumb across my cheek.

The fire in the pit of my stomach reignites.

"It's the same for me too. But if tonight is our last time together, then I want you. All of you."

He leans in, kissing me softly. I'm afraid I'm going to break into tiny fragments. Gently, he pushes me back on the bed, covering my body with his. The fire burns brighter between us, and the urgency returns. Until I feel Rikkon go rigid on top of me and grunt not out of pleasure, but in pain.

He rolls over with a fisted hand pressed against his chest. "It's the damn bond."

My stomach bottoms out as realization sinks in. The bond will never let us be together like that.

Rikkon shoots to a sitting position so suddenly that it scares the crap out of me.

"What is it now?"

"I can feel Eriel moving closer. She's coming here."

"Why?"

"I don't know. I think she might have felt the bond at work too."

I glance to his bedroom door, wide open and leading to the living room. "Can she get in uninvited?"

"No. My quarters are warded."

"But I could walk the wind here."

"They're not warded against you." He smiles wearily only to wince again.

"I'll go then." I jump out of bed, but then stop, not knowing how.

"Shit. She's just outside the door."

"Can she sense that I'm here with you?"

"No, I'm masking your presence."

"We have a problem; I don't know how to walk the wind back to my apartment."

"You might not be able to. I suspect that was a one-time only deal, a gift from my mother."

That makes total sense. For whatever reason, Queen Maewe wants me to hook up with her son at all costs.

"Can't you take me back?"

"I could, but Eriel will sense I left. I don't want to draw her ire on you again." Rikkon stands and walks to the window.

"Don't even think about it. I don't think I can float back to my room."

He gives me a perplexed look. "That's not what I have in mind."

Rikkon faces the window again and whistles softly.

"What are you doing?" I stop next to him and look out.

Everything is under the shadows of the night with the moon now hidden behind a cloud. I can't see anything, but I can hear the flapping of wings getting louder.

"Come on." He takes my hand and steers me to the double doors that lead to the veranda.

Fili, the beautiful oversized immortal bird, is already waiting for us. She croons when Rikkon steps next to her to pat her head.

"Thanks for coming, Fili. I owe you one."

He glances over his shoulder, extending his hand to me. "Ready?"

"No, not really." I accept the offer and let Rikkon help me up the bird.

"You'll be fine. She's not going to let you fall."

"What about you? What are you going to do about Eriel?"

His eyes become shadowed. "Nothing. She can stay outside my room all night for all I care. I'm not letting her come between us, Mir. I promise."

I know he means that, but is he strong enough to keep his word? I don't know what to say, so I give him a tight smile.

Right before Fili takes off, I lean forward and whisper, "Please don't disrupt any wards, okay? I'm out of crystals."

Thirty-Three

RIKKON

Last night, I returned to bed after Miranda flew away with Fili and pretended I couldn't sense Eriel just outside my apartment. This morning, I found a note slid under the door not from her, but from my mother. It was an invitation to breakfast. I turned the piece of paper into dust.

The bond's tug is relentless, but I brace against it and ride the pain. I won't be controlled by it, nor will I be manipulated by fate. The vision I had feels more like a curse, and I'll do everything in my power to prevent it from coming to pass.

I leave my apartment early with every intention of seeking out Castiel and asking about his project. I can't help but think it's related to last night's attack. It's a nagging suspicion, not one of my absolute certainties. If I was sure he was involved in it, I wouldn't be so blasé about it. I'd be tearing down his door and demanding he destroy everything he's worked on even if it went against my father's wishes.

It turns out, I don't have to look for him. I find Castiel just outside of Miranda's apartment, fist raised and ready to knock on her door. The red-hot rage surges within me again as jealousy sinks its sharp teeth in my heart.

"Good morning, Rikkon." He smiles.

"What are you doing here?" I almost growl.

His eyebrows arch and his smile wilts. "Queen Maewe asked me to escort Miranda to breakfast. I can, naturally, leave that task to you if you desire."

He knows very well I can't be seen with Miranda alone.

"I don't appreciate your sarcasm. I'll walk with you both."

"And what about your fated mate? Shouldn't you be sniffing around her quarters instead?"

My back stiffens. "I didn't come here for Miranda. I was actually on my way to find you."

"Oh?"

His surprise is genuine this time, which baffles me. Why did he think I wouldn't want to talk to him about his ongoing project after last night's attack? Did he think I forgot?

"I want to see the lab."

Shadows darken his greenish-blue eyes, and the corners of his mouth tighten. "Of course, but I'm afraid it will have to be after breakfast. The queen doesn't like to wait."

"Sure. I'm looking forward to it."

The door opens and Miranda appears on the threshold like a sun goddess sent to the world to torture me with her beauty. She's wearing a gold dress this morning, not as glimmery as the one from last night, but ostentatious enough to showcase her ranking in court. No doubt a selection from my mother to not-so-subtly piss off Eriel.

"Hi. I thought I heard voices outside," she says with a smile, but her eyes don't linger on me.

It chafes me more than I care to admit.

"And you just opened the door without checking who was outside first?" I ask, not pleased with her lack of caution.

She glowers at me. "I recognized your voice."

There's nothing I can say to that, so I just swallow my annoyance and let her through. The door closes automatically, and the wards protecting her apartment lock back in place. Castiel throws me a fleeting glance before he offers his elbow to Miranda. She doesn't even give me that small attention before accepting his arm.

He and I are equally ranked, but protocol dictates that I take the lead since we're in my court. But that means I can't watch them. So I linger and wait for Castiel to take the hint that he should start walking.

"Uh, are we waiting for something?" Miranda asks.

Castiel spares me another look. I point forward with my head. "Go on. I'll follow you."

Understanding dawns in his eyes. "As you wish, Your Highness."

There's a hint of irritation in his tone. I couldn't care less that he's not pleased with my actions. The feeling is mutual.

Miranda and Castiel converse politely, and I take note of every inflection in their words, of every gesture of their hands. With every step I take, the urge to tear them apart increases. The topic of their chatter is mundane and innocent enough, but it doesn't matter. I'm acting like a bonded male, but toward the wrong female. This is what I should feel toward Eriel, and maybe, if I caught her near a male, I might feel this way too. Only this feeling festering in my chest is stronger than the bond. It's raw, it's primal.

When we approach the entrance of the ballroom, Miranda's spine tenses visibly. There isn't a shred of evidence of what happened here last night. The rubble is gone, the gaping hole fixed, and the tall double doors replaced. I can't even detect the smell of blood anymore.

"How can this be?" she asks in awe.

"The palace staff is efficient," Castiel replies.

Miranda turns her head to keep looking at those doors even after we walk past them. Lines of worry mark her otherwise smooth forehead, and her lips are nothing but a thin, flat line.

"How many people perished last night?"

"Twenty-one," I reply before Castiel can.

She looks over her shoulder, her face visibly paler now. "That's horrible."

"Yes, it is. When I find out who's responsible for letting those creatures in, we can add another number to that list."

Castiel's shoulders stiffen visibly—almost an admission of guilt. For the male to let me see that reaction means he's deeply worried about what I might find out.

"You think you have a traitor in your midst?" Miranda's voice drops a decibel.

"It's a possibility," Castiel replies. "But let's not discuss these matters out in the open. Here, the walls have ears and eyes."

MIRANDA

I shouldn't be shocked to find a rather large group of courtiers at the queen's breakfast. I count at least thirty in total, all acting as if last night's disaster didn't happen. How can they be so blasé about the deaths of twenty-one Nightingales?

Don't be a hypocrite, Miranda. Last night, you weren't thinking about the ones who lost their lives either.

No sooner do we step foot in the room, than I move away from Castiel, thanking him for his company. I didn't want to accept his elbow earlier, but it seems customary for males to escort females here. It was hard to follow the conversation with him when I was keenly aware of Rikkon's presence behind us, burning a hole through my head.

I could feel his magic, wild, intense, passionate. It brought my mind back to his bedroom, to his bed. Arousal had begun to unfurl in the pit of my stomach when I noticed the fixed entrance to the ballroom. The fire quickly sizzled as I remembered the terror of facing those monsters, and how close I came to death.

Rikkon stops next to me and whispers, "Did you make the trip back to your room all right?"

Why is he asking me that question here, where I have to pretend he didn't say he loved me? All I want is to be able to pull him closer to me and bask in his heat and attention. I couldn't even say the words back because there was no time. Does he know, though? He has to know.

"I'm in one piece, aren't I?" I reply.

"Mir," he starts.

"Where's your fated mate, anyway? Shouldn't she be here?" I cut him off. I can't let him say anything that's going to make my bones melt and my heart overflow with emotion.

"She's not far. She'll be here in a minute."

"I hate that you know that," I blurt out, instantly regretting my uncensored comment.

"I do too. We'll fix this. I promise."

No, Rik. I will fix it, even at the cost of condemning my soul to damnation.

I spot the queen, standing bored next to two female courtiers who prattle on about something. She catches my stare and beckons me to walk over.

"Well, your mother needs me. I'll talk to you later."

I'm halfway across the room when I sense a shift in the air. I glance over my shoulder and see that Eriel has arrived. Rikkon automatically turns in her direction like a puppet being pulled by a string. I look away, not wanting to see him greet his mate with a kiss. One would think it would be easier now that I know he loves me, but it's actually the opposite. I want to jump the princess and gouge her eyes out with my bare hands for daring to come near Rikkon.

Queen Maewe smiles from ear to ear when I stop in front of her and curtsy. It's almost like she just read my thoughts.

"Your Majesty," I say.

She breaks away from the two females and laces her arm with mine, steering me to the long table where food that's almost too pretty to eat is spread out. Almost. I'm really famished.

"I hope you managed to get some sleep after our conversation," the queen says.

"You love to do this, don't you?"

"Do what, my dear?"

"Ask questions to which you already know the answer."

She chuckles. "Well, I supposed I do enjoy watching people squirm. But you're different from anyone I've ever met. Actually, that's not true. You remind me of... someone."

The pause was noticeable. Whoever that person was, it made a great impact on her. *Who could she possibly be referring to?*

"I take it that person is no longer in your life?"

"No," she replies icily.

Great. I remind her of someone who pissed her off in the past.

She stops in front of a tray of mini fruit pies. She picks one up and offers it to me. "Try this. It's to die for."

I eye the bite-size morsel with suspicion. "Is it going to do something to me?"

"Yes, it will fill your belly. You'd better eat well, child. There won't be anything like this during your trip to the Cygnus court."

Dread drips down my spine. "When is that happening?"

"Today, before lunch."

"So soon?"

"The sooner you depart, the sooner this nightmare will be over."

"How long should I wait to... you know?"

"Use your best judgment. Now eat."

Wow, thanks for the advice. Like I ever killed anyone in cold blood before or killed anyone, period. I pick up a plate and fill it because a hollow stomach won't help me accomplish my goals. I sense the queen's departure, even though I wasn't looking in her direction. I let out a sigh of relief, but it's short lived. I nearly drop everything on the floor when I almost collide with Eriel. *Fuck.*

She's staring at my forehead with a frown. "Who healed you?"

"The queen," I lie.

And it seems it's a bad one, from the way the princess is looking at me with distrust. "The queen healed you?"

"That's what I said." I walk around her, but she grabs my arm, digging her nails into my skin. Immediately the area becomes ice cold.

"I don't trust you, witch. You've done something to my mate, and I'll get to the bottom of it."

"I've done nothing to your mate besides help him get back to you. You should be more thankful," I grit out.

She drops my arm, taking a step back. "He's linked to you in a way that's not normal. Perhaps it's gratitude, and I hope for your sake that's all it is."

"Is that a threat?" I throw the glare right back at her.

She laughs in derision. "Interpret it however you like. Rikkon is mine, chosen by fate, and nothing will get between us."

She leaves before I can offer her a retort. I follow her with my eyes while thinking that I might actually enjoy cutting the bitch in two.

Thirty-Four

RIKKON

Hoping that Miranda won't turn back to look at us, I let the bond take control for a brief moment. I kiss Eriel when she arrives for the breakfast feast my mother put together. But despite the fire of desire that goes through me, it doesn't burn as hot or as bright as it did when I was with Miranda.

I barely listen to the words coming out of Eriel's mouth. I'm too distracted thinking of a way I can leave and not have to play the couple in love in front of the woman who has truly captured my heart. I don't want to cause her any more pain.

So when I spot Castiel, lurking in a corner, I decide to kill two birds with one stone. I excuse myself to Eriel and seek out my friend. I'm not sure yet if I can still call him that. It will depend on what the visit to his lab unveils.

He glances at me, showing the phantom of a smirk. "Ditched your mate already?"

"I'd like to see your lab now," I tell him, ignoring the jab.

"I haven't eaten yet."

"You can do it later."

He looks over my shoulder. "Ah, I see. You don't want to be in the same room with your mate and your lover."

A rumble goes up my throat, a sound akin to a growl. "Don't talk about Miranda like that."

Castiel's eyes widen, then understanding shines in them. "I didn't realize your feelings went deeper than a meaningless romp."

"Watch it."

"I'm not trying to be disrespectful. Cool your head, my friend. I'm not the enemy."

That remains to be seen. I don't want to discuss my fucked-up love life with him, especially not in a room full of gossipy courtiers.

"Shut up and let's go."

I don't wait for him to take the initiative to start moving this time. I walk out of the room knowing he will follow me.

"What's with you this morning?" he asks as soon as we're in the hallway.

"I don't know. Maybe the resurrection of our ancient enemies, or the twenty-one courtiers who died last night?"

Castiel has the decency to look remorseful. "That's not how I operate, Rik, and neither did you. We didn't dwell on the past, no matter how awful it was. We learned from it and moved on."

"I was not coldhearted like that," I seethe.

"I'm sorry. I forgot how long you've lived among humans and all their emotions. You might not act like that now, but that's how you were before your banishment."

Was I really like that before? Am I looking at my memories through rose-colored glasses? I can't worry about that now. Even if I was as ruthless as he's painting me to be, it's in the past.

"Absorbing from other cultures leads to evolution. Perhaps the Nightingales can learn a thing or two from humans and vampires."

Castiel considers me for a few seconds without saying a word or revealing anything in his expression. He has his poker face on, inscrutable. I wonder what he's thinking about, what part of my speech struck a chord.

"You wanted to see my lab," he finally says. "Follow me."

We don't stay in the main hallway for very long. Castiel takes us through a maze of less-used corridors that are meant to disorient anyone trying to get to the lab. I make sure to pay attention to every single detail along the way just in case I have to return here on my own. Finally, we reach a carved door that opens with a skeleton key Castiel has around his neck. *That's interesting.*

"How many people have a copy of that key?"

"Just me."

"Not even the king? I thought you were working on this project because of him."

"He's never shown any desire to come to the lab. He's only interested in my progress reports."

I find that hard to believe. I inherited my inclination for the sciences from my father. If he went through all the trouble to request Castiel's presence here—which must not have been easy, since he's now the heir to the crown of Lynx—he'd be all over this project.

The door opens to a spiraling staircase going up. The stone wall is rougher and darker here, and the stone steps are slick from constant use. No one has bothered to renovate this area, which means very few individuals know about it. It also tells me exactly where we are.

"Why did you move the lab to one of the south towers?"

"It wasn't my decision. When I arrived, the king simply told me where everything had been set up."

At the top of the stairs, we come to another door. It opens with the same skeleton key from before. Castiel unlocks the door and motions for me to go in first. The strong scent of framalaine hits my nose, almost causing me to go into a coughing fit. I forgot how bad it is in the beginning when one's senses aren't yet used to the smell. I cover my face with the back of my forearm before moving farther into the room.

"Over a thousand years away from that stuff will do that to you," Castiel chuckles.

"That, and also, it has been recently used." I approach the display of horrors.

Several glass containers taller than me and twice as wide are in neatly arranged rows. Inside them, swimming in framalaine, the liquid that prevents flesh from decomposing, are the monsters that almost decimated us millennia ago. A chill runs down my spine looking at them up close. These were the ones we brought in alive, and after my mother was done interrogating them, she allowed me to keep them alive for research purposes. It led nowhere, but then again, I was banished to the human realm not much later. Perhaps if I'd had more time, I could have discovered their secrets.

Castiel stops between two containers and taps the glass. "These are the ones from last night."

"They're headless."

"Yes, Miranda decapitated them. I couldn't locate their heads afterward."

"The heads simply vanished?" I move closer to one of the glass cases and squint.

The cut through the neck is clean. A starfire sword is capable of doing that, but only when the person wielding it is skilled enough. I shouldn't be surprised that Miranda did that. She has shown me time and time again she's fucking amazing at everything she does. Pride makes my chest warmer, and I wish she were here so I could tell her how much she inspires me.

"Yes. Or perhaps the remaining shadowbeasts took the heads with them." He moves across the room to a slab covered by a white sheet.

My stomach rebels and I'm glad I didn't have a chance to eat this morning.

"What do you have there?"

Castiel removes the sheet, revealing another slain shadowbeast. This one still has its head attached, but the rest of its body is in shreds. Even with its glowing red eyes closed and its mouth shut, it's a ghastly sight.

"This was my kill," he says, keeping his eyes glued to the monster's face.

"Your only kill?" I raise an eyebrow.

He lifts his chin, meeting my gaze. "Yes, Rikkon, my only kill."

A grin unfurls on my lips. "Miranda killed two."

"Indeed, and you got none. Even Eriel managed to freeze one of these bastards."

My amusement wilts into nothing. I clear my throat, trying to hide the shame that washes over me. I was an utter failure; I couldn't save any of the slain courtiers. I couldn't even sense the shadowbeasts until they were upon us. One of these monsters could have killed me, but instead, it pushed me out of the way and went after Eriel. It didn't make any sense, just like the one that had Miranda at its mercy left her alone in the end.

"Where did you go, Rik?" Castiel asks, bringing me back to the here and now.

I must have shown my mind was miles away from here. I shake my head. "Nowhere. What do you plan to do with this one?"

"Since he's already cut into ribbons, I thought I'd do an autopsy to figure out if there's anything different about this new generation."

"That's a good idea."

"I can do it now. Do you want to watch?"

I clench my jaw, trying to keep the bile that has risen up my throat from spilling out. Castiel knows I never enjoyed this part of the process, so his question feels more like a challenge than anything else. He already made me feel like a piece of shit earlier. I won't have him hold this over my head as well.

"Yeah, I'll take notes."

Thirty-Five

MIRANDA

Following Queen Maewe's advice, I stuffed my face at her breakfast extravaganza. Not even bitch-face Eriel could make me lose my appetite. The encounter and her threat worked to actually make me even hungrier. I need my full strength to put an end to her.

Emboldened by my purpose, I left the social event alone. I didn't need an escort. Rikkon and Castiel disappeared earlier and never returned, anyway. I'm curious about where they went, obviously, but seeing Eriel look for her mate and her gradual annoyance when he didn't come back for her was the cherry on top of a fantastic cake.

I'm so full when I return to my apartment that all I want is a nap. Maybe my eyes were bigger than my stomach. The queen said we would be leaving for the Cygnus kingdom before lunch so that means I have a few hours. And since I have no possessions, I don't need to pack anything.

As soon as I enter the apartment, I sense another presence inside. I tense and glance around for anything I could use as a weapon in the living area. The starfire sword is in my room, and I forgot to bring a river stone with me to breakfast. Not that it would do me any good anyway. It barely has any energy left in it.

"Relax, little witch, it's just me." Selor walks out of my bedroom, drying his hand on a towel.

"You again? What were you doing in there? Never heard of privacy?"

He gives me a droll stare. "I had to use the restroom."

"Ew. Why are you here?"

"The queen sent me. You have a few hours before your departure, and she wants me to give you a few combat lessons."

"I've had training. I'm a samurai."

Selor scoffs. "Who are you trying to bullshit? You didn't complete your samurai training."

How the hell does he know that?

"Fine, but I have experience, and I killed two of those shadow-beasts last night."

"You got lucky." He widens his stance by placing his legs farther apart and folds his arms in front of his chest. "Now stop being difficult, get your sword, and let's go."

"God, you're annoying. I think I liked you more when you were trying to kill me."

"Sure you did."

"I have to change." I point at my fancy dress.

"Fine. If you're not back here in two minutes, I'm coming in. We don't have much time."

"Go into my bedroom again without permission and I'll stick another dagger in your gut."

He chuckles. "You're funny when you're delusional. Now go."

I give him a death glare as I walk around the mountain-like male in order to get into my room. I bang the door shut using a simple spell that doesn't require an amplifier. I can't let my witchcraft get rusty. I'm a witch before I'm a warrior.

I'm all riled up and eager to show him I'm not a puny human. Now that I have a magical sword as well, the field is a little more evened out—at least I hope it is.

Knowing Selor will make good on his promise to barge in here, I yank my dress off, not caring if I snag the fabric. It's not likely I'll ever wear it again. Pity. The look on Rikkon's face when he saw me this morning would be a good reason to pack the garment and bring it on the trip, but I know there won't be any opportunity for me to put it on again. The plan is to never make it to the Cygnus court.

I open the armoire where I found exactly what the queen wanted me to wear to every single occasion. Instead of a beautiful gown, I find a dark wool shirt, simple but clearly well made, a pair of brown leather pants, and a matching vest. This time, undergarments were provided, thank heavens. I'm tired of going commando everywhere. It's like the queen wants to give Rikkon easier access to my goods.

I change quickly and then look for my own boots from the mortal lands. They're in the same corner I left them, only they look brand new now. Stuffed inside them is a pair of long woolen socks. When I put the boots on, they fit even better than before. The queen is clearly dressing me for winter. I don't mind the season, but I'm not looking forward to facing it in a foreign land. The issue is that I'm still in Aquila and I'll probably melt wearing all these thick layers.

The door opens a fraction and Selor's head sticks in. "Are you ready or not?"

I jump from the chair and grab my sword from the desk. "I told you not to come in here."

He flashes me a manic grin. "Technically, I'm not inside your room."

"Ha ha. You kill me with your sense of humor."

I stride in his direction and yank the door open all the way. He steps to the side to let me through, but I don't go far. His beefy hand takes my arm and off we go, walking the wind.

We land in an open field where the grass has gone yellow from lack of water. I brace my hands on my knees and wait for the dizziness to pass. I thought I was getting used to it. I almost felt nothing when I traveled the wind by myself into Rikkon's bedroom.

"Why is walking the wind so bad?"

He shrugs. "Maybe because humans aren't meant to travel like that."

I bite my tongue and don't tell him I've already done it on my own. It's possible he knows, but if he doesn't, there's no need for me to bring it up.

I stand to my full height and look around. We're on higher ground. Behind me, there's a thick forest and opposite us, I spot a village in the distance at the bottom of the valley. No sign of the palace though.

"Where are we?"

"Still in Aquila territory."

"How far are we from the castle?"

He arches his eyebrows. "Why do you want to know? Fancy heading back on foot?"

"No. I just want to know my location."

"Don't worry, little witch. I won't leave you stranded. You have an important mission to complete."

"You know about my mission?"

He nods. "I'd do it myself if I could. It's a great honor, you know."

I raise my chin higher. "I'm not doing it for the honor. I'm doing it for Rikkon."

"Ah, young love," he curls his lips into a sardonic grin.

"Shut up. I thought we didn't have much time, so why are we wasting it with inane conversation?"

The mirth vanishes from the warrior's face in a flash.

"You haven't earned the right to tell me to shut up, witch."

"I believe I have, or have you forgotten the dagger sticking in your side?"

He lets out a gruff. "That was pitiful."

"We escaped your clutches, didn't we? What are you showing me today?" I ask because we are getting sidetracked.

"Let's start by learning how to conceal your weapon. You didn't have it on you at breakfast, so you obviously didn't read the notebook I gave you."

"I did back at home, and there was nothing in it about concealing the starfire sword," I grit out.

Selor looks at the sky. "Heavens, give me patience." He drops his annoyed gaze on me again. "The notebook is enchanted. The content is never the same."

I throw my hands up in the air. "You should have told me that before."

"I'm telling you now."

"Fine. I'll read it again. But I thought this was going to be a lesson in combat."

"It is. You've proven you can wield the sword, but that won't be enough to slay the princess of winter. You need the element of surprise, and that will be gained by hiding your starfire sword."

"She already knows I possess the sword."

"Does she? Did she see it glowing when you came into the ballroom?"

"I don't have a clue."

"My bet is that she didn't, or she wouldn't have bothered you at breakfast."

How the hell does this dude know so much about everything?

"To her, it was just an ordinary weapon, and it is in your best interest to let her think that," he continues.

A heavy weight settles on my chest. *I'm really doing this. Fuck. The pressure is on.*

"Got it. Okay, what do I need to do?"

RIKKON

I leave the lab with a heavy conscience and an even heavier heart. Castiel looks as grim as I feel. It didn't take long for us to realize the shadowbeasts that attacked us last night weren't the same as the ones that terrorized us in the past. There's been a mutation.

Castiel showed me the progress reports he has given to my father and in the last one, one detail raised several alarms in my head. He had been able to isolate the magic that makes the shadowbeasts invisible to us.

Some Nightingales have chameleon abilities and can blend in with the background. But the glamour doesn't work on someone like my mother, for instance. Yet not even she can see the shadowbeasts. Isolating the magic means we could actually turn an entire army invisible to even the most powerful Nightingale royals.

"Can you please put up your mental shields, my friend? You're blasting your inner turmoil to everyone who cares to listen," Castiel tells me.

Shit. I can't believe I'm still doing this.

"I'm out of practice."

I focus on elevating the barriers that protect my mind from intrusion, imagining they're made of impenetrable steel.

"That's better," he says. "You're leaving for the Cygnus court today, aren't you?"

"Yes," I grit out.

More than ever, I want to delay the trip. This new situation with the shadowbeasts is too important, too dangerous. I can't say my trust in Castiel has been restored completely, even though I couldn't find anything amiss in the lab or his reports. But he's a master of keeping secrets.

"What are we going to do about this new information we've discovered?" he asks.

"I'm not sure. Maybe you should keep it out of your progress reports for the time being."

I watch Castiel from the corner of my eye, noticing how his jaw is set in a hard line. "Yes, there's no need to alarm the king."

His words ring false in my ears. My father wouldn't be alarmed by this new discovery. On the contrary, he'd be excited. What's Castiel hiding from me?

We part ways once we return to the heart of the palace. We spent hours in the lab, so I'm sure the breakfast feast is over by now. Not that I wanted to return to that nonsense. Using the bond, I search for Eriel. She's back in her quarters, which are conveniently in the opposite wing of mine and Miranda's. My mother once again at work, no doubt.

The lab was heavily warded and therefore, I doubt Eriel could sense me there. She must be going out of her mind, wondering where I went. Now that I'm back from the most secluded location in the palace, the invisible link connecting us is stronger again. I won't have much time alone until she comes looking for me. I want to talk to Miranda one more time before we depart. There won't be many opportunities for privacy once we're on the road.

I walk the wind, stopping in front of her apartment door. Her quarters aren't warded against me, so I could simply appear inside. But I don't want to invade her privacy like that. However, I don't feel her presence on the other side. She's not there.

Worry gnaws at my insides. I doubt she found someone to escort her back, and who would she ask? I give myself a mental slap. She wouldn't ask anyone.

The hairs on the back of my neck stand on end, and goose bumps break out on my arms. Eriel is coming near. The feeling isn't pleasant as it should be. She can't walk the wind, that's a gift specific to the Aquila kingdom and those who were trained here like Castiel, but she has other means to move with speed.

She can't find me lingering in front of Miranda's door. With regret, I return to my apartment and prepare to once again avoid being alone with her.

Thirty-Six

RIKKON

I'm not back in my quarters for even a minute when Eriel's soft knock sounds on the door. I can't use the same excuse as the last time, that I was too exhausted to sense her outside my door. I glance at my immaculate apartment and have an idea. She doesn't know what kind of male I am, but I know there were rumors I was some type of mad scientist. I'll feed the lies and let her believe that.

With a wave of my hand, I turn my quarters into chaos with things out of order—papers, clothes, objects all scattered everywhere. I run my fingers through my hair as well, making sure it's properly messy, as if I have been pulling it back at the strands in frustration.

"Rikkon?" she calls.

With my back to the door, I lower the wards, and call, "Come in."

There's a moment of silence before she asks, "What happened here?"

I whirl around, making sure I look like a veritable maniac. "What do you mean?"

"This room is a disaster." She frowns, not pleased at all with the sight.

It's almost comical to see her wrinkle her nose as she scans the area.

"Well, I was packing, or trying to pack."

She arches her eyebrows, her eyes going wider with it. "Why? Don't you have servants to do that?"

"Are you mad? I'd never allow servants to touch my things."

"Never?"

"No."

"That's something we'll have to work on. You'll be my husband, it's not appropriate for you to do manual labor. It might also offend our servants. They consider it an honor to take care of us."

I give her a deranged look. "No one touches my stuff, my love. I'm very particular about it. Besides, they have to respect the wishes of their rulers. Or have things at the Cygnus court descended into madness? I've never heard of masters bending over backward to please their servants."

The jab hits the mark. Eriel winces visibly, showing a hint of hurt in her eyes. It doesn't give me joy to treat her this way. She's as much a victim of the bond as I am.

"Before the bond took effect, I didn't think I'd be lucky enough to have a fated mate. Then it happened and you went away. I thought destiny was punishing me for something I'd done in the past. Now you're here but somehow, I still think I'm being punished."

Way to make me feel guilty as hell. My instinct is to comfort her, but if I do that, then this entire ruse had no purpose.

"Have you ever considered that maybe the bond magic doesn't always bring the right people together?"

Now, you've really done it, Rikkon. Eriel is staring at me as if I've suddenly sprouted a second head.

"No, that thought never crossed my mind. The bond is sacred, and to even think for a second it might pick the wrong partner is almost blasphemy." Her eyes take on a hint of fanaticism. "Why are you bringing this up? Are you questioning our bond?"

Damn everything to hell.

"Humans don't have bonds and I lived with them for almost a millennium. My views about things might have shifted. And I'm a male of science. It's my job to question things."

My answer seems to mollify Eriel. The crinkles on her forehead smooth and the tension in her shoulders eases off. I was afraid she'd mention Miranda and blame my actions on her.

"We don't know each other very well, do we?" She gives me a peace offering in the form of a smile.

I smile in return, but it's not entirely genuine. I feel like I'm an actor, behaving according to the script.

"We have the trip to remedy that."

Her cold eyes spark with renewed intentions. She walks over, now smiling in a seductive way. *Shit.*

"We're not leaving for a few hours. We could start to get to know each other now."

Her arms wrap around my waist and then she's invading my space. The scent of her arousal hits me at full blast, and when she places a kiss in the hollow of my throat, it takes everything in me to not yank her head back and kiss her hard and deep. My body is reacting to the bond, to the urge to consummate our mating. I've been fighting this for so long that it won't take much to push me over the edge.

I picture Miranda in my head, how beautiful she looked this morning, how her sweet lips can unravel me with a single taste, how my heart yearns for her desperately. If I bed Eriel now, I'll be sealing my fate. There won't be a way to break the bond. And I want Miranda, only Miranda.

Eriel kisses the corner of my mouth while her hand presses against my erection. Miranda's image dissolves into the wind. I'm on the verge of snapping, of losing control.

The arrival of an unexpected visitor clears some of the lustful fog that invaded my brain. I lean back, never happier to see Selor in my life than I am now.

He clears his throat when Eriel won't unlatch from me. "Sorry to interrupt, Your Highness."

Eriel finally drops her arms from my waist and steps aside, but her ire is unmistakable. It's crackling around her body.

"How dare you come into the prince's quarters without permission?" she asks.

Selor stares at her, unaffected. "You're not my queen, I owe you no explanation."

I sense her power gather around her and the temperature in the room drops several degrees. I place a hand on her shoulder in an attempt to calm her down.

"Sadly, he outranks even me in certain matters," I tell her. "Why did you come, Selor?"

"There's been a change of plans. You must depart in thirty minutes."

"Why?" Eriel asks.

"I'm just the messenger, Princess. I wasn't given the reason. The birds will be ready to take you to the border. From there you'll have to use the ground mounts until you reach Cygnus."

"Mounts? I thought the giant birds could carry us all the way to Cygnus."

"Winter doesn't agree with them," I reply.

She turns to me. "I know you can't travel through the ice portals I create, but why can't you walk the wind to Cygnus and take me? Your belongings can come later."

I sense the brush of Selor's power touching my mental shield. He's trying to tell me something, but when he can't penetrate my barriers, he gives me a meaningful glance instead.

"What did I tell you earlier, my love? No one touches my things."

The fight gathers in her eyes but then she seems to think better of it. "Fine. I'll go get ready." She rises on her tiptoes and kisses my lips fully. I can't help kissing her back even if I hate myself for it.

Thankfully, she keeps it short. She walks past Selor and gives him a look so cold, I'm surprised he doesn't actually turn into ice. He holds her stare, though, not hiding the contempt in his gaze.

When she leaves my apartment, I tighten the wards, making sure no one can eavesdrop on our conversation.

"Okay, now she's gone. What's the reason we're leaving earlier than planned?"

"Are you daft, boy? You were a second from fucking that ice stick. I came to run interference. The change of plans was just an excuse."

"So the change of plans was a lie?"

"Of course not. We *are* leaving earlier, thanks to your inability to keep your dick in your pants. Gee, what do you see in that ice-cold bitch?"

"I can't help it, it's the bond," I grit out. "And what do you mean by *we*? You're coming too?"

"Unfortunately, yes. I've been appointed your chaperone."

I don't know if I should be glad or annoyed.

"Don't look at me like that," Selor continues. "If you stick your dick into that freezer, it's game over. There's no breaking the bond then."

I pass a hand over my face, glancing away. "I'm not sure it is even possible."

"Ah, but it is. Remember, true love is capable of many things, even the impossible."

I whip my face to his. "What's with the romantic bullshit, Selor? Did you hit your head?"

His face twists into a grimace. "Ask your little witch friend."

"Wait. What does Miranda have to do with you suddenly spouting poetic nonsense?"

"I was referring to the hit to my head comment." He rubs his temple.

Sudden anger surges through me and I don't attempt to

control it. Wind gathers around me, making even more of a mess in the room.

"Why were you with Miranda?"

"I was teaching her how to conceal her starfire sword, among other things."

I rein in my temper and the wind dies. "I could have taught her that."

"When? You can't even peek at the little witch without your jailer going berserk."

As much as his comment annoys me, he's not wrong. I swallow the angry retort and glance around, trying to decide what I should bring to Cygnus.

Selor seems to guess my train of thought for he says, "Just bring your sword and comfortable clothes for the trip. I have a feeling you won't be staying in Cygnus very long."

"What makes you say that?"

"A hunch," he replies with a shrug before vanishing into thin air.

Fuck, what the hell is Selor planning? Whatever it is, I know he's not coming on this trip only to be my chaperone. My mother is meddling again, which means I have one more thing to worry about.

Thirty-Seven

MIRANDA

Selor had to cut our training short, and I don't think it had anything to do with the rock I smashed against his forehead. To be fair, he totally deserved it. He said I was as stealthy as an elephant on roller skates in the middle of an IKEA store. I sent him that flying rock and he didn't even see it before it hit his head.

When he dropped me off in my apartment, he told me to pack up because we were leaving earlier than anticipated. It wasn't like I had much to pack, and yet I wasn't surprised to find on my bed a small leather satchel, my bag with all the belongings I brought from home, and my starfire sword, all ready to go.

With everything taken care of for me, I decide to clean the sweat off my body. Who knows when I'll have a chance to bathe again once we're on the road? I'm assuming Ellnesari is like Middle Earth and there aren't many lodgings along the way. I could be totally wrong, and they have the Nightingale version of Best Western hotels sprinkled everywhere.

I don't linger in the humongous bath—seriously, it looks more like a mini-pool than a bathtub. I half expect Selor to pop back in and catch me naked, so I dress as quickly as I can. Not a minute later, I hear tapping on my veranda door. I grab my things and find a great shadow blocking the sun from outside. And then I catch a glimpse of radiant turquoise.

"Fili," I say as I open the door. "What are you doing here?"

The bird coos in answer and then comes near to nuzzle my face with her head. It tickles and I laugh.

"Did you miss me?" I return the caress with my hand, but she only lets me pat her for a few seconds before she steps back and makes another sound, hard to describe. It's a cross between a chirp and a shriek, I guess.

"What is it?"

She lowers her body and then I understand what she wants.

"Oh, so you're my ride?"

Fili doesn't answer this time, just remains in that lower position and waits for me to hop on. It's a little harder to get on her back without assistance while I'm carrying the extra load. After I struggle for a bit, I attempt the levitation spell I used to save my life and Rikkon's. I don't have a crystal with me, but somehow, it works. I float off the ground and get onto Fili's back without effort. I guess my powers have been growing since I arrived here. Maybe it has to do with the queen's touch on my shoulder at the ball that infused me with her strange magic. Sometimes, I can still sense it swirling in my chest.

I curl my fingers into Fili's feathers and tell her, "I'm ready."

She spreads her wings and lifts off, making my stomach drop. I let out a gasp and my legs tense around her body. It takes me a moment to get used to the feeling of flying on the back of a giant bird. It helps if I don't look down.

The trip is a short one. Fili circles down right in front of the palace, descending at a gentle angle until she lands on the soft grass of the manicured lawn. Other giant birds like her are there, waiting for the rest of the party to arrive, I guess. They're bigger than Fili and I notice the harnesses they wear around their bodies, and the loaded cargo attached to the bottom.

Shit. If we're going to fly all the way to the Cygnus kingdom, when am I going to have the chance to complete my mission before we reach princess Eriel's domain? Fili fidgets under me, perhaps picking up on my nervousness. I pat her back, trying to calm her down.

I was wrong in my assumption though. She's not reacting to me, but to the approaching ice princess who is followed by her entourage. They all look like ice statues, so I assume she brought her own servants here.

Selor, Rikkon, Castiel, and Queen Maewe appear out of thin air. The king is nowhere to be seen.

Eriel's frosty gaze alights on me, making Fili even more agitated. "What's the human witch doing here?"

"Miranda is one of Rikkon's advisors," the queen replies calmly. "She'll take up residence in the Cygnus court as well."

"Excuse me?" She glowers at her mate. "Why am I only hearing about it now?"

"There hasn't been much time to discuss anything, has there, my love?" he replies sweetly, immediately giving me a toothache.

It grates on my nerves when he does that. It's so fake. *Shouldn't you be glad, Miranda? It would be much worse if he sounded sincere.*

Eriel gives me a haughty glance, and then turns to Rikkon to beckon him closer with a smile.

Bitch. She did that on purpose.

He answers her call, pretending I don't exist. Fili notices his indifference and lets out a pitiful sound that somehow matches the sorrow in my heart. I run my fingers through her soft feathers, trying to soothe her and myself at the same time. Selor and Castiel both aim for their birds. *Huh?* I didn't know he was coming too, or Selor, for that matter.

The air whooshes out of my lungs painfully when Rikkon leads Eriel to the biggest bird in the flock. Naturally, he'd fly with her. My eyes sting at the sight, so I purposely keep my gaze down, pretending I'm admiring the colors of Fili's plumes.

Don't fret, my child. It will all be over soon, the queen whispers in my head.

I lift my chin, meeting her gaze. Her face is a perfect mask of neutrality, but I see beyond that. I see the ruthlessness that she hides. Chills run down my spine. That's the female who banished her children to a millennium of misery. She's only friendly to me because I have a purpose in her grand scheme. I have to remember that once I complete my mission, she'll have no use for me, which means I'll be on my own again. I don't dare to hope Rikkon will want anything to do with me after I kill his fated mate in cold blood. Who wants to date a murderer?

Someone says something—I don't know who spoke or what they said—and at once, all the birds take flight. This time, my stomach doesn't plunge nor do I tense my legs around Fili. I'm looking forward to the distraction this trip will provide.

RIKKON

I'm glad we won't be using the birds to travel all the way to Cygnus. Traveling pressed against Eriel is an exercise in self-restraint. We land an hour later at the border of Hydra, the neighboring kingdom. The change in the air is impossible to miss. We're near the swamps, and the heat and humidity levels are already making me wish for a cool dip in a lake.

Using my powers, I will my body to adjust to the change in temperature. It's an ability all Nightingales have, but it manifests more strongly in members of royalty. After a minute, I barely notice the oppressive heat.

Guards from the palace came earlier with our mounts and are waiting for us in the clearing.

I jump off my ride as soon as it touches the ground, then extend my hand to help Eriel down. My fingers tingle with the contact, and a burning fire seems to spread up my arm. My head is getting more muddied by the second as the bond lust spreads through my body.

"Your Highness, a word, please," Selor, my official chaperone intervenes, earning a glower from Eriel.

I drop her hand, glad that with the loss of contact, the desire that had begun to take root recedes. Selor walks away from Eriel, forcing me to follow him. She stays behind, but her glare is now pointed at the back of my head. It feels like little shards of ice prickling my skull.

Bond or not, that pisses me off. I unleash my gift, creating a gust of wind that pushes her power back. She gasps, but I don't bother to look over my shoulder. More and more, I'm certain that the bond doesn't necessarily indicate the best match. Even if I wasn't in love with Miranda, I doubt my union with Eriel would be a happy one.

"What is it, Selor?" I grumble.

"Nothing. Just doing my job." He smirks.

"She's not dumb, you know. She's probably already figured out your role in this trip."

He lifts his shoulders in a what-can-you-do shrug. "It doesn't bother me at all if she knows what I'm up to."

"So, what's the plan?" Miranda asks, stepping closer to Selor, not me.

I stiffen, feeling the weight of her detached stare. I know we can't show our attraction around Eriel, but staying away from Miranda is becoming harder and harder, even more painful than when I act against the bond.

"Now we travel on the rombolos." I point at our tall mounts, which are similar to the buffalos you find on the plains in the human realm, but twice as large and tall. Their fur is also lighter, the color of wheat, save for their dark gray broad faces.

Miranda follows my line of vision. "Okay, they look friendly enough."

"Yeah, just keep your hands away from their mouths and you'll be fine," Selor laughs.

Castiel approaches, earning my attention. "Well, this is where we say goodbye, my friend." He gives me a hug, pats my back, and whispers, "Don't worry, I'll find out who let those shadowbeasts into the palace. You have my word."

When we ease apart, I hold his stare. "And it shall be done."

Magic ripples between us. Here in Ellnesari, bindings can be made by simply voicing promises to the wind. He won't be able to rest until he fulfills his vow.

Fili walks over, almost hesitant. She first nudges Miranda, who leans into her caress. My heart seems to expand in order to contain the love that keeps growing for her. Of course Fili would like Miranda, she's loyal, caring, the best person I've ever met. I can't imagine my life without her. There's a painful tug underneath the heady feeling—the damned bond, but it's not as strong as before.

I wait for Fili to come to me, but she refuses to leave Miranda's side.

"Traitor," I say under my breath. "Fine, I'll come over."

Miranda tries to sidestep, but Fili keeps her in place with her wing. I stop on the other side of my avian friend, which brings me as close to Miranda as I'll be able to get on this trip.

"I'll miss you, Fili." I run my fingers through the soft short feathers on her head, and she closes her eyes, leaning into the cuddle.

I sense Miranda's stare, and even knowing I should avoid making eye contact with her, I turn. Our gazes lock, making the air between us loaded with all the words we want to say to each other but can't.

I love you. I send the thought toward her even though speaking mind to mind was never a gift I possessed. But her eyes widen a fraction, shining with emotion so raw that it burns me. She glances away in the next moment and pretends to survey the comings and goings of the guards transferring our loads from the birds to the rombolos. I say pretends because I can hear the sound of her heart beating faster and I can see how her cheeks are rosier.

She heard me and she's trying her hardest to conceal how my confession affected her.

I give Fili another pat and seek Castiel's attention again. "You'd better make sure Fili is okay."

He frowns. "I've been taking care of Fili for almost a millennium. I think I can manage a few more weeks."

"Weeks?"

Castiel's sheepish expression is a novelty. He never reveals things by accident.

"Safe travels, my friend." He smiles broadly, purposely ignoring my question.

Miranda and Selor have already moved toward the rombolos. He's pointing at the mouth of the closest one and making exaggerated hand gestures. Probably warning Miranda to keep her hand clear of those blunt but dangerous teeth.

Eriel is perched atop her ride, looking regal despite the expression of deep disgust on her face. "These creatures reek."

"Breathe through your mouth then, my love."

I walk around mine, checking that all my belongings are already stored in the cargo compartment attached to the harness on the animal's sides. An unnecessary measure to avoid the princess. Did she notice that I allowed the Aquila guards to transfer my belongings without making a fuss about it? I'm sure she did. I don't think her shrewd eyes miss much. At this point, I don't care if she can see through my lies. I brace one foot on the stirrup and lift myself onto the animal.

Selor approaches us on his rombolo. Miranda is next to him, looking a little tense as she grips the reins of the beast.

"Relax, Mir. It can sense your discomfort," I tell her.

"I never liked horses, and this is ten times worse."

"They're fine to me," Eriel chimes in. "Perhaps you shouldn't come. No one is interested in listening to you whine."

I whip my face to her, incredulity shining in my eyes. "You were complaining about the rombolo smell a second ago."

Her eyes spark electric blue with annoyance, and her lips

become nothing but a slash on her face. "Are we going, my love? I want to reach the border to Lynx before nightfall."

Selor and I trade glances, and I read the question in his gaze. I should be the one leading this trip, but I've been gone too long, and I don't know what the best route is anymore.

"Lead the way, Selor. We'll follow you."

Thirty-Eight

MIRANDA

I try to keep my head focused on the journey, but the easy trot of the rombolo and the sounds of the jungle in the background make it easy for one to get lost in their own thoughts. I heard Rikkon loud and clear in my head when he said he loved me. I didn't imagine it. The boy wears his heart in his eyes when he forgets to be careful. He caught me by surprise, and I couldn't school my face into Switzerland fast enough. I hope his bitchy mate didn't notice our exchange.

I shake my head, trying to force my brain to let go of memories I shouldn't be replaying. I feel sluggish and this damn heat is not helping one bit. Selor is riding ahead, all mighty in his warrior armor. How he is not melting under all that metal is beyond me. I'm dying here.

Rikkon and Eriel follow right behind him flanked by two Aquila guards on each side. I ride in the midst of Eriel's entourage, a stranger among people so cold, I actually get chills despite the tropical temperature every time I glance in their direction. If only their frosty nature worked like an AC unit, I wouldn't mind the open hostility directed toward me so much.

There are four of them, two riding in front of me and two behind. I feel like a prisoner being escorted to the gallows. It's clear this arrangement is intentional. Eriel doesn't want me close to Rikkon. Only she doesn't know he's not the one to whom I want proximity. Her entourage presents a problem, though. *How am I going to get the princess alone to off with her head?*

We ride in silence for roughly an hour, and I'm already dying for a break. My legs and back are sore from sitting stiffly on the rombolo, and the moisture in the air clings to my skin in an unpleasant way. My heavy tunic is drenched, and the fabric is glued to my back. I've already put my hair up in a ponytail, but it only helped a little. There's no breeze here. The air so stifling.

I reach for my water canister once again, wincing when it feels too light in my hand. I toss my head back, lapping the last drops. I do have another full canister, but I don't want to touch it before I refill this one.

"How long until we come across a water spring?" I ask.

Rikkon looks over his shoulder, slowing the pace of his mount. "Why? What's the matter?"

The two guards in front of me shift closer, blocking my view of him. *Dumbasses.*

Rikkon turns around and forces his rombolo between them, creating a path toward me. I pull on the reins, stopping my beast when I realize Rikkon's intention. The entire procession comes to a halt. *Great.* Now we have several pairs of eyes on us. *Nice job, Rik.*

"One of my water canisters is empty," I answer his earlier question.

His eyebrows shoot up. "You drank the whole thing in an hour?"

"Yeah. It's too hot in this jungle."

It's then that I notice Rikkon doesn't have a strand of hair out of place or a drop of sweat dotting his forehead. *Why am I the only one who's melting in this sauna?*

"Shit. I didn't realize you would be so uncomfortable traveling through the Hydra swamps. We're able to condition our bodies to adapt and withstand different weather."

"Well, sorry, but this human here doesn't come with her very own portable AC unit. As you can see, I'm sweating like a pig, and I'm parched."

"Pathetic," Eriel pipes up from the front. "Can we resume our trip now?"

Rikkon glowers at her. "No, we should find a source of drinkable water first."

"We won't find any for miles," Selor butts in.

"It's okay, Rik. I'll drink more sparingly."

"Rik? You should be addressing him as Your Highness," Eriel interjects again.

I curl my fingers tighter around the mount's reins and count to ten in my head. I don't want to show my hand yet.

Rikkon clenches his jaw tight until I can hear his molars grinding together. But he doesn't offer a response to Eriel, and that aggravates me.

"Here, Miranda. You can have my canister. I won't need it as much as you."

I notice he didn't call me by my nickname this time, and it hurts more than I care to admit.

"Thanks." My answer is clipped.

I reach for the offering, accidentally brushing my fingers against his. Sparks seem to fly with the touch. I pull back fast, utterly shocked by it. Then, remembering where we are and our audience, I glance at the stony faces of Eriel's guards. I see no reaction, only blank expressions. They didn't see anything. It must have happened only in my head.

The animals in our party begin to shift uneasily on their feet, and make small, nervous noises. I can feel their restlessness and fear. Something has spooked them. Rikkon must have noticed the same thing. He's frowning as he scans the jungle.

I strain my ears as well, trying to pick up any sound of approaching danger. I itch to pull my starfire sword from its invisible sheath, but I was instructed to keep it concealed until it was time to use it for my task. I should have grabbed a regular dagger too, because right now, I have no weapon save for my wits and my magic.

"What's going on?" Eriel asks.

"Shhh. Listen," Rikkon says.

"I don't hear anything," I reply.

He glances at me, worry shining in his eyes. "Precisely. The jungle has grown quiet all of a sudden."

The crack of a whip cuts through the silence, and a split second later, a thick vine wraps around Rikkon's neck and middle, lifting him off his mount.

"Rikkon!"

Out of reflex I jump, trying to reach his legs, but I miss them by an inch, falling on the ground on my knees. White-hot pain makes me see stars, but I still manage to look up just in time to see him vanish behind the canopy of trees.

Chaos ensues, the guards dismount and try to climb the trees to go after Rikkon. Selor vanishes into thin air, no doubt going after his prince. Eriel does what she does best: she freezes all the mossy trees surrounding us.

Fucking cunt. She's going to freeze Rikkon too like that.

What can I do? I don't have the powers the Nightingales have.

Not true. You know how to fly, Miranda.

I know a floating spell is not the same as flying, but it worked to get me up on Fili; it has to work to follow Rikkon. After everything we've been through, I can't lose him to a mossy jungle. I don't have any energized crystals, so I dig my fingers into the dirt, grabbing fistfuls of mud in my hand as I recite the memorized spell. It's the connection with nature that I need. Like the crystals, the soil becomes warm in my hands until they burn, but I don't let go. I visualize shooting high up in the sky, like an arrow cutting through air.

Slowly, my body rises as if lifted by invisible hands. My ascension increases in speed until there's no doubt that I'm actually flying, not floating on air. I straighten my body and I raise my arms over my head. I don't know why Superman does it, but if it's good enough for him, it's good enough for me. I discover it was the right decision as I breach the first branches and giant leaves. I need to use my fists to protect me from hitting a trunk head on.

But I can't simply fly without direction, so I do something I've only tried once before. I recite another spell while keeping the current one going. This could very well be the end of me. Flying is much more taxing than creating a mist like I did back at Bloodstone. I'm flying so high now that a sudden fall would definitely kill me. It's a risk I have to take. I must find Rikkon.

We just touched, so to find him, I simply picture him in my mind and let the magic do the rest. I drop a few feet suddenly, hitting a branch below. I curl my arms and legs around it, not wanting to lose my grip. Grinding my teeth, I re-shift my focus to the flying spell and don't let go of the piece of wood that prevented my fall when my body becomes as light as a feather again. I need to be able to hold both spells first.

I attempt to find Rikkon again, putting every spare ounce of magic I have into forming that golden thread that should link me to him. My vision becomes blurry from the effort, and when I feel moisture above my upper lip, I know my nose is bleeding.

Finally, I see the faint line. I push myself toward it, honing all my senses on keeping that link visible. It leads to a denser part of the jungle where the thick vines and moss present as much of an obstacle as the trees themselves. And then it drops suddenly, and I almost don't have time to adjust my body to follow it.

The thread is becoming thicker and brighter. It means I must be getting closer. I try to slow my descent, but apparently, I don't have a good grip on this newfound ability yet. I break through the cover of trees and crash against one of the males holding Rikkon hostage. The impact sends us both rolling around in the mud, and I end up getting a mouthful of it. When the motion finally stops, the small male is stunned, but I'm not. I push him off me and jump to my feet, finally pulling my sword from its sheath. It glows brightly, which doesn't help me much right now. It's making it harder to count how many enemies I have to fight. My ears are also ringing from the fall and subsequent tumble.

A crack sounds nearby and a vine wraps around my wrist so tightly that I can't keep holding the sword. It falls to the ground, the glow fading.

"Don't hurt her," Rikkon begs. "It's me you want."

More vines appear out of nowhere, turning me into a green mummy. My movements are contained, but I won't stop struggling against my restraints.

I glower at our captors, who look more like people made out of clay and bark than Nightingales. They're short and stocky, their hair has the texture of straw, and it's chopped unevenly, perhaps with a knife, and their dark skin is textured to resemble a tree. *Jesus, how easily can they blend in this swamp?*

Rikkon is bound like me by the vines and there's a gash on his forehead, which bleeds, but it's already healing.

A smaller creature with a hunched back steps forward, moving slowly with the assistance of a cane. The lines and cracks on her face run deeper than in the others, and the whites of her eyes have more yellow in them. She must be an elder.

"Do you know why you're here, prince of Aquila?" she asks Rikkon.

"I have no idea. Why don't you clue me in?" he grits out.

"You're here to pay for the sins of your kingdom."

"What sins? We've never bothered you before." He struggles against his bindings, and his face gets redder with the effort.

Rikkon knows who these creatures are?

"Liar!" she shrieks.

The vines squeeze Rikkon tighter, drawing a grunt of pain from him.

"He's not lying!" I yell. "He's been gone from Ellnesari for almost a millennium. So whatever sins Queen Maewe committed against you, he doesn't know anything about it."

The elderly female turns to me, cocking her head as she

assesses me. "You're not a Nightingale, but you have powerful magic in you. What are you, child?"

"I'm from the human realm."

Better to not reveal I'm a witch.

"Ah, I remember your kind now. Warriors from your realm crossed the veil and helped rid our world of the shadowbeasts."

"Yes, that's right."

"And as a thank you, the Nightingales turned them into monsters themselves," she retorts.

Well, I can't argue with her there.

"What sins has the Aquila kingdom committed against the marsh people?" Rikkon asks.

The elderly female whirls around. "You truly do not know?"

"I swear I do not."

She glances at two male warriors and, with a nod of her head, commands them to do something. They break from the circle that has formed around us, disappearing from my limited view. I can't really turn my head with the vines circling my neck. I'm only able to breathe and talk because these folks are letting me. One squeeze and my airway will be blocked.

While we wait for the return of those males, I direct my awareness inward, focusing on the magic Queen Maewe gave to me. I sense nothing, not even a spark. My own magic seems to be dormant, and it's not a far-fetched guess that these vines are blocking my access to it. It must be doing the same thing to Rikkon.

Shrieks sound in the distance, and the blood in my veins freezes. It's the same sound the shadowbeasts made. Are we under imminent attack? If so, then captive like this I'm totally screwed. Our captors don't seem bothered by it, though. The shrieks become louder and a moment later, the two males return, dragging a bound shadowbeast with them.

It thrashes against the vines, snarling and foaming at the mouth. It looks more rabid than the ones that attacked the palace, and the sight sickens me. I look away, my gaze clashing with

Rikkon's. His face has gone ashen and his eyes are round, but not with fear.

"This is what we have against your kingdom, Your Highness." The elderly female points at the shadowbeast, making no effort to hide the contempt in her voice.

Rikkon's swallow is noticeable, even from where I stand. "I had no idea of this. You have to believe me."

No idea of what? What the hell is going on?

"Are you implying that Queen Maewe let loose a bunch of shadowbeasts? The palace was just attacked recently," I chime in.

"That's not what she's implying, Mir," Rikkon replies. "That's not an ordinary shadowbeast. That's a marsh male, changed into a shadowbeast."

"Oh my god. How is that possible? And who would do such a thing?"

His gaze turns dark. "I know exactly who."

Thirty-Nine

MIRANDA

Rikkon's statement drops like a bomb in my head. Unfortunately, it doesn't change our captors' stance. We're still trapped, and the elderly female is scowling openly at him. By the way Rikkon's eyes are burning with fury, I have one suspect in mind. *Castiel.*

This betrayal had to come from someone he didn't expect. If it had come from Queen Maewe or her husband, I don't think he'd be this angry. If that's true, then I was also a fool. I actually liked Castiel.

"Oh, enough with this nonsense, Marja." A male even older than the female stands from his seat and strides toward the center of the circle.

He's also a bit shorter than her, but wider, reminding me of a talking log, if such things existed. Maybe it does here. There's definitely a plethora of creatures I couldn't imagine even in my wildest daydreams.

He stops in front of Rikkon and begins to sniff him like a dog. Then he snaps his fingers and a young male rushes forward, carrying a stump of wood in his hands. The elderly creature steps on it, which brings him at eye level with Rikkon, who recoils when the male leans in.

Making a tsking sound, he grabs Rikkon's face between his dark hands and forces him to remain still. Rikkon's eyes widen, and his face gets red. *What the hell!*

"Stop it. Don't hurt him, please," I beg.

Like an idiot, I jump forward, which only results in me falling face-first to the forest floor. Pain shoots up my nose and expands over my forehead. Damn everything to hell. If the ground had been harder, I might have broken my nose. With effort, I manage to roll on my back and avoid suffocation in the mud.

"Hmm, he's not lying. Interesting."

"It doesn't matter if he didn't know, Erkon. He's a son of Aquila and we should make an example out of him," Marja spits back.

I have to twist my neck to be able to see what's happening now, which only makes the vises around me tighter.

"He's a male of science. Maybe he can help cure those who were affected by this wicked magic."

"I can definitely try. You have my word," Rikkon chimes in.

Marja curses in a language I don't understand, probably the marsh people's dialect, and then strides away, not bothering with her cane anymore. Maybe she doesn't really need it. The elderly male jumps off the log, and with a swishing motion of his arm, the vines release Rikkon and me. I take in a huge breath, letting it fill my lungs completely with a loud gasp. I didn't realize my airways were so constricted.

Rikkon rushes to my side and helps me to a sitting position. "Mir, are you okay?"

I rub my face, keenly aware that I have dirt all over it. "I need a moment to answer that."

"There's blood on your face." He furrows his eyebrows.

"And on your forehead too," I say.

"It's nothing. May I?" He lifts his hand, letting it hover an inch from my nose.

"It's not broken, Rik. It bled a little when I was holding two spells at the same time."

He lowers his hand, but the furrow between his brows remains. "How did you find me?"

The circle of marsh people closes in around us, making me tense. "Let's talk about it later."

Rikkon and I get back to our feet and when he throws his arm over my shoulders, I melt into him unashamedly.

"You need to rest your body and mind if you're going to help poor Loomir," Erkon tells us.

"Do you want me to try to find a cure for him *here*?" Rikkon asks in a slightly high-pitched tone.

"Naturally. The word of a Nightingale has no value to us, only actions. We can't let you leave until you cure him."

"What if he can't?" I ask.

The male's eyes darken. "Then I'll let Marja do whatever she wants with you."

I feel the lick of dread behind my neck and try in vain to suppress a shiver. Rikkon pulls me closer, tightening his hold on me.

"Now, follow me. I'll take you to your lodgings."

We trade worried glances, but that's all we're able to do before we're forced to follow Erkon. Unencumbered by the vines, I can now survey the area and hopefully think of a way to escape.

This is a small village where the houses are nothing but huts made of husk, wood, and dried mud. As we near a cluster of them, the small children who were playing outside hurry to hide behind their mothers. Everyone stares at us with either hate, suspicion, or both. *Yikes. They really have a grudge against Rikkon's family.*

The leader stops in front of the smallest house in the settlement and pulls the canvas flap back, revealing the entrance.

"We'll bring you water to wash off and food. You're not to leave unless I come for you."

"What if I need to use the restroom?" I ask, doubting there's a toilet inside.

The male frowns. "Use what?"

"Where do we relieve ourselves?" Rikkon asks, and I fear the answer.

Someone in our welcome party shoves a wooden bowl into Rikkon's hand.

"Use this," the leader says.

My stomach bottoms out. *Hell to the fucking no.* I can't pee or poop with Rikkon in the room. I will die of embarrassment. No eating then.

Rikkon lifts his eyes from the bowl. "When are you bringing water and food?"

"When it's time. Now go before I change my mind about our agreement."

Agreement? It's more like coercion. Do this or you die.

Rikkon enters the dark hut first, no doubt to make sure it's free of danger. But I follow close behind him, not wanting to spend another minute with our hosts. The air is stale and stuffy, giving me a sense of claustrophobia. A moment later, a little breeze comes through, making it easier to breathe. Rikkon's doing.

There's nothing to be done about the dimness though, unless... I reach behind me, finding nothing but air. *Shit.* I forgot I dropped my blade earlier. But Rikkon didn't. He draws his starfire sword, and the glow illuminates our little prison. It was better when I couldn't see. There's nothing around, not even a mangy cot to sit down on. I guess we're resting on the dried mud. That's better than the potty bowl though.

"So, what's the plan?" I ask.

"We should rest and eat first." He sets the bowl down.

"And then we figure out a way to get out of here, right?"

Rikkon clamps his jaw tight. "I would like to try to help that poor soul."

He doesn't want to escape. He actually wants to help them, and it's easy to see why. He feels guilty for what happened to Loomir, or whatever that creature was called.

"Is Castiel responsible for this?"

He runs a hand through his hair and looks away. "I didn't want to believe it, but he's been studying the shadowbeasts for years, trying to figure out how their magic worked. Who else could have done it?"

"What makes you think he was the only one studying those monsters?"

"My mother said we were the only ones."

I snort. "And you believe her? No offense, but your mother is not the most trustworthy person in the world."

"I have other reasons to suspect Castiel, but I won't worry about them now."

The creases on his forehead smooth out and his eyes, which were covered in shadows before, become brighter. He walks over, keeping his gaze glued to mine. My heart takes off, drumming away as if trying to escape my chest.

"You came after me," he says softly.

"Of course I did."

"Why?"

His question makes me pause. I balk for a moment. I'm not sure I'm ready to confess everything, not when he's bound to another woman. It might be stupid, but if I say "I love you" out loud, and then lose him, the blow will be harder.

"Why? What kind of question is that? I'd follow you even if you crossed into Hell."

Just like Aurora did when she went after Saxon. The difference is, I don't have a bond enhancing everything I do or feel. My emotions are my own, one hundred percent.

He cups my cheek, rubbing his thumb back and forth. I must look disgusting with all the dirt and blood on my face, but Rikkon is looking at me as if I'm the most beautiful girl in the world. It robs me of air.

"I'd do it too, Mir. I'd follow you anywhere. Even if it ripped me apart, I'd follow you."

I let out a gasp, which Rikkon swallows when he brings his lips to mine, searing my tongue with his. The glow from his sword fades, dipping us in the gloom again. If I thought I was unraveled before, now I'm truly undone. I kiss him hard, licking the top of his mouth, then grazing my teeth over his. Who needs food and water when I have him, worshiping my mouth with his tongue, turning my bones into fire with his touch?

The sound of a throat clearing makes me jump back. Two females are standing by the entrance of our hut, each carrying a large pot of clay. One has steam coming off of it. A strong aroma soon takes over the small space, but at least it's not unpleasant. My stomach grumbles, and yet, I know I won't touch anything. I definitely don't want to use that bowl in the corner.

They set the pots down and then one of them lingers. Unlike the other villagers, she doesn't stare at us with hatred.

"Do you think you can cure Loomir?" she asks Rikkon.

"I'll try my best."

She nods, then turns her attention to the bare floor. "You need to rest well tonight in order to be in top shape tomorrow. I'll bring blankets."

She hurries out the door before we can get another word in. But yay to blankets.

Rikkon walks over to the pots, and then digs his hands in the one with water. He splashes his face, dripping water down his shirt and hair. I don't know why, but he looks sexy as hell doing that. He turns around and beckons me by curling his index finger.

"Come on, Mir. Let me wash off all that grime."

I narrow my eyes into slits. "I can clean myself."

The young female returns with the blankets she promised. She sets them in a corner and vanishes without making eye contact with us. I spare a glance at them. They seem fairly fresh, cleaner than us for sure.

"Come on, Mir. Food is getting cold, and you know you can't have supper without washing up."

What's up with him? Is he still under the effects of our kiss?

The corners of his lips twitch upward as he watches me walk over. I drop into a crouch next to him and peer inside the water pot, hoping to see my reflection. But it's too dark now without the glow of the sword.

Faster than a cobra, Rikkon dips his hand in and splashes cold water on my face.

I jump back, falling on my ass. "Ugh, you jerk."

Rikkon just laughs at my expense. *Oh, he wants to play games, I'll give him games.* I scoop water with my hands and using my magic, create a ball of water, floating on air. His eyes widen when he sees what I have.

"Mir, come on. There's a lot of water there."

"So? You said yourself, we can't eat unless we wash off first."

I throw the water ball at him before he remembers he has powers that can deflect my attack. It hits him right in the middle of his chest, drenching his shirt even more. Now the white linen fabric is see-through and clinging to his chest. *Shit, maybe that wasn't such a smart move.*

"Oh, you're on."

Thinking he's going to pounce, I jump away from the water pot, but Rikkon sends a gust of wind my way that wraps around my waist like an invisible lasso, and then he yanks me forward. I fly straight to him as if I weigh nothing, crashing against his wet chest and mouth.

There's a new kind of fire in this kiss. It burns hotter than before, frying every single thinking cell in my brain and with them, any argument that I might have had against surrendering to this moment. My back lands on the blanket softly and Rikkon is half on top of me.

But then he abandons my mouth and stills, hiding his face in the crook of my neck.

"Rik? Is something wrong? Is it the bond?"

Leaning on his forearms, he pulls back. "No. The bond is weaker here. Maybe the magical vines surrounding the village are blocking it. My magic is also diluted, isn't yours?"

"Yeah, it was when I was trapped by the vines, but I didn't sense anything different just now. Is that why you stopped?"

"No, I stopped because I don't want to take advantage of you."

"You're not taking advantage of me. I want this."

"Do you want to give yourself to me in this filthy hole? You deserve more than that, Mir."

I push him off and sit up so he can't see the tears that have gathered in my eyes. *God, why am I so pathetic when it comes to him?*

"Did I upset you?" He pulls my hair back and rests his chin on my shoulder.

"No, of course not." I turn my face toward the rough wall when a rogue tear rolls down my cheek.

"I want to be with you, Mir, but when that happens, I'll be whole, not torn up by some ancient magic."

I bring my knees up and hug them. The only way Rikkon can be free is if I kill the princess. The chances of that happening are pretty slim right now, considering we're prisoners of the marsh people.

The flap of our cell is pushed open to allow Erkon to walk through. He eyes the food we didn't eat and twists his face into a scowl.

"The food was to strengthen you for your task," he says in a disapproving tone.

"We aren't hungry." Rikkon stands up. "I'm recovered enough. I'd like to see the shadowbeast now."

Forty

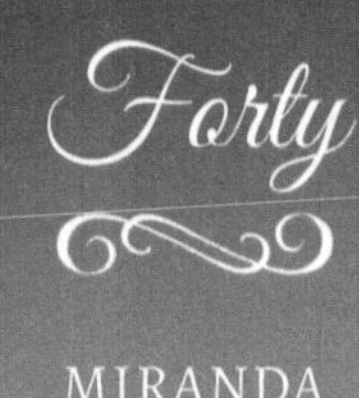

MIRANDA

I'm still reeling from the conversation with Rikkon as I follow him out of the hut. The sky is getting darker despite the fact the trees block out most of the sun. The villagers have started a fire in the center of their settlement, and next to it, pots of varying sizes have been laid out. More food, perhaps.

I understand Rikkon's determination to help the poor male who was turned into a monster, but he said Castiel spent years studying those beasts. If he indeed is responsible for Loomir's transformation, what chance does Rikkon have to revert his condition? Besides, his magic is not working at full capacity thanks to the vines protecting this place.

I search for my own magic and find it as bright as ever. Maybe the vines only affect me when they are wrapped around my body.

Loomir is brought back from wherever it is they keep him, still bound. But he's not thrashing and fighting to break free as before.

"What have you done to him?" Rikkon asks.

"We gave him a sedative. It won't last long. We didn't want him lacerating your pretty face when you come closer to examine him," Marja replies with a perverse grin.

Bitch. I mark her as one to watch out for. Even if Rikkon manages a miracle and cures Loomir, I wouldn't be surprised if the shady female stuck a knife in our backs.

"And what are those?" Rikkon points at the pots I noticed earlier.

"Anything we could steal from the Nightingales in the hopes of helping Loomir," the young female who provided us the blankets replies.

Marja throws her a quelling look, which makes the girl cower and lower her head.

Rikkon proceeds to inspect each container, sometimes smelling the contents or sticking his finger inside. When he straightens to his full height, his gaze settles on Erkon. "These will help me little. What I need is full access to my magic."

A wave of murmurs echoes among the crowd, but it's Marja who voices her disagreement the loudest.

"What do you take us for? Fools? The moment we lower our shields, you'll whisk your lover and run away."

"I won't. You have my word."

"Like I said before, your word means nothing to us," Erkon replies.

I can see the desperation in Rikkon's gaze. He truly wants to help the poor male. I begin to understand his reason. He must feel responsible somehow for what happened here.

"Use me as leverage," I volunteer. "Tie me up again. He won't escape without me."

The look of sheer horror Rikkon gives me feels like a blast of cold wind, prickling my skin.

Mir, no. His voice sounds desperate in my head.

"I'm sorry," I mouth.

The vines spring from different directions, wrapping around my body like before and pinning me in a vicious grip. I sense my magic wane until all that's left is a flickering light.

Marja shares a meaningful glance with Erkon, who nods. In a

powerful whoosh, the shield protecting the village lowers and the sounds of the jungle beyond our little bubble reach us once again. I hadn't realized they were missing from our surroundings until now.

Rikkon's eyes shine with guilt. I want to tell him I put myself in this situation, but I don't think anything I say will make him feel better about it. He turns to the shadowbeast and raises a hand over him, palm facing down. His shoulders rise and fall with his deep intake of breath. His magic flares up next, creating a shimmering shield around him.

I glance at the crowd, finding them watching Rikkon in the same way as before. Curious and leery. Can't they see what's happening? Am the only one who can actually see Rikkon's magic at work?

His palms become brighter while his eyebrows scrunch together. He keeps his eyes closed as the minutes go by. Loomir begins to writhe on the ground, still knocked out. When his movements become more agitated, I want to warn Rikkon to step back. But I don't do it, afraid to break his concentration.

What happens next draws a desperate scream from my lungs. The creature awakes and breaks free from its bindings as if they weren't tight enough. *Did fucking Marja do this?* The shadowbeast leaps on Rikkon, jaw wide and ragged teeth exposed, teeth meant to shred him to pieces. But Rikkon walks the wind, escaping the sudden attack by a second. The villagers scatter, screaming as well. *Hell.* I'm still bound and unable to use my magic.

With the shadowbeast free, I can see the lacerations on its chest and arms. That's why Rikkon could see it, otherwise he'd be invisible.

I don't have time to wonder how it broke from its restraints. I'm the only one around who isn't running away, and thus, the easiest target for its blind rage. It charges and I close my eyes. Then my body turns into pure air for a split second. When I'm solid again, I open my eyes, and see that I'm in Rikkon's arms, but we're still in the village.

"We need to go, Rik."

"We can't, Mir. I have to help them." He cuts my vines with his glowing sword, setting me free.

His determination to help the marsh people makes me feel small and selfish. Yeah, I want to save our skins because they sure don't care if we live or die.

Suddenly, the air becomes freezing cold, and the small hairs on the back of my neck stand on end. Rikkon's spine turns taut as he scans the jungle surrounding us. I'd do the same, but movement on my peripheral catches my attention.

"Watch out." I body-slam into Rikkon, pushing him off the path of the freed shadowbeast.

We fall on the hard ground with me on top. I look over my shoulder to see where the shadowbeast went and find it frozen into a statue.

A wail of despair echoes above all the noise. I search for the source, finding the young female who was kind to us rushing toward Loomir. I'm paralyzed as I watch the scene unfold, my heart breaking. What if that had been Rikkon?

I'm still staring when he hauls me back to my feet, pulling me out of my stupor. I notice then that the jungle has turned into a winterland, and when I breathe, I create a white mist with my exhale.

"Eriel. Stop it! They're not the enemy," Rikkon yells.

The Cygnus princess and her guards are freezing anything that moves, even children. My hate toward her increases tenfold. I reach behind me, ready to draw my sword, when I remember I don't have it anymore. *Fuck*.

The magic I received from Queen Maewe unfurls in my chest, spreading through my body at the speed of sound. It mixes with my own magic and fury, creating a tornado inside of me that I direct toward the bitch. Satisfaction surges in me when my twister swallows Eriel, stopping her killing spree.

My ears are buzzing with power and my hair is flapping madly, dancing in the wind.

"Mir, stop it." Rikkon's voice sounds far away.

I can't stop, won't stop until the princess is dead. It's the only way to free Rikkon.

He appears in my line of vision, blocking my view of the tornado. He grips my shoulders and shakes me.

"Please, Mir. Don't do this."

The agony in his voice breaks my concentration. I lose control of the leash I had, and my spell dissolves. He begged for her life and that felt like a punch to my gut. I step back, my vision going blurry with unshed tears.

Released from the tornado, Eriel drops into a crouch and then lifts her murderous gaze toward me.

"You tried to kill me," she seethes as she stands to her full height.

"She was trying to make you stop. The marsh people are not the enemy," Rikkon intervenes, but she ignores him.

She knows what I did, and she's going to make me pay.

"I'm done putting up with your interference, witch." A blue glow appears in Eriel's cupped palm as she gathers her powers.

I have no fight left in me. Rikkon chose her over me, and thanks to our linked fate, I can't hope to return home. I don't tense my muscles, preparing to jump out of the way. I don't attempt to create a protective shield around me. It's over.

Rikkon grabs her wrist, preventing her from unleashing her fury on me. "Don't even think about it."

She turns her furious glare on him. "You're protecting her after what she tried to do to me?"

"You won't kill Miranda."

She doesn't answer for a moment, but it feels like an eternity to me. "Fine, I won't kill your precious pet."

Rikkon releases her, stepping away. Did he really believe her?

"But I can send her far away so she will never get between us again."

She flicks her arm, creating a powerful maelstrom of cold magic behind me. The winds howl loudly as my body is pulled back in the vortex. The last thing I see before I'm swallowed whole is Rikkon yelling for me.

Forty-One

RIKKON

When I see Miranda get sucked through the portal Eriel created, there isn't a shred of doubt in my mind. I walk the wind after her. The seconds-long trip is brutal. My incorporeal self is blasted by ice shards which run through me painfully, even though I don't have a body.

I land hard on a snowy bank, rolling with the impact. My breathing is coming out in bursts as I try to get air into my lungs by the time I come to a stop. It doesn't help that I ate a mouthful of snow. Bracing on my hands and knees, I lift my head and take in my surroundings. Everything is stark white and with the sun glaring down, it's almost painful to look at the landscape. I fell on high ground, peppered with ancient trees that seem to speak to the wind. It's a miracle I wasn't impaled by their spear-like branches.

On the valley below there's a frozen lake, and on the other side, a small bank that vanishes into a dense forest of dead trees. No sign of Miranda.

Knowing it's a risk, I frame my mouth with my hands and call her. "Miranda!"

My voice echoes in the valley below, but no reply comes forth. Fear that Eriel might have changed the destination of the portal when she realized I meant to follow Miranda grips me. What if she's not in this frozen wasteland?

The crack of a twig behind me makes me whirl around. I don't call Miranda's name this time, for I sense what's hidden behind the twisted branches and rocks is not her. A low growl follows but I don't wait to find out what's stalking me. I walk the wind and reappear by the edge of the lake.

Once I get some sense of control of my nerves, I can think properly. Miranda and I are linked by a blood spell. If she's nearby, I can find her. I close my eyes and focus on the magic that binds me to her. It's more difficult to find it than I expected. The bond magic lurks like a cobweb, ready to trap me if I get too close. The thread that links me to Miranda is on the other side of it, pulsing, calling to me.

Fuck it. I'm risking it. I need to find Miranda.

The sounds of racing pads on the snow and heavy breathing pull me out of my inner thoughts. A growl warns me of danger nearby. I turn as the white beast with electric blue eyes and teeth as long as my arm pounces on me. No time to walk the wind this time. I raise my arms to protect my face from being swallowed by the huge animal and use the wind to prevent a fall that would be fatal.

Its teeth sink into my forearms, slicing them open, and its sharp claws cut into my sides before I'm able to envelop the creature in a tornado similar to the one Miranda created earlier.

"Rikkon!" she yells, as if I summoned her with my thoughts.

Wincing, I turn. She's running across the frozen lake toward me. Behind her, a similar creature to the one that attacked me chases her. It stops short of the sheet of ice though. It knows not to cross. *Shit.* The ice must not be thick enough.

"Miranda. Stop!"

She skids to a halt right in the middle of it. And then she's gone with a yell when the ice underneath her gives way.

"No!"

I walk the wind, even though it costs me a lot more than it

should. I'm bleeding too much from my wounds and they aren't healing as fast as they should. I land softly on the edge of the hole and see nothing but my own reflection in the dark water.

I don't think twice about it; I jump after her, but at least I have the forethought to create a bubble of air around my face. I can't see anything at first, the water is too murky and dark. I try once again to find Miranda by using our blood link. I don't hesitate to plunge through the threads of my bond to Eriel. I blow past them until I'm grasping the thread to Miranda with both hands.

A glow appears below me, revealing Miranda's form. She's sinking fast. I kick my legs and swim after her as quick as I can. When I hook my arms under hers, she feels like dead weight. I'm losing strength by the second, so I use the little bit I have left to propel us upward and out of the gelid water. I'm able to take us far from the lake and the beasts roaming there, but not to a safe area by any stretch of the imagination. We're deep in the forest now, and who knows what else is around looking for prey.

Miranda is like a block of ice in my arms; she looks like death.

"Mir, please. Wake up." I touch her face, then check if she's breathing.

I get nothing.

No!

In a panic, I set her down and begin CPR. I don't have any training, but I've watched enough shows on TV to know more or less what to do. I lose track of time as I repeat the steps over and over again.

"Please, Mir. Don't go," I beg through the tears that freeze on my cheeks.

It's over, Rikkon. Give up. She's gone.

I don't know whose voice is in my head. It could be my own cruel conscience. She wasn't under for that long. She has to come back.

My arms have gone numb; I don't even know the count anymore. When I press my lips to hers to blow air in, I linger, breaking into a million pieces when I get no reaction. Something snaps inside of me. I pull back and let out a roar that reverberates through the trees. When the sound finally dies, I sit on the balls of my feet with my shoulders hunched forward. The forest is quiet save for my ugly sobbing.

Minutes seem to go by, and I feel nothing besides a void in my chest where my heart used to be.

Then, a cough.

I open my eyes and find Miranda trying to come back to me. Her coughing continues as water spurts from her mouth. I turn her on her side and massage her back to help. She gasps loudly, opening her eyes once the coughing subsides. I pull her to me, crushing her limp form against my chest.

"You're alive. Thank God, you're alive."

She starts to shiver violently. "I-I'm so-so cold."

"We need to get you some place warm."

Her eyes drop, making my chest tight once again. I can't let her fall asleep. She might not come back. "Stay with me, Mir. Please."

"Tired."

Fuck. She's going into hypothermia. I have to leave this place. I stand up, lifting her in my arms. I focus on getting us back to Aquila, but we're deep in Cygnus territory and my magic is severely depleted. I need to go somewhere closer. An old cabin in the woods near the Lynx court castle comes to mind. When I went to visit Castiel's family once, we spent most of our time there. I hold on to that image and will my body to become one with the wind.

We both dematerialize, but it takes much longer to complete the journey. When we land, I'm weak as fuck, yet I still let out a sigh of relief. We're in front of the cabin from my memories, and the building seems to be in good shape. I was afraid that after nearly a millennium, it wouldn't be here anymore.

With quick steps, I head for the door, using my magic to open it. I detect a faint smell of fire and ashes, but it's old. There hasn't been anyone here in a while. It's a small space, not meant for comfort. There's a small living room with a fireplace and an area to store food, but nothing like a human kitchen. I set Miranda on the old couch and go in search of blankets. I only find a ratty thing that wouldn't cover half of her body.

Shit.

Fire. I need to get a fire going. Mercifully, there are some logs left. Unfortunately, I don't have fire magic, but my sword gets hot enough when glowing, I just need to find kindling. Quickly, I raid the cupboards in search of alcohol. I find a lonely dark bottle tucked in a corner, covered in dust. Pulling the cork out, I confirm it's indeed potent spirits.

I drench the useless blanket and the logs with it, and then I press my scorching blade against the fabric. It hisses as it burns and soon a flame flickers to life. It quickly spreads over the rag, and I hope it stays hot enough to ignite the wood. I use a little bit of wind to help and only move away when I have a good blaze roaring.

It didn't take me more than a minute to start the fire, but when I return to Miranda on the couch, her eyes are closed.

"Mir, wake up, darling. Please." I shake her, noticing how cold her skin is to the touch.

I press two fingers against her neck to feel her pulse. Worry takes hold of me when I find it weak and uneven. I have to get her warm ASAP but the fire alone won't do. First, I push the couch as close as I can to the fireplace, then I remove Miranda's wet clothes. It's the first time that I've seen her naked, but I care little about that. All I want is for her to wake up. Knowing she needs as much heat as she can get, I take off my clothes too and lie on top of her, hoping it will be enough.

MIRANDA

When the awareness of my body returns, the first thing I notice is how toasty warm I am. My eyelids are heavy though, and it takes me a few minutes to force myself to blink them open. Rikkon is on top of me, resting his cheek across my chest—my very naked chest.

Oh my god.

Did we have sex? My mind spirals out of control as my body tenses.

Rikkon stirs, and then he lifts his face to mine. His sleepy eyes become alert, followed by the crack of a smile.

"You're awake. Thank God."

"What happened?"

"You don't remember anything?"

I swallow hard, and it's perceptible. "The last thing I remember is running for my life."

"You fell into the lake. I was able to get you out, but you weren't breathing, and..." he pauses, fighting through his emotions. "I thought I'd lost you."

"I drowned?"

"Almost. I got you breathing again, but you developed hypothermia. I was only strong enough to bring you to this cabin in the Lynx territory, but the fireplace alone wasn't getting you warm fast enough, so..." A blush creeps up his cheeks.

He leans on his forearms and starts to move off me, but I stop him.

"You saved my life. Thank you."

"There's no need to thank me, Mir. I'd be lost without you. I couldn't bear the thought. I love you so damn much."

The earnestness in his eyes and the tightness in his voice undoes me. "I love you too, Rik. More than you'll ever know."

I pull his face to mine, needing to feel his lips, to taste his tongue so I can be sure I'm not dreaming. Rikkon groans against my mouth, devouring me with gentle ardor that makes me forget the rest of the world. Desire swells in the pit of my stomach and pools between my legs. I'm all too aware of our naked bodies pressed together, of Rikkon's hard length pushing against my belly. Raw need goes to my head and I surrender control to it. Our bodies begin to move in sync as we both mimic what we've been craving so deeply.

Rikkon's hands trace the outline of my body, leaving goose bumps in their wake. I arch my back, opening my legs to accommodate him between them. His cock nudges between my legs, pressing against my clit. A zing of pleasure travels all the way to my toes. I gyrate my hips, trying to increase the friction and ease the sweet agony down below. We quickly create an inferno between our bodies.

"Oh my god, Mir. You taste so good. You *feel* so good," he whispers against my lips before plunging his tongue into my mouth again.

I get lost in that kiss for a moment, but there's something I have to say. With reluctance, I break away from him.

"I don't want to wait anymore. I want to *be* with you."

His heated gaze narrows. "Are you sure?"

"Yeah, aren't you?"

"I want this more than anything in my life, but you deserve more than this old cabin."

"It doesn't matter where we are, Rik. As long as we're together, I'm happy. I don't want to wait another minute, another second."

Because we might not have that.

He slants his lips over mine, branding me, while he grinds his hips against mine. I'm slick with desire and the movement brings the tip of his cock to my entrance. Involuntarily, I tense underneath him.

"I'll go slow, Mir. We can stop at any time."

"If you stop, I'll kill you. Unless you're in too much pain."

I remember then the fucking bond that tortures him whenever he's with me.

His eyebrows crunch together. "I haven't felt the bond's tug since I rescued you from the lake. It's like it's not there anymore. I think it's broken."

My eyebrows arch. "For real?"

"Yeah."

I don't dare to hope that's true. Queen Maewe said the only way to break the bond was if I killed the princess. Maybe the bond is only dormant. Right now, it doesn't matter. It's giving Rikkon a reprieve and we're taking advantage of that.

I lift my knees, opening myself even more for him. Rikkon moves only an inch, and I can sense his reluctance.

"It's okay, Rik. I won't break."

"You're so damn tight, Mir." He rests his forehead against mine.

"I hope so, you're the first explorer."

Rikkon leans back and stares at me in surprise. *Shit.* I can't believe I blurted that out.

Lacing my fingers behind his neck, I say, "Ignore what I said."

I pull him to me, kissing him hard and deep to hide my embarrassment. He follows my lead with his mouth, but not with the rest of his body. It's almost like he's terrified of hurting me. *For fuck's sake.* I lift my legs, hooking them at the ankles behind his ass, and nudge him forward. He slides in almost all the way. I feel a pinch, but the pleasure overrides the pain. Rikkon stubbornly halts again.

"Rik, please," I beg against his lips.

"Are you okay?"

"Yes."

"I felt your wince." He leans back to peer into my eyes.

"I'm fine. But I won't be if you don't mo—" He thrusts all the way in, filling me so completely that I lose my train of thought. "Yes!"

He leans down again, only this time, his warm tongue finds my neck instead of my lips. He licks a path toward my ear while pulling his cock back almost completely. When he slams back in, he bites my earlobe softly, drawing another moan of ecstasy from me. I can't lie still; I need to meet his thrusts pound for pound. My nails find his exposed back, and when I run them over his skin, scratching him, he hisses against my mouth.

Sudden urgency takes hold of us. Rikkon increases the pace, getting larger inside of me. I clench my walls around his cock, loving the sensation that's quickly building below. I'm torn between wanting the grand finale and prolonging the journey.

"Mir, fuck," he breathes out, fanning hot air against my mouth.

I thought I had more time, I thought I could hold on longer, but when the climax comes, it devastates me. It levels me to the ground. I cry out, digging my nails into his back so hard that I know I draw blood. Rikkon gives another final hard push and then he's unraveling like me. His body shakes as he rides his own wave of pleasure. He doesn't slow down, though. He keeps pumping in and out as if he too doesn't want this to end. Only when the tremors running through his body subside does he slow down.

"Holy shit," he murmurs against the crook of my neck, sagging on top of me but careful not to squash me.

I can't even reply to that because my thoughts are adrift in the galaxy. All I can do is try to catch my breath.

"Mir?" he asks, rolling off to the side. "Are you okay?"

"Never been better in my entire life."

"I didn't hurt you too much?" He frowns.

Seeing him so worried fills me with emotion. My heart swells, overflowing with my love for him.

"Not at all. You were amazing."

His concern melts into the most radiant smile I've ever seen. It's contagious, and it melts my bones. I reach for him, finding his cock still hard. I curl my fingers around his length and tug a little. His eyes become hooded, blazing with need.

"Is this Nightingale stamina?" I ask.

"No, this is hunger for you." He bites my shoulder lightly, and in response I pump his shaft, loving how he grows larger in my hand.

"I'm game for the second round if you are," I say.

"God, yes."

"But I want to ride you this time."

His lips curl into a crooked grin. "As you wish."

My pussy clenches in anticipation, but a knock on the door erases any ideas of fun time from my mind.

Forty-Two

RIKKON

Miranda tenses in my arms, widening her eyes. I press my index finger against my lips, signaling for silence, and then I listen beyond the cabin. The moment my awareness reaches outside, I recognize Castiel's essence.

"Rik, I know you and Miranda are in there. This is an emergency."

Miranda sits up, covering her breasts with her arms.

"Give me a second," I say.

I hand over her clothes. They're still damp, but it's better than letting Castiel see her naked.

"I'm sorry, they're not dry yet."

"It's okay. At least they're not freezing cold anymore."

While she gets dressed, I put my own clothes back on. In another minute, I'm opening the cabin's door and finding Castiel pacing in front of the building.

"What's the emergency and how did you know I was here?"

He gives me a sardonic look. "You've crossed into my territory. I knew the moment your ass landed in front of this cabin."

Right. I had forgotten he's now the crown heir, and thus, more connected with the magic of his land.

"What's the emergency?" Miranda asks as she sticks her head outside.

Castiel's gaze softens. "I'm glad you're in one piece, Miranda. The reports I received from Selor were disturbing."

"What's going on?" I ask.

"Eriel destroyed the marsh people's settlement. She froze everything in a five-mile radius. Queen Dunkara of Hydra is incensed and she's blaming Aquila for Eriel's actions since she's your fated mate. On top of that, King Titus has given Queen Maewe an ultimatum. If she doesn't deliver you and the witch to him, he's declaring war against Aquila."

Son of a bitch.

The certainty I had that if I succumbed to my feelings for Miranda are coming to fruition. A war between Aquila and Cygnus would be disastrous for the entire realm. Kingdoms will form alliances and the conflict will last centuries. Meanwhile, no one will care about the vampires, who are dying without our magic. And without them, we can't fight the threat of the shad-owbeasts.

"That's bullshit," Miranda pipes up. "Eriel killed innocents without a care. She tried to kill *me*. Rikkon is not the bad guy, nor should he be held responsible for that psycho bitch's actions."

I pass a hand over my face. "It doesn't matter, Mir. King Titus will use any excuse to come after us. He's been dying to conquer Aquila for millennia. I just gave him the perfect excuse."

"Nothing is lost yet, Rikkon. You can still stop the war from happening," Castiel chimes in. "Marry the princess of Cygnus."

"No," Miranda blurts out. "He can't."

I don't move as I process Castiel's words. He's not wrong. If I marry Eriel, there's no war. I always knew that was the only outcome possible, but I was selfish and dared to hope I could carve out a different future for Miranda and I. But we'll never be happy while thousands of people suffer.

My heart is shattering as I turn to her. She reads the agony in my eyes and her face falls. Fat tears roll down her cheeks.

"Rik, you can't possibly be considering this," she says in a small voice. "There has to be another way."

My vision is blurry, and the lump in my throat is almost too thick for words. "A sacrifice has to be made, Mir, and it must come from me."

"If you marry her you will die," she sobs.

"No, I won't. But if I don't marry her, thousands will for sure. *You* will die. I can't allow that to happen."

"Your mother saw it!" she yells. "She told me she had a vision. If you marry Eriel, you will die. Please don't do this."

I pull her into my arms, needing to feel her body pressed against mine one last time. I kiss the top of her head, and murmur against it, "I'm sorry, Mir. It has to be me."

"No, it doesn't."

I look at Castiel. "Where's Eriel now?"

Miranda stiffens in my arms.

"You can't sense her anymore?" he asks.

"No, somehow the bond has been broken."

"My latest report told me she was heading back to Aquila, marching with her father's forces."

Miranda hasn't moved or said a word, so I pull her back to look into her eyes. What I see gleaming in them chills me to the bone. Then the vision comes clear in my head. Miranda sprawled on the grass of Aquila's gardens, her blood everywhere. Shocked by what I see, I don't react in time when she presses her lips to mine and steals my sword.

"Miranda, no!"

She's gone in the next second, vanishing like a ghost.

"What the hell!" Castiel pipes up. "Did she just walk the wind?"

I turn around while my heart is hammering inside of my chest. "Yes. She's going after Eriel. And she's going to die."

MIRANDA

I didn't say goodbye, I didn't tell him I loved him. There was no time. I had to act fast. When I heard what Rikkon intended to do, give himself up to Eriel, I couldn't let him go through with it. With my despair came the solution, as clear as day, followed by the magic that I needed to pull it off. I realized then that Queen Maewe had created a link between her and me. The idea wasn't mine, just like the magic wasn't either.

I don't care though. When I land on the outskirts of the palace, just at the edge of the Sacred Forest, I'm ready to do what I must. I'm ready to fulfill my vow. Magic crackles between my fingers as I hold Rikkon's starfire sword. A twig snaps nearby, yet I don't turn to investigate. I know who is approaching.

"Hello, Selor. Glad to see you've made it back to the palace unscathed."

The warrior stops next to me, but keeps his gaze locked ahead.

"I did go after the prince, but I lost track of him in that damn jungle. You found him though." He gives me a sideway glance. "And you broke the bond."

Frowning, I turn to him. "*I* broke the bond?"

"Well, your near-death experience did. Don't ask me the details. Queen Maewe only told me the bare minimum."

I turn my attention back to the forest. "It's not enough though. Rikkon still feels obliged to marry the princess to avoid a war. I have to end this; I have to end *her*."

"It won't stop the war from coming," he replies solemnly.

Guilt makes my chest heavy. I'm willing to condemn thousands of lives in order to save one. Rikkon might never forgive me for it, and in the end, I will end up losing him anyway. But I can't stand aside and let him die, even if it's the moral thing to do. I'm resigned to my fate. I'll become the villain in the story so he can live.

"I'm aware of that," I reply.

I sense Selor give me an appraising glance. "I didn't think you had it in you, little witch. I won't deny it, if it weren't for my vow to not harm you, you wouldn't be standing here."

"I know."

"But I'm glad I couldn't kill you. You're making me damn proud."

I give him a quizzical glance. "You're proud that I'm willing to let thousands perish in order to save Rikkon?"

He snorts. "Fuck yeah. I'm here to help."

"How?"

"The princess is traveling with an army. Getting to her will be impossible. But she'll break away from the safety of her knights if she believes Rikkon is calling for her."

I glance at Selor again, finding him grinning like a veritable psychopath. "And how are you going to accomplish that?"

"I'm going to recreate the magic of the bond and lure her to you."

"She must have sensed the bond is gone."

He shakes his head. "Nah, she's too fanatical about it. She believes the bond is unbreakable."

"You seem to know a lot about Eriel for someone who's been gone for centuries."

"It's my duty to know thin—" He stops speaking abruptly and faces ahead, his spine going taut. "They're approaching."

I strain my ears, but I hear nothing. "Are you sure?"

"Yes, I'm sure. Get ready and hide." He shoves me to the side, almost making me fall.

Fucking asshole. Grumbling, I pick the first tree I find. Any will do since the tree trunks are so wide an elephant could hide behind them. My heart beats staccato, too loud for my liking. With the Nightingale enhanced senses, I'll be found out soon. I have to somehow conceal my presence.

A spark of magic in my vest pocket catches my attention. There's something inside it now. I'm not even surprised when I pull Tom Mularkey's notebook from it. I had packed it in my bag, but I thought I had lost it when I went after Rikkon in the Hydra jungle. There's no point wondering how its magic works. For all I know, Selor is able to move the object with his mind without needing to be near it or touch it.

He told me its contents change. Maybe there's a spell in here that will shield me from detection. I hear the sound of hooves and paws on the forest ground now, which means the soldiers and Eriel are getting closer. Not wanting to sheathe my sword, I try to flip the pages with only one hand. But I'm shaking uncontrollably, and it isn't helping.

Duh, Miranda. Use your magic. This is the simplest spell.

Holding the notebook on my open palm, I make the pages turn slowly enough that I can quickly scan the text. The literature is still the same as the first time, and I begin to suspect Selor lied, until I finally find a story that portrays exactly what I'm trying to do.

There once was a fair maiden
Her beauty was a thing of wonder
But happiness it did not bring her
Only envy and obsession
She wished to disappear from the world
So she begged the Dark Moon goddess
For the power to become invisible at will
Only the goddess couldn't grant her wish
Instead she gave her the power to hide in plain sight
Recite these three words, she said
Praetexo, abrogatio, praetereo
And think of me
No one you pass will sense you
It will be like you were not there

All I have to do is repeat those words like a mantra and think about the Dark Moon goddess. I have no clue what she's supposed to look like. The noises of the army are much louder now, and no doubt, Selor already set his trap for Eriel. I have to act fast. I close my eyes for a second and the image I conjure up in my head of the Dark Moon goddess is basically Castiel's female version. I hope it works.

I sense no change, no tingling over my skin to let me know if the spell took effect. *Damn it.* I guess I have to trust it did. The army is moving away from us now, which means they're continuing their march to the Aquila castle. However, I pick up the noise of a sole mount coming closer.

Eriel.

All my muscles tense as I hold Rikkon's sword with both hands. My heart is beating so fast I'm afraid it's going to burst out of my chest.

"Rikkon?" Eriel's voice echoes in the forest.

This is it. It's now or never.

I stick my head out and see Eriel atop a white-furred creature. It looks like the beast that was chasing me in that winter wasteland. *Damn it, how am I supposed to cut her head off while she has the advantage of the higher ground?*

Simple, Miranda. You fucking fly.

With a fortifying breath, I step away from my hiding place. There are dry twigs on the ground, but they don't snap and thus alert the princess of my presence, nor does her animal sniff out my approach. My legs tense a second before I break into a run. She begins to turn in my direction, forcing me to leap before I intended. The words of the flying spell pop into my mind, and I don't even have to say it out loud for it to work. It seems my magic is supercharged, indubitably by Queen Maewe. I raise my sword above my head and let out a war cry. Eriel sees me then, but she doesn't have time to react save for widening her eyes.

My blow doesn't land where it should though. A powerful gale knocks me off course and sends me to the ground. I get the wind knocked out of me and lose my grip on the sword. My vision is spotty and blurry for a second. When it finally clears, Rikkon's face appears above mine. Anger surges through me, giving me enough strength to shove him off.

"What the hell, Rikkon!" I yell.

"I couldn't let you kill her, Mir. I couldn't let you destroy your soul for me."

I want to argue, to hit him in the chest out of frustration. I was so close to freeing him. But the air around us crackles with cold magic, raising the small hairs on my arms.

"This is the second time you've tried to kill me, witch," Eriel seethes. "Nothing will save you now."

Rikkon gets in front of me again. "No. Stop it, Eriel. There's no need for this."

Quicker than a snake, she sends bolts of ice our way. Rikkon screams when his feet become encased in blocks of ice. Eriel's long hair flies around her head as she gathers her powers, and her rage-filled eyes turn electric blue.

"You were my mate, but you chose to turn your back on the most sacred magic in all Ellnesari for that whore. You broke our bond. I'm not going to end her, I'm going to end you both, and then, I'm going to freeze everything in Aquila."

A massive ball gathers between her hands. She just created a storm system. We're seconds away from turning into ice statues forever. I focus on walking the wind and taking Rikkon with me, but the magic doesn't work. It seems whatever Eriel did to him is also keeping me from accessing my magic.

Selor. Where the hell is he?

Eriel's mount rears on its hind legs, roaring as if in pain. Not expecting the sudden shift, she falls off, out of sight, and then Selor is there, bloody sword in his hand. He rushes to us and presses his glowing blade on Rikkon's ice shackles.

"Go on. Take Miran—"

He never finishes his sentence for he turns into an ice sculpture even as his mouth forms the words.

"No!" I scream.

My voice is swallowed by the sudden void and lack of physical form. When I regain the feel of my body once again, we're out of the forest, but I'm too disoriented to recognize my whereabouts.

Rikkon's arms are still wrapped around my body, and he's blocking my view.

He jumps to his feet, dragging me with him. "Come on, Mir. We need to get you to safety."

My eyes widen in horror when a dark blue portal appears behind us, and Eriel steps from it. She's got another freeze ball in her hand, ready to strike.

"Watch out!" I push Rikkon off me with all the strength I have as I jump back.

Her strike lands where we were standing a second ago. Shouts in the vicinity catch my attention, but I don't dare to investigate who is approaching. The biggest threat is this cunt from hell.

Now that Rikkon and I are split, she can't attack us at the same time. It's no surprise she focuses her aim on me now.

Use the gift I bestowed upon you, Miranda, Queen Maewe's voice sounds in my head.

She's the most powerful queen in Ellnesari but she's choosing to not get directly involved. No, she's using me as her puppet, so she can claim I was acting alone. I've allowed her to turn me into a mindless drone and now there's nothing for it.

Before Eriel can create another freeze bomb, I aim my hand at the ground beneath her feet and command giant roots to spring forth and trap the bitch, just like Rikkon and I were trapped when we arrived here. My order is heeded; the ground does open to allow the roots to rise up. But Eriel freezes them before she is ensnared.

Rikkon jumps in front of me, creating a buffer between Eriel and me. "Enough, Eriel. If you want to take your revenge, kill me."

Ugh. What's up with him willing to sacrifice himself at every turn?

Annoyed, I use Queen Maewe's wind magic to shove Rikkon out of Eriel's range and fly toward the bitch, hitting her odious face with my fist before she can freeze me to death. We fall hard on the ground, tangled and fighting for dominance. She's trying to freeze my arms but somehow, her magic is not finding leverage. Either my punch stunned her or something else is afoot.

But for all my rage, she manages to pin me down and wrap her icy fingers around my neck.

"You will die, witch, one way or another."

I try to pry her hands off me, but she's awfully strong. Even with borrowed magic, I can't make her budge. Black dots appear in my field of vision. I hear Rikkon scream my name, but his voice sounds far away. I'm about to pass out when a shadow collides with Eriel, pushing her off me. Without the constriction around my neck, I try to draw air in, but there's something wrong with me. A gurgling sound escapes my lips as I try to gasp. With a shaking hand, I touch my neck, finding it warm and wet. Blood. I'm drowning in my own blood.

Forty-Three

RIKKON

Everything happens so fast, I can hardly keep track of what's going on around me. Miranda once again tapped into the powers of the Aquila royal line and used it against me. Somehow, my mother has given her the ability for her own nefarious gain. But Eriel is stronger and Miranda quickly loses the upper hand.

I prepare to walk the wind and tear Eriel off Miranda when Cygnus soldiers break through the forest, ready to engage in battle. Behind me, my mother's soldiers materialize and prepare to defend the castle. I'm caught in the middle of the two fronts, stuck between a surge of power belonging to two formidable armies.

I did everything fathomable to stop this from happening and it's all for nothing. But I can still save the love of my life.

A chill licks the back of my neck as a sense of dread drops from the sky like a bomb. My blood runs cold when I recognize what's coming for us.

"Shadowbeasts!" I yell.

I turn just in time to see Eriel fly backward and then get ripped to shreds by an invisible foe. Her screams soon become muffled by the sound of soldiers either panicking or attempting to fight the shadowbeasts. There's no time to react, no chance to try to save her life. The shadowbeast turned her body into something unrecognizable. No healer in this world would be able to put her back together.

I walk the wind to where Miranda is and freeze as I come face-to-face with what I saw in my vision. A huge gash sits starkly on her neck, blood everywhere. Shuddering, I drop to my knees and pull her into my arms. Her eyes are wide and fearful as she reaches for my face.

"No, my love. You can't die on me." I press my hand on her throat, trying to stop the blood from flowing out, but that's not the only problem. She can't breathe.

"Miranda!" a female yells nearby.

I lift my face and see Aurora running across the field followed by Saxon. A moment later Vivienne and Lucca appear, and then Ronan, Manu, Karl, Cheryl, and finally Solomon. The vampires and wolf shifters see the shadowbeasts and immediately engage in battle. I'm too lost in my despair to wonder how they managed to cross into Ellnesari.

Aurora reaches us first, stumbling to her knees.

"What happened?" she asks through tears.

"A shadowbeast got her. I couldn't stop it from happening," I answer through my hopelessness.

"You got your powers back, Rik," Vivienne, who has just reached us, chimes in. "You can heal her."

Naturally, she can sense that I'm not an empty shell anymore.

Miranda's eyes begin to shut so I shake her. "No, don't go yet. Please."

"If you can heal her, do it now!" Aurora screams in my face.

My hands shake as I attempt to close the gash and stop the blood from spilling, but as hard as I push, the magic is not doing its job. I'm failing her again.

"She's gone, my son. Let it go," my mother tells me in her cool tone.

I look over my shoulder and find her there, serene, as if the love of my life wasn't dying in my arms.

"She's not dead yet. I can feel her heartbeat."

She links her fingers together. "It's only a matter of minutes now."

Aurora jumps to her feet and, quaking with fury, shouts, "If you can save her, why are you just standing there?"

"Because my mother is a heinous bitch who cares about no one," Vivienne snaps.

She ignores Vivienne in favor of answering me. "Miranda has served her purpose. She freed you from the bond with Princess Eriel, and indirectly, she killed her. She was never meant to be your consort, Rikkon."

"I don't care about what she was meant to be. I love her! I'm begging you. Save her."

"Oh, for fuck's sake, Maewe. Enough with the petty games," my father replies as he walks over, unfazed by the shadowbeasts that are still giving hell to the Cygnus soldiers.

As a matter of fact, only the Cygnus soldiers seem to be in trouble.

"This is not a game, Ruel. I'm not about to lose my son again to someone who is not good enough for him."

"Not good enough for me?" My voice rises to a snarl. "Have you stopped to consider that maybe I'm not good enough for her?"

My throat is raw from yelling. I have never felt more like an utter failure than I do now at the mercy of the whims of my odious mother. And then comes the worst blow. I see the ugly truth in her eyes and with that comes the unshakable, absolute certainty that every word out of her mouth since we got here has been a lie. She didn't have a vision of my death. The only reason she condemned me to almost a millennium of torture, the only reason she wanted to break my bond to Eriel, was so I wouldn't tie Aquila to Cygnus through marriage.

"Well, too fucking bad." Dad crouches next to me and touches the side of Miranda's neck.

"What do you think you're doing, Ruel?" Mom asks, incensed.

The gash on Miranda's neck knits back together, and her face that had already taken the color of death becomes rosier again. With a loud gasp, she opens her eyes.

"Rik? What happened?" she croaks.

Pushing Dad out of the way, I pull her tight against my chest and kiss her forehead. "It doesn't matter now, Mir. You're back with me. You're back with me."

"I can't believe you flouted my wishes!" my mother shrieks.

Dad stands to his full height and faces her, sporting a smirk. "Oh, I did more than that, my dear. I made her immortal."

I glance at Miranda again, and then notice the difference in her aura. She's no longer human, she's a Nightingale. All these years, and I had no idea Dad had that kind of power.

Mom's face turns scarlet, something that doesn't happen often. I jump to my feet, carrying Miranda in my arms, and step away. She is about to blow, and I don't want to be near her.

"How dare you? I'm the queen and you went against my desires. I ought to have you killed for treason."

"And who is going to take care of that for you? Selor? Isn't he dead?"

I catch a small wince from Mom, but she puts the irate mask back in place. *She did care about that psychotic male. Who knew?*

"You won't do anything, because you can't," my father continues calmly. "I might not have political power in your court, but you need allies more than ever, now that King Titus has shown his hand. Kill me and you lose the support of the Vega kingdom."

"Your sister cares about you as much as I do."

"She might not like me much, but she hates you more. Besides, technically, I didn't go against your wishes. You never told me not to heal the witch girl or not to make her immortal.

Like you never told me not to restore Vryenn's powers." He extends his arm, pointing at Vivienne.

Shimmery magic shoots out from his index finger and hits my sister right in the middle of her chest. Her back arches forward as the magic returns to her center. She gasps loudly as her entire body begins to glow from within. Her hair strands twist wildly as a gust of wind envelops her, lifting her off the ground for a moment. I hear a male call her name, no doubt Lucca who must be freaking out at the sight.

"You vile male!" my mother screeches, gathering all her power into her frame.

A dark storm cloud forms above her head, crackling with energy. She's gone berserk and she doesn't care if her actions will create more conflict in Ellnesari. Queen Merissa, Dad's sister, won't hesitate to avenge his death even if they're not close as siblings.

Dad doesn't look worried about what Mom is about to unleash, though. He crosses his arms in front of his chest and watches her with a smug expression. The sense of foreboding returns, making my spine go taut. Shadowbeasts are approaching.

"Behind you, Rik," Miranda warns me.

I whirl around, ready to walk the wind and take her to safety. Lucca, who has found his way back to my sister's side, holds his sword at the ready.

"Don't worry, son. They're not going to harm you. The queen, I'm not so sure about," Dad tells me.

Mom's eyes widen a fraction before she furrows her eyebrows. "You are behind this!" she hisses.

From the corner of my eye, I see Castiel approach us, looking grim and guilty. Disappointment washes over me. He was the one behind these mutated shadowbeasts just as I suspected. When he stops next to my father, he meets my stare for only a fleeting moment before he glances at the ground.

Motherfucker. He experimented on the marsh people. And then Eriel decimated them. I'll never forgive him for that.

"Was I?" My father arches an eyebrow, answering my mother's accusation.

Right. He will never confess to something so atrocious. He'd lose any support from the other courts if they discover he brought the shadowbeasts back to life.

Telar Nyrk, Selor's younger brother, strides in our direction. His brow is creased, but other than that, he doesn't have a hair out of place. After all, the shadowbeasts only attacked the Cygnus soldiers.

"The enemy has retreated, Your Majesties," he announces.

"Excellent," Dad replies.

I sense the approach of more people and I'm not surprised when Ronan, Saxon, Manu, Cheryl, Karl, and Solomon join our group. The tension in the air increases exponentially, but the animosity is stronger from Manu, who is glaring openly at my mother.

No one utters a word. We're all waiting for the ruler of Aquila to speak her mind. It's clear to me what needs to be done though.

"What are your orders, my queen?" Telar asks when all Mom does is continue to glower at our group in silence.

"Return to your station. It seems you weren't needed after all."

The slight narrowing of his eyes tells me Telar is not happy about her dismissal. He's a male of honor and his loyalty to Aquila is far superior to what Selor's ever was. He wants retribution, I can read him clearly.

"My father is aware of King Titus's treachery. He's called for a grand council meeting," Castiel chimes in.

"That's unnecessary," my mother replies, looking bored already.

Back to her games, I see. How quickly she can change from being a second away from bringing the power of storms down to this pervasive aloofness.

Castiel seems to grow taller. "Forgive me, I misspoke, Your Majesty. He's not asking for your permission. There will be a grand council meeting whether you choose to attend or not. All the other rulers have confirmed their attendance save for the heir of Tenebris."

Her nostrils flare, another disruption of her cold mask. "Where will the grand council meeting take place?"

"I suggested here, Your Majesty. But if you're not willing to attend, then we can easily host it in Lynx."

"No. We'll have the meeting here. We're the kingdom that Titus attacked, after all. The meeting will take place tomorrow. I don't want to give that snake time to regroup."

She glances at Miranda and me for a second with eyes brimming with hate. She'll claim all the suffering she put me through was to save me from marrying Eriel, but the reality is, she doesn't care about my happiness. She just didn't want an alliance with Cygnus. And to think that for a moment, I actually believed she had good intentions. She snorts in derision before she walks the wind and vanishes from sight.

"Rik, you can put me down now," Miranda tells me.

She's covered in blood still and I'm hesitant to let go. "I don't mind carrying you, my love."

"Aha! I knew you were sniffing around her skirt," Saxon pipes up.

Aurora hits his chest with the back of her hand. "Sax, we talked about that."

"Miranda is the woman I love," I reply. "You'd better get used to it."

The cocky vampire's expression softens. "That's good to know. Then you have my blessing."

Aurora turns to him, mouth agape. "Okay, we really need to have a serious conversation about your role in our family."

"Now that my lovely wife is gone, I'd very much like to know how you lot managed to find a way back into Ellnesari," Dad chimes in.

Solomon takes a step forward. "I can answer that, Your Majesty, but not before we're all rested and fed."

My father's lips split into an amused grin. "Very well. It shall be done."

"Wait. We're not going back home now?" Miranda asks.

Solomon turns to her. "I'm afraid we're going to need some assistance from our hosts for that."

Fuck. If he means he needs my mother's cooperation, they might be stuck here for a while.

Forty-Four

MIRANDA

The king made good on his promise and assigned everyone in my rescue party luxurious apartments. Understandably, the vampires weren't keen on staying in Ellnesari, especially under Queen Maewe's roof. I feel the same way. She used me to further her agenda but was happy to let me die. If it weren't for the surprising benevolence of King Ruel, I'd be gone. I still haven't wrapped my mind around the fact that he turned me into a Nightingale. I don't feel any different than before.

Rikkon insisted that I stay with him, which caused a little bit of an argument between him, Aurora, and Saxon. I had to put my foot down and tell them there was nothing they could say that'd keep me apart from Rikkon. We've gone through too much to be separated now.

Now that I'm alone with him, I don't know what to do with myself. All the events from the past twenty-four hours weigh heavily on my shoulders, leaving me quite numb.

"Mir, are you all right?" Rikkon stops in front of me, touching my arms gently.

I lift my chin so I can meet his concerned gaze. "I don't know what I'm supposed to feel now, to be honest."

"You're still in shock. It's okay. I'm here for you if you want to talk, cuddle, or sit alone for a while."

"I don't want to be alone," I reply quickly, dreading the idea.

He cups my face tenderly, rubbing my cheek with his callused thumb. The caress sends a ripple of pleasure down my spine.

"Then I shall be glued to your side like chewing gum on the bottom of a shoe." He gives me a tentative smile, and it acts like air fanning over a small fire, feeding it until the flames grow larger and brighter.

"I think a bath is in order," I say.

He nods. "I'll set it up for you."

"I want you to take it with me."

His eyes widen a fraction before his face breaks into a broad smile. "As you wish."

He takes my hand and steers me to his bedroom. My gaze focuses on his enormous bed and a blush creeps up my cheeks as I remember the last time I was here.

"Definitely better than that old, dusty couch," he says as if guessing my train of thought.

I don't reply because as unattractive and uncomfortable as that old cabin was, I'll always cherish that memory. Rikkon saved my life that day and what happened after was just a beautiful thing.

His bathroom is twice the size of mine, and so is the bathtub —more like a medium-sized pool. I'm not surprised it's full and ready to be used. Steam is wafting off the water, which has made the space pleasantly warm. If I was alone, I'd probably fall asleep in the water, but that won't happen in Rikkon's presence. I'm too in tune with him and the electric sparks that crackle between our bodies.

"Do you need help with your clothes?" he asks.

"What? No. What made you ask that?"

My face is on fire now, and I know I'm blushing ten thousand ways to kingdom come.

"Because you were staring at the bath for a whole minute without speaking." He chuckles.

"Was I? I didn't realize."

"I'll turn around and wait until you're in."

It would probably help with my sudden jitters, but I won't take him up on his offer. It would be foolish. He's seen me naked before.

"No need."

I unbutton my vest first, which is stiff thanks to the dried blood. It's the same deal with my tunic, which I toss as far away from me as possible. I never want to see that piece of clothing again. Rikkon's eyes drop to my exposed breasts and I swear they grow larger. When he swallows, it's audible. I lose my nerve right before I unbutton my pants because he's standing there, watching me with heat in his gaze.

"Do you plan to bathe wearing your clothes?" I ask.

He blinks a couple of times as if to clear his mind from a daze. Then his face becomes beet red. Seeing him flustered so easily makes me feel better about my own awkwardness.

"No, of course not," he says at last.

I wait until he catches up with me to continue undressing myself. But maybe I shouldn't have done it because now that he's shirtless, I'm the one ogling and unable to move a muscle. Rikkon is not as buff as the vampires, but he's seriously shredded. *Wide chest? Check. Washboard abs? Check. Impressive, muscled arms? Check.* And he's all mine. Now it's my turn to swallow loudly.

He raises an eyebrow, smirking. "Do you plan on bathing with your trousers on?"

"Nope."

My hands are shaking as I pull my pants and underwear down. I try to do so as gracefully as I can, but afraid to look like a one-legged kangaroo, I recite the floating spell under my breath. Rikkon, missing nothing, chuckles.

"What's so funny?" I throw my pants in his direction, hitting him in the chest.

The amusement vanishes from his stare in an instant. "Nothing, absolutely nothing."

I sense his intention. He's going to shorten the distance between us and slant his mouth over mine. I yearn for that, but I'm too aware that I'm covered in dirt and blood. I turn around and dive into the bath—pool, whatever—forgetting to ask if it was deep enough. Lucky for me, it is, and I don't split my skull open on the bottom.

Still underwater, I hear the splash of Rikkon jumping in too. When I break the surface, he's behind me, pulling me flush against his chest. His arms wrap tightly around my waist, and his erection is pressing against my ass when he kisses the curve of my neck, giving me goose bumps despite the heated water.

"Rik," I mumble, shutting my eyes for a second. "I'm filthy."

"I don't care," he whispers in my ear.

I manage to turn around in his arms, putting myself in an even more dangerous situation. His cock is now closer to where I desperately need it to be. And looking at his beautiful face, I can barely concentrate.

"Where's the soap?" I ask, almost out of breath.

His lips twist into a crooked grin. Without breaking eye contact, he lifts his arm and using his magic, flies the bar into his hand.

"Neat trick," I say.

"You can do the same, you know."

"Yeah, using my floating spell."

He shakes his head. "Mir, you have the same magic as I do now. You can control the wind."

My eyebrows shoot to the heavens. "Really?"

"Can't you feel the power inside you, swirling in your chest?"

"I-I don't know. My mind is still whirring. I'm an immortal now and I'm not sure how I feel about that yet."

He runs his soapy hand across my cleavage, and then up the column of my neck. "I can tell you how I feel. I'm over the moon. I'm the happiest male in the universe that I'll never have to say goodbye to you. Well, if you want me by your side for all eternity, that is."

My heart is beating so fast now, it feels like I have a drummer trapped inside.

"Yes." The answer whooshes out of me in a powerful gust. "I'm confused about my new reality, but there's no doubt in my mind of how I feel about you. I love you with all my heart, with all my soul."

"Thank heavens." He captures my face between his hands and kisses me deep and hard.

I open my lips to him, welcoming his sweet invasion, while I wrap my arms around his waist. Rikkon releases my face to run his fingers down my back until they reach the curve of my ass. The seed of desire that had taken root before we got into the pool grows like a savage weed. I'm burning for him, for his fiery touch and kisses.

With little effort, I bring my legs up, and hook them behind Rikkon, opening myself for more friction, more of him. He groans as he adjusts his position, bringing his cock flush with my clit.

"Rik. That feels amazing."

"I want to make you feel even better, my love."

He glides to the edge of the pool, keeping his lips locked with mine. But then he releases my mouth and before I can protest, he lifts off and sets me down on the ledge.

"Rik, what are you doing?"

He nudges my legs wider and places an open kiss on each of my inner thighs. A shiver runs down my spine, and my nipples pucker, turning into pebbles.

"Now that there's no bond, no running for our lives, I want to take my time savoring you, Mir. Will you let me?"

My throat is suddenly parched, making it hard to reply. It feels like my tongue is stuck to the roof of my mouth.

"Yes," I breathe out.

Rikkon keeps his eyes locked with mine as he places a soft kiss on my pubic bone. I gasp loudly, unprepared for the sensation of his lips so close to my core. He rewards me with a crooked smile, before he nudges my clit with his nose and then sweeps his tongue over my bundle of nerves. Curling my fingers around the edge of the pool, I throw my head back and moan out loud. My voice echoes in the room, which would normally make me blush, but I've already passed the point of caring.

The noises coming out of my mouth seem to motivate him more. Gripping my hips, he pulls me even closer to him and launches a merciless attack with his tongue, licking and sucking as if I were the most delicious meal in the world.

My body quickly melts like ice cream in the sun, and to make sure I'm not dreaming, I thread my fingers through Rikkon's hair. When he nibbles my clit lightly, I twist my fingers around a lock of his hair and yank.

He leans back and looks at me. "Should I stop, Mir?" His tone is taunting, matching the wicked grin on his lips.

"No, I want more, much more."

"Your wish is my command."

He resumes his tongue work, but he brings the torture up a notch by inserting two fingers inside of me. The pressure keeps building, only it's ten times more intense than during our first time. It's almost like all my senses are enhanced. This could be related to me being a Nightingale now or to the fact Rikkon is getting better at making love to me. Either way, the room is spinning, and my boneless body can only take so much before it shatters.

I lean back on my elbows, biting on my lower lip to keep my moans from turning into screams of pleasure. It's pointless. When my release comes, it equals the force of a category EF5 tornado. It levels me to the ground, turning me into dust. Not even my elbows can sustain the weight of my upper body now. I collapse on the floor, not caring about the tile's hard bite, and try to catch my breath. Only Rikkon doesn't give me the chance. Using his wind magic, he whisks me into his arms and flies us back to his bedroom, to his bed.

"We're drenched," I say when we both bounce on the soft mattress.

He's lying partially on top of me with his arm across my belly and his leg between mine.

"I don't care. I was selfish and didn't stop to think that position at the pool wasn't comfortable for you."

"Do you think I noticed that?" I laugh.

"Still, I'm sorry." He kisses my neck, turning me into goo again.

I push him off me and onto his back. "It's my turn to play now."

"Oh?" He raises an eyebrow.

"I said I wanted to ride you the last time, and I plan on sticking to the plan."

Smiling from ear to ear, Rikkon pulls me astride him, bringing my pussy right over his erection. "I love your commitment."

Using my hand, I guide him to my wet center. I'm still sore from the last time but the pleasure overrides the pain. Slowly, I impale myself on him, loving when his eyes roll back in their sockets followed by a throaty moan.

"Fuck. You feel so good, Mir."

"It's about to get much better."

I lift my hips, unsheathing myself from him almost completely, only to lower again fast. Rikkon hisses, narrowing his eyes as he digs his fingers into my skin. I repeat my movement one more time before Rikkon takes control, setting the pace. He bucks his hips forward, thrusting into me fast. I don't care who is in charge to be honest. I'm too lost in the feel of him inside of me, in the way he looks at me with love and passion. I surrender myself to the moment until I become nothing but stardust again.

RIKKON

After our ordeal over the past few days, one would think rest was a sure thing. But Miranda and I couldn't sleep as we tried to erase all the ache of not being able to be together for so long. We made love all night, and only when the first rays of light began to drift through the window did exhaustion finally take over.

I have no idea what time of the day it is now. But my body is awake and hungry for more. Miranda is tucked nicely in my arms, resting her head on my chest. I run lazy fingers over her shoulder, making her purr like a kitten.

"Don't tell me it's time to get up yet," she murmurs.

"We don't have to leave this bed if all you want to do is stay in." I kiss the top of her head.

"I love that idea, but only if we can get room service. It feels like I haven't eaten in forever."

I chuckle. "That can be arranged. I have something for you right now if you fancy a—"

She lifts her face to mine and glares. "If you say a tube steak, I'm going to lose it."

I bite my tongue, fighting the laugh. "Fair. I won't say it. How about a sausage?"

She pushes off me, pretending to be angry. "Good grief, Rik. You'd better acquire a better vocabulary. You're an immortal, for crying out loud."

"You didn't mind my dirty vocabulary last night." I lean on my elbow and bite her arm playfully.

A flush colors her cheeks, and when she nibbles on her lower lip, it takes everything in me not to pounce on her right away.

I reach behind her head, tangling my fingers in her hair, and say, "Come here."

She doesn't put up a fight as she leans over and lets me greet her properly. I only planned on an innocent kiss, but the moment our tongues touch, an electric spark runs through my body, reminding me that I just can't do innocent when it comes to her.

She pulls away, laughing. "Wow. Aren't you tired?"

"Never when I'm around you." I try to capture her lips again, but she leans back and then flicks my nose. "Hold that thought. I need to pee first."

Dejected, I sink back on the mattress. "Fine. But hurry back."

No sooner has she disappeared through the bathroom door, than I sense Castiel's presence outside of my apartment. In an instant, the bliss of this morning is gone. The last thing I want is to look at his duplicitous face, but part of me wants to know why he did what he did.

I get out of bed and put my pants back on. Miranda returns to the room then, and seeing me standing half dressed, frowns.

"What's the matter?"

"Castiel is here."

Understanding dawns on her face. "Oh. I'd better get dressed then."

I nod. "Join me when you're ready."

"You don't want to speak to him alone?"

"No. I have nothing to hide from you, Mir. You're part of my world now, so you should be privy to all the details, even the not-so-great ones."

"Okay. I'll be out in a moment."

On my way to the living room, I grab the shirt draped over a chair and only let Castiel in when I'm fully dressed.

I lower the wards, opening the door using magic from my spot near the window. Castiel enters, sporting a downcast expression in his eyes and a hard-set jaw.

"Thanks for letting me in."

"My curiosity worked in your favor. I want to know how those new shadowbeasts came to be."

He shifts on his feet, shoving his hands in his pockets. I've never seen him look so downtrodden.

"Shortly after the portals to the human world were sealed shut, rumors reached Lynx and Aquila of a possible betrayal by King Titus. He wasn't happy your mother banished you, knowing you and his daughter were mates. The only thing keeping him from declaring war was Eriel's hope that you would return to her soon."

"I know that story. She told me. What's that have to do with your disgusting experiment?"

Castiel's eyes flash with annoyance, but then Miranda's arrival catches his attention, and his gaze softens. That doesn't sit well with me. Immediately, my spine goes rigid. I pull her flush to my side in a possessive manner and I'm not even sorry about it.

"Tensions were brewing for centuries before the shadowbeasts appeared. You know that. My father knew it was only a matter of time before a new war broke out. When your father came to him with his idea, he didn't hesitate to let me return to Aquila and continue our project."

"What was the idea? Kidnap innocent villagers and turn them into monsters?" I grit out.

Castiel's eyes are shadowed with remorse. "That wasn't the scope of the project. I managed to isolate the magic that grants the shadowbeast their power of invisibility. The mutation of the marsh people was at your father's hands. I suspected it, but didn't have confirmation until that day in the lab when we performed the autopsy."

"Is there a cure for the mutation?" Miranda asks.

"I don't know. But it's unlikely King Ruel will be interested in that. He got what he wanted. An invisible army to set loose on his enemies."

"He's controlling the shadowbeasts. How?" I ask.

Castiel laughs ruefully. "Like I said, I don't have any involvement with that part. I don't know how he's doing it."

I pass a hand over my face. My father will never reveal that to any of us.

"I always knew he wasn't happy with his role in the Aquila court, and that he secretly coveted power. Now that he finally has the upper hand over my mother, he's going to hold on to it for as long as he can."

"I know what was done to the marsh people was horrible, but your father's beasts stopped the Cygnus forces from storming the castle," Miranda says.

I get what she's not saying. His beasts also killed Eriel before she could kill Miranda. Maybe that's why my father decided to spare her life in the end—out of guilt. He never intended to harm Miranda in the process. Unlike my mother. The memory alone makes me see red.

Everything starts to make sense though. Miranda and I were spared by the shadowbeasts during the attack in the castle. As a matter of fact, the beasts had been intent on killing Eriel.

Shit. He was trying to help me, which makes my guilt double. I was the one who started the project with Castiel.

"I wanted you to know the truth from me," Castiel continues. "I'm going back to Lynx after the grand council meeting."

"I believe that's the best choice for you." My gaze remains hard. I want him to know he's no longer welcome in Aquila even if I don't plan on staying much longer.

"Take care, Rikkon. For what it's worth, I *am* sorry for my part in this." He switches his attention to Miranda. "It was nice to meet you. Take good care of my friend."

He spares me another fleeting glance before he whirls around and walks out.

"Rik, I'm so sorry." Miranda rubs my back.

Frowning, I glance at her. "Don't be sorry, Mir."

"He was your best friend. I know how you must be feeling."

I touch her cheek gently, giving her a small smile. "I guess that spot is now taken by you."

"And Fili. I hope she's okay."

"She's okay. I can sense her flying above the castle."

Miranda lets out a relieved sigh. "Good. I wish we could bring her back with us to Salem. I mean, you want to go back, right?"

I see fear shining in her beautiful eyes and it kills me. "Of course I want to go back. Why would you think I wouldn't?"

"Because you had a miserable time in the human world and this is your homeland, for better or for worse."

"I did, until I met you. Even as a stranger, you made my world brighter, you breathed life into me. I love you more than all the stars in the universe combined, Mir." I pull her into my arms. "We're going back to Salem, and I see no reason why Fili can't come."

"She's a giant bird. People will notice her."

"So? Aren't there dragons in Salem?" I raise an eyebrow.

Suddenly, I sense a disturbance in the room. Someone is trying to break through my wards. I release Miranda and we prepare to defend ourselves. Tense now, I focus on the magic pressing against mine, but I can't discover who it is before the wards break and my father materializes in front of us.

"What the hell? Was that really necessary?" I ask, annoyed as hell. "I'd have let you in."

"I couldn't risk coming through the front door. We don't have much time. If you and your friends want to return to the human realm, it needs to happen now."

"What about the grand council? I should stay for that."

"It's because of the damn council that you need to leave now, all of you. I won't be able to protect your vampire friends if you stay."

"How come that wasn't brought to our attention yesterday?" I ask.

"Yesterday your mother hadn't thought of a counterattack. I should have known she'd retaliate quickly."

"Are the others in danger? Should we go to them?" Miranda asks, her voice rising in panic.

"They were the first ones I brought to safety. They're waiting for you at the edge of Hornet's Gardens."

"What? *That's* the safe place you thought to bring them?" I throw my hands up in the air.

"They're wearing the proper attire. The hellionflares won't bother them. You should make haste; the wards I set in place won't keep them hidden from your mother's guards for much longer."

He lifts his hand and points at my forehead. An image appears before my eyes of the exact location where the others are.

"Go now and don't look back."

"Where are we supposed to go from there? Who is going to open the portal to the human lands?" I ask.

"You, my son. You will open the portal. I just gave you the means to."

Dad vanishes from sight, leaving me reeling. But I can't dwell too much on this conversation now. He's not lying when he says we don't have much time. I was too stupid to not foresee Mom would strike back. Too bad the sight is not something I can control and it only manifests willy-nilly. A sooner warning would have been ideal.

"We're really going right now?" Miranda asks me. "What about Fili?"

"We can't fly with Fili to the rendezvous. She's too easy to spot. We have to walk the wind."

"Okay."

I pull her into my arms, making sure there's no chance in hell we'll get separated during the trip. "It's going to be okay, Mir. I promise."

"I know."

The trip only lasts a split second. When we land in the spot my father showed me, the entire gang is there.

Aurora sees us first, and rushes to steal Miranda from my arms. "Are you okay? I barely had a chance to talk to you yesterday."

"I'm fine, Rora."

"Rik, did Dad tell you what's going on?" Vivienne asks me.

"He was vague. Mother is plotting something. We need to leave Ellnesari at once."

"And who is going to open a portal for us?" Saxon puts his hands on his hips, looking as arrogant as ever.

"I will," I say, equally proud.

The gleam of surprise in his eyes is priceless. I think putting the cocky vampire in his place will be my favorite pastime when things return to normal.

"Well, if you're gonna do it, let's go. This place gives me the creeps," Solomon pipes up.

"Right. Everyone, gather around. I can only do this once."

Dad said he gave me the means to do it, but I have no fucking clue what he meant by that. I bring my focus inward, blocking out everything else. The first thing I sense swirling in my chest is my own power. It never felt brighter than it does now. It's not exactly a solid mass of energy, but tendrils that pulse in sync with my heartbeat. I plunge deeper and finally find my father's magic, pulsing in a different rhythm and color. I reach for it, discovering it's slippery, as if it doesn't want me to utilize it. I hold it tight with my hands and entwine it with a tendril of my own power. It resists at first, so I add another tendril, and another, until I can barely see it throbbing underneath. Finally, its pulse matches my power's rhythm, and a moment later, the colors almost match. The words for the spell appear as clear as day in my mind. I let the magic flow through me as I extend my arm. Power whooshes from my outstretched hand as the maelstrom gathers around me. I finally open my eyes and see the portal in front of me. I can't see what's on the other side though.

"You have to cross it now," I tell them.

I sense their unease. There's nothing in front of them but an opening with a blinding light that crackles with ancient magic.

"Do it!" I yell. "I can't hold it open for much longer."

"Oh, for fuck's sake. I'll go first." Solomon steps into the light and vanishes from sight.

Vivienne takes Lucca's hand and together they step into the portal. Aurora glances at Miranda and beckons her to cross together with her and Saxon, but Miranda shakes her head.

"I'm crossing with Rik."

"Come on, Rora. She'll be fine." Saxon tugs Aurora's hand.

She allows her mate to steer her into the portal, but she keeps her eyes on Miranda until the light swallows her.

Manu, Ronan, Karl, and Cheryl are next, but no one moves.

"What are you waiting for? Can't you see the strain on Rikkon from keeping the portal open?" Miranda yells at them, frustrated.

"Come on, Karl." Cheryl tries to drag her brother, but he glances at Manu, who makes no motion to step closer to the portal.

"You guys go ahead. I'll follow you," she tells them.

Karl and Ronan hesitate, and I'd push them with a gust of wind if I thought I could hold the portal open. Miranda, as if reading my mind, does exactly that. She pushes the trio closest to the opening through using her wind powers. Manu, who was out of Miranda's range, jumps even farther away from the portal.

I feel my hold on the magic slip, and the opening becomes visibly smaller.

"You have to cross over now, Manu," I grit out.

She shakes her head. "I'm not going back."

"What do you mean you're not going back?" Miranda's voice rises to a shriek.

"Tell Lucca that I'm sorry." She turns around and breaks into a run, vanishing from sight.

"What the hell!" Miranda takes a step in her direction, but I block her path.

"Mir, you can't go after her. If you do, you won't return home."

Her eyes go round, and I can see how torn she is about the decision looming in front of her. So I wrap my arms around her and jump into the portal. Miranda screams, just as she did on the trip here, but mercifully, it doesn't last as long.

The portal opens high above the ground and I barely have time to slow our fall. I realize then that the magic concealing Lucca's mansion prevented the opening from appearing any closer to the property. When we land, everyone turns to glare at me. It seems they took the brunt of the sky drop.

"Couldn't you have brought us closer to the front door?" Saxon complains.

"The wards surrounding the mansion prevented it," Miranda replies for me.

She steps away from my arms, avoiding my gaze. Is she angry that I didn't let her go after Manu?

"Where's my sister?" Lucca asks, frowning.

"She didn't want to come back," Miranda replies in a small voice.

"So you just left her behind?" Karl takes a step forward, glowering at me.

"She made her choice," I reply through clenched teeth. "She took off before we could force her through the portal. Going after her would mean getting stuck in Ellnesari. I couldn't do that to Miranda again."

"So now Manu is stuck there?" Lucca asks, narrowing his eyes.

"For now." I nod.

"Why would she want to stay?" Vivienne asks, hugging her middle.

She looks devastated by the news, and I understand why. She knows what fate awaits Manu in Ellnesari if our mother catches her.

"For revenge," Ronan replies, eyes growing dark. "She stayed in Ellnesari to kill Queen Maewe."

Lucca whirls around and faces his friend. "How do you know that? Did she tell you?"

"No, but I know Manu. The hate she feels for the queen has been festering all these years."

"Goddammit, that female!" Karl pulls his hair back, yanking at the strands.

"If that's her plan, it's foolhardy. Killing my mother is almost impossible," I say. "She'll get herself killed or worse."

"What's worse than dying?" Cheryl asks.

Vivienne and I trade a loaded glance. We've heard the awful stories about the fools who betrayed our mother. She sees death as too mild a punishment. It took millennia for Dad to finally go against her and he only did once he was sure she couldn't retaliate.

"You don't want to know," Vivi replies.

"Fuck. There's nothing for it now. We have to go back and drag Manu's sorry ass home," Lucca pipes up, glancing pointedly at me.

"The magic my father shared with me was for a one-way ticket only," I say. "How did you cross into Ellnesari?"

"We used the Taluah Mirror, but unfortunately, it was destroyed in the process," Vivienne replies, and everyone stares at Solomon.

His face twists into a scowl as he points his chubby finger at the group. "Don't you dare give me that accusatory glance. I warned you that would happen."

Karl walks away from us and stares at the forest that surrounds the property. "There has to be another way," he says in a desperate voice. "We can't abandon Manu in Ellnesari."

"Why not?" Cheryl asks, earning a growl from Lucca, which she ignores. "She had no problem abandoning *you*."

Karl looks over his shoulder. "You don't understand. You never will."

"I *do* understand, Karl. More than you know." She glances briefly in Ronan's direction before focusing on her brother again.

The tall vampire remains quiet, but his jaw hardens. I'm new to the group, but anyone with eyes can see there's something going on between Cheryl and Ronan. The tension is impossible to miss, but it seems everyone has chosen to ignore it for whatever reason.

Vivienne steps closer to Lucca. "We'll find another way into Ellnesari, Luc. I promise."

"Vivi, you cannot return," I tell her.

"Why the hell not?" She stands straighter. "I have my powers now."

"Exactly. Against Mom's wishes. She won't hesitate to come after you or Lucca."

The vampire prince pulls Vivi closer to him in a protective gesture. "She won't lay a hand on Vivi. I won't allow it."

Cheryl snorts. "No offense, dude. But what can you do against that female? Nothing. That's why going back to Ellnesari after Manu is a suicide mission."

"I don't care if it's a suicide mission. I'm going after her," Karl grits out.

"Karl—"

"Do you want your brother to die?" Ronan cuts Cheryl off. "If Manu dies in Ellnesari, so does Karl."

The blood seems to drain from Cheryl's face. She must have forgotten that detail. But quickly her consternation turns into ire. Her eyes flash bright yellow and her canines elongate. "And that's the only reason she's kept her head attached to her body."

Her body trembles and a moment later, she turns into a gray wolf and races off into the forest.

"You're back!" a male voice says from the front door.

I turn and find Vaughn there. He's smiling from ear to ear until he catches the gloom hanging over our group.

"What happened?" he asks.

"There's much to discuss. Let's all head inside and cool off. We can't rush into things," Lucca says.

"You go ahead and discuss all you want. I have to report back to Isadora," Solomon says, then turns to Miranda. "You should be heading home, sweetheart. Your mother is worried about you."

"I will in a moment." She turns to me. "I'll come back as soon as I can."

"Wait. You don't want me to come with you?"

She arches her eyebrows in surprise. "I didn't think you'd want to."

I capture her face between my hands. "What did I tell you before? Gum on the bottom of a shoe."

Forty-Six

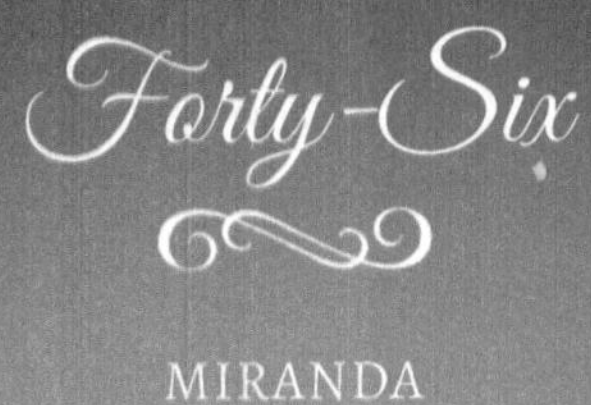

MIRANDA

Rikkon and I walked the wind straight into my mother's living room, successfully scaring the crap out of her and Niko. Solomon agreed to wait until I talked to her first before giving his report.

He was right, she had been worried about me. After the shock of my sudden appearance vanished, she hugged me for a good minute and cried. We both did. Then, in the most surprising turn of events, she hugged Rikkon too, thanking him for keeping me safe.

We're both sitting on the couch, holding hands and waiting for Mom to speak. I just told her everything that happened to us in Ellnesari—minus the racy bits.

Niko is the one who breaks the silence first. "So, you're an immortal now."

"Yeah."

"And you're more powerful than Mom, Solomon, and even the king!" she continues.

I want to deny it but Rikkon speaks before I can. "Yes, she is."

Niko widens her eyes even more. "Awesome. Wait until I tell everyone at the institute about it. Oh, I can't wait to watch those hateful Belmonts tremble in fear."

"No, we're not disclosing that to anyone," our mother finally chimes in. "It's not wise considering what's at stake. Jacques is at large and Nightingale blood is still a coveted asset."

"I agree," Rikkon pipes up.

Niko's enthusiasm deflates. "That sucks."

"We have another problem on our hands. Manu is still in Ellnesari and God knows what she's going to do," I say.

Mom shakes her head. "That foolish girl, always getting into trouble. There's no question about it. We have to rescue her before she does more harm to herself and others."

"Yes, but how are we going to open another portal into Ellnesari? The Taluah Mirror was destroyed," I reply.

"Can't you and Rikkon open another one?" Niko asks.

"No, the magic I used to get us out of Ellnesari is gone," he replies. "I'm not even sure how my father was able to give me that ability, to be honest."

"I think your father is more powerful than he lets people believe," I say.

"After what I learned, I don't doubt that."

His gaze becomes troubled. He's probably thinking about the shadowbeasts.

The doorbell rings, disrupting the heavy moment. Mom frowns and prepares to check who is at our door when Niko jumps from the couch.

"Don't worry. I'll get it."

She runs to the front door, making me suspect she knows exactly who is outside. Unbidden, I travel with my mind to the front door and see a tall young man standing there. Niko walks out and proceeds to talk fast, gesturing with her hands. With a snap, I return to the living room. *Holy crap. What was that?*

"Everything okay, Mir?" Rikkon asks.

"Yes, I'm just tired."

"I'm sure you are, darling. You've been gone for almost a month," Mom tells me.

"A month!" I yell.

"Why are you surprised?" she asks me.

"Time moves differently in Ellnesari, ma'am. It's only been a few days for us," Rikkon replies.

Mom's eyes soften. "Oh Mir, you missed your eighteenth birthday."

"It's okay, Mom. I got what I wanted anyway." I smile at Rikkon.

He brings our joined hands to his lips and kisses my knuckles.

"Hmm." Mom stares at us through slitted eyes. "Well, Solomon is waiting for me. So I'd better go see him immediately. Then I'm going to check on the king."

"How is he?" I ask.

A shadow crosses Mom's eyes. "Not good. The disease is spreading fast. I'm not sure how much longer we have until he forgets who he is."

"I'd like to see him if possible," Rikkon says.

She cocks her head to the side. "Why?"

"I think I may be able to slow down his mental deterioration."

Mom's eyes widen. "You have healing powers?"

"Yes, ma'am. Vivi does too. Perhaps the two of us can buy the king more time."

"I'll speak to him." She stands up. "I assume you need to recover your strength though."

Shit. Is Mom dismissing Rikkon already? I don't want him to leave.

"It's probably a good idea." He stands as well, catching on to Mom's not-so-subtle hint that she wants him gone. "I'd better go back to the mansion."

Mom turns her attention to me, and I don't know what she sees in my face, but whatever it is, it makes her sigh in resignation.

"You don't need to go. You're more than welcome to spend the night."

I jump from the couch, latching myself to Rikkon's arm. "Really? He can stay?"

"I'd rather he stay here than the other way around. It's bad enough that I never see your sister anymore."

It's the first time I've seen Mom talk about Aurora as if their estrangement pains her. Maybe my disappearance affected her more than I thought.

She clears her throat, putting the cold mask back in place. "Anyway, I probably won't return until early morning. Please, try to stay out of trouble."

"Don't worry, ma'am. I'll keep Mir safe," Rikkon replies. "And Niko too."

She frowns. "Speaking of Niko, where is she?"

"I'm here, Mom." She runs back into the living room, looking a little flustered.

I wonder if the boy outside is Troy, the son of the leader of the rogue mage guild. I hope not. We definitely don't need more complications in our lives.

"Who was at the door?"

Niko's eyes go rounder. "No one. Probably some stupid kid playing pranks. I'm gonna hit the sack. I'm tired."

Faster than a ninja, she hurries to her bedroom. *Shit.* There goes my hope that Niko will stay out of trouble.

"You keep an eye on her, Mir. Out of the three of you, she's the one who gives me the most white hair, and that's saying a lot considering what you and Rora put me through already."

I don't know how to reply to that. It's not like I went looking for trouble. But Mom leaves before I can think of something to say.

When the front door bangs shut, Rikkon lets out a loud exhale. "Holy moly, that was intense. I swear I thought your mother was going to eat me alive."

"She was surprisingly nice to you," I laugh. "Probably because you offered to heal the king. Do you think you can really help him?"

"Honestly, I don't know. But it's worth a try. If I had been allowed to stay for the grand council, I'd have pushed for the other kingdoms to open the veil and return their magic."

"Do you think that can happen?"

"It's a possibility now that my father has resurrected the shadowbeasts."

"We have Manu to consider in all this. What could she possibly be planning?"

"From the little I know of her, nothing good or smart." He pulls me into his arms. "But let's not worry about that now. We do need to rest if we're to be of any use tomorrow."

I melt into his arms, despite my worries and anxiety about the future.

"When you say rest, do you mean sleeping or just going to bed?"

His lips curl into a crooked grin. "How long until your sister falls asleep?"

"I don't know. Hopefully soon."

"Well, we can cuddle." He leans down and kisses me softly on the lips.

"Or we can make out like teenagers."

He laughs against my mouth. "I'm thousands of years old, my love."

"Yes, but you have the vocabulary of a high school dude."

He kisses my neck and then whispers in my ear. "Just confess, Mir. You have a thing for old men."

I'd reply but he bites my earlobe, obliterating my ability to speak. My body becomes vapor and whole again in a flash. And then we're in my bedroom, doing what I suggested: making out like two horny teenagers. There's no hurry this time, though. There isn't a deranged psycho trying to separate us or foul creatures chasing us. Tonight, I can finally be with Rikkon and pretend we're just two people in love.

** THE END (FOR NOW) **

Savage Vow

BLUEBLOOD VAMPIRES BOOK FOUR

Five hundred years ago, I fell in love with a vampire. It was a crimson fever that consumed me. I gave up my home, my family, and my pack to be with her. She obliterated my heart at the first opportunity.

Our fates are bound whether I like it or not. If she dies, I die.

She may have a death wish, but I don't. When she decides to risk everything for revenge, I have no choice but to stop her and find a way to be free of the vow I made. But surviving the dangers of Ellnesari together might not have the outcome I expect. Instead of freedom, I learn who Manu Della Morte truly is, and that reignites a passion I thought I had lost.

About the Author

USA Today Bestselling Author Michelle Hercules always knew creative arts were her calling but not in a million years did she think she would become an author. With a background in fashion design she thought she would follow that path. But one day, out of the blue, she had an idea for a book. One page turned into ten pages, ten pages turned into a hundred, and before she knew it, her first novel, The Prophecy of Arcadia, was born.

Michelle Hercules resides in Florida with her husband and daughter. She is currently working on the *Blueblood Vampires* series and the *Filthy Gods* series.

Sign-up for Michelle Hercules' Newsletter:

Join Michelle Hercules' Readers Group:
https://www.facebook.com/groups/mhsoars